For Fiona, Seán, Rían, and Liadh

A FURORE NORMANNORUM LIBERA NOS, DOM-
INE

*"From the fury of the Northmen deliver us, O
Lord."*

- a litany of despair spoken across 9th century
Saxon England

ONE

Hundr grasped at a clump of weeds trying to haul himself up, but the plant tore free from the soil peppering his face with muck. He spat gritty coarse mud and cursed as his arm slipped, skinning his elbow on the riverbank scrub.

He grunted and scrambled up and over the bank's ridge and cursed again as his foot gave way in loose gravel, almost spilling the spare arrows strapped to his back. Hundr straightened his load, fletchings banging against his head as he shuffled them securely into their quiver. He ran, heart thumping, to catch up with the rest of the ship's crew, who loped through the undergrowth ahead. The warship Seaworm lay safe at a wide turn in a Northumbrian river behind him, an impressive vessel whose oars were manned by hardened men. Thirty warriors that ship carried from the cruel cold North down to the soft, lush greenery of Saxon springtime. Men prepared to leave their homes and risk their lives on the seas in search of reputation, glory, and silver.

The crew came together to huddle in a bracken-filled field. Hundr peered over the shoulders of the gathered warriors, breathing in the rich, earthy odour of their leather armour, the acrid smell of their sweat, and feeling the palpable sense of excitement amongst them as they waited to attack. Those men crowded to hear how their Lord would lead the raid, and they shuffled and jostled, laughed and talked in hushed voices and thumbed at the fine edges on their axes and spears. Hundr itched to own such a weapon, hungered to walk with a warrior's pride and a shining war axe looped at his belt. He was at the back of the huddle because that was his place as bail boy, spare arrow carrier, and general dogsbody-lowest-of-the-low member of the warship Seaworm's crew. Hundr sniffed and cuffed at his running nose. He might not be a warrior yet, but he was ablaze with the thrill. He was about to be part of his first Viking raid. After all, this was why he had left home in the first place, to become a warrior.

Hundr shouldered past two of the younger and skinnier warriors to get a better view, but they were full crew members, or *Carls*, and higher in the pecking order. A lanky warrior shoved Hundr back with his elbow.

"Piss off you, get to the back," said Kraki Horse Face, sticking his mossy green buck teeth in Hundr's face, daring him to challenge. Horse Face waited for two heartbeats, leering, then sniggered and turned his back. Hundr closed his eyes and imagined beating on those furry anchor stone teeth until they shattered. It had been Kraki who had named him Hundr, which meant Dog in Norse. It would do as a name, for now. They all spoke Norse, all these Danes, Svear, and Norway men. Hundr spoke Norse too, but with the Eastern clip of his homeland.

The warriors were mumbling and giggling like children as they huddled around.

"Shut up, shitworms," said Halvdan, the bull-necked shipmaster of the Seaworm in a low growl, and then moved aside for his Lord. The Jarl, their leader, was Einar Rosti. In Norse, that meant Einar the Brawler, and he was a tall slab-faced man whose flat cold features were grim even amongst the ghastly. He wore a coat of mail, which marked him out as a Battle Lord and a successful warrior. Few could afford to have such a coat made or have the fighting skill to strip one from a defeated foe and prevent others from murdering you for it in return. The mail coat shimmered like the scales of some great beast, with hundreds of interlocking iron rings forged with skill and which could deflect a sword or axe blow.

"Here we go, let's get in and out, boys, no messing around." Einar's lips curled away from his teeth as he spoke and accentuated the sheer brutality of his severe features to radiate pure violence. Hundr almost pitied the Saxons they came to raid, almost.

"Kveldsson brothers out on the flank with your bows, Horse Face and Brownlegs take the other side," the men laughed as Ufketil Brownlegs shook his head at his nickname. He sighed and strung his bow, bending it around the back of his right leg and securing the string in its horn nook. The long braid at the back of his otherwise shaved head was swinging around as he readied his weapon.

"Make the wedge on me. We want their silver and their gold and whatever else the bastards have. Anyone gets in your way, do them quick. No fires, lads, we don't want Saxon warriors heading us off up river. Remember, we are sea wolves and known men. Let's get rich," said Einar.

With a clipped roar, they set off, weapons in hand and blades thirsty for blood. Hundr remained at the back as they strode through a boggy field towards a cluster of nondescript buildings ahead. The steading was a collection of long low rendered buildings roofed with dark thatch and one larger like a barn mounted with a wooden cross. Hundr couldn't see a wall or gate. Nothing to protect the lambs from the wolves.

He ran alongside the crew, their weapons and armour jangling and clanking loudly against the quiet of the surrounding fields and pastures, their faces set for the fight to come. One day he would become a warrior, other warriors would know his name, and he would have their respect. He just needed to convince Einar he could do more than bail out the ship's bilge. He needed a place as a Carl, a fully-fledged fighting member of the crew with an equal share of the prizes. But you didn't just ask Einar for a place; that had to be earned.

Hundr dodged a pile of cow turd and almost slipped as his foot landed in a field divot, snapping him from his dreams of future glory. As they came closer to the buildings, the wedge got tighter with Einar at its tip. The archers fanned out running at a low crouch; arrows nocked and ready. Hundr's heart raced as the wedge's pace quickened before him and his walk turned to a run. Cries rang out from the buildings, intertwined with thrumming bowshots loosed by archers on the flanks. Einar bellowed, waving his axe in the air, and the crew whooped and charged. Hundr's heart pumped in his chest, his face flush and warm with the thrill of the fight to come. He breathed out of his nose and reminded himself to keep to the back. He was unarmed, save for the two spare sheaves of arrows on his back and the three empty hemp sacks tucked under his arm. Even with those items, he could subdue a gaggle of shaven-headed Christ Priests.

So, no, this was not the time for him to fight and show his skill, skill developed from a lifetime of training. Einar would not notice his abilities slaughtering these Holy men like pigs before a feast. A drengr, a warrior, didn't build a reputation by butchering skinny unarmed priests.

Hundr quickened his pace again and followed the warriors between two buildings. In the narrow space ahead, he watched as Kraki Horse Face and one of the Kveldsson brothers slaughtered three priests in a flurry of axe blows as the Saxons cowered and screamed. Kraki flailed and swung his axe like a washerwoman beating a wet tunic against a rock, spraying bright crimson blood against the greyed and yellowing building walls. Hundr would have laughed at Kraki's ineptness if it wasn't so pitiful a sight. The priests were short and thin and dressed in dull, sack-like smocks and made no attempt to defend themselves. It would have been harder to kill a quick chicken or a slow pig. No glory to be had on this day, then. Hundr made his way to an open square, where Ulfketil Brownlegs burst out of the barnlike building mounted with the darkened timber cross. He was laughing, clutching a large silver plate under one arm and holding a huge candlestick aloft in the other. Hundr stopped and laughed at the joy on Brownlegs' face. Anything Brownlegs did was amusing; even his name was funny; earned from shitting in his pants on some past voyage. However, his mirth cut short because of the sheer size of the man who had emerged lumbering from the cross-gabled hall behind Brownlegs. He was old with long silver hair, a thick white and grey peppered beard, very tall and broad in the shoulders.

"Put that bastard down," Halvdan shouted, twenty paces away, pointing his axe at the old man. Hundr imagined that was easier said than done. The old man's nose was twisted and bent, broken in some fight long ago, and even at this distance, Hundr could see the scarring on his face and arms, scarring that you didn't get praying or taking coins from Saxon villagers. The enormous man lumbered over to stand in front of a tiny mouse-like priest spattered with the blood of his friends and kneeling and wailing in the square's grass whilst one of the crew threatened and jabbed him with a spear. Two crewmen dashed over with spears outstretched, but the old man did not flinch, and his hand flashed out at incredible speed, grabbing one shaft below the spear point wrenching it free. He then swayed back to avoid a thrust from the second.

"Let this man live," the old man roared in Norse, and the entire crew stopped and stared as he hopped around, waving his arms in front of the cowering Priest. Hundr dropped the sacks and spare arrows; this at least was interesting. The raid was a disappointment, no fighting, just slaughter. But a Northman, and a huge one at that, living here with the Christ men? The Sea-worm crew had butchered a gaggle of defence-less Saxon Holy Men to steal their plates and candlesticks, which was not the glorious com-bat Hundr had imagined the day would bring. *What in Thor's balls was a hulking, scarred-up old Viking warrior doing in this place?* He could feel something, some sort of tingle at the back of his mind, just like the tingle when he first saw Jarl Einar back in Jutland. He didn't know what that tingle meant or what to do about it, but it was *something,* and it was giving him a nudge to say this was a moment where something important could happen.

Hearing a Norse voice among the screaming Saxons put an end to the slaughter. Most of the pitiful monks were dead or had fled, save for the big old Viking and the Christ Priest he had tried to protect. Those two sat in the open monastery square whilst the crew was busy gathering any-thing they could find of value and making a pile of loot near a withered Sycamore tree. It was Hundr's task to put the smaller items into the sacks he had carried from the ship, and the crew would take the larger items. Hundr picked up a cloak pin that had gone green and mottled with age, and he couldn't tell what animal its maker had attempted to craft. It looked like a disfigured cow, and he couldn't imagine anyone wearing it, never mind paying silver for it, which about summed up the raid on Northumbria so far. He worked slowly, placing the paltry trinkets into the rough spun sacks whilst craning his neck to listen to Einar and Halvdan, who whispered only ten paces away. Unfortunately, he couldn't pick out all of their words. Still, the gist of it was that Halvdan wanted to kill both prisoners, which wasn't a surprise because Halvdan wanted to kill anything that moved. Einar, however, appeared curious about the old warrior. Halvdan shook his head and followed Einar as he crossed the open square where the prisoners knelt unguarded. When Kraki offered to guard the prisoners, Halvdan laughed.

"Guard them against what?"

Which was fair. They could try to flee if they wished but wouldn't get far before a pitiless Northman introduced skull to iron. Hundr stuffed a yellowed horn cup into a sack, left the loot, and then skirted around the edges of the grass square, stopping to lean on a poplar tree within earshot of Einar and the prisoners. He wanted to hear greybeard's story and see if Halvdan got his wish and would send the two miserable captives to the afterlife.

"You can understand us?" Einar barked at the old man.

"I can."

"You are a Dane?"

"I was once."

"How long have you been here with the Christ men?"

"Maybe six summers, but it's ten summers since I was on the Whale Road."

"What is your name, greybeard?" said Einar.

"Sten."

"Your father's name?"

"Rognvald,"

"Very well, Sten Rognvaldsson, what are you doing here, and how did you get here?"

"It's hard to talk," said Sten, rubbing at his throat, "some water or ale for me and the good brother here."

"Soil scrabbling bastard," Halvdan said and cracked Sten across the head with the butt of his spear.

That was brave, brave, or stupid.

"I need to piss. If you want to live, think of something valuable to tell us when I return." Einar said, sighing and strode off with Halvdan to inspect the loot pile; Einar then disappeared behind a building to piss.

The old Dane was a warrior, a big man criss-crossed with scars. He still wasn't sure why but

Hundr sensed an opportunity here. He still had that tingle nagging him, that same sense as when it feels like someone is watching or following you. Unnerving but also useless if not acted upon. Hundr pushed himself off the tree and took a few steps towards the prisoners.

"How does a spear Dane find his way here, old one?"

"Who says I'm a spear Dane?" replied Sten giving him a sideways look. Hundr pointed at Sten's left hand, where half of his little finger was missing, and then at the scars on his forearms and his twisted nose.

"You didn't get those pulling cabbages or milking cows," Hundr said, smiling.

"You haven't seen the cows here, lad."

Hundr laughed.

"We're taking no prisoners, friend. So if you have anything you can use to keep yourself alive, now is the time to talk. Halvdan back there would love nothing more than to cut off your head and use your beard as an arse wipe."

"You're no Dane, and you've no weapons laddie, are you a slave?" Sten asked. Hundr bristled and pushed his shoulders back. *Some cheek on this old dog.*

"I am from the East and am no slave, grandfather. Have you anything of value before we send you to Hel to be a nithing wandering like a beggar until Ragnarök?" Hel was the afterlife for people who didn't die a warrior's death, to wander as a nithing wraith for eternity. It was a warrior's worst nightmare to die this way, and Hundr hoped to get some sort of reaction out of the big bastard with the threat of eternal damnation. After all, what could be worse than that? There must be something about this old warrior. What was the use of all this neck tingling if Halvdan buried his spear in the old goat's gullet? Sten looked at the quivering priest next to him and then down at the puddle of piss the little man had made. Sten sighed and shook his head.

"Maybe I have something, boy. I know these Saxon lands, and I have my name. That name and my deeds of long ago have some value, I dare say. I know the sons of Ragnar Lothbrok would be happy to see Sten Sleggya again. Much time has passed, but if they live, I'd say the sons of my old friend have some name and reputation wherever Northmen sail. For was it not I who taught Ubba to wrestle and Sigurd Snake Eye the cuts of the sword." Sten straightened his back and lifted his chin.

Hundr realised he was staring open-mouthed, so he closed his teeth and feigned indifference, which was hard. Ragnar Lothbrok was the greatest of all Viking warriors and revered across the North for his exploits, he had died years ago, and his sons were famed Sea Kings. So, the tingling had been worthwhile after all.

"Run along, lad and tell your master who you have stumbled across and let him come talk to me."

"Grand words, old one, but all I see is a grizzled old farmer sat in a pool of piss with his boyfriend. I should kill you now with my eating knife and have done with it," Hundr said, smiling. "But I will get the Jarl and let him decide." Hundr was about to walk away, but he held back. What if the old turd was a great man and had, in fact, sailed with Ragnar and knew the Ragnarsson's? Then maybe Sten could be a means to an end. What if Sten could be a way to get close to the proper warriors of reputation, the real known men? What if he, Hundr, could fight alongside Ivar the Boneless himself, the most famous son of Ragnar Lothbrok and the Champion of the Northmen? Then he would have made it. Hundr imagined himself sailing home in his own warship, showing his father and his crusty old weapons master what he had become, showing them all that he had become greater than any of them ever believed possible.

"If I save your life, can you get me an audience with the sons of Ragnar Lothbrok?" Hundr asked. Sten touched at the bruise on his head where Halvdan had struck him. He spat into the piss-soaked grass and looked Hundr straight in the eye.

"Beware young pup, that way lies blood, death, treachery and deceit, axe and sword. But If they're alive, I daresay I can grant you an audience. If that's what you want."

This was good timing because Einar had finished his piss and was striding across the square, flanked by Halvdan. The stocky, thick-necked shipmaster had left his spear with the loot and now brandished a short hafted axe whose head was too large for war and was more likely used by the Saxons for trimming tree branches for the fire. Halvdan swung the thing as he marched.

"Sten Grey Beard, do you have anything of value to share with us before Halvdan here sends you to Hel?" said Einar.

Hundr took a step towards Einar and was about to speak when Halvdan reached out and pressed the top of his axe haft into Hundr's chest, pushing him backwards.

"Make yourself useful, boy, find a cart and start loading," said Halvdan. Hundr took a breath and tried not to panic as Halvdan's eyebrows turned into a frown, creasing his forehead.

"Lord Einar, I believe this man..." Hundr said. Einar tilted his head and fixed Hundr with a puzzled stare, tucking his hands into the top of his brynjar, the shining mail coat which protected him from neck to knee.

"What are you doing here bastard, piss off, away with you," said Halvdan, interrupting as Hundr made to speak again.

"Lord Einar, I have spoken to this man and I.." Hundr didn't get to finish as Einar nodded at Halvdan, who took a step towards Hundr with his axe outstretched. Hundr, without pause, darted to his left and then forwards, grabbing the Halvdan's thick meaty wrist and twitching the axe from it. Hundr spun it backwards in his grip, and now it was he who pushed Halvdan's chest with the axe head. Men nearby shouted and grabbed for their weapons. Halvdan's face looked beyond anger. His cheeks were blood red, and his eyes bulged as though they would pop from his skull. Einar just glared. *That may have been a mistake.* He had acted on reflex rather than thought.

"I did not ask for this, Lord," said Hundr, "I tried to talk, to tell you, but Halvdan, he…."

"Out with it, boy or I'll take your head," said Einar, placing a hand on Halvdan's chest to stop him from charging at Hundr like a maddened bull.

"This man is Sten Sleggya, and he says he fought alongside Ragnar Lothbrok and knows the sons of Ragnar. He also knows these lands; he can be of help to us, to you, Lord," said Hundr. Halvdan and Einar looked at each other. Einar scratched at his beard and chewed at his bottom lip.

"As your last gamble to cling on to your shit, miserable and dishonourable life," said Einar, "you claim you are Sten Sleggya, known wherever Vikings sail, Champion of Ragnar Lothbrok? First over the wall at the siege of Paris, killer of Ketil the Black, Jarl Thorgrim Redbeard, and so on?"

"My name's Sten, and once men called me Sleggya," Sten said.

Hundr stared at Einar and then at Sten. The old goat was a hero. Hundr had known there was something about him. Halvdan sprang forward and snatched the axe out of Hundr's hand, turned at the hip, and slammed its blade into the piss-soaked Christ Priest's forehead. The thick blade thudded like a cleaver into meat, and as the priest's skull cracked open, blood and bone pieces sprayed across those closest, and Hundr flinched as he felt the warmth of it slapping his face. He scratched at his cheek, trying to wipe the Priests' brains off, and watched as Halvdan put a foot on the priest's chest and yanked at the axe. It took three heaves to pull it free. The burly shipmaster grinned as he coiled for another blow, and Hundr stepped forwards, raising his arms.

"Wait," he shouted, "Lord Einar, I claim the right of combat. I vouch for this man and ask for a place on your crew. Any man who disputes that is a liar and a turd, and I will fight them," It was a desperate chance, and his words sounded stupid, but Hundr felt sure that this was his time. He swallowed hard at the thickening ball in his throat. Hundr had bailed the filthy bilge of the Seaworm from Jutland to Northumbria and kept himself quiet, kept his ambitions to himself. He had to trust his instincts. This was the moment. He looked at Sten, who had one hand on his mangled and dead priest friend, and stared wide-eyed at Halvdan.

"You little shit, you can have some too," growled Halvdan, taking a step towards Hundr with his wood axe dripping gore onto the grass. But Einar held up his hand, and Halvdan paused.

"So, you claim the laws of the drengr, boy?" asked Einar. Hundr knew from listening through the long nights onboard the Seaworm that Einar prided himself on being a drengr, a warrior. A drengr followed drengskapr, the warrior's way. They had brought Hundr up in the ways of the drengr, his weapons master, and his lore master, both keen to instil drengskapr in the young warriors and the path to Odin's hall Valhalla. He knew the drengr laws, and so he knew Einar would let him fight a Holmgang, a fight within a square of hazel rods. The Holmgang was the root of all law for Northmen, for why would the Gods allow a liar to win a fight? The winner of the duel within the square had the right in any dispute.

"Yes, Lord," said Hundr. "I will fight for Sten because of his exploits of old and because he knows this land and can be of help to us. But also for myself. If I win and prove myself in the Holm-gang square, I will have a place on your crew and swear myself to you, Lord."

"And if you lose?" asked Einar frowning.

"If I lose, then my life and his are forfeit. That's the law."

"You have no rights here, shit weasel, Einar let's just do them both and get back to the ship," said Halvdan, losing whatever fragment of patience he still possessed.

Hundr swallowed, trying to choke down the burning fear which had kindled in his belly and now travelled up to his head. It was screaming at him to run, make for the trees beyond the build-ings and flee from Halvdan's bloody brain coated axe blade. He hadn't come all this way to run; he had come to be a warrior, and a drengr did not run. It seemed to take an age as Einar scratched at his beard and thumbed the blade of his axe in its belt loop. Hundr noticed the crew had gathered around, and he could see Kraki Horse Face grinning over Einar's shoulder.

"Do him Halvdan," said Kraki. Some of the crew mumbled agreement. Finally, Einar shook his head and spat.

"You can fight, boy. If you win, I'll give you an oar, and grandfather here can live. If you lose, then Halvdan will send you both to Niflheim,"

"Lord..." growled Halvdan, but Einar shook his head.

"We follow the Laws of the drengr in my crew. He can fight. If he's the balls to do that, then he deserves an oar. Who will fight the pup? He can't fight Halvdan being only a bail boy. Who will fight him?"

A grizzled warrior in a leather breastplate stretched over an enormous stomach, and striped trews gave a loud laugh and planted his spear in the ground.

"Toki will fight the pup. Let's at least have a laugh whilst stuck in this shit hole," he shouted, and the crew cheered and banged weapons on shields. Hundr had shared a bench with Toki on the Seaworm, and he had been good company, and Hundr liked him. *Why him, why hadn't Kraki put himself forward, the useless turd?*

"Toki fights the bail boy, make the square. Let's get this done fast and get gone," said Einar, and he stalked off towards the loot pile again. Hundr turned to Sten with a grin, but as he moved, Halvdan punched him in the ribs and yanked him up by his hair as he doubled over. Then, as his head rose, the shipmaster head-butted him on the corner of his eye, making his vision explode with white flashes, and pulled him towards him.

"I'll have you, boy. Make a fool of me, would

you? I'll have your stinking scalp if Toki doesn't kill you first," he hissed and pushed Hundr to the ground.

Hundr rolled and came up to a crouch, but Halvdan had gone. He shuffled backwards to sit next to Sten, touching one hand to his eye and feeling blood there, and another to his ribs shot through with lancing pain.

"What do you think you're doing gambling for my life, pup?" said Sten, glaring.

"Saving it, greybeard."

"Do you know how to fight?" asked Sten, and Hundr shrugged.

"We are about to find out," he said, trying to seem confident, but he was aware of how alone he was and how vulnerable. He was one man, new to this world of Viking adventurers, with no friends among the crew. Hundr had left his home to seek his way in the world of warriors, and now his fate stood on a knife-edge. All that stood between him and an axe blade in the skull was Jarl Einar's steadfast adherence to drengskapr, the way of the warrior. Even if he won the Holmgang, Halvdan and the rest of the crew might cut him down anyway and leave him here to rot with the butchered Christ Priests.

TWO

The Seaworm crew gathered in tight around the fighters. Hundr watched their faces, flushed and eager for the combat to come, and struggled again to push his fear back into the pit of his gut. The crewman named Bush had stripped some branches from one of the tall Elm trees dotted around the buildings and created a crude fighting square. Kraki Horse Face ambled across the square, grinning his stupid buck-toothed sneer as he sauntered towards him. Hundr crouched on his haunches, waiting for the combat to start, trying not to look like he was shitting himself. Kraki drew close and handed Hundr a linden wood shield with flaking paint, which had once been painted half blue and half red but had become battered-looking and faded with age. Hundr tilted the rim upwards, looking for the grip. There was a worn leather loop and a sodden hemp rope. He glanced at Kraki, who blew his cheeks out and raised his eyebrows.

"Frigg's tits, bail boy, you are going to be slaughtered. You put your arm through the loop and grab the bloody handle, and don't let go, here," he said, waiting as Hundr put his arm through the loop. The shield was heavy, and it dragged his arm down, its edge banged on the grass. The crew laughed, and Hundr reddened. Kraki shook his head and handed Hundr an axe. It had a fine tapered beard-shaped blade and a blackened wood haft. He took it low on the grip, and Kraki guided his hand higher up.

"Better balance. Good luck and don't die, dog. We need a fool to bail the bilge."

"Why are you helping me? You wanted Halvdan to kill me just now?"

Kraki shrugged.

"I don't give a dry shite if you live or die, turd, but if you die, then I have to take a turn at bailing. So try to live, bail boy."

Kraki turned and walked back across the square, guffawing at his own humour even though no one else laughed. Hundr held the shield in front of him and let the axe dangle at his side. The wooden haft was slick and bare of any leather or wool binding. A warrior would often add some material to the haft to help with grip. When some murder crazed bastard was trying to cave your skull in, the last thing you wanted was to drop your axe. At least the shield was fine, with a strong iron boss, and the boards did not seem cracked or rotten. Hundr breathed deeply. It was a fine Spring day, and he closed his eyes and said a prayer to Odin, the favourite but fickle god of all warriors. He prayed that today wouldn't be his last; he prayed to Odin to grant him favour and to not make a foot slip or his grip slide. Hundr turned to Sten, who stood behind him.

"Any wise words, grandfather?" he asked. Sten looked him up and down and shook his head.

"Can you even lift that bloody shield, boy? You don't look like much of a fighter."

Hundr shrugged his shoulders.

"I'll do my best. But, if I lose and Toki kills me, well then I'll see you in Hel," he said, which he thought sounded good and brave.

"Bloody fool," said Sten, dripping scorn, and touched at the wooden cross hanging around his neck. Hundr hadn't noticed the trinket until that moment. So, the old man had given up on the Gods in favour of the Christ God. That wouldn't go down well with the crew if he survived the Holmgang.

There was a movement on the opposite side of the square, and a low growl of anticipation rumbled around the gathered crew as it became time to fight.

Toki took up a position opposite Hundr, also armed with an axe and shield. The grizzled warrior was laughing and joking with the surrounding crew, and his baggy striped trews flapped in the light breeze. Einar shouldered his way through the crowd and walked around the square.

"By the laws of Gods and men, we have a Holmgang to decide the fate of these men. If you lose the fight, boy, you will die. You can't go back to bailing after this. On the other hand, if you win..." he said with a flourish of his arms, and the crew laughed and banged their weapons together. "If you win, you join the crew as a Carl like the rest of the men, and this one comes with you," Einar gestured towards Sten.

Einar left the circle, and Toki grinned and raised his weapons out wide. Toki was of middling height, but years at the oar had made him broadshouldered and thick-necked; he wore his hair in a long thin plait down his back. His beard and moustaches also plaited into a chunky rope that bounced on his chest as he twirled his weapons to show his skill. The crew cheered a ferocious, bloodthirsty roar, and Hundr turned to Sten and winked, enjoying the surprise on the old man's face.

Hundr shuffled forward, crouched low behind his shield peeking over the rim. His axe held close, tight to his torso and inside the shields' bowl so that his entire body below his eyes cowered behind the relative safety of its boards. The crew laughed because it was clear Hundr had little or no experience with weapons. With the axe tucked in so close, he could not strike, so Toki gave a great whoop as he smelled blood and leapt forward to slash his axe down hard on Hundr's shield. Hundr let out a scream as the weapon thudded like thunder onto the middle of the boss, and the clanging impact jarred up his arm. He jumped backwards, breathing hard, much to the delight of the crew. Many of them laughed so hard at his complete battle incompetence that they had to put their hands on their knees to stop falling over.

"Bury the whelp," one Warrior cried.

"Chop his balls off," called another, setting the crew off into more creasing laughter.

Hundr kept low behind the shield, the smells of the damp twisted rope strap and the bitter iron boss swamped his senses, and he allowed himself a slight smile. Toki was laughing himself now and mimicking Hundr's scream, which set off the crew's howls of laughter again. Hundr was smiling because he was enjoying this now. He tried his best to appear panicked and desperate, but in his heart, he was strong and confident. Hundr looked around at their hungry faces; Kraki held his stomach; he was laughing so hard. *You won't be laughing soon, Horse Face.* Toki came on again, sweeping his axe at Hundr's legs, Hundr let his shield fall to catch the blow, but this time he took it square on the shield, just as he had done in practice every day of his life for as far back as he could remember. Toki recovered then swung backhand. But this time, Hundr just left the shield low and swayed back away from the axe's blade, leaving Toki's arms spread as his arm followed the momentum of the axe swinging wide. Hundr watched it pass, feeling the waft in the wet of his eyes. He snarled and darted in, head-butting Toki as hard as he could, Toki's face mashing under his forehead. He then ducked under Toki's rising shield arm and drove his foot into the back of Toki's knee. Toki fell to his knees off balance and let out a gasp, and Hundr kicked him hard into the mud, where he writhed and twisted.

The watching crew was silent and baleful now, and Toki struggled to his feet in a rage. Hundr took two quick shuffled steps towards him, feinted low, and then slashed his axe across Toki's bicep. He enjoyed the thrill as he saw the red bloom of blood on Toki's sleeve. His heart was beating fast, and he clenched his teeth. This was what Hundr lived for, the thrill of combat and the glory of a warrior showing his weapon craft. Hundr stood straight and let his shield drop to the ground, staring over at Kraki. *Not laughing now, are you, you horse-faced bastard?* Hundr used the blunt back of the axe and slammed it into the back of Toki's leg as he darted by. He flipped the axe to his left hand and wrested Toki's axe from him, and drove the butt of that weapon into Toki's head, ending the Holmgang as Toki collapsed in a heap of striped trousers and crushed pride.

Hundr turned in a circle in case the crew turned on him. He had won, but he sensed the tension and threat oozing from their flinty stares. No one cheered his victory. He held the two axes firm and looked at each set of cold eyes surrounding him. He wanted to enjoy the elation of his victory, of glorying in his weapon skill, but fear festered deep in his belly. As he turned, he saw Kraki the fool standing there with his mouth wide open, as did the rest of the crew. Halvdan was snarling and drawing his axe from its belt loop. *I must swallow this fear, this weakness. I am a warrior, and none here could stand against me. Who is the bail boy now?* He set his jaw against the fear and replaced it with what he hoped was a stern look of confidence. The fight had been easy. Feigning ignorance of weapon skill had bought him some time, but he could have beaten Toki anyway without the pretence. It felt good to hold weapons again, and he twirled them in circles, enjoying the weight and balance, wondering what his weapon master back home would say. He would shout and bully and order Hundr to finish the bastard off, more than likely. This was what he had trained all his life for, to be a warrior and use his skill to build a warrior's reputation.

Einar was frowning and spat as he strode into the square with his axe drawn.

"You have won, boy. You are more than you seemed. But, be careful; men don't like tricks. You know the trickster God Loki as well as I. Maybe this is Loki's work, maybe not. You have your place on the crew, and you, grandfather," he held his axe out, and Hundr and Sten knelt before Einar and swore their loyalty to him and kissed his blade. Einar nodded and turned to the crew.

"Enough, get packed up and back to the Ship. We will be with Ivar before nightfall."

The crew grumbled and mumbled. Ulfketil and Kraki moved to help Toki, who lay slumped in the Holmgang square.

"Come on, you lazy bastards, let's go. Now," said Halvdan as he shoved and jostled the crew into action.

A heavy hand pressed on his shoulder, and Hundr turned to see Sten grinning beneath his silver beard.

"So, you can fight, laddie. You deceived us all," he said. Hundr nodded his appreciation. He was part of the crew now, which was all he had wanted since leaving home. But the furtive and resentful glances soured the victory. Toki's humiliation stung the group, and it didn't sit well that Hundr had pretended he couldn't fight. It was one thing to be part of a crew, but it was another to be hated by his new shipmates, shipmates who were also vicious killers.

"Where'd a whelp like you learn to fight like that?" Sten asked. Hundr slung the shield over his shoulder.

"We can talk later, grey beard. You owe me your life. Come on."

THREE

The crew rowed the Seaworm downriver and back into the wide embrace of the open Sea without incident. The flow of the river made rowing easy, and Hundr had taken his turn at an oar with glee, no longer a bail boy. Her shallow draft made the Seaworm the perfect warship, as comfortable on the heaving swell of the Whale Road as she was in the twists and turns of inland rivers. Sten had been sullen throughout the day, and Hundr had left him alone, watching instead as they entered the coastal waters off Northumbria. The Seaworm cut through the wave swell like a knife, long, sleek and low sided, all danger and threat. Hundr enjoyed the salty spring wind blowing through his loose brown hair, which he had untied in the refreshing breeze, and he allowed his mind to wander.

Before the Seaworm, Hundr had spent some months on board a Knarr Trading Ship. She had been fat-bellied and high-sided trudging from port to port across the trading route, which picked its way westward from the flat grassy lands of the Rus across to the high rocky fjords of the Svear. He had left that ship at the end of its route before it turned for home. That same day he had approached Jarl Einar on a moss-covered slippery jetty at a miserable trading post south of the Jutland Peninsula to beg for a berth. All despite not knowing the Jarl nor any of the crew and looking like a beggar. The Seaworm had stood out that day amongst the gloom and drabness of fish and sheep-stinking traders. She had been like an image from Hundr's dreams, right there before his eyes. This skillfully crafted vessel carried Viking warriors to glory and Valhalla. The Jarl would have seen a broad-shouldered but slim-built youth with his long dark hair scraped back from his face and tied with a piece of cloth, dressed in a travel-stained tunic with few belongings. Hundr had sold most of what he owned for food on the long journey from home to the coast. He had expected a kick or a curse, but Einar had stared hard into his eyes, and to Hundr's surprise, had agreed and let him come aboard, and here he was.

The crew called their leader Jarl, or Lord. Amongst Northmen, a man could call himself a Jarl if he was a leader of men and could lead ten men or a hundred. Hundr had worried about approaching the Jarl. Not afraid of the man himself, but fearing that being a masterless man and plain to all a runaway that he would not find another berth. Odin only knew what might have become of him otherwise, alone in a trading port, no silver or belongings to speak of. He had left the safety of the Trading ship because he was not a trader. They had not trained him for war his entire life to spend his days lifting bales of wool.

"Hundr," came a growl from down ship, but he couldn't see which man had called him as they moved forward and back at their oars, grunting and pulling in unison like some magnificent beast from legend.

"Boy, ale. Fetch ale," called another voice. This time he saw it was Kraki Horse Face. It was hard to find clean drinking water to fill barrels for men to drink on board, so men drank ale to stop their guts running. He looked up at the Jarl, who, with the smallest nod, gave the approval. Hundr scrambled, splashing between the rocks in the bilge and the dark, battered sea chests the crew used as rowing benches. The ship surged, and spray lashed at his face again; he felt his leg slip against a ballast rock under the bilge water. He sprawled forwards, just catching the ale barrel with his left hand and hauling himself upright, cursing under his breath. Most of the crew didn't notice or care, but Kraki guffawed as he heaved his oar backwards.

"Still not found your sea legs, boy?"

Kraki spoke between bursts of laughter, spittle clinging to his buck teeth. He had teased Hundr relentlessly since joining the crew, and he was not that much older than Hundr, which made it even more maddening when he called him "boy." He didn't have to take this harrying from Kraki anymore. But he had yet to decide how to deal with his tormentor. Hundr closed his eyes and again imagined himself smashing in Kraki's huge discoloured teeth, and it lifted his mood.

Hundr dipped the horn cup into the barrel and brought it to Kraki, who drank deeply and passed the cup back. He shouldn't have to bring ale to the crew, now that he was a Carl, a Warrior like the rest, but he did it anyway. He felt their menacing looks and whispers behind his back ever since the Holmgang, and he knew that a push over the side would be all too easy and doubted if the Jarl would care enough to stop the ship and pull him in. Better to fetch ale than find himself at the bottom of the Saxon Sea. So, he cursed Kraki as a buck-toothed bastard under his breath, dipped the cup and went to the bow and back again, giving each man a drink between pulls at the oar. As he passed the barrel again and for a third time dipped the cup, he went to move around the mast, but a foot shot out and tripped him. He slipped, knees and wrists crashing into the freezing ballast stones. The horn cup flew from his hand, and he watched it sail through the air and strike a brawny, stringy bearded warrior on the knee. The man kicked out, connecting with Hundr's shoulder, sending a dull ache down his arm.

"Clumsy bastard," the brawny man said. Hundr turned to see Kraki Horse Face laughing. Kraki had tripped him, the swine. *Who else but that irritating turd?*

"If you don't find your sea legs soon, boy, we might feed you to the sea monsters," said Kraki, laughing at his own jest. None of the crew joined him, and Hundr held himself fast. The rage fired inside him like a flame on dry kindling, and he knew he could have his axe buried in Kraki's head before you could say, *over the side with him.* A voice bellowed from the steer-board.

"Ten more pulls and get the sail up, winds changed. Boy, ale." Einars voice carried down the Ship, sonorous and clear even above the din of the crew and the force of the surrounding Sea.

The wind was changing, and the men cheered each of the subsequent ten oar strokes. Hundr grabbed the cup and dipped it again, ignoring the stinging pain in his knees from the fall. This time, as nimbly as possible, he hopped and jumped up the length of the hull to the steer-board. Reaching up with the cup, he looked into the broad flat face of the Jarl and his grey eyes, colder than the sea itself. He had not yet learned how Einar had earned his name, *the Brawler*, but it was a good name for a warrior, one Hundr would be proud of.

Einar drank, watching the men as they groaned and heaved, bringing their oars in and stuffing the oar holes with wooden plugs, then scurrying around untying and retying seal hide ropes to let the vast sail out. As the wind filled the wool cloth sail, it billowed and snapped taut, spraying icy water over the crew, and they cheered again as it soaked them. A single faded raven stood proud on the yellowed white sailcloth in defiance of the weather. Einar handed back the cup and eyed Hundr, judging him with those cold grey eyes. The moment dragged until it became awkward, and Einar grunted and cast his gaze back to the crew. Hundr swallowed and picked his way back up ship. *Timid bastard*. He cursed himself for not talking to the Jarl, for not being the confident warrior he told himself he could become. Hundr could have asked practical questions: what would his additional responsibilities be? Or who should fetch ale? Now that he was a Carl like the rest of the crew, surely he was above those tasks. But, instead, he had just stared at Einar like some sort of dumbstruck lackwit. His old weapons master had said that confidence was half the battle. Act and look like a warrior, and people would consider you one; until the blades clashed and blood flowed at least. Hundr cursed his weakness again and returned to his seat in the bows next to Sten, who was fingering the small wooden cross at his neck and staring back at the Northumbrian coast where his priest friends lay butchered and soaked in blood. He thought about asking the big man why he wore the cross and why he had forsaken Odin and Thor, but looking at Sten's sour brooding face, he decided against it. *Who gives a shit what the old fool believes in, as long as he is who he says he is.*

Hundr watched Kraki at his work. Even the way he tied rope was annoying, grimacing at each pull, baring those ridiculous choppers in his mouth and fumbling around with knots. On his first night aboard the Seaworm, Kraki had asked his name, and Hundr had not wanted to say. So Kraki had given him his dog's name meant as an insult to the new boy bailing the bilge, but Hundr didn't mind it so much. He was the lowest of the crew and the lowest of men. He had nothing when he boarded the Seaworm, no silver, no weapons, no arm rings, and no reputation. Yet he had known that would change; that was why he was here. Already he had become a Carl of the crew, equal to Kraki and the rest. He had an axe secure in a loop at his belt. Einar had allowed him to keep it after the Holmgang, so although his name was Dog, his lot was improving and he was doing what he set out to when he ran away. He was making his way as a warrior. *So, call me Dog, and I'll show you what a dog can do.*

Hundr fished a biscuit he had kept back from his rations and took a bite, sitting in silence as the crew finished securing the mast and stowing the oars. He rolled his shoulders and stretched his neck, still sore from the days bailing the bilge, knuckles still pink and raw where he had scuffed them on the ballast stones as he bailed.

"Sore, lad?" came a question from across the deck. He looked up, and it was Bush, a balding warrior with a paunch. Hundr smiled and nodded.

"Wait 'till you row proper. Don't mind that Horse Faced bastard; he's full of piss and wind. I remember when he joined the crew, the bastard was sick for days."

Hundr smiled again and nodded thanks, "How long have you been with the crew?"

Bush blew out his cheeks, removed the stained leather helmet liner he wore, and scratched his balding pate.

"Must be on for five summers now, five with Einar."

"Is Bush your proper name?" Hundr asked, and the man next to Bush laughed.

"We called him Bush because once he got shot

by an arrow in the arse whilst having a turd behind some bushes."

"Well, there's no explaining needed for your name, Blink," said Bush, and they both grinned.

Hundr looked at Blink and found it hard to meet his eye. The man's eyes opened and closed so rapidly. Bush was right; the name needed no explanation. Blink's face was long, open and honest, and Hundr liked him. He was the cook for the crew, and truth be told, his food was terrible, but no one else wanted that responsibility.

"Mostly we stay with rest o 'the Ragnarsson Ships," said Bush, "but we're often sent on special jobs. Ivar likes Einar, and we get the job done. Five years I'm with Lord Einar, more than that with Ivar though..." he said.

"I'm a Seaworm man for six years now, love these boys I do," said Blink, stuffing a biscuit into his mouth amid frantic blinking.

"Who is Ivar?" Hundr asked. Bush sat up in shock, and the crew stopped their chatter to look at him. He reddened as he felt their gaze. Of course, he knew who Ivar the Boneless was. But Hundr wanted to hear what the relationship was between Ivar and Einar and what opportunities lay ahead if the useless old warrior next to him did indeed prove to be a man of reputation who could gain Hundr favour.

"Ivar Ragnarsson is our Lord, and Jarl Einar

serves Lord Ivar. You know of the Ragnarssons?" said Bush, with a look of incredulity on his round face as he scratched at his belly. Hundr shook his head and shrugged. Bush leant forward, wagging a finger at Hundr.

"Ivar's the Champion of all Northmen, the son o' Ragnar Lothbrok and brother to Sigurd Snake Eye, Ubba, and Halvdan Ragnarsson. How d'you not know these names? Where are you from boy, I don't recognise your accent?"

"East, I come from the East, and we hear little of the great deeds of the men of the West," he said, worried that he took playing dumb a bit too far.

"You've much to learn, lad. You're on a Drakkar, a warship owned by Ivar Ragnarsson and captained by Einar Rosti, both men of reputation and renown," said Blink.

Hundr had obviously heard of Ragnar Lothbrok, supposed friend of Sten, and how he had travelled far to get here to the shores of the West, paving the way for other Vikings.

"So Hundr, you have an accent like the Rus Vikings, are you Rus?" asked a young man with a thick plait of golden hair hung down over one shoulder onto his chest.

"No, I am from a small island near the coast."

"This is Bjarni; we call him Lack beard," said Blink, and Bush sniggered.

"My beard will grow, Bush, but you will always be an ugly bald bastard," said Bjarni, and the entire crew laughed.

"Shut your holes," said Halvdan, a few benches down, growling and glaring between Blink, Bush, and Bjarni. "You three shitworms joking and talking to this turd who tricked Toki makes me sick. You aren't part of this crew, turd, neither you nor that miserable old bastard next to you." Halvdan nodded backwards to Toki, who huddled under a blanket, nursing his wounds and his pride.

They fell silent for a minute, but then Bush leaned forwards and gestured to a crewman a few benches down.

"It won't be far now. Thorkild tell us a story to pass the time," he said, fitting his helmet liner back in place, covering his bald spot, and the crew grunted approval. A greying Carl with a lined and weather-beaten face pulled at his long moustaches, staring into a pot of ale for inspiration.

"I will tell a tale of the Gods," Thorkild said and winked at Hundr. "Of how Loki the trickster turned himself into a salmon and hid beneath a waterfall, and how mighty Thor caught him as he leapt above the rapids." Thorkild started his tale, and his mellow voice eased all the men to relax. Hundr leaned back, his eyes becoming heavy as the ship rocked with the gentle swell of the waves.

The brief journey south was pleasant, the swell was gentle, and the wind blew just enough to fill the sail, and they furled it as they turned inland through a maze of sandbanks and tidal rivulets. The crew removed the wooden oar plugs and extended the oars. Then, with Einar guiding the ship through withies driven into the river bed to guide ships away from the treacherous shallows, the rowing began. The Seaworm had sailed into the wide mouth of the River Mersey and along its silted banks until they came to an old Roman hill fort. Most of the famous dressed Roman stone was still standing, dominating the mouth of an estuary thick with ships like a forest of war.

They moored the ship, and Hundr followed the crew along the timber jetty. He marvelled at the impossibly close joins of the fort's colossal wall stones as they passed through a half-crumbled gateway. The stones were so big and cut so tight to one another that they seemed crafted by Gods. He looked behind him and could see all across the Peninsula from where the Fort perched atop its rise.

"Easy to see why the Romans picked this spot," he said, glancing at Sten, who gave a low grumble in agreement.

"Rome folk knew how to build, lad," Sten said,

sniffing, and then sighed and trudged after the rest of the crew. Einar and Halvdan were talking with a man in a mail brynjar, similar to Einar's. His arms were thick with rings, and he had a sword at his belt, which was rare. Only a wealthy or powerful warrior could afford a sword. The blade and brynjar marked the man out as a leader or a great warrior. Anyone who killed such a man would be rich himself, with mail coat, sword, and arm rings, all worth a small fortune in silver. Hundr scampered to catch the conversation.

"No, the Boneless isn't here yet," he heard the warrior say.

"The snake eye?" asked Einar, referring to Ivar the Boneless' famous brother Sigurd Snake Eye. Not a renowned warrior like Ivar, but a Sea King and clever in battle, or so they said. The warrior shook his head and spat into the mud.

"No Ragnarssons here, just him up yonder."

He nodded his head up towards the central keep of the fort, which rose to two stories topped by old rotten thatch. Then, almost on cue, a jarring voice cut through the afternoon carrying across the hilltop from the keep.

"Einar Rosti, here to put the cursed Saxons to the sword," the voice called. The sword warrior sighed and shook his head.

"Good luck," he whispered and winked at Einar, sidling away.

"Bastard," Halvdan said. Hundr assumed he was referring to the man at the keep. It was hard to tell with Halvdan because he used that word in most situations and to describe most people.

The man trotted down the short stairs from the keep and strode towards Einar, flanked by two giant warriors, long hafted axes resting on their thick shoulders.

"Lord Hakon," Einar said as the man drew close. He was of similar height to Hundr with a sharp-pointed face framed by a well-tended chin beard, draped in a bear's fur cloak, which made him look broad in the shoulder. Hundr caught the glimmer of a brynjar underneath the fur, and he wore a bronze circlet on his forehead, much like a crown. Not a son of Ragnar then, but still an important man to get away with wearing a crown, or a sort of crown, anyway.

"Einar the Brawler, good to see you, old friend," Hakon slapped Einar on the shoulder, and Einar almost grimaced but stopped his mouth from twisting just as it turned down at the corners. "Halvdan, grim as death as always, eh?" Hakon said and chortled as Halvdan's left eye twitched with barely concealed rage.

"Lord," said Halvdan, and it seemed to Hundr that were he pressed to speak further, Halvdan might fall into an uncontrollable slaughtering spree. Luckily Einar spoke first.

"Is your father here, Lord?" Hakon shook his head and pushed his shoulders back.

"No, Einar, I am in command here. My uncles Ubba and Sigurd have already marched East."

"When is Lord Ivar expected, Lord?"

Hakon narrowed his eyes and pursed his lips.

"I am in command, Einar, as I said. Anything you want of my father, you can ask of me."

Einar just stared at Hakon, towering over the son of Ivar the Boneless. Einar was a head taller than most men. There was something about his slab face and flat stare, which looked calm but gave off an undercurrent of implacable violence. As far as Hundr could tell, Hakon had done nothing to set off Einar's latent rage, yet there was no mistaking the concealed fury behind Einar's grey eyes. Men close by stopped to watch the tense encounter. Hakon glanced around and pushed his shoulders back again, and jutted his chin out.

"Einar, do we have a problem? What is it you have to tell my father that you can't say to me?"

Hakon's voice rose in pitch, and his feet shifted. Einar raised an eyebrow, and Hundr watched as Halvdan's mouth gaped.

"No problem, Lord, I need to talk to your father about the work I am returning from, that's all. So I'll wait until he arrives," Einar said and took a step to the side as though to keep walking, but

Hakon held up a hand.

"You may not have noticed Einar, but I am in command of an army here. The Jarls look to me as their leader, and I have been making plans for this campaign. You should show me more respect."

He almost spat the last word, and one of his guards raised his axe a fraction from his shoulder and took a small step forward, which was a mistake.

"Move again, and we'll make the square," Einar growled at the guard, whose face flushed red as he looked to Hakon for support. Einar took a pace towards Hakon, looming over him.

"I am sworn to your father, not you. If you want my respect, you earn it. You are where you are because you are Ivar's son, nothing more," he said, and Hakon took a small step back.

This one is weak, Hundr thought; a warrior with pride would never have backed off like that from a confrontation. *Hakon was no drengr*. The Seaworm crew gathered close around Einar. A whisper and a murmur of excitement and challenge coursed around the watching warriors in the fort.

"I'm warning you, Einar, back off," said Hakon wagging a shaky finger up at Einar, "what do you know of being Ivar's son? All you have to do is, as you are told, sail here, kill there. What do you know, Einar the Brawler, with your simple life? Now back off!" He was shouting now, his face blood red.

"Or what?" Einar said, raising his voice. Hundr's heart raced. If there was to be a fight here, it was hard to see how many of the warriors in the fort supported Hakon. There were hundreds of warriors milling around that hilltop, and it could be a massacre should blades be drawn and blood be spilt. Before Hakon could respond, a loud low horn boomed its humming call from the riverbank reverberating across the hillside and then sounded again. More ships were arriving. Men craned their necks to see the sails or standards of the four Drakkar cutting through the Saxon river like a dragon through the skies of legend.

"It's Ivar. Ivar is here," came the call. Ivar the Boneless, son of Ragnar Lothbrok, Champion of the Northmen and father to Hakon, had arrived in Northumbria to make war. The Viking warriors gathered in that old fortress cheered and clashed weapons in greeting. Hakon Ivarsson just glared at Einar, and then at the ships. He gestured as though he would speak again, but Einar had moved away, and the moment passed. Hakon instead clenched his fist and pounded it onto his thigh, and turning on his heel, he stalked away. But after a few steps, he paused next to Halvdan, and they exchanged a few words which Hundr couldn't hear above the commotion of Ivar's arrival. Hakon shot a glance in Hundr's direction and pointed.

"Who are those two? Einar is scraping the barrel for warriors if this is the best he can muster. A crusty old slave and a vagabond," Hakon said, this time loud enough for Hundr to hear. Hundr glanced down at himself, dressed in a faded tunic and trews. He had the axe belted at his waist, but amongst the Viking warriors on the hilltop in their war finery, he was as a beggar, a far cry from the cloth he would have worn back home. He felt his face turn scarlet and couldn't stop it. Halvdan snorted a sneering laugh, and Hakon grinned at him. The feeling of shame yielded to anger, and Hundr's hand drifted to his axe just before he felt a big hand grab his arm, and amongst the din of cheering, Sten leant in close to Hundr's ear.

"Let this one go, laddie, don't touch your blade. He'd gladly make a show of you after Einar hurt his pride."

Sten was right. Hundr mastered himself and cast his eyes back towards the river and the approaching ships. Hakon laughed and clapped Halvdan on the shoulder and marched back to his keep. *That shit is everything I'm not.* Just because of his birth, Hakon had reputation and power. He had warriors loyal to him because he was of the line of Ragnar and Ivar. Hundr looked down at his clothes and brushed at the stains and creases; he didn't look like a warrior. He clenched his teeth and ignored the burning feeling that everyone was looking and laughing at him. Hundr told himself he would rise and be like these warriors, these men in fine brynjar mail coats with shining arm rings. He would show Hakon Ivarsson and the bastards back home what he could become.

FOUR

Warriors gathered in groups on the slope, talking and laughing, many standing on their tiptoes to get a better look at the approaching hero. They thronged the area close to the dock, pushing and jostling to get to the front, to get within touching distance of Ivar the Boneless. Hundr also wanted to run down the hill and force his way to the front, but he held back. Ivar would laugh if he saw Hundr's clothes and appearance or ask him to fetch ale or clean his boots. So, he stayed with Sten behind the crowd, feeling like a warrior but looking like a beggar.

Ivar Ragnarsson was the most famous of all Northmen. His deeds, alongside those of his father, were retold and embellished at firesides across the Viking world. It was beyond the hopes of most men's miserable lives to meet such a legend. That, along with the promise of silver and reputation, drew the Viking Ships to Northumbria to join the sons of Ragnar as they assaulted the Saxon lands. The desire to escape the humdrum of everyday life drove Northmen to their ships to go Viking. For those brave enough to risk their lives on the Whale Road and in battle, the rewards were huge in this life and the next. Warriors who worshipped Thor and Odin thought only of dying a glorious death in battle. Of dying with weapon in hand and going to one of the great halls of the afterlife, Valhalla for Odin or Thruthvangar for Thor. Once there, you would feast, swive, and fight all day until you fell, only to rise the next day to do it over again. For Northmen who sat in freezing huts swaddled in furs eking an existence from rocky ground and thin soil, to go Viking was a dream. Ivar the Boneless was the epitome of that dream. A peerless warrior, rich with plunder and the respect of warriors the world over.

"They are beautiful, aren't they?" Hundr said, nodding towards the ships.

After an uncomfortable silence, he glanced at Sten, who grunted in agreement. The hulking old warrior had been sullen and withdrawn since joining the crew, but he had stopped Hundr from making a grave mistake with Hakon and likely saved him from an axe in the face. So Hundr thought he would try the miserable old sod with conversation again. It was like trying to get blood from a stone. Hundr switched his attention from his surly companion to the lead ship, where a figure in bright mail and a green cape billowing perched high on the prow of the leading vessel. The figure raised a shining sword high. The warriors on the shore cheered and chanted.

"Ivar, Ivar, Ivar,"

The green caped warrior leaned over the side

and let his blade catch the surface of the water, making long ripples whose ridges sparkled in the Spring sunshine. Hundr supposed the green caped warrior must be Ivar. The gathered crowds continued to chant his name whilst also clashing weapons on shields, creating a reverberating din that made Hundr's heart thump. The Boneless called back to his crew, and the ship's oars came up as one and held a position level with the ship's sheer strake. Ivar the Boneless in full mail brynjar then hopped up on the first oar. The men on the hill roared their cheers even louder. Ivar leapt to the next oar, lurching into a sequence of running jumps as he ran the oars bow to stern and back again, completing the daring feat with ease. A mail coat was heavy. Hundr had worn them for weapons practice in his youth to develop the strength needed to move and fight under that weight. Should Ivar slip into the water, it would carry him down to the depths of the God Njorth's underwater kingdom.

"Difficult that," grumbled Sten, and Hundr looked up at him.

"What?"

"Running the oars, never mind with bloody mail on. Not easy. Suppose he is the Boneless, though. Ragnar used to say it's the spectacle of brave and fearsome acts keeps men loyal."

"What does his name mean?" Hundr asked,

"Boneless? He can twist and turn around blades as though he has no bones at all, fast as bloody Hel. Or he was when he was a lad anyways," said Sten.

So maybe the old goat was the Sten of legend and did know the sons of Ragnar.

"So, you can talk."

"What d'you mean?" Sten shot back, frowning.

"You've barely said a word since the Holmgang."

Sten shook his head and chewed at his bottom lip.

"Those men you lot killed were my friends, good men, Holy men… you lot butchered them for a few candlesticks and plates. D'you ever think on that?" Sten said, eyes blazing.

Hundr kept silent because he hadn't thought about that. Maybe the old sod had a right to be miserable. Everything Hundr knew told him the strong preyed on the weak, and a man should be able to defend himself. As he watched Ivar jump back to the prow of his ship, he remembered the words of his old lore master;

"What does the eagle fret for the fate of the mouse?"

Which at the time he had thought was a load of shit, as was most of the lore master's prattle. But that was how Northmen lived. A Lord should protect his people with warriors, and a man should be ready to defend himself and his family. He decided against telling Sten about the wisdom of the eagle. The old bastard was built like a stone shithouse, and Hundr wasn't sure yet that Sten wouldn't twist his head off and roll it down the hill if the mood took him.

The approaching ships had stowed their oars and drifted into the dock. Ivar leapt ashore and raised two swords aloft. The crowd of warriors cheered him as he strode among them, heading towards the keep. Hundr noticed warriors bowed their heads, and any who wore helmets took them off as Ivar passed. *That must be what it feels like to have a reputation, to be respected.* Hundr imagined himself making that walk and how it must make Ivar's chest burst with pride. The crowd of warriors shoving and jostling to get a look at their Champion forced Hundr back, so he couldn't get a good look at Ivar as he passed by. Hundr craned his neck and stood as tall as he could, but the shields and shoulders of the warriors ahead of him obscured the view. Finally, Ivar reached the keep and hopped up its staircase. As the excitement dissipated and the crowd dispersed, the Seaworm crew huddled together close to the hill's summit.

Halvdan barked orders to find food and ale and provided some hack silver to buy it. Hundr had used all of his hack silver weeks ago to get his berth on the trader ship and it was merely shards of silver hacked from rings or jewellery, which people would accept as payment for goods. As they sat and waited, the day drew on into the early evening, and crews nearby made small fires waiting for orders from the Lords and Jarls. Hundr had learned from Blink that they would soon march East to join up with the other sons of Ragnar. He asked why the Ragnarsson's were here, why so many ships and men, and Blink had called Thorkild to tell the tale. Thorkild loved to talk, and his blue eyes flashed as he shuffled into a comfortable seating position. He held up a gnarled hand where two of the fingers were missing to silence the crew as he told his tale.

"Ragnar Lothbrok was the greatest Viking in all the North, sacker of cities, voyager to the ends of the World, warrior of warriors. Returning from a glorious adventure where he had sailed South to where the sun burns men's skins black. A monstrous storm took him one fell day, and Ragnar found himself shipwrecked off the coast of this very land, Northumbria, where the Saxon King Aelle took him prisoner. Aelle hates all Vikings, and in vengeance for past raids, Aelle cast Ragnar into a pit of snakes, those poisonous Loki worms. This pit Aelle had kept ready out of hate of all Northmen, and he'd prayed to his God that one day he would catch one. But before the viper worms could kill Ragnar, he called loud and clear to the Gods, 'how the little pigs would grunt if they heard how the old boar died'. The Gods made sure that message came to Ragnar's sons. Those sons took an oath of vengeance against Aelle and all the Saxons, an oath of blood and axe. So, the little pigs have come with a Great Army to make war on Aelle."

Hundr had heard bits and pieces of that story before but never in that awe-inspiring detail. He had visions of the writhing snakes biting and snapping at Ragnar and of the anger and fury that death had fired in Ragnar's sons. It stirred Hundr. An end like that would ensure Ragnar's name would live on forever.

"Did it happen that way?" asked Kraki, but before anyone could answer, Halvdan cut in.

"Shut your mouths, worms. No one wants to hear bollocks stories and bullshit. So keep it down until the grub gets here." Halvdan stared across the crew, challenging them with his bulging eyes and creased frown.

Hundr leaned towards Sten.

"You knew Ragnar, did you know about all that?" he whispered.

Sten just frowned at him,

"Aye, I knew."

Hundr shook his head.

"Well, thanks for sharing your side of the story Sten, you've really brought the tale to life."

Sten ignored him and lay back with his hands behind his head. Trying to get Sten to talk felt like trying to get a donkey to sing a tune, difficult and not really necessary. It was becoming tiresome.

Hundr heard a creaking of timber behind him. He turned to see Ivar coming through the faded door of the keep trailed by his son Hakon and a shambling, dusty-looking figure who hobbled down the stairs behind them. The trio was striding in his direction, and he gulped hard and shuffled behind Sten's huge frame.

"Einar Rosti," Ivar shouted, a wide grin splitting his handsome face. Hundr had expected Ivar to be a hulking brute with battle scars and snarls to match. Instead, Ivar looked like a warrior in his mail, and two fine swords belted at his waist, but his face and features were gentle and unscarred. He had shining black hair tied back from his face in a plait, and his green cloak stood out among the browns and greys of the Viking warriors in the fort. He was of average height and build and walked on the balls of his feet, balanced and smooth. Ivar raised a hand as he approached, and Einar gave what passed for a smile on his broad, severe face, and the two men clasped forearms.

"Lord Ivar," said Einar, "running the oars with your brynjar on," and he shook his head in mock disapproval and smiled his strange smile where the corners of his mouth turned down rather than up. Ivar clapped him on the shoulder.

"Got to give the lads a spectacle, Einar."

Some of the crew laughed along, and Ivar nodded, recognising a few of them, including Halvdan.

"So, how did you get on up North?" Ivar asked,

"We got the job done," Einar said.

"Good. How did it go?"

"He grovelled and apologised for not sending his warriors. I hurt him, roughed up his son, and burned his barn down."

"Good, Einar, bastard won't do it again."

Ivar clapped Einar on the shoulder again, nodding his approval. He looked over his shoulder and beckoned Hakon to join then.

"I sent Einar to punish Jarl Hrafn Rafnsson in Vankjir. Why did I do that?"

Hundr noticed that the Boneless' eyes were

different colours. He had one blue and one brown eye, which made him hard to look at, the blue, bright and piercing and the brown deep and pitiless.

"Because Einar is your dog, father," said Hakon, looking as though he was about to yawn whilst glowering at Einar.

Ivar turned to his son.

"What reason, boy, for what reason did I send Einar?" Ivar looked Hakon up and down.

"To punish Jarl Hrafn father."

"To punish him. If other Jarl's heard that Hrafn the fat lazy nithing had refused my call to arms, then other Jarl's sworn to me might do the same. So, Einar, Halvdan, and these men sailed North and slapped him around as an example," said Ivar, his voice rising as he spoke.

"I am sure fat Hrafn and his farmhands didn't put up much of a fight," Hakon said, tilting his head towards his guards, and they chuckled along with him.

"Einar Rosti is a drengr and a Sea Jarl. He's fought alongside me more times than I can remember," Ivar was shouting, and the men around shuffled backwards, "He fights like a demon, like, like...." Ivar had become enraged now, his face twisted and furious. He had gone from calm to rage in a heartbeat and almost could not speak he was so incensed, "who are these turds with you? Who are you two who stand here amongst warriors? You there, turd, you look like a whore with your hair like that, a turd whore," Ivar bellowed, pointing at one of Hakon's guards.

Hundr edged away from the furnace of Ivar's rage. It had erupted in an instant. A minor slight from Hakon and Ivar had exploded. Hakon and the other guard stepped away from the unlucky sentinel who had incurred Ivar's wrath. Hakon was shaking and looking from his father to the ground. The insulted guard swallowed hard and shifted his grip on the long-handled war axe resting on his shoulder, using his right hand to brush the offending long loose fair hair back from his face. Ivar whipped one of his swords free and pointed it at the guard.

"You touched your axe at me, pup... you touched it... I'll have your head... I'll have your head," Ivar thundered. The guard looked to Hakon for help again, but Hakon looked away, leaving his man alone to face Ivar. Hundr could feel that wrath, and it was like a blacksmith's forge, too hot to be near, forcing men away from its intensity. Ivar took a few steps and turned his blade in a wide circle.

"Get back, give me room," he said, quivering. The warriors in the vicinity, including Hundr and Sten, had retreated from Ivar. The guard had realised there was no way out and instead set his jaw and readied his axe. Hundr thought the man had seen a chance to make his reputation, to be the warrior who killed Ivar the Boneless. Worth a try, he supposed, given that he was going to fight the Champion of the North whether he wanted to or not.

"Come then, hero," taunted Ivar.

"Odin," roared the guard and leapt at Ivar, swinging his axe in great sweeps around his body in a blur. Ivar moved at an impossible speed between the arcs of the axe and got behind the guard, kicking him forward off balance. The guard stumbled and then spun, swinging the long axe wide in a blow that would cut Ivar in half, but Ivar just swayed away from it and stepped in as the blade passed by and slammed the pommel of his sword into the guard's face. The guard gurgled and groaned as his nose burst open, spraying blood. He tottered as the crimson liquid sheeted down his face and onto his mail. He held the shaking axe out, but Ivar tipped it aside with his own blade and, with a grunt, drove its length deep into the guard's chest, twisted it once and pulled it clear. Hundr heard the sickening crunch as the blade crushed bones. The guard fell to his knees and dropped his axe. Ivar leapt forward, dropping his own weapon and grasping the axe as it fell. The guard fell onto his back, and Ivar scrabbled across the dirt to clasp the axe haft into the dying warrior's hand.

"Take this warrior to Valhalla, Odin. He will fight well on the day of Ragnarök. He will wait for me there, and we will drink together and feast together until the end of days," Ivar called to the sky. He rose to his feet, picking up his own blade, and levelled it at his son.

"He died like a drengr. Learn from that."

The anger which came so fast and burned so bright left him like a cloak falling from a man's shoulders. Ivar stood with Einar and ignored the looks of fear and surprise from those around. Putting the weapon in the dying man's hand assured his place in Valhalla. Hundr watched as men nodded at one another. Even though Ivar had flown into an incandescent rage over next to nothing and snatched a man's life away, he had given the guard an honourable death. A death all warriors aspired to. Ivar had put on another show for his warriors, showing them his skill and ferocity, ensuring the men had the right amount of fear and respect.

The gathered warriors avoided Ivar's gaze and wandered away, leaving a wide space around the Seaworm crew. Sten was holding the wooden cross at his neck again. His eyes were closed, and he was talking under his breath.

"What are you doing?" hissed Hundr, fearing if Ivar saw the Christ trinket, he might fly into another murderous rage. Sten stopped and opened his eyes.

"Praying."

Hundr clenched his teeth. Sten's brusque manner of speaking, or lack of it, was giving Hundr a pain in the arse.

"Well, don't. Nobody gives a shit about your pox-ridden Saxon God; it might get us both killed." Hundr spoke as quietly but with as much force as he could without risking the rage of the Boneless.

"What am I doing here? I left all this behind bloody years ago," Sten mumbled.

"What?" asked Hundr, but Sten closed his eyes and did not answer.

Ivar and Einar were talking, so Hundr tried to listen to them rather than persevere with his attempts to get words from the stone that was Sten.

"You will stay with my son and his three crews," Ivar said, "I will leave at first light tomorrow with the rest."

"Lord, I.." said Einar, but Ivar shook his head and cut him short. "You wait for the last few ships and march with Hakon. We will meet when we join with my brothers in the East. Hakon needs your experience, Einar. We will march across Saxon lands full of warriors, and we can't lose men."

Ivar strode away, and Hakon lowered his eyes as his father went by and then followed him, his remaining guard trailing behind. All the fort was humming with hushed talk of Ivar's fury and the unnatural speed he had shown in the fight. Hundr turned to Sten.

"Thor's balls, I wasn't expecting that," he said.

"Well, you're amongst wolves now. No time for weakness or pity here."

"Doesn't look like Einar likes Hakon very much," Hundr said, and Sten gave a harrumph.

"Sounds like we're to march out with his men soon enough, lad, so we'll see how they get on, whose supposed to be in charge, and whose actually cock o 'the roost."

FIVE

Ivar was true to his word, and most of the army left with him early the next morning. The precious ships stood moored on the Mersey, where they would remain protected by a holding force of three crews. It was a cold but bright morning, and it had been a glorious sight to watch the crews march out behind Ivar and his captains. Ivar led the way, with his gnarled Holy Man, Kjartan Wolfthinker, riding alongside him. Three Volva trailed that wizened figure, witches clothed in filthy robes and festooned with charms and animal bones. The long column followed down the hill and across the deserted Saxon farm land and its patchwork of greens and browns. They slithered along like a long winding serpent, weapons and mail catching the sun like scales.

The Seaworm crew remained in the Fort with Hakon's men and the three crews who would guard the flotilla. The Seaworm men gave Einar and Halvdan a wide berth because they were in a foul mood, which Hundr found difficult to differentiate from their usual disposition. Bush had assured him they were as prickly as pigs balls at being forced to stay and play wet nurse to Hakon, and Hundr took his word for it. Halvdan had growled at the crew to shut up more than once already that morning. So they hung around at the quayside, waiting for Hakon's late ships to round the river's broad meandering bend.

Hundr sat with Sten, who had spoken little during that morning or the previous evening. After the excitement of Ivar's arrival the day before, the morning dragged, with little to do but watch and wait.

"So, how did you end up in the land of the Saxons?" Hundr asked, hoping grandfather's life story would pass the time but expecting the old sod to grumble and say nothing. Instead, Sten looked at him sideways and sighed.

"Keep your nose out. That's my affair."

"Listen," Hundr said out of frustration, "First, I saved your life. Second, the rest of the crew don't want to talk to us, what with Toki still all banged up. The least you could do is try to be less, well, less surly. We should be friends, Sten."

Sten just huffed again and fingered his wooden cross pendant.

Hundr glanced across the river bank to where Toki was hobbling back from a piss into the river water, and Kraki Horse Face ran to give Toki an arm to lean on. Hundr thought Toki was milking the sympathy; he hadn't hurt him that badly. Toki and Kraki sat with a few of the other Seaworm crew, the Kveldsson brothers, Asbjorn Luckyfeet, and Styrr. As Toki sat down and groaned, they shot Hundr a murderous stare and Styrr spat in his direction, just to confirm their hatred of him in case there was any misunderstanding.

"You are the only friend I've got," Hundr said, half under his breath and tried to skim a flat stone across the surface of the river. It made four bounces before he flitted back to the unfortunate fact that his fellow murderous crewmen wanted his blood when all he wanted was to be one of them, to be a warrior and a Carl of the army.

A rumbling thunder vibrated around the hilltop, interrupting his melancholy, and Hundr turned to see a band of mounted warriors entering the fort. All the men lazing about the river noticed the commotion and rose to see who it could be.

"Come on," he said to Sten and hiked up the hillside towards the keep. Hundr had taken only twenty paces when the mounted troop cantered around the hill, and he had to jump out of the way to avoid being crushed by their horses. They reined in, swirling and ambivalent of the gathering crowd, their horses' hooves churning clumps of mud into the air. Hundr leapt back, shoving Sten away from the danger.

"Bloody hell," the warrior next to him said in surprise, realising at the same time as Hundr that the riders were all heavily armed women. There were ten in total, and their leader was stocky, with a closely shaved head. She had a patch over one eye, and scars ran across her scalp in a patchwork demonstration of her experience in battle. Hundr had heard tales of women warriors before and knew there would be many with the army, but he never expected anything like this. They were well-armed and carried the powerful re-curved horn bows famous in the East, and half of them wore mail brynjar coats marking the band out as serious warriors. Their one-eyed leader yanked on her reins and turned her horse in an elaborate circle, showing her skill with the beast and sneering at the gathered warriors who stood open-mouthed and staring.

"Ivar Ragnarsson," she called towards the keep in Norse with a heavy Svear accent.

Hakon Ivarsson appeared at the top of the keeps wooden staircase, baleful in his fur cloak.

"I am Hakon Ivarsson."

Hakon grasped the timber rail outside the door, and even from this distance, Hundr could see the whites of his knuckles he clenched it so tightly.

"My father has left. Who is this who shouts in my camp as though they were the Champion of the North?"

The woman patted her mount's neck and kept it still.

"Sigurd Snake Eye and Ubba Lothbrokson sent me here to bring the forces of Ivar to join the army, Lord."

"My father left yesterday, and we are leaving today. Who are you, woman?"

"I am Ragnhild of the Valkyrie. Priestess of Odin All-father and guardian of the temple of Uppsala," she said, straightening her back as she spoke. A murmur spread across the fort. The warrior next to Hundr took off his dented helmet and clutched it to his chest.

"Thor's ball's, has Odin sent his Valkyrie to fight alongside us?" he said. All men knew of the Valkyrie, Odin's harbingers of souls for his Einherjar, but they were of the Gods, not the world of men. A man behind them laughed.

"They are not Gods, friend. They are warriors like you and me. I have heard of these women, they are Svear and serve the great Temple of Odin there. They have a fearsome reputation, and it should honour us they are here to fight alongside us," he said.

The Valkyrie leader Ragnhild nudged her horse a few steps towards Hakon.

"We will escort you to the East to join your uncle's camp. They itch for battle."

She turned her horse in a circle again, grinning at the gathered warriors, "And the All-Father wants your souls."

Ragnhild's mirthless grin sent a shiver down Hundr's spine. She barked an order at her riders, and they dismounted and tended to their steeds. Hakon was retreating behind his door when Ragnhild shouted.

"We leave in an hour."

Hakon paused as though he would reply but stalked back into his keep without another word.

"Ships!" Came a shout from the quayside, and Hundr saw two wide bellied Knarr's coming around the Mersey's bend and turning for the fort. He hoped these were the ships Hakon was waiting for, so they could get marching. The Valkyrie had set Hundr's mind racing. These were proper warriors, a fearsome war band. He smiled to himself. He was now among the likes of Ivar the Boneless, Einar the Brawler, and now Ragnhild and her Valkyries. His friends back home would never believe him. His dream was coming alive; he was a warrior among warriors.

The ships docked, and it seemed to be just more

of Ivar's warriors arriving from his forces in Ireland. Hundr was about to turn away when he glimpsed a splash of colour amongst the brown and grey drabness of ships and men. He craned his neck to look over the crowd.

"Well, would you look at that," said Sten. Hundr looked. Indeed, he couldn't stop looking as stepping from ship to wharf was a woman draped in a green and yellow cloak, her hair shimmering, with a fine ivory comb holding it up, glinting in the sunlight. Another well-furnished and delicate lady accompanied her. Hundr almost toppled over as he stood on his tiptoes to get a better look.

One of the arrived crew stopped to talk to Bush just in front of Hundr.

"Is the Boneless still here?" the Irishman asked in a lilting voice, and Bush shook his head and gestured Eastwards.

"He left this morning, friend, with most of his men. Where did you boys sail in from?" said Bush, scratching his beard and looking at the weapons and gear of the crew, appraising their quality.

"Dublin. We have the bride of Hakon Ivarsson on board."

Bush laughed and frowned,

"What's he want his wife here for? Can she

fight?" he asked, and the men around laughed. The Irishman spat on the ground.

"Freja herself only knows, friend. War is no place to bring your wife."

"Not when there are pretty Saxon maidens to be had."

Hakon Ivarsson's wife was beautiful. She had a long gentle face with a wash of freckles across a delicate nose. As she glided past, Hundr listened to the newly arrived crew explain she was the daughter of an Irish tribal chief. Her name was Saoirse, which meant freedom in the language of the Irish. Hundr could not tear his eyes off her, and their words faded out as she picked her way gracefully towards the keep.

"I've seen it all now, lad," huffed Sten, snapping Hundr from his trance.

"What?" said Hundr, still thinking about the Princess and her shining hair. There had been women back home, of course, but not like this.

"A bloody Lord bringing his bloody wife a'Viking. Bloody fool," said Sten, shaking his head. *Why would Hakon bring her to war when she should be safe from harm?* If she were his wife, Hundr would bring her everywhere for fear of missing a moment of her beauty. He supposed Hakon felt the same.

Sten and Hundr mustered outside of the fort

with the rest of the warriors. Halvdan had found a couple of battered old shields, which they now had slung across their backs. Sten was already moaning about its heavy strap chafing his shoulders and how his back ached from standing for so long. They waited for the other crews to gather in the space between the fort and the fields beyond.

"What am I doing here?" Sten grumbled again, and Hundr ignored him this time, becoming tired of the old goat's whingeing. Hakon rode out of the fort on a fine white mare flanked by the impressively named Svein Bonebreaker, his second in command, and Jarl Einar. Next came an escort of three warriors with Hakon's wife and her handmaiden, all astride horses of chestnut and black. Sten dipped his head in respect as they rode past, as did Hundr.

The leaders rode up to join the Valkyrie, who had already assembled outside of the fort. They headed off at a slow trot with the rest of the warriors marching behind them. This force that trailed Ivar by a full day totalled four crews, around a long hundred men of Irish and Viking warriors. The column set off following the muddy track Ivar's force had left, a great brown scar snaking over the hills ahead, where that tremendous iron Ragnarsson dragon had slithered over Northumbria's fields.

So far, Hundr had not seen an armed Saxon. He

found it strange how these people had allowed the Ragnarsson forces to land without challenge, but Ivar's troop was large and well-armed, and his Irish warriors were wild and fierce. It would take a well-organised army to throw them back into the Sea.

Half of the Valkyrie force galloped off to scout ahead for the roving bands of Saxon scouts and warriors who would be out of sight but would nonetheless be peppering the hills and copses, monitoring the Viking advance. The column marched west for a day and a half, making camp and resting where Hakon chose, passing burned and deserted villages. Twice they saw mounted men on hilltops watching them, spear points wavering against the skyline. Those Saxon forces would be somewhere, waiting for the right time to avenge their murdered people and hit back at the Viking marauders who had already cut a swathe across Northumbria. Hundr wondered how this Saxon enemy fought and if they were fearsome, assuming any men whose home and families were under attack would fight with venom and anger. And who was to say there hadn't already been a battle in the East where the rest of the army gathered. He hoped not. Battle was a chance to forge a name and a reputation, and he longed for it.

On the second day of the march, the track led into a wood at the foot of a range of hills. The forest thickened and continued up a vast hillside spotted with tilled fields stretching into the distance. Ivar's force had come this way, so the road was clear, and although his shield chafed at him, Hundr breathed in the thick woody dampness of the forest and listened to the chittering of birds. It felt good to be in the open marching with the prospect of battles to come. Sten marched along in familiar grumpy silence whilst Hundr tried to talk to his crewmates and diminish their hatred of him since the fight with Toki.

"When battle comes, that's when reputations are made," said a bright-eyed young Dane with the confidence of a seasoned warrior who had countless battles behind him. Yet with his fresh soft face and wispy beard, he looked like he had barely left his mother's tit. The Dane looked even younger than Hundr, Erik was his name, and they had struck up together as they marched along.

"Aye, and fortunes," Hundr replied.

"So the bloody poets say," said Sten through a sigh over Hundr's shoulder. Hundr shot him an annoyed frown. He had saved Sten's life and risked his own to do it. So far, it seemed to have been for nothing. Maybe the promise of an audience with the great and the good of the army was just a fantasy, concocted by Sten to save his life. *What if it was a fantasy I've allowed myself to be drawn into like a fool?*

Hundr was about to question Sten again about how he had ended up in Northumbria in the first place when he heard a commotion up ahead. Men up the column were shifting shields from their backs into defensive positions, but Hundr couldn't see what was going on. He could hear shouting in the distance and men looking at one another as they hefted shields and checked for weapons. An arrow whipped past Hundr's face making him flinch as it buried itself with a bloody thump into the head of the man in front of him, killing that man and causing the others around to duck and look from side to side in case more deadly missiles flew. *In a thick forest and arrows on the flanks, shit. Smells like an ambush.* More arrows thudded and slapped into the flesh around him, and men were shouting and crouching, trying to bring shields to bear but banging them into their shipmates as they panicked. Hundr hunched down, trying to keep his head low, unable to see where the missiles came from.

"Arrows. Keep your head down, boy," growled Sten, stepping close to Hundr with his shield raised high. Hundr scrambled to get his own shield into position. Four riders galloped down the column, shouting for warriors to form two shield walls facing either side of the track. One rider was the Valkyrie leader, Ragnhild. She waved her axe as she bellowed at the warriors to hurry.

"Shield wall, shield wall," she called, pointing her axe at Hundr and Sten.

Hundr braced himself, shield ready and axe drawn. It was a reflex drilled into him since the time he could lift a shield and practised a thousand times until it became second nature. His heart was pumping hard, and he searched to see where the threat was coming from but couldn't, so he just raised his shield and kept himself ready. A rumbling began deep in the trees to his right, which then became thunder erupting from within the forest as a huge wagon crashed from the undergrowth and thundered through the middle of the Viking column. The attackers were riding double, and men jumped off the horses' backs to swing hammers at the wagon's wheels, smashing them from their axles. Those men jumped back on their mounts before the Vikings could respond. In the blink of an eye, they were away, riding at full gallop back into the safety and cover of the trees. The wagon had cut the column in two. The forest around the Vikings erupted with the roar of warriors baying for blood, a deep undulating call in the Saxon tongue, which Hundr didn't understand. Still, he understood that there was an army of Saxon warriors keening their murderous rumbling battle song, and the Viking warriors tried not to shake or quiver as they waited for those hidden warriors to attack. Hundr backed into Sten.

"Is it the Saxons?" he said, knowing that it couldn't be anyone other than the bloody Saxons but wanting to speak to settle the fear coursing through his body.

"It's the Saxons," said Sten. "ready yourself for a charge boy, and keep your shield up. Overlap your shield with mine and with the man next to you...."

"I know how to fight in a... shit!" snapped Hundr as an arrow slammed into his shield, and the force of it banged the rim into his face.

Before he could respond, the charge came hard from both sides as Saxon warriors tore into them with heavy spears and blades, screaming their war cries. Hundr braced his shoulder behind his shield just in time as a spear smashed into the upper edge of it, banging the iron rim onto his head again. He cursed, grunting as a Saxon shoulder charged him, but he held his ground, shoving back using his legs to drive back at the onslaught. Hundr was breathing hard as a blade beat at his shield. He looked at Sten, who heaved his shield back at the Saxons with all his might. Hundr was being pounded into a crouch. The Saxon Warrior wielding the sword, which thudded and hacked at his shield, was screaming and spitting curses, mad-eyed and furious. All around was chaos, men shouting, screaming, hacking at each other. Hundr could smell shit as dying men voided their bowels, mixed with the metallic, ferrous smell of blood and the sour smell of sweat. The Saxons had attacked from both sides of the forest in a well-planned ambush, and it was utter carnage.

"Shield wall, shield wall," came the call again in Norse above the din as the Vikings gathered their senses amidst the onslaught. Hundr glanced around, and it was too late. The enemy was among them all down the line. Soon, they would roll them up in a great slaughter and a famous Saxon victory over their hated invaders. He couldn't see any of the Seaworm men, no sign of Bush or Blink or Kraki. Instead, he looked to his right just in time to see Erik take a spear thrust to the belly. As the boy dropped his shield, grimacing in shock and pain, the spear blade pulled free and thumped into his eye in a gush of blood, dropping the young Dane and ended his dreams of glory. Hundr snarled, letting out a roar and shoved back at the foe still beating on his shield, creating a few seconds of space.

"Cover me, quickly," he called to Sten and dropped his shield, whipping his axe free of its belt loop, and on one knee, Hundr swung it hard across the shin of his attacker, and the man toppled. Hundr rose to his feet, driving the axe tip into the Saxon's armpit, screaming into his bearded face. Then, without pause, Hundr rolled around the man's body and sliced his axe across the belly of the next enemy. He was among them, swinging and chopping, and they backed away from his ferocity. He had acted on instinct and attacked when he should have kept the shield wall solid, but he would not die here in a shit stinking forest. Then, suddenly, an ear-piercing scream rattled his senses and Ragnhild, the warrior priestess, charged into the gap Hundr had created. She lay about her with an axe in one hand and a knife in the other, cutting and slashing like a demon.

"Odin!" she shouted above the battle din as she pressed forward, and she and Hundr carved the enemy line in two. Then, as Sten banged a man out of the way with his shield, Hundr swung his axe into the belly of another Saxon and could smell ale on that man's fetid breath as the air blew out of him. Another Valkyrie followed her leader into the fray. They were turning the tide, but the enemy was too many, and they were flowing around the cart, which meant the other part of the Viking force was surely lost.

"We need to move," Sten shouted above the battle din and moved towards Hundr. The four of them formed a circle, the two Valkyrie, Hundr and Sten.

"Into the woods," said Ragnhild snarling, and they backed away from the fighting, their attackers already preferring to loot the fallen rather than tackle their formidable blades. The four ran deeper into the dense trees, a victory roar undulating behind them, making the hair stand up on the back of Hundr's neck. They ran on, crashing through the bracken and branches until the din of Saxon victory dwindled. The band came to rest in a small clearing, each one of them panting and dropping their hands to their knees, gasping for air, and looking at each other in despair. They had marched as a strong, confident force of Viking warriors. But now, they were a defeated, ragged band of four, alone in a foreign land and surrounded by enemies.

SIX

"Ambush," spat Ragnhild, panting, her scarred face grimacing, "Hakon's scouts weren't worth shit."

"I thought you were scouts?" said Hundr.

"Watch your mouth, boy," said Ragnhild with venom, "that fool Hakon preferred to use his own men."

Hundr held a hand up in apology, and his breathing slowed. He could feel blood wet on his face and hands, so he wiped it on the sleeve of his tunic. He felt a pang of shame that he had fled his first actual battle, but he knew he had fought well. Saxons had fallen to his axe, and Hundr had carved a way through them with Ragnhild, who had fought with a ferocity and skill the Saxons could not match. Hundr, Sten, Ragnhild and one of her Valkyrie warriors were in a clearing in the forest. In the distance, they could hear the laughter and shouts of the victorious Saxons, mixed with the screams and calls of the fallen Vikings.

"What now, then?" he asked.

Ragnhild stood straight and brushed herself down, returning her blood crusted axe and knife to her belt,

"Keep moving East towards the Great Army," she said, "Any other survivors will go that way. I came from the Ragnarsson camp, and they were only waiting on Ivar before they start the war with King Aelle. So we keep going until we find them."

"I thought we were in Northumbria?" said Hundr. Ragnhild looked him up and down, which made him blush and stand straighter. He knew his clothes looked poor, but he had fought beside her, and so he hoped she would see him as a warrior and not as a bail boy.

"It goes from West to East coast, the western part is a shit hole, Aelle has his city in the East," said Ragnhild.

There were no objections to that plan. On the contrary, it seemed the only sensible thing to do. One thing was for sure, to stay where they were was to die.

"How many days East is the army?" asked Sten.

"Three on foot," Ragnhild said.

Hundr watched as she gave Sten the same appraising look she had subjected him to, and he noticed a sneer at the corner of her mouth as she glanced at the unbloodied axe in Sten's belt. Sten could not meet her gaze, and so he cast his eyes down and shifted his grip on his shield. Sten was alongside Hundr in the fight, he had seen him and heard weapons beating on the old man's shield, but Sten had not struck with his axe or attacked any Saxons. That was clear as day. *Some bloody legend.*

Hundr glanced from Sten to Ragnhild. Hundr could feel the unspoken tension between them. He thought she was about to accuse Sten of his inaction when a high-pitched shriek echoed around the treetops.

"That's a woman," said the other Valkyrie warrior, her eyes going wide and her long fair hair billowing as he searched for the direction of the scream.

"It came from that way," said Hundr, nodding at a hillock visible through the foliage.
The sound had been clear, but he couldn't see any actual movement through the dense wood. He reckoned it had to be Viking survivors or prisoners, and it had been a woman's sound. Hundr didn't wait to think. He moved off in the scream's direction, but none of the others followed. He turned to Ragnhild, who remained in the clearing.

"Are you afraid? Would you like grandfather here to hold your hand?" he said.

"Piece of shit," she growled, drawing her axe.

"Come on," Hundr said, running through the undergrowth, leaping over a fallen and rotting log. Now that he was moving, it dawned on Hundr that he did not know what lay ahead. It could be one Saxon with a prisoner or the whole Saxon army. He felt the heat of fear rising, and the sense of danger thrummed behind his eyes. He paused with his back against a moss-covered trunk and turned to check the others were following, and sure enough, the two Valkyries had broken into a run. Hundr smiled to himself as Sten blew hard and wiped the sweat from his brow rising from his crouch; the old warrior hefted his shield set off, grumbling as he shuffled and increased his pace.

"Bloody young fools," he said, but at least he followed.

They reached the crest of the hillock and crouched behind a cluster of mossy rocks jutting from the leafy bracken. A scream tore through the air again, followed by the low rumble of men's laughter. Hundr put his hand on the cold, wet stone and peered down into the dell below. Five Saxons guarded two women. One was a Valkyrie, her breastplate marking her out, and she looked bloody and beaten. One of her Saxon captors, a short, thin sandy bearded man, was examining her recurved bow, stretching the string and looking at the fine horn work on the weapon. The other prisoner was Hakon's wife. She stood, head bowed, her hair ruffling lightly in the breeze. A thick set and helmeted Saxon laughed and poked his spear point at the hem of her dress, and she gave a small yelp and leapt backwards, bumping into the Valkyrie. The Saxons laughed.

"Hrist," Ragnhild whispered, and the other Valkyrie nodded.

"We must free her," Ragnhild said to Hundr, "Hildr and I will skirt round to their flanks and shoot at them. You two attack down the middle when you hear my signal."

"What signal?" asked Hundr as desperately as whispering would allow.

"You will know it when you hear it, boy," she said.

"I am not a boy; why does everyone insist on calling me a boy?"

"You want me and him to attack five Saxons whilst you two shoot bloody sticks at them?" said Sten. Ragnhild looked him up and down, her grim face twisted into a sneer.

"Just charge them, old man, don't worry, we will do the axe work," she said, and she set off keeping low and darting to the left whilst Hildr cut right.

"We can't charge five men, lad. We'll be slaughtered," Sten hissed.

"You are as big as three of them put together," said Hundr and grinned. "Besides, we are going to rescue a Princess. That will deserve a reward and a story at least."

"A story? Bloody Idiot."

"Now!" came a shout through the trees and down the slope, Ragnhild's unsubtle signal. The Saxon warriors spun to look in her direction.

"For glory, old man," said Hundr, grinning again as he set off down the hill.

"Bastard."

Sten stumbled after him, and they charged down the hill into the dell, roaring at their enemies. Hundr's heart pounded, and he clutched at his axe as the Saxons panicked and looked around, seeing they were being attacked from three directions. A Saxon warrior cried out as an arrow thumped into his chest, dropping him to his knees, and another fell to the ground with an arrow jutting from his neck. Quick as a flash, the Valkyries dropped two Saxons, arrows piercing their leather armour as though made of cloth.

"Odin," Hundr shouted as he closed on them. Reaching the first Saxon and leaping inside the wild swing of that man's spear, he cut him down with a slash of his blade across the warrior's face. Blood sprayed everywhere as he halted the charge to spin, swinging at the next Saxon. In a blur, Sten bowled that man over with his shield, charging and bellowing at full tilt, crashing the man to the floor and driving a few steps past him before he could stop his momentum. Hundr turned to look for the remaining enemies to see Hrist, the captured Valkyrie, jump onto the back of the final Saxon. She clawed at his face, screaming with battle joy as the Saxon flailed his arms around, trying to shake her off. Then, in a few heartbeats, it was over. Ragnhild cut the throat of the man Sten had dropped and tossed her axe to Hrist, who butchered her former captor, snarling as his blood splashed on her face and hair.

Once the Valkyrie slaughter ceased, Hundr ran straight to the Princess, who crouched shaking in the bracken with her hands held over her face.

"My Lady, are you hurt?" he said, falling to one knee. He held out a hand to comfort her but flinched back, knowing he shouldn't touch her. And not knowing what to do, he just held it there, wanting to help but aware that he looked like a fool. The Princess reached out a delicate, trembling, pale hand, and in between sobs, she grabbed his hands in thanks. Hundr gasped at the cold soft touch of her skin, wanting to pull her close and tell her everything would be well, but shouts of alarm disturbed him.

"We need to move," said Ragnhild as she tossed

the captured bow back to the freed Hrist. "Get up, lack beard, stop fawning," she said to Hundr, smirking as his face reddened with embarrassment.

Hundr knew he had turned the deepest shade of red, and he faced away. Ragnhild had embarrassed him in front of the Princess, but he had fought well. Only a few days ago, he had begged Jarl Einar to let him join his troop, now he was a full member of a Viking warship's crew, and today he had rescued a Princess. Hundr had come a long way. He helped the Princess to her feet, and she nodded thanks, keeping her gaze cast at the undergrowth as they moved off to follow Ragnhild. Hundr paused as he passed a fallen Saxon. Then, gesturing the Princess to walk with Sten, he knelt and tore the leather breastplate from the dead Saxon. He pulled it clear of the man's head and pulled it over his own. It fit well enough, loose around the chest. But it was armour, and now, it was his.

He ran to catch up to Sten and the Princess, who followed close behind Ragnhild, Hrist and Hildr. The Valkyrie moved through the forest, arrows nocked on their bows, ready to fire if an enemy showed themselves. The Princess walked with Sten, so Hundr went to his opposite side.

"I saw you laughing at me," he said, annoyed that the old giant had sniggered at his efforts to comfort the Princess.

"What? We've just been bloody ambushed, and we're lost in a Saxon forest surrounded by enemy warriors, and you're worried about me laughing at you?"

Hundr peered around Sten's frame, rolling his lips against his gums. But the Princess hadn't heard.

"I know well the shit we are in, thanks," said Hundr, "just haven't heard you laugh since we met. Strange that you thought that now was the time to lighten your mood."

Sten huffed and chuckled.

"You fight well, boy, but you're a bloody fool charging around like a hero. Maybe I am getting used to this life again, haven't had this much fun in years." Sten said and shoved Hundr's shoulder. "Come on, little one. You're safe now. Me and the glorious hero here will keep you safe." Sten cast a mocking look in Hundr's direction.

They left the blood and death of the ambush behind, marching Eastwards away from the Saxon cheering and the screams and cries of dying Vikings. It was not the glorious war that Hundr expected it to be. They had barely left the security of their Roman hilltop and had already suffered defeat by the Northumbrian Saxons, who had proved wily fighters. Nevertheless, Ragnhild assured him that the Great Army was in the East, where Sigurd Snake Eye and Ubba Ragnarsson waited for Ivar's men.

Ragnhild was adamant that Hakon was to blame for the ambush, and she cursed him to the Gods for bringing this defeat and shame upon her. As they marched, the Valkyrie fanned out into a wide line to watch for Saxon forces or Viking survivors, and Hundr walked with Sten and the Princess. Hundr felt and looked more like the warrior he wanted to be, with his axe and knife belted at his waist and his looted Saxon hard-baked leather breastplate over his chest. It was a simple breastplate, but it was armour nonetheless, and it belonged to him now, earned in battle and taken from the fallen as was his right.

The Princess marched next to Sten, seeming to gain comfort from his silence and hulking frame. The old man himself trudged on with his shield slung over his broad back and his unused axe in its belt loop.

"I have some ale, Princess, if you are thirsty?" Hundr said, holding a half-empty skin of the warm but clean liquid. She shook her head beneath her downward gaze, and Hundr's heart quickened as he glimpsed her pale green eyes beneath the shadow of her long dark hair.

"Please, call me Saoirse," she said, only just audible above their steps and jangling of their equipment. Saoirse. It was a beautiful name, and Hundr wanted to hear more of her soft Irish lilt.

He struggled to come up with another question to ask her, and he almost tripped over his own feet in the thinking.

"You ever been ambushed before?" he asked Sten, knowing it was a stupid question but wanting to break the silence. Sten gave one of his harrumph's and nodded his head.

"More than a few times, lad." Sten adjusted the shield on his back. *That was the end of that discussion, then.* Hundr marched on.

"Tell me again how you ended up in Northumbria?" Hundr asked, and Sten chuckled.

"I ain't given the tale yet, and don't plan on it neither," he said. One of his great paws swiped the ale skin from Hundr, giving him a wink.

"I'll see if they need ale," he said and quickened his pace to catch up to Ragnhild, Hildr and Hrist.

Hundr and Saoirse walked next to each other. She had her arms folded about her and continued to walk with her eyes fixed on the ground. Hundr swallowed hard.

"So, where in Ireland are you from?" he asked and held his breath.

"Close to the Black Pool, from Dublin," she said, and he exhaled.

"What's it like?"

"Same as here really, my father is a King there,

so I don't get out beyond his halls much," she said.

"How long have you been married?"

"Not long, a few months." She looked sideways at him. She looked sad. Hundr was sure that the assault and capture by the Saxons had terrified her. Still, there was deep melancholy there, stretched across her face and behind her eyes. Something more than her recent troubles.

"Had you known Hakon long?" he asked, and she shrugged.

"I'd never met him before. My father arranged it with the Boneless."

"Arranged, why?"

"To make peace, to stop the fighting. So now my father's warriors are here with Ivar and my husband, and our people have accord and harmony," she said. *So Saoirse was a peace cow, and Hakon was a lucky bastard. He was born into a noble family of warriors, inheriting reputation and wealth, and gifted a beautiful Irish Princess for a wife.*

They marched on, climbing a long slope towards a rise of hills that grew in size ever Eastward. The day was turning to dusk, and Hundr thought they should find a safe place to hide for the night, but he didn't suggest it at risk of being belittled by the more experienced Ragnhild, Hildr, Hrist, or Sten.

The three Valkyrie scoured the land ahead, focused on their surroundings and scanning the horizons all around the group for signs of danger. They had encountered no trouble since leaving the forest, and Hundr walked next to Saoirse. They walked mostly in silence, but the march was not awkward. She had unfolded her arms, and as the afternoon wore on, her head had come up, and he could steal glances at her, and he hoped to Thor that she hadn't noticed.

"I just realised I haven't thanked you," she said as they neared the crest of the slope.

"Thanked me for what?"

"You rescued me. You and others. I thought,... well I thought.."

"I just did what any man would do. We couldn't leave you with the Saxons," he said, cutting her off to help her avoid stating the obvious.

"No, not every man would have risked their life like that. Most would have hidden or fled. But, thank you, anyway," she said and smiled at him. Her face gleamed around that smile, her green eyes glittered, giving Hundr a warm feeling in his belly and chest. *By the Gods, she is beautiful.*

That night they found a cave high on a rocky rise, shielded from the wind by the surrounding hills and woodland. That afforded them the chance for a fire and to take stock. It surprised Hundr that the Valkyrie were also skilled healers and fine warriors. The three applied salves and dressings to their own wounds and the cuts and scrapes Hundr suffered in the ambush. Sten remained uninjured save a swelling on his old knee, which he grumbled about as he dropped his shield to the cave floor, and an ache in his back that he said never went away. Hildr, the Valkyrie, massaged Sten's knee and bound it with linen. The old warrior lay back and left her to her work, maintaining his sullen silence.

Ragnhild and Hrist shot two rabbits and a bird, and they were cleaned and roasted on wooden spits across a small fire as deep in the cave as possible to avoid a visible glow in the night. Hundr found a small brook with babbling cold water and refilled his skin, allowing the Princess to drink and wash the dirt of the day from her face and hands. He sat next to her now as they waited for the food to cook, and she didn't seem to mind, which made him happy.

Sten sat up from where he lay at the mouth of the cave and thanked Hildr for helping him. She asked him to remove his heavy tunic, to which Sten grumbled but eventually took it off. Next, she probed his body for wounds and knots in his muscles, feeling at the spot in his back where he showed that the aching throbbed.

"You are a big man," she said, kneading at the base of his back, making Sten groan and twist his torso with relief. Hundr marvelled at the heavy scarring on Sten's body, but more so at the faded black whirls and markings under his skin which writhed like a nightmare as he moved. Hundr had heard that Viking warriors would cover their bodies with tattoos telling the tales of their campaigns and deeds to remind the Gods of their achievements. But he had not seen such markings before.

"You have been around old one," Hildr said, looking at him with a grin.

"Long time ago. Different life," he said, waving his hand to quieten her. She didn't push him any further, and Ragnhild called to say the food was ready, and so they ate.

Once the small meal was over, Ragnhild led the Valkyrie in prayer to Odin for the fallen. Hundr joined in. He didn't know the incantation the three said in unison, but he knelt and raised his hands to Odin all the same. Sten just frowned and fingered at his wooden Christ pendant whilst Saoirse watched, her eyes glowing in the firelight.

Warriors of the North could not abide defeat. The loss that day was a dishonour to Odin, and Ragnhild made a vow to the All-Father to avenge that loss with Saxon blood. Hundr did not doubt she would see that oath through. What made that day's attack worse was that it had been warriors of the Christ God dealing out the slaughter. God against God, the Christ God had won. Of course, Odin would be furious, and the walls of Valhalla would tremble with his anger.

Hildr finished helping Sten with his aches and pains, so Hundr took a succulent piece of rabbit from its spit and went to sit with him at the mouth of the cave.

"Here, it's good," Hundr said, handing the food to Sten and wiping the grease on his trews. Sten blew on the hot rabbit and a bit off a chunk, the juices running into his beard.

"Do you think we will find the army?" Hundr asked. The thought of being lost in Saxon Northumbria had nagged him all afternoon. Not only that worry but also the likely problem of running into another Saxon force. They had been lucky so far, only coming across the five Saxons guarding Hildr and Saoirse. No doubt bands of bloodthirsty Saxons were combing the countryside looking for Viking survivors.

"She seems to think so," Sten said, nodding in Ragnhild's direction, which she did. Ragnhild seemed to know that they would reach the army in the next day or so, and if so, then all would be well. Hundr thought he might even get a reward from Hakon Ivarsson for rescuing his bride.

"Looks like you're cosying up with the Princess there," said Sten as he chewed his meal. Hundr frowned at him.

"What of it?" he said. Sten wagged a thick finger at him.

"A woman like that'll get you killed faster than the plague, lad. Watch yourself is all I'm saying. Men kill for three things. Power, silver, and women."

"What would you know of it? When I want your advice, I'll ask for it. Remember, grandfather; you said you could get me in front of the sons of Ragnar, get me a place on a top crew." Hundr wanted less of his miserable advice and more talk about his old life and what standing he might have with the sons of Ragnar.

The old man chewed his rabbit and raised a bushy grey eyebrow in his direction. Hundr was starting to think the old dog was telling the truth about his past. The tattooes combined with the snippets of information Sten had let slip gave weight to his claims. Maybe he was the Sten Sleggya of the old tales.

"Sleep now," Ragnhild called as she lay down on the stony soil of the cave, "we have a journey ahead tomorrow."

"Will we make it to the army tomorrow?" Hundr asked.

"If we push hard," said Ragnhild.

"Saxons will be everywhere. So we must move carefully," said Hrist, as she was replaiting her long blonde braid.

"If they catch us, we all die. You two will be the lucky ones," Hildr said, gesturing to Sten and Hundr. Which was true, Hundr knew, the men would simply be killed, but the women's death would be more prolonged and infinitely more painful.

Hundr found himself a spot close to the fire and lay down, enjoying the warmth of it against his face, but it was impossible to sleep. His head swirled with terrible visions of what would happen to Saoirse should they capture her and thoughts of his own death. Yet these were interspersed with ideas of how he could spend more time with Saoirse tomorrow on the march. He would make sure they travelled together. Talking to her made him happy and his heart warm. Although married to Hakon Ivarsson, there was no love in the relationship; it was an arrangement between great Lords, but not one geared towards her happiness. Hundr wondered if he could make her happy, if he would give up his dreams of reputation and warrior respect for a quiet life with her. *Yes, maybe he would. Would she, though, does she enjoy talking to me, or do I annoy her?* After all, she was a Princess, and he was just a warrior with a dog's name, for now.

These thoughts and fears swam around his head, and as he watched the low flames of the fire dance and crackle, the lids of his eyes became heavy. Then, as they closed and sleep took over, one final thought forced itself to the front of his mind; *what if she could love me and we could be together?* That he knew would mean that the peace with her Father and Ivar the Boneless would be in tatters. Ivar would lose his Irish warriors, putting the whole Great Army at risk of dissolving, and Hakon would swear revenge and death on them both. *Was she worth all that? Yes, that and more.*

SEVEN

Einar Rosti held a mug of warm ale in both hands and took two short sips. The warmth passed through his body, helping his shoulders relax. He closed his eyes as the comforting heat spread through his chest. Bruised and sore, and feeling the tightness leave his muscles, the desire to sleep washed over him. They had travelled across the Saxon countryside for days, down babbling rivers and across ripe green fields before finding the main army.

Twenty of them escaped the ambush. Survivors who had met as they crashed through the forest fleeing the Saxon slaughter came together as desperate fugitives to find the main Viking force. Others had made a similar journey and survived. Twenty escaped with Einar, yet only eight had survived the expedition to join up with the army. Roaming bands of Saxons picked off the rest along the way. Einar had lost count of how many Northumbrian warriors he had killed in the escape. Hakon Ivarsson had made it, *mores the pity*.

A long hundred men marched out from the Mersey days earlier, and the Saxons had massacred them. It should not have happened. Hakon, the idiot, sending out his own scouts despite advice from the Valkyrie to leave them to do it, and Hakon's men failed to spot the Saxon force. Einar wondered how it was possible to miss an entire Saxon army. It was a spectacular defeat and a bad omen for the start of the war with King Aelle. Einar fought in three skirmishes on the journey eastward following the attack. As he sipped at his ale, his wounds throbbed. He had heavy bruising on his ribs where a horse had charged him and a deep cut on the back of his scalp, which made his head pound and his shoulders stiff.

The warm ale was like a gift from the Gods, soothing his head. He slumped back, allowing himself to rest. Einar felt old. He looked at his travel-stained clothing and his mud and blood-encrusted weapons and brynjar. *Better get them cleaned.* They spoke of days sleeping cold-arsed in the dirt, of fighting for his life toe to toe with vengeful Saxon warriors. Maybe he'd sailed for too many summers now; he couldn't remember how many. *Too many.* He should be sitting in front of a fire, a dog at his feet, and a wife sat beside him to listen to the stories of his days at sea. Einar yawned and rubbed at his eyes. *Odin's balls*, he could sleep for a week.

Men in the camp said that Hakon fought in the ambush and the escape, but not well, and other men died to protect him. Good men gone, all to save a shitworm like Hakon. *What a waste.* Einar had seen Hakon and his guards under attack from the Saxons and had waded into the fray. No doubt he'd saved Hakon's life. *Would have been better if the turd had died.* Most of the Seaworm men made it through. Some of the newer lads, like young Erik, had been killed, but the older hands had made it. *Tough old bastards.* No sign of the boy Hundr and old Sleggya. Most of those lads had sailed with Einar for summers beyond memory. Some had wives and children back in Ivar's lands. It would be time to settle down soon, time to grow old.

The log door to his small room creaked open on its leather hinges, and a red-haired, red-faced warrior poked his head in.

"Ivar wants to see you, Lord, in the main hall."

Einar nodded and sighed. He knew the summons would come. Facing Ivar with bad news could well mean death. Ivar would not take the revelation of his son's failings well and might look for someone to blame. It would shame Ivar in front of the army, the defeat and his son being a bloody idiot. A hundred men were three long crews, and the army could not replace those men until next Spring. That was always the great weakness of Viking armies; they had to be cautious when they fought. To lose too many men meant campaigning was over. Einar drank his ale and got to work making himself presentable.

He said a prayer to Odin, asking for luck, and rose, holding his ribs, his knees clicking and shoulders yelping in protest and strode out of the door. He had combed his hair back into a tight ponytail and cleaned down his mail coat and weapons. Being a drengr was everything. It would not do for other men to see him dirty or brought low. Einar had built his reputation, which was all he had, and he protected it like a father would protect a daughter. He had returned filthy and bloodstained from his escape across Northumbria, but now he was clean, and his mail shone and glinted in the torchlight.

The Viking army camped in a large town taken from the Saxons a week ago by Sigurd and Ubba. Einar didn't know its name, more than likely something unpronounceable and in need of a good Norse renaming. The hall in the town centre was different to a Danish hall, darker and smaller. But it was still large and a wonderful prize. Men said this land the army occupied was not, in fact, Northumbria but was in the Saxon kingdom of East Anglia. The weak East Anglian King Edmund had bought peace from the sons of Ragnar with two hundred horses and chests of silver. *Bloody fool*. The Vikings could now put fast-moving mounted raiders into the field, and the hungry Jarls would have their appetite whetted by the silver, making them hungry for more.

Tonight, there was a feast in that captured Saxon hall to celebrate winning the town, horses and silver, even though there'd been no fighting to secure it. No glory or brave deeds for the men to boast in their cups. Einar crossed the mud-slicked walkway where men drank ale and laughed in the streets. These were the Carls of the army and warriors without enough prestige to warrant a place in the hall at the feast with the famous warriors and Jarls. Einar had been such a man once and remembered his old hunger for silver and reputation. This assault on Northumbria was the best chance for these men to prove themselves, to become known men through deeds and skill. It would also be the closest they would come to death and the opportunity to die with blade in hand and secure a place in Valhalla. Einar still burned with that hunger and that fear. He walked past a young man hobbling along on a crude wooden crutch with one leg missing below the knee. *There would be more poor bastards like that before this war is over.* A drengr did not show fear, but Einar knew all men feared as he did. He feared the pain of the terrible battle wound that didn't kill, denying a warrior his place in Valhalla and cursing him to a life as a cripple. The biting fear of all Northmen, Einar included, was dying without a blade in his hand. The Hall drew closer, and Einar shuddered as that horror prickled up his neck, and he went to meet Ivar the Boneless.

The doors to the Hall were wide, dark, oak re-enforced panels fashioned in the shape of giant leaves and hinged with ornate metalwork painted black. The woodwork of the hall was fine craftsmanship, with ornate window shutters and carvings above the doors. Two burly guards flanked the doorway. They weren't guards in the sense of guarding the hall against intruders because those inside needed no protection. Instead, the guards were there to make sure no one below a certain rank wandered in, and those that entered must leave weapons at the door. Drunk Northmen vying for prestige in front of their Lords was not a good idea, so they drank unarmed. A neat pile of swords, axes, and long knives were gathered to the right of the entrance. Einar stopped to look at the weapons. There were the best Frankish blades sheathed in ornate scabbards studded with precious stones and huge double-bladed war axes and long curved knives with jewels at their hilts. All worth a fortune enough to make any man rich, but those fine weapons could lie in the middle of the town square, and no one would touch them. His own axe was a plain, unadorned thing.No jewels or runic inscriptions, but he was sure she had sent more souls to Valhalla than most of those fancy blades.

The two guards leaned against the wooden doors, not concerned with Einar at all. He drew his axe and long knife and handed it to the guard closest to him, who didn't even raise a hand to take the weapons or acknowledge Einar's presence. Einar sighed, and his face creased into a frown.

"Just leave it there with the others," the guard said, nodding at the nearest stack. *This pup has got some cheek. He must be a pet of the Snake-Eye to feel so confident.* The guard pricked Einar's pride, but he bit his tongue even though the drengr rage had set alight in his belly. Einar was not a Jarl in the truest sense; he didn't have lands to back him. He was a Sea Jarl of only one crew. He could have been the King of Norway, for all this bastard seemed to care. Ivar the Boneless, the Champion of the North, had raised Einar up and given him the title. But Einar had earned it and would have respect from the Carl's of the army. Einar's arms were thick with the warrior's rings a Lord gave to his warriors as payment for their deeds, but these two also wore rings, though not as many as he.

"Leave your weapons here, Lord," Einar said.

"What?" replied the guard.

"I am a Jarl, and you call me Lord." Einar raised his voice and did not wait for the guard to respond. "I have to go in and see Ivar."

The guard closest to him stood. He was as tall as Einar, which seemed to surprise the man a little. Einar was a head taller than most men, and no doubt the guard hoped to look down on him once at his full height. The guard stared at Einar for an awkward, silent minute, and Einar returned his belligerent gaze. Then, after a suitable amount of time passed, Einar just laughed, shook his head, walked past the guard, pushed one of the heavy doors open, and entered the hall. They did not stop him.

The heat inside the hall hit Einar like a wave. There was a cloying closeness in that vast room. It pulsed with the heat from the central fire pit, and the sweat of the prominent men of the army crammed into the long hall. The fire glowed and crackled. Its smoke swirled up and out of the hole at the centre of the thatched roof. At the top of the hall was a raised bench that seated the Lords of the army, the senior Jarls and Kings. Other benches filled the rest of the space, and men without seats clustered around the edges, talking, drinking and laughing.

Einar could see Ivar at the top table, his hair plaited, and his fine Frankish mail was shining in the firelight. His famous and formidable brothers flanked him. The wealthy Norse Jarl Guthrum was also there, but he didn't recognise the rest of the rich and powerful men. He searched the Hall for Hakon because his seat, or at least its distance from Ivar, might offer some sign of Hakon's current standing with his Father. But he couldn't see him among the smoke and bodies.

Einar waited at the back of the hall for a moment, just watching. He knew he must approach Ivar, and to skulk at the back was not the way of the drengr, but better to get a feel for the mood in the room than blunder into a wasp's nest. Einar couldn't sense any hostility or bad temperaments from the ambush, so he strode forward. A Saxon slave walked past him, sweating and red-faced, carrying a wooden tray crammed with cups of frothy ale. Einar grabbed one. The liquid was warm going down his gullet, and he wiped the froth from his beard. Ivar looked up from his food, and his strange eyes pierced the gloom, staring straight at Einar. His stomach tightened. Einar always found it unnerving that Ivar's handsome face concealed such monstrous and unpredictable rage. His angular face gave away no sign of his mood. Immediately, Ivar raised a hand and beckoned Einar forward, so he nodded in greeting, swallowed down the unwelcome fear, and went to meet his Lord.

Einar approached the top table, and men nudged each other as he passed, and a quiet hush swept over the hall. Einar felt his guts twist, and his mouth was dry. *Should have saved a swig of that ale.* He skirted the fire pit and its ring of stones and then glimpsed Hakon Ivarsson two rows back from the top table. Hakon grinned at him from beneath his ale-soaked beard. *Little Bastard.* Einar stood in front of the top table in the space between it and the fire pit and tucked his thumbs into his belt, standing straight with his shoulders back. Ivar raised his hand, and the hall went quiet.

"Where is my son," Ivar said in a low growl. Men turned their gazes to Hakon. As he stood, Hakon banged his knees on the bench and cursed. Some watching warriors in the hall sniggered, and Ivar's odd coloured eyes flashed around looking for those who mocked his son.

"Here, father," Hakon said. Ivar paused, threw down the food in his hand and pointed at the space next to Einar. Hakon stumbled between the tables and seated warriors as he passed the fire. Einar saw Ivar's cheek twitch as he watched his son, and Ivar took a long pull of his ale and wiped his hands on the skirts of the slave girl behind him.

"I hear you have lost your wife?" Ivar said. There was a rumbling murmur across the hall, men nudging and whispering.

"They captured her, Father."

"I also hear that you have lost crews of warriors," said Ivar, picking through his food, "sword and spear Danes we will need for the wars ahead. How was she captured?"

Before Hakon could answer, a voice shouted across the hall.

"What did he bring his wife for?"

"Maybe she is good with a spear shaft," shouted another. The hall erupted in laughter.

Einar looked at Hakon, who stared at the floor, face reddening. Ivar sprang to his feet, knocking ale and food into the air, and slammed his eating knife into the tabletop with a loud thud. The hall went so quiet that Einar could almost hear the mice running through the rushes scattered over the hard-packed earthen floor. Ivar scowled around the place and vaulted over the table, landing just in front of his son, causing Hakon to stumble backwards. Einar saw the look Ivar gave Hakon, and it dripped with contempt and disappointment. Einar could feel the fury pulsing from Ivar as he stalked back and forth in front of the fire like Fenris, the giant wolf who guarded the doors of Hel. The fire glinted from his brown and blue eyes.

"Stand up the men who said those words," he said. Ivar did not shout; he did not need to. Einar was close, and he fought against the desire to step backwards away from the glare of Ivar's fury as he watched him shake. One man stood, a brave man, with a defiant look on his face. Ivar nodded and waited. There were murmurs and movement from a darkened corner of the hall, but no other men stood.

"Stand up, you filthy drunken coward, wherever you are." This time his rage overcame him, and Ivar bellowed, spittle flying from his mouth and his face twisting into a rictus of hate and spite. Then, finally, a man towards the back of the hall stood up. He was a fat man with a droopy moustache, clutching a pot of ale, and he had to steady himself with a hand on the table to stop from toppling over.

"Holmgang tomorrow," said Ivar, pointing at the two men. "After second watch. You can fight me both at once or one at a time. I don't care. Now bring more ale, and let's feast."

Men talked and ate as the two challenged men sat down, stony-faced and pale. There wasn't much they could do, Einar supposed. The challenge was fair, and to appeal it would embarrass them and be pointless. Ivar would kill them anyway. Ivar turned his glare to Einar and Hakon.

"You shame me again, my son." Ivar placed a hand on Hakon's shoulder.

"Father, I live only to please you and...."

Ivar raised a finger to stop his son. He instead looked across at Einar.

"Einar, the Gods favour you today. Those two drunken fools will distract the men from your failure when I kill them tomorrow," Ivar said and nodded to dismiss the pair. As Ivar stalked to the high table, a tall man with many arm rings and a shining brynjar stood from the same table as the portly man Ivar had called out.

"Jarl Ivar," the tall man called, but before he could finish, Ivar spun, pointing at him.

"It's King Ivar, you snivelling pig. Shout at me again, and I will cut your black heart out and feed it to my dogs. If you want to fight instead of your man tomorrow, so be it."

The tall man sat down, red-faced and spluttering, and Ivar waved an arm before returning to his chair. Ubba nodded at his brother and shouted for more ale, and the feast continued. Einar turned and strode through the hall as calmly as possible. He forced down the desire to run away from Ivar's wrath but held himself back.

"Thank you, Thor," Einar said under his breath, touching his Mjolnir hammer pendant. Tomorrow Ivar would take out his anger on other men and distract the army from the embarrassment of the ambush. Ivar had referred to it as Einar's failure, so already he was being tainted by Hakon's ill-luck or ill judgement, whichever it was. Einar knew if left unchecked, men would talk of the defeat, and they'd fear it was a bad omen. Worse still, the warriors would talk like old wives, and in a matter of days, the Saxons would be as giants and warriors of peerless skill. So, they had to be distracted, and what better way than for Ivar to show his fighting prowess. The feast that night was to celebrate Sigurd's success in extorting the East Anglian King. Still, all men spoke of the attack and defeat in Northumbria.

Einar saw the torches outside glinting through the gap in the vast hall doors and blew out his cheeks in relief. He had avoided a questioning from Ivar in front of the eminent men of the Viking world. That would have harmed his reputation for good. Einar was about to raise his arm to open the door when a hand clapped on his shoulder. He closed his eyes, sighed, and turned around to see Hakon, red-faced, swaying, and staring at him.

"That was a close one," Hakon said.

Einar clenched his teeth as Hakon grinned. Hakon belched, and the foul smell of his ale breath made Einar turn his head away with a snarl. They had escaped the ambush with their lives, Hakon the useless bastard had not sent out adequate scouts, and good men had died. Men that would be sorely missed in the war to come. Hakon didn't give a shit about his captured wife, not even asking for men to search for her before he fled for his life. She had no business being here in the middle of a war. Hakon was a fool, a constant disappointment to his father and had a poor reputation. *I should have found him and cut his miserable throat in the forest.* To be associated with him harmed Einar's reputation and even being in his company was unpleasant. *I am sworn to Ivar, not Hakon.*

"What do you want?" Einar said with a sigh.

"That's no way to talk to your Lord."

Hakon tried to square up to Einar, but he was too short and had to look up. Tilting his head threw him off balance, so Einar barged him with his chest knocking Hakon backwards, causing him to stumble.

"You are not my Lord. I am sworn to your father. I saved your life in the forest, you miserable bastard. Reward me, and then keep away from me." He spoke with more venom than he intended and regretted it. There was nothing to be gained in making an enemy of the son of Ivar. Hakon bared his teeth but then mastered himself, managing a forced laugh, and slapped Einar on the shoulder.

"Enough jesting, Einar. I need you again, old friend. My father has given me twenty men and horses, plus mounts for my own men."

"Good for you, Lord," he said, emphasising the

last word, "what do you need me for?"

"He has also given you and your crew to me to get back my Princess."

"Bastard," said Einar, half under his breath but loud enough for Hakon to hear.

"Come now, Einar, this is a chance to restore your reputation. My father will be pleased if we are successful. He will distract the battle-hungry army tomorrow with the spectacle of his Holm-gang, and all will be well."

"Restore my reputation..." said Einar through his teeth. He stopped himself from saying any more and strode on through the door.

"We leave after the Holmgang tomorrow, Einar, be ready," Hakon called after him. Einar stormed out of the door, cursing to himself as he walked past the guards. The sentry who Einar engaged in a staring contest earlier sniggered as he passed. Einar stopped and stared at him again. The guard just smirked and continued to loll against the hall wall.

"Get me my weapons."

The guard laughed and looked at the other sentry.

"Get them yourself."

Einar shook his head.

"Get my axe, now."

At that, the guard stood from where he was leaning and took a step towards Einar. The pent up anxiety from facing Ivar and the anger Hakon stoked within him all boiled over, and Einar gave freedom to his rage. The guard was about to say something smart when Einar head-butted him hard and full in the nose. He felt the soft gristle there give way against the rock-hard force of his head. Blood spurted and splashed on his face, and the joy of combat washed over him. The guard's beard was long, and Einar grabbed it and yanked his head down twice into his knee. He fell to the floor, scrabbling and gasping, and moved his hand to his sword, but Einar kicked him in the throat, and the guard toppled onto his side. The accompanying sentry approached to help his friend, and Einar pushed him hard back against the hall. Einar hit him in the stomach as he came forward again, doubling him over, and Einar kicked his head against the door. Both guards were writhing and groaning half senseless on the cold stone of the hall entrance. Einar sighed and stretched his back, and put his hand to his sore ribs. It felt good to hurt someone after his encounter with Hakon. All Einar was, had come from violence. He was good at it, and he gloried in it. A small crowd gathered around the hall, and some had weapons drawn.

"My name is Einar Rosti, and I serve Ivar Ragnarsson," Einar said, "these men insulted me, and I have taught them their lesson. Any man who has an issue with that can challenge me now or any time."

No man moved. A rumbling murmur crept amongst the crowd as they spoke in hushed voices. Einar retrieved his weapons and walked back to his lodging. *That's how a drengr responds to a challenge. That's how you built a reputation.* He was Einar Rosti, Einar the Brawler, and he hadn't risen to be a Jarl in the forces of Ivar the Boneless by cowering in front of nithings. Tomorrow he would watch Ivar fight and then ride out with Hakon the turd to find his lost Princess. He was getting old, but Einar knew nothing else. This was his life. What would he do on a farm with a crusty old maid and mangy dog?

The Great Army gathered outside the town, ceded to the Vikings by King Edmund. The warriors formed in a large circle, and men swarmed the town palisade walls to get a better look at the fight. Einar waited at the centre of the ring. He had two shields for Ivar and a bucket of water for washing after the skirmish. Ivar had honoured him by asking Einar to act as his second for the Holmgang. Einar was grateful for the opportunity if a little suspicious as to why Ivar had asked him. But of course, he had accepted. Refusing Ivar didn't boost life expectancy, and it wouldn't harm his reputation to be seen as a trusted companion to the Champion of the North. The throng was buzzing with chatter and excitement as men spoke of fighting styles, weapons, and the usual bluster accompanying Holmgang duels. The gathered warriors were about to see the greatest warrior of the North fight, the son of the legendary Ragnar Lothbrok and a living legend in his own right.

Einar had seen Ivar fight many times, and the lads were in for a treat today. The army needed amusement, Einar knew. These were not average men like farmers or millers; they were warriors hungry for excitement, glory, blood, and a tale to tell. Most of the army had landed in the East and so had escaped the Northumbrian ambush.

The East Anglian King had paid them off, and not a Church sacked. The Jarls had sailed expecting war and plunder, yet not a single spear blade had been bloodied in anger, so Ivar must amuse them.

Einar saw Hakon out of the corner of his eye. He stood with a Norse Jarl, a colossal bear of a man with masses of wiry brown hair and an enormous stomach stretching at his jerkin. It was Guthrum from the top table the night before, and Einar recognised him as a powerful Jarl who had eight ships of his own and warriors to crew them. That Jarl could call himself a king if he so wished, but doing so would risk the disapproval of the sons of Ragnar, and no man risked that lightly. Hakon grinned and nodded at Einar before draining a mug of ale and chuckling with the Jarl. *Slimy bastard.*
Einar would ride out again with that shit today to get his wife back. A bloody fool's errand. The Seaworm crew would not thank him for it. They were getting poorer by the day, spending their hack silver on ale and women. Ivar had forbid Einar and Hakon from raiding because of the truce; no killing East Anglians. *Hopefully, Northumbria isn't too far away.* A rumble of a cheer starting in the town grew to a roar and awoke Einar from his melancholy thoughts as the men on the palisade shouted and clapped, stamping their feet. Ivar the Boneless was coming.

Einar looked across the fighting square at the two men who had affronted Ivar the night before. The man who had stood up first in the hall stood straight-backed and seemed ready to fight. He had a shield resting against his leg and his axe in a loop at his waist. His second stood next to him with a spare shield, and those men showed no fear. The other man who would fight looked like he was about to shit himself. He was a fat, short man with a scruffy beard and a balding head. He, too, had a sword and shield and second. If he had allowed himself to run to fat like that, then he was no drengr. He wouldn't be able to hold that shield up for more than a few minutes at a time, nor trade blows for more than a few heartbeats without losing his breath and lowering his arm. Such a man couldn't pull an oar. He couldn't fight. Ivar would butcher him and send him screaming to the nithing world, the afterlife of those who were not lucky to make it to Valhalla.

The Ragnarssons emerged from the town gate, and in the middle of that group was Ivar, holding up his two famous swords, Hugin and Munin, to the army. Those two swords were legendary and named after Odin's twin ravens, Thought and Memory. Ivar, flanked by his brothers Sigurd Snake Eye and Ubba, was stripped to the waist and his tattooed body glistened in the sunlight. His long hair was loose about his head, and he roared at the crowd, whipping them up, twirling his blades in a dazzling display. A young warrior carried behind them the Ragnarssons Raven banner, and it fluttered limply in the breeze. The army was lapping it up. Finally, Ivar approached, and he was shouting.

"Holmgang."

The army echoed his chant. Ivar loved to fight, as did all the Ragnarssons. These fights built their reputations of fear and awe. Men fought Holmgang's across the North to settle disputes and feuds. The winner of the battle would have the right of the argument, and if they killed a man, there would be wergild or payment owed to that man's family. Ivar walked into the centre of the circle and around its edge, acknowledging men he knew and glaring at his opponents. He completed his full circle and came to Einar.

"Good day for a fight, Einar."

"Yes, Lord, they are shitting in their pants."

Ivar grinned, and his odd eyes flashed.

"I heard you had a fight of your own last night."

"I am a drengr Lord, and they disrespected me."

"They won't do that again, will they? They were Sigurd's men. But don't worry, he isn't angry with you. What is the point of having two guards if one unarmed man can defeat them?"
Ivar smiled and shook his head as Einar offered him a shield.

"Help my son get his wife back, Einar. He is a fool, and he should have left her in Ireland. His jealousy is not the way of the drengr; you know that. Help him build his reputation, and I will make you a landed Jarl here once we take this land from the Saxons, or back in Ireland wherever you want." Ivar fixed him with those strange eyes, and Einar felt a shiver run down his neck. Ivar nodded and moved to the middle of the circle, armed with only his swords and no shield.

A landed Jarl. That was Einar's ambition since he had been a young carl in Ivar's ships. Einar had been first a carl, then a captain, then a Sea Jarl. To be a landed Jarl meant wealth and power. Einar would have his own ships and his own hall, enough to support the crew and their families. He would marry and have sons. Einar would have made it, secure into his old age. But to reach that goal, he had to help Ivar's whelp get his bloody wife back and make him into a famous warrior. Ivar roared the crowd to silence.

"These men shamed and challenged me in front of my brothers and the Jarls of the army. I am a drengr and will settle the insult by right of Holmgang today. Do you wish to fight me together or one at a time?" Ivar levelled his blades at the two men.

The tall warrior did not move or speak but stood still and solemn. The fat man still looked petrified, and he called out.

"Together, we will fight you together."

Einar watched the man. His eyes looked enormous as he shifted from one leg to another, licking his lips. The tall warrior just shrugged his agreement. He knew it did not matter. Ivar was the Champion of the North and the Boneless one who moves faster than an arrow and can bend and twist around sword and axe blades. *If it were me, I would make myself ready for Valhalla and make sure I died well, weapon in my hand.*

Sigurd Ragnarsson, the Snake Eye, shouted out the rules of the fight. Each man could replace his shield and weapons once if damaged, and the battle was to the death. It was always this way with Ivar, *to the death*. The first cut would settle a dispute for most warriors, but not Ivar. Sigurd also shouted that Ivar had waived his right to a shield and would fight with his two swords, Hugin and Munin. Ivar's swords were famed wherever Northmen sailed, and few men had enough silver to own two swords, never mind fight well with the two blades. In long grey robes holding an outsized spear, a tall man strode to stand next to Sigurd and Ivar and gave a low rumbling incantation to Odin. He waved his silver Gungnir spear to the heavens to get Odin's attention. The High Priest was Vattnar of Uppsala, and it was he who commanded the Valkyrie. Vattnar was a long and thin man with a grey beard slashed with deep black. He had long and pointed eyebrows and carried that spear everywhere with him; it had an oversized leaf-shaped head made of pure silver inlaid with runes. It was a dedication to Odin's own spear named Gungnir, fashioned by dwarves and inlaid with magic.

The Ragnarssons and the Priest fell back to join the circle, and Ivar twirled his swords to the delight of the watching warriors who cheered him. Ivar beckoned on his adversaries. The tall warrior braced his shield and stood in his fighting stance with his axe held low and moved towards Ivar. The fat man fell in behind him. What they should have done was make a two-man shield wall and try to bully Ivar backwards, but the fat man was quaking and so stood back. Ivar shot forward with incredible speed and banged his swords on the shield of the first man driving him backwards, and then, leaping forwards, Ivar spun around to cut low at the fat man's legs. The man dropped his shield to block the blow. Ivar hit him hard in the face with the pommel of his other sword. The crowd cheered for Ivar as he strode away, lifting his blades and playing to the masses.

The fat man had dropped his shield to hold his bloody face, and Ivar took three quick steps towards and kicked him between the legs. The crowd laughed at that, and Ivar bowed in mock salute. He turned now to face the taller man again, who was a proper warrior. *This one is a drengr, showing no fear*. The man had made a mistake last night to call out in front of Ivar. Too much ale. But he was straight-backed and unafraid and now faced the Champion of the Vikings as a warrior should. Ivar stepped in towards him, and they clashed, the tall man taking blows on his shield and attacking with his axe. He even drove Ivar back for a second, but Ivar recovered. Then, in a dazzling display of sword skill, he got inside the man's guard, cut him in the shoulder, and slashed his other blade across the man's knee. The tall warrior buckled but straightened himself. He dropped his shield, and his second moved to pass him his replacement, but he waved it away. Ivar nodded in respect and set himself for the killing blow.

"Always I have fought in the front line," called the warrior, "I did not mean to insult you, Lord Ivar," he said.

"You have fought well today, like a drengr. I will make sure men remember you," said Ivar as he moved in, feinted one way and then struck the man down with a cut to the throat. The warrior dropped his sword as he fell, and Ivar dashed forward, dropping his own blades, to put the sword back into the dying man's hand. Ivar held it there and whispered to the warrior as he died. Einar closed his eyes and whispered a prayer to Odin to thank him for the death the warrior deserved. Dropping his blade could have cost him his place in eternity, and Ivar had saved him that shame. The man would wait for Ivar in Valhalla. There they would fight and drink together until the end of days.

"Save a place for me at Odin's table," Ivar said as he stood again so that the gathered warriors could hear.

The crowd went silent in respect at that gesture. The dead man had a reputation in life and had fought well, and Ivar had assured his place in Valhalla. That was the way of the warrior. Nevertheless, the fat man still clutched his face and whined in pain, and Ivar rose to his feet, snarling at him.

"What of this pig?" Ivar called to the crowd.

"Niflheim, Niflheim!" they chanted. *Every warrior's nightmare.* Niflheim was the lowest realm in the afterlife reserved for the basest of men. Ivar nodded.

'I condemn you to Niflheim. You are a nithing." Ivar twirled his blades and cut the man down, stabbing both hard into his chest. For a fleeting moment, Einar pitied the man. To walk in the netherworld for eternity was the most feared nightmare death. *He should have fought harder.*

Ivar walked back to his brothers and retrieved

a pouch of silver, which he tossed to the second of the tall warrior. He did not make any payment to the second of the disgraced man. *A good day's work.* That would keep the men amused for a day or two before the army rode north to King Aelle. Fighting, raiding, and maybe a battle. Lots of opportunities for the men to get some silver and win some glory. Einar watched Hakon Ivarsson shake hands with the Norse Jarl Guthrum and head off towards the town. Einar followed.

EIGHT

Hundr breathed the fresh Saxon air deep into his lungs. He walked like there was a cushion of that light fragrant air under his feet, bouncing along and smiling. He marched next to Saoirse, and they talked of Ireland and her life there, of her father's rolling green lands and of the ways of her people. The Spring sun warmed his face and made her eyes sparkle like emeralds, and when she smiled, he thought he had never seen anything so beautiful.

This was their second morning since the ambush. Ragnhild was sure they would find signs of the Viking forces that day, having guessed the journey would take only two days. Every time Ragnhild mentioned how close they drew to the army, Hundr felt a knot in his stomach. He wanted this march to last forever. Once they reached the troop, they would reunite Saoirse with her husband, and more than likely, Hundr would never see her again. She had been shy on the first day, but they had talked a great deal since then. He had asked as many questions as he could about her life, building in his mind a tapestry of where she came from. She had, of course, asked him similar questions, and he had been as vague as possible. However, Hrist had also quizzed him about his weapons training, and he had been lucky to deflect that question. Talk of home and his old life would do him no favours. His life was here and now.

As they had since the ambush, the three Valkyrie warriors ranged ahead. They scouted for any sign of danger, looking for Viking scouts or any signs of the Great Army. The Vikings would have scouts all across the countryside memorising the lay of the land to report back to the Ragnarssons. These reports helped build a picture of the Saxon landscape to plan camps and potential battle sites. If the band of fugitives could find one such scout, they could then join the army and return to safety.

They marched in a broad line across a tilled field ready for planting with the thick soil lush, soft and prepared for seed. Sten was at the rear of the group as always. He had continued to say as little as possible and had tried to keep away from the Valkyrie since Hildr had seen his tattoos and asked about his old life. Hundr glanced back at Sten. He trudged along with his shield strapped to his back and nodded to Hundr as he caught his eye.

"Hundr, walk with an old man for a while," Sten said. Hundr held back and then fell into step.

"What's wrong greybeard, do you want me to carry you?"

Sten laughed.

"That'll be the day, laddie. I see you and our Princess have become fast friends."

"We have; she is good company. Don't you think?" Hundr smiled and felt his cheeks reddening. He tried to keep himself in check, not to let Sten see how he really felt. It was hard. She was the first woman he had spent any significant time with. Back home, the only women he knew were his mother and her maids. There had been some short trysts with serving girls, but not actual conversations. Those were reserved solely for his limited interactions with his masters and friends and were primarily concerned with fighting, wrestling, and the varying merits of the serving girls.

"She's a fair lass," Sten said, "*and* she's the wife of Hakon Ivarsson."

"I know, I know, but she is miserable. And besides, we are only talking."

"Well, lad, who says it's anyone right to be happy? Women of high station, it's not their lot in life to choose their husbands. There aren't many choices in this life, son, for people of any station."

"I think he beats her Sten, he's weak, and he beats her," said Hundr, grabbing Sten's arm.
Sten sighed and rubbed his beard. Hundr took his hand away and regretted his passionate outburst. He knew Sten thought he was a fool, and maybe he was. Falling for a woman with whom he could have no future.

"That's as maybe," Sten said, "but a husband may beat his wife, lad. It's none of your business."

"She needs to be protected," said Hundr, hearing the feeling in his own voice. *Shit, I have fallen hard.*

"Suppose you're the one to protect her, are you?" said Sten.

"I can protect her, yes," said Hundr, looking at Sten with his brow furrowed. Sten stopped walking and put his hands on Hundr's shoulders.

"Listen, lad. You saved my life and since then...." He tailed off, struggling for the words.
"Look, you can't protect her, son. If you disrespect Hakon, he'll kill you for it. So you must stay away from his wife, no matter how pretty the lass is."

Hundr shook his shoulders free.

"I can protect her." He picked up his pace to catch up with Saoirse again, tired of the old man's talk. No matter how right the bastard was.

Ahead, the two Valkyries Hildr and Hrist, were running back towards the group. They reached Ragnhild, and the three warriors talked, gesturing towards the horizon. Sten, Hundr, and Saoirse quickened their pace and caught up to them.

"We need to get off the road," said Ragnhild, "there is a settlement up ahead. Small, but big enough for a palisade. Therefore Saxons will be around looking for Viking stragglers."

The group lurched into a run, following Ragnhild. Saoirse almost tripped as her foot slipped into one of the field's furrows, but Hundr grabbed her by the hand and caught her. She blushed and smiled as he pulled her towards him to keep her upright. He felt himself also turning scarlet as he looked into her eyes, and they ran, following the others, keeping a tight hold of one another's hands.

"The village is through the valley ahead, and we can skirt around it over the mountains to the North," called Hrist as they ran. She had her recurved bow cradled in her arm, and her quiver rattled as she moved. "That takes us away from our path Eastwards, but we can head back that way once we get past the village."

"How large is it?" asked Hundr.

"Large enough. It has a palisade and a hall."

"Likely means a Lord and retainers," said Sten.

"It means trouble for us if they spot us and raise the alarm across the countryside," said Ragnhild, "I will go on ahead to scout more closely. Hundr, you come with me. The rest of you keep moving; we will meet you at the top of that hill to the North before nightfall, the large hill crested with trees surrounded by black gorse," she said, pointing towards the middle of three large hills to the North.

"I need to..." said Hundr before Ragnhild cut him off, raising a finger.

"You need to come with me. There might be fighting, and I will need you," she said. Hundr stood straighter at her approval, and he nodded in agreement.

"If there is any trouble, we will find you," Ragnhild said to the others, "skirt on the inside of that copse and then follow the shepherds' wall up the peak. Stay on the east side of the wall."

Hundr and Ragnhild scouted close to the Town whilst the rest of the group pushed Northwards towards the hills, following Ragnhild's orders. Hundr followed Ragnhild's example and moved in a low crouch alongside a track leading to the settlement. After travelling through some clawing briar, the trail became furrowed from regular use, and Hundr saw the settlement sitting atop a small rise.

It was a collection of drab, weather-worn, thatched buildings with thin trails of fire smoke wafting in the breeze. The town had a log palisade wall and a wide gate. The wall was not in good repair, and some logs looked rotten. However, it still spoke of a Lord who protected his people and who would therefore keep a force of household warriors in his hall. Hundr looked at the village. He thought of places in terms of attack and defence; they had drilled it into him for as long as he could remember. He could almost hear his old war master's gravelly voice in his head. *Look at the land, the high and low ground, water, rocks. Look at the defences and where the weak points are. Take your time, make the right decisions.* Hundr pushed all thoughts of home and those years out of his mind.

Ragnhild skirted across to him, the snapping of twigs under her feet breaking Hundr from his daydream. She reached him, and they huddled low to avoid any sentries who may have been out of sight.

"All quiet here, no warriors that I can see outside the palisade," she said, "let's head back to the others. We can take the route to the North East through the farmsteads."

Hundr nodded, "We should bring back some food and water," he said.

They headed off through the undergrowth and out onto a field where the Spring crop was already waist height. Again, keeping low, they travelled silently, observing in every direction for Saxon enemies, or indeed for Viking scouts from the Great Army.

"Where did you learn to fight?" Ragnhild said without looking at him. He glanced across at her in surprise. She had not spoken more than a dozen words to him or anyone in the days they had been travelling together. Her stern and battle-scarred face always seemed focused and prepared, not in the least bit open for any sort of conversation.

"I picked up a few things back where I was raised," he shrugged.

"Where was that?"

"A small place, east of Hedeby," he said and then turned to look around, checking again for signs of warriors from the town, and then moved off away from Ragnhild.

"East of Hedeby could be anywhere. The entire world is East of Hedeby. What are you hiding, boy?"

Hundr didn't answer and continued to peel away. He could not risk being hunted by his past, not until he had built his reputation to become a warrior in his own right. Ragnhild followed him; her scarred faced turning into a frown.

"Somebody trained you as well as I, which means every day, weapons and drills since being a small child. So your family must have been rich to pay for a warrior to train you, not a family who tills fields or tends animals. Who is your father?"

Again, he ignored her and pressed on. He sniffed and spat and adjusted his axe in its belt loop to stop it from chafing against his side.

"Are you a bastard?"

He laughed at that, how many times he had wished to be someone's son instead of someone's bastard. Being a bastard was a curse. Knowing his father, watching his wealth and the status of his sons, but always on the outside. He glanced at her now and shook his head.

"What then? Who gave you your dog's name? Was your mother a whore?" said Ragnhild with a sneer.

His mother. He had spent many long nights thinking about his mother. Why had she abandoned him? His first memory was of being a small boy, running wild around a beautiful Palace surrounded by Lords and Ladies, smells of perfume and soft fabrics against his skin. Then the training started, discipline, weapons, combat.

"You must be a slave then, maybe a man slave for an eastern Jarl. You have an Eastern accent. Were you a lover for a Rus Jarl?" She laughed this time.

"If all women looked like you, maybe that wouldn't be a bad idea," he said with venom and then laughed himself, as her laughter turned into anger. He looked her up and down as if appraising her body and then shrugged.

"Bastard," she said, spitting through her missing teeth; she lunged at him, throwing a straight punch with her right hand. Ragnhild was fast, yet he batted her away and then blocked the follow-up blow she aimed at his stomach with her left hand. Hundr lifted his leg to avoid her foot as she tried to rake it down his instep. He sprang backwards.

"Not bad, for a woman. But maybe you should stick to sewing?" he said and then laughed again as she screamed, her face contorting into an animal snarl. She ran at him; a flurry of punches and kicks flew at his head and body, and he moved backwards through the crops blocking her attacks. Then, finally, she caught him with a kick to the shin, and he stumbled, allowing Ragnhild to crack a punch off his ear. Pain flashed through his skull, and his ear felt like it was on fire.

"Bitch," he shouted as he cannoned into her. They tumbled to the dirt and rolled through the crop sheaf's, wrestling for holds. She tried to get inside his guard, *Thor's balls she's strong*, but he manoeuvred his hip and flipped her over into a rear choke. Or at least he thought he had. Ragnhild had tricked him, and she rolled him over and had his arm caught in a lock of her own. *She wrestles like a bloody champion*. As he lay there panting and grimacing, thinking how to get free, he looked up and saw horsemen move into the field, plodding along with no urgency. He pointed across the field with his free arm.

"Look there, mounted warriors, not ours." Hundr could tell they were not Northmen by their hair. All the horsemen wore their hair short in the Saxon style, whereas Vikings wore their long and styled and elaborate, as a sign of their confidence and prowess. She let go, and Hundr rolled away, scrambling to his feet but trying to keep as low to the top of the crops as possible, as did Ragnhild. They glanced around, both breathing hard, but there was no shelter. Hundr cursed himself for his foolishness. He should not have allowed Ragnhild to anger and distract him. There were five horsemen, and the leader of the band spotted them and waved his spear, ordering his men into a line. The horses cantered through the crop. Ragnhild and Hundr both looked around for a way out, heads turning fast in every direction.

"You and your bloody questions," hissed Hundr. They were both out of breath from their scuffle, but all that had to be forgotten now. Hundr scanned around him. There was nowhere to hide or flee. The closest place that was not open ground was a farmer's hut across the next field.

Ragnhild didn't speak. She reached back into her quiver and took out five of her arrows and planted them into the ground before her, where they had crushed the sheaves in their fight. Hundr drew his axe and moved a few paces to her left to split the horsemen when they charged. They were close now, and the warriors had lowered their spears, so they bristled at different levels, wavering like iron-tipped trees in the wind. It would be an easy kill, and they came on without fear. A woman and man alone in a wide field. It did not matter to the horsemen whether they were invaders; they were still armed warriors on their Lord's land without leave.

Ragnhild took two deep breaths and then notched her first arrow. She drew the recurved bow back to her ear and loosed the string. The power of the wood and horn thrummed as it exploded the steel-tipped arrow into a low arc. Hundr heard it creak as she drew the thing and the violent twang as she released its power. The arrow flashed and slammed into the right-most horse's chest. Before the horse even screamed or reared, Ragnhild had loosed her second shot. It flew wide past the shoulder of the left-most horseman. The first horse had fallen now, screaming terribly, trapping its rider's leg under its weight. *How is she so fast?* He watched again as Ragnhild loosed two more arrows. She had dropped one man, and firing at either end of the line had forced the horsemen to bunch together to avoid her missiles. This made her targets easier to hit and harder for them to ride in line as they clattered and hindered each other's progress. Their leader barked in Saxon, and they tried to quicken their pace.

She had the final three shots off in less than twenty heartbeats, and all three shots found their mark. Another horse was on its foreleg knees with its rider clinging onto its back. A warrior bellowed, clutching at an arrow in his thigh, and a third had an arrow shot through his shoulder and dropped his spear. It was all panic and shouting now, horses wild-eyed and screaming and bloody amongst the crops. The Saxons could not even kick into a charge with the carnage she had wrought among them. Ragnhild dropped her bow and drew her axe from its belt loop, and without hesitation, she charged them.

Hundr whooped and followed her. He couldn't believe she was charging mounted warriors, but his heart was pounding, and the battle joy coursed through his body. He went for the left-most horseman who had the arrow in his shoulder. The man had his spear across his saddle and struggled to drag it back across the head of his mount. Hundr leapt into the air and swung his axe, banging the blade hard into the man's face, spraying blood bright across the golden wheat. The man slumped and hung sideways with his foot caught in a stirrup. Hundr spun around and chopped his blade twice, dropping the Saxon as the horse bucked and reared in panic. Ragnhild was hacking at another horseman inside his spear reach. Hooves pawed and pounded the earth, and the attackers shouted at each other wide-eyed and furious, trying to return the vicious attack. One horseman kicked out of the melee and was screaming in panic. He rounded his horse, and seeing his men defeated, he galloped off away from the fight.

He watched Ragnhild drag her man from the saddle and sink her axe into his throat as he hit the ground. She had beaten five mounted warriors almost single-handedly, a feat that should not be possible even for the greatest of warriors. She strolled to the man trapped beneath his dying mount; the horse had been making an ear-piercing screaming sound since it fell. Ragn-hild braced herself and swung her axe, hitting the horse square between the eyes to silence its pain. The warrior was shouting at her in Saxon, holding up his hands in surrender, but Ragnhild had no pity. She raised her hand to the sky and whispered a prayer to Odin, then she pinned the man with her knees and strangled him with her bare and bloody hands. Hundr had never met a woman like her, not a woman who could fight like that. He had heard of women warriors before but never thought there had been one such as Ragnhild. She was one of the finest warriors and most skilled fighters he had ever seen.

Hundr heard a shout, and over his shoulder, he saw the Horseman who had fled the skirmish wheel back around. The Saxon kicked his horse into a gallop, letting out a great war cry and lev-elling his spear. Ragnhild was still throttling her sacrifice to Odin and seemed not to notice the horse thundering towards her. Hundr snatched up a fallen spear and ran towards her, but the horse was closing too fast, and he knew he could not make it in time. He shouted her name twice as he ran. At the second call, she looked to see him charging and pointing. Ragnhild jumped to her feet and spun around. The rider was almost upon her, his face twisted in anger. She tried to move out of the way, but it was too late as the spear point slashed across her shoulder, knock-ing her off her feet. Hundr threw the spear but missed as the man galloped away. The horse war-rior shouted a challenge and then turned, riding hard, back towards the village.

His heart was in his mouth as he sped to Ragnhild and knelt as he turned her onto her back. The blow had torn her mail and left her shoulder bloody, and she was unconscious from the assault. She was breathing, but the wound was deep. Hundr went to the dead Saxon close by and tore cloth from his jerkin; it was not clean, but it would have to do. He pushed the fabric in between her clothes and the wound to stem the blood flow and then tied it around with a longer piece of torn cloth. He searched the fallen men and found some hard bread and cheese and two skins of ale. One horse grazed nearby, and Hundr led it by the halter over to where Ragnhild lay. He retrieved as many of her arrows as he could from the dead and slung her quiver and bow across his back. Then Hundr hauled her into the saddle so that she lay across the horse's back before him, and he jumped up to sit behind her. Ragnhild did not wake as he dug his heels into the beast's sides and drove it ahead.

Hundr knew the escaped rider would raise the alarm in the village, and the Saxon warriors would be back in force. They would think that they had located two Viking scouts and would try to hunt them down before others followed. His horses' tracks would be easy to follow, and he would lead any pursuing Saxons to the rest of the group. But he had to get Ragnhild to Hildr and Hrist, who were experts at healing, as well as killing. He rode slowly, keeping her balanced in front of him by holding his arm across her shoulders. There would be enemies all around them before nightfall, and Hundr feared what would become of them if captured by the vengeful Saxons.

NINE

Einar rode at the front of the column. His East Anglian horse was a fine mount. He had never been much of a horseman, but he liked the animals. This horse was chestnut with a white burst on its forehead. It was a gentle beast and had given him little trouble so far. He patted its muscular neck and thanked the foolish King Edmund again as he gazed at the Saxon countryside. It was lush. Farmers had cleared the brush and forest and made fields surrounded by low stone walls to mark their land.

Around the fields grew thick copses where birds nested and squirrels fed. Beyond the trees, Einar could see a set of three hills whose brown hue stood stark against the surrounding greenery. *No wonder men fought over this place*. This Saxon kingdom contrasted to the lands in Norway and Denmark, where farmland was harsh and scarce. Einar allowed his mind to drift, wondering what land he would own once Ivar made him a landed Jarl. He imagined a hall and a wife and fields full of grain and livestock. All he had to do to make that dream a reality was help Hakon the whelp find his bloody wife.

They would need to find a place to camp for the night soon, having covered much ground that day riding back towards the ambush. Tomorrow they would be deep into Mercian territory, then on into Northumbria. And then, only Odin knew how, they would try to pick up some sort of trail of the lost Princess. Hakon rode ahead of Einar with his huge and baleful Captain Magnus No-Ear. Einar was happy to hang back; he just wanted this job to be over quick. The less time he had to spend with Hakon, the better. Hakon led three crews; all mounted on the fine horses provided by the East Anglian King. A long hundred mounted Northmen moving through the Saxon countryside. They passed two villages that day, still in East Anglia, and therefore forbidden to raid or risk breaking the peace the sons of Ragnar had made.

Ivar had ordered them not to cut a fiery swathe through Mercia either. He did not want the Mercian King provoked, nor did he want to fight Mercia before the Great Army could destroy the Northumbrian King Aelle. Worse still, Mercia and Northumbria could unite against the Vikings. Ivar had made Einar and Hakon swear an oath to keep the peace. They were to find out where Hakon's wife was and then try to ransom her back or take her by force if necessary. Few of the Northmen spoke the Saxon tongue. Still, the Seaworm man Styrr's mother had been a Saxon, and he could speak and understand the basics of the language well enough.

Einar shifted his weight in the saddle. They had been riding most of the afternoon, and his arse was sore. He looked at Hakon, who was in high spirits, laughing and joking with Magnus. A chunk of Magnus' ear was cut or bitten off in a fight some years ago, so men called him No-Ear. Magnus was proud of that name and his reputation as a fighter. Magnus was a drengr and respected throughout Ivar's forces. Einar hoped that some of Magnus' reputation would rub off on Hakon. It baffled Einar that Hakon, the bastard, was so happy and laughing as he rode. He had brought his wife to war, then lost her, humiliating his incendiary father.

"We should make camp for the night soon," Einar called ahead. Hakon turned around and grinned at him.

"We should indeed, Einar; when the scouts return, I will choose a place," Hakon said something under his breath to Magnus, and they both laughed. Einar spent the next few moments imagining removing Hakon's head and using it to beat Magnus No-Ear to death, and that thought lifted his mood. Halvdan rode up the column and fell in alongside Einar.

"Will we camp soon, Lord? My belly thinks my throat's been cut."

Einar chuckled.

"I just asked our great leader the same thing. We're all hungry. We just await the return of the scouts."

"Scouts, eh? Bastards learned his lesson then," said Halvdan, and the two men shook their heads.

"Where do we even look for the woman?" asked Halvdan.

Einar wiped his nose. It was a cold day with a chill wind, making his nose run into the moustache of his beard.

"First settlement we reach, we get Styrr back there to ask the Saxons where she is. We tell them that if they don't tell us what they know, then we'll kill them all and eat their children. Or something to that effect," said Einar. "The men who captured her will have sent out news of their victory, and I imagine every Saxon knows of the ambush and the prizes captured by now."

"Don't you think it's strange they haven't tried to ransom her?"

It was strange. It would be clear from the Princess's clothing and jewellery that she was of high rank, and any man would know he could get a good price from the woman's family in ransom. Men made good livings from such kidnappings.

"It is strange. You have me worried now. I hope there isn't another twist in this bloody sorry tale," said Einar gnawing at his beard. He hoped they could find out who had the girl, pay them a bag of silver and get back to the army. Then Ivar would be happy, and Einar could get away from Ivar's idiot son. They rode for a while in silence, listening to the sound of the surrounding wood. The trees creaked, and the birds sang. Finally, a scout rider approached ahead and reined in his mount before Hakon. They spoke for a while, and then Hakon turned to Einar.

"There is a small village up ahead, and we will reach it before dark. We camp there."

Einar looked at Halvdan, who shrugged. Surely they were still in East Anglia. To lead the men to a ripe town in a foreign land would be beyond provocation. If there were no peace agreement and the men were on any other campaign, they would loot the place and burn it to the ground. There had been no prizes taken yet, no excitement other than Ivar's Holmgang and a defeat. The men were restless and hungry for silver. As soon as they saw the town, the talking would start, and the blood madness would take over.

"Maybe we can find a place away from the town," Einar said to Hakon. Hakon sighed and looked at the ground, shaking his head. Then, he turned in the saddle and glared at Einar.

"Who commands here, Einar, you or I?"

"You command, Hakon Ivarsson," said Einar. This was embarrassing. Hakon was humiliating him in front of his own crew. Einar could not put up a challenge in front of the men, and if word got back to Ivar, it would be Einar's neck on the chopping block. So he gripped his reins and swallowed his pride.

"Yes, I command," said Hakon, shifting in his saddle and puffing out his chest, "so I say when and where we camp. When I want your advice, I will ask you for it."

The column moved off. Einar just stared ahead and clenched his teeth. He mastered himself and continued onwards. As much as he wanted to drive his horse forward and bury his axe in

Hakon's head, he was oath sworn to Ivar and must follow orders. So they rode on.

Not long after, the column stopped to allow men to relieve themselves and take a bite of whatever food they had with them. Einar sat on the grass and chewed at some hard bread from his pack. He winced as he saw Hakon approach him, clutching a skin of ale.

"Einar Rosti, we are old friends, and we should not have cross words. So let's drink some ale together," Hakon said. Einar no more wanted to drink with Hakon Ivarsson than he wanted to wrestle a bear, but he nodded and smiled.

"I shouldn't have snapped at you like that in front of the men, but I can't be seen to lose face," said Hakon.

Gods forbid you lose face, as though you had any left to lose.

"It's fine, Hakon, I understand," he said, taking the skin and drinking deeply. It was good ale. "Hopefully, we will pick up a trail on your wife soon."

"With Frey's blessing, we will," said Hakon, taking the skin back. "My father likes you, Einar. He has always liked you."

Einar shrugged, "Ivar is a good Lord, a good ring giver. I have always tried to please him."

"I remember when I was a boy, and you were a young Carl. My father used to like to watch you scrapping and brawling with the other warriors. Was it not him who gave you your name, Rosti, the brawler? It's a good name."

Einar remembered that day. He had been caught up in a fight with two Carl's from Ivar's crews. They had beaten him senseless, but he had given as good as he'd got. Ivar had laughed, and from that day on, he had been Einar Rosti. Einar had been in many such scrapes. His father had not been a wealthy man but had sailed and raided like many other Northmen. He had made sure Einar had found a place on a good crew, one of Ivar's crews. Einar knew he could fight; he was bigger than most men, and when he was younger, he liked to fight. Einar felt at his gnarled and scarred face. He liked it that way; it showed the life he had led and told men to beware of his ferocity.

"I remember, Lord. Ivar has been good to me."

Hakon nodded, taking a pull at the ale.

"Do you know Einar; I often think my father loves his warriors more than he loves his own children."

Einar raised an eyebrow. Ivar had three sons. One was in Ireland keeping things safe there, one was too young yet to fight, and then there was Hakon.

"Your father is proud of you, Hakon. It's just...."

"Just what?" said Hakon, his eyes blazing.

"Well, he wants you to be more..., more like him."

"More like him," said Hakon, laughing. "It's difficult to be the son of Ivar the Boneless and the grandson of Ragnar Lothbrok. Every day I try to live up to what they expect of me, Einar, every day. It's not easy."

Einar knew it could not be easy; Ivar was not like other men. He was the Champion of the North and had forged his own kingdom in Ireland, and his grandfather Ragnar was a legend. But why should it be easy? Life was hard, either scrabbling in the soil as a farmer or risking all in battle.

"It cannot be easy, Lord, but look, let's get your wife back; then there will be many battles to fight here against the Saxons. You will have the chance to make your father proud," said Einar.

Hakon flashed him a wide-eyed look of anger.

"You mean he is not proud already? What does he say to you of me, Einar, when you talk behind my back?"

"Nothing Lord, he doesn't talk of you to me."

"You know he hates me," Hakon said. Then, rising to his feet, he pointed at Einar, "I hope you are on my side; I hope you aren't talking to my father against me. That would be a mistake, Einar." Hakon turned on his heel and walked off towards Magnus.

What happened there? Did I offend him?

As the day drew on, the company wound their way through the countryside without coming across any Saxons. The Saxons would have seen the Northmen many times on their journey, and the news of their coming would have travelled for miles around. Families would gather belongings and look for safety in large towns and villages or seek the security of high ground or difficult to access terrain. On their descent into a broad valley, the column passed a handful of empty farms, all deserted with tools left outside and ripe crops ungathered. They rode next to a narrow stream, and the village Hakon was aiming for came into view. It was a collection of hovels with some sheep and cows. Up ahead in the road, three armed horsemen sat abreast, still and calm. Hakon ordered the column to halt and called up Einar's man Styrr who could speak the Saxon language. They spurred forward, and Einar followed.

The three Saxons looked like warriors, well-fed and well-armed. One had a fine mail coat and a sword, and the other two had stout leather breastplates and spears. Hakon reined in, forcing his horse into a slow trot. The Saxons remained silent, unmoved and stone-faced. Hakon leant back towards the translator Styrr.

"Tell them my name is Hakon, son of Ivar the Boneless, King of Ireland. Ask them if this is East Anglia or Mercia," he said. Styrr translated with pauses and fumbles over certain words, which made Einar nervous in case the bastard muddled the messages and incited a fight that would break the peace he had sworn to. The man in mail replied with a brief answer.

"He says it's East Anglia," said Styrr.

"Bastards," said Hakon. "Tell him we are looking for survivors of a cowardly ambush inflicted on us by Mercians or Northumbrians. Tell him we want to know where the survivors are being held."

Styrr's face flushed.

"I don't know some of those words, Lord," he said. Hakon glared at him.

"Just give him the gist of it, you idiot."

Styrr said the words, and the Saxon in mail stared at Hakon. He spoke flatly, and Styrr repeated the words.

"He says they had news of some Viking raiders in the next valley who broke the peace. They assumed they were brigands, and men are hunting them."

Hakon clenched his teeth.

"Ask him if there are any women with the brigands."

The Saxon nodded yes,

"He says yes, Lord," said Styrr. Hakon snarled at him and kicked his leg out towards him.

"I understood that much, you shit," he said.

The Saxon raised an eyebrow and scratched at his beard. Einar just stared ahead. *How had the apple fallen so far from the tree?*

"Tell them we will camp outside their walls tonight, and we will leave in the morning to find the brigands. We expect to be treated as guests," Hakon said.

Styrr translated, and the Saxon set his jaw and straightened in the saddle. He spoke severely, and Styrr nodded.

"He says that you and your companions are welcome to dine in the hall this evening, Lord."

Hakon nodded and waved the column on. Einar kicked his horse forward level with Hakon as the

Saxon rode away.

"Do you want me to send a column ahead to find them?" he asked.

"We can find them together in the morning. One more night won't make a difference, Einar."

"They have men hunting for your wife, Hakon. Who knows how many warriors there are. Your wife might be with our survivors, those brigands, as he called them. If they captured them..." said Einar. Hakon nodded and pursed his mouth. Einar thought he was imagining what might happen to his wife if a band of Saxon warriors unaware of her royal status captured her.

"Go, Einar, take your men with you. We will follow tomorrow," said Hakon. Einar nodded and wheeled his horse around.

"Halvdan, get the men ready to leave at once." Einar felt his mood lifting already. At least now, he would be free of Hakon. He would find the fool's wife and get her back to Ivar and be one step closer to becoming a landed Jarl.

TEN

Hundr kept tight hold of Ragnhild as the horse picked its way across a lumpy field of wild grasses. Ragnhild groaned and raised her hand to her injured shoulder, interrupting the peaceful sound of sheep braying and the rhythmic clicking of Ragnhild's quiver at his back. Finally, she came to her senses and craned her head around to see who was holding her.

"What are you doing?" she asked, jerking to get free of him, her speech slurred.

"Getting back to the others before the Saxons find them. I patched you up a bit, but your wound needs proper dressing."

"The bastard skewered me. Get me up." Ragnhild grunted and clutched her shoulder as she twisted and threw her leg around the horse's neck to sit astride the saddle.

"He did. You were busy throttling the life out of one of them and didn't see him."

She nodded, "Let me get behind you. Don't want you getting the wrong idea."

Hundr laughed.

"Don't worry, pretty as you are; you aren't my type." He climbed from the saddle and held out his arms to help her down. They both laughed as she flashed her gap-toothed grin at him. She slid off the saddle, and he caught her shoulder whilst she clutched her injured one, wincing as she landed. He jumped back up to the horse's back and pulled her up behind him.

"How long before we reach the others?"

"Not long, that should be the hill there," he said, pointing at the peak to the North. The horse plodded on for a while in silence.

"You fight like a demon," Hundr said over his shoulder.

"I serve Odin, wouldn't want to be a mewling girl, would I?"

"How did you lose your eye?"

"So, you are the one with the questions now. I lost it fighting a bear when I was a babe," she said. Hundr snorted a laugh,

"Come on now, tell me the story to pass the time."

"I lost it in Frankia. A spear took it in the shield wall. It came over the top of my shield and laid open my face. The wound brings me closer to Odin All-Father, and I am glad of it."

"Can you see the future?" he asked. All who worshipped the Aesir knew Odin had sacrificed his eye and had hung on the mighty tree of Yggdrasil to gain the power to see the future.

"Yes, I can see a boy with a dog's name who talks too much getting a slap round the head."

They both laughed again, and she jerked with the pain at her shoulder.

"Your turn now. Why are you called Dog, and where did you learn to fight?" Hundr had told no one of his past, it was far behind him, and he liked it that way.

"When I joined Jarl Einar's crew, the men gave me the name. I was the bailing boy." He worried Ragnhild was about to probe him further when they caught sight of Sten and the others gathered around a wind slanted beech tree halfway up the hill slope.

"They made it," he said and kicked the horse into a canter. Ragnhild clutched her aching shoulder as they jerked up the slope.

Sten helped Ragnhild down from the horse. Hildr ran over and lay Ragnhild flat to look at her injuries.

"What happened?" said Sten.

"We ran into Saxon warriors," Hundr said, "didn't see them coming."

"Dog's name here saved my life," said Ragnhild through clenched teeth as Hildr pulled back the makeshift bandage.

"It needs to be cleaned and stitched," said Hildr tutting, and she reached into her pack for bone needle and twine.

"Get me some water," she said.

Hundr grabbed a waterskin from the saddle and handed it to Hildr. As she washed the blood away from the wound, the puncture oozed dark blood. Then, without hesitation, Hildr pinched the edges of the wound together and stitched them closed. Ragnhild clenched her teeth but did not let out a cry or a shout. *Her resolve is hard as iron*, Hundr thought, believing that he would have cried out to all Asgard if Hildr stitched that wound on his body.

"You're a drengr Ragnhild, and no mistake, Odin's watching," Sten said to encourage her. She stared at the old warrior with her one eye blazing wide with the pain. Hundr turned and saw Saoirse standing there, bright against the darkness of the hill behind. His heart lifted to see her safe and well. She had her hand over her mouth as she watched Hildr put Ragnhild back together. Her eyes grew wide as he approached, suddenly aware of the blood on his clothes and breastplate.

"They hurt you," she said in her soft voice, and her hand reached out for his. He smiled.

"No, I'm fine. The blood is Ragnhild's. Are you alright?" Her hand snaked away, and Hundr turned to see Sten approaching, breaking up the moment. Before he could tell Sten to get lost, Hrist shouted.

"There on the edge of the line of pines to the West." They all searched the horizon where she pointed, and there was a glint of the sun off metal.

"Warriors, must be. I can't see how many. We need to move; we're exposed here," said Hrist. They gathered their things together, and Hildr helped Ragnhild back astride the horse.

"We must head back towards the valley, there was a stone bridge at the bottom of the dale, and we can follow the river to hide our tracks. Bastards'll find us for sure if we carry on in the open," said Sten.

"We must find a place to hide?" said Saoirse. She looked from person to person for an answer and took a step closer to Hundr, wringing her hands. She had come from a life of comfort and privilege at her father's hall in Ireland. Yet the idiot Hakon Ivarsson had brought his pretty young wife to war to show her off, and here she was scrubbing around in the dirt and blood with a lost band of warriors.

"They'll kill us if they find us, Lady," said Sten, and paused, "be worse for the women. But, if we must, we can defend that bridge back in the valley where the river runs deeper. If there aren't too many and we are lucky, we can kill maybe six or seven of the buggers and the others might lose their belly for the fight and retreat," he said.

It surprised Hundr to hear the old man talking this way. He hadn't seen him swing a blade in anger, despite his claims to a heroic past.

Ragnhild pulled the reins of her horse with her good hand.

"We go to the bridge. There will need to be fifty of the bastards to take us alive," she said.

Hildr and Hrist smiled and urged the others on. They hurried down the hillside towards the stream in the valley bed. Once they reached the valley basin, Hundr looked at the surrounding area. The hill they had come from was steep. It was rough grass and weeds with a few miserable bushes here and there. There were no trees or rocks to break the enemy's advance. As the hill levelled out, it was flat for twenty paces before a drop of two paces into the stream. The stream itself was fast flowing with icy mountain water and looked thigh deep, hence the bridge.

The bridge was of sturdy wood in good repair and was narrow with maybe enough room for two men to walk shoulder to shoulder and spanned around fifteen paces. Bridging the river was a necessity because of the steep banks on either side and the fast-flowing water. Cattle or people would have a problem making the crossing, and the next ford must have been far downstream.

Hundr stamped his foot on the bridge twice, and it held fast. The land went flat again on the far bank, and then it led into a low-lying marshy bog with pockets of ash and elm trees dotted across the landscape.

The enemy was coming over the crest of the hill. There were at least twenty riders, perhaps more, and they were in no hurry. Ragnhild certainly wasn't in any shape for a fight. Her shoulder was immobile, and she was weak from blood loss. Hundr doubted she could draw a bow or swing an axe. The others came scurrying down the hillside. They were a sorry bunch, an old man with a shield who would not fight, and a Princess who was as much use in a skirmish as a turd in the bilge, beautiful though she was. The two Valkyries had plenty of arrows and the ferocity of five men. And then there was him. He would have to hold the bridge whilst the Valkyries shot at the attackers from the flanks of the bridge to prevent them from entering the water and encircling them. If they could kill a few of the bastards, it would be a stalemate, and they would retreat to look for a ford. That was their only hope. Or, the Saxons would swarm through the river and surround them, and their deaths would be short and bloody. Sten reached him first, and Hundr gestured to the shield on his back.

"You will all cross to the other side; I'll have to hold the bridge," he said. He did not ask Sten if it was a good idea or if he thought he could hold the bridge. It simply had to be done. Sten nodded, handed Hundr his shield, and walked to the other side. The rest of the group followed him across and made their preparations. Hildr and Hrist unslung their bows and made sure the strings were nice and taut. Their bows would usually be unstrung to preserve the power in the recurved horn and wood, but now since the ambush, they had left them strung in case of immediate need. Each carried a spare string should the actual bowstring become wet or snap, and they took their places at either side of the bridge.

The Saxon line fanned out, and there were a lot of them. Hundr started to count them but stopped himself. The only thing that counting achieved was to make his stomach churn and his mouth dry. They were all well-armed men on splendid horses. There were a few with good mail coats, and all carried spears; some had swords. They were approaching, almost in contempt of their prey. Sten approached Hundr, and together they watched the approaching Saxon warriors as they made it down to the flatter part of the valley. They looked like the hearth champions of the local Lords, all big well-fed men and well-armed. They may have been at the ambush or heard of these invaders on their land. It didn't matter. Their job was to defend their Lords' farmers and churls from attack, to protect them from raids. They were all warriors, unafraid and confident.

Hundr felt Sten's eyes upon him, and he looked up. The old man chewed his beard and clapped Hundr on the shoulder, and nodded. Sten's eyes had a softness, and his mouth twitched as though about to speak, but he just nodded and strode across the bridge to stand with Saoirse and Ragnhild. *I could do with the old Sten, the Sten Sleggya of legend. He would make a stand with me.*

Hundr was silent. He picked up Sten's shield from where it rested against his leg, put his arm through the leather loop, and grabbed the wooden handle. He weighed it, and it felt alright. It was a little heavy, but it would take a few heavy blows to break the boards, and that was good. He raised it twice above his shoulder to loosen the muscles and then moved into the fighting stance. The shield was of regular size, and in his battle crouch, it protected him from nose to knee. He stood straight. The strap and handle were sturdy, and there was no risk of them coming loose. He removed his hand from the strap and lay the shield to rest on the bridge rail. He rolled his neck from side to side to loosen the muscles there and stretched his arms backwards to relax the muscles in his chest. These exercises were second nature to Hundr. His weapons master often told of men who ran straight into the fight without loosening limbs, tore the muscles in their arms or shoulders, and could not hold a weapon.

The Saxons paused at the opposite end of the bridge. One man rode forward; his mail was of excellent quality. It was a fish scale brynjar, bright and shining, less effective than the traditional chain mail made of hundreds of sets of four round links joined into one central link. Still, it looked magnificent and marked the man out. The enemy warrior shouted words to them in Saxon, and whilst their languages were similar, Hundr could not understand what he said. Ragnhild barked an order, and Hildr and Hrist nocked arrows to their bows. The Saxon lowered his spear and nudged his horse towards the bridge, and an arrow hit the beast square in the chest; it reared, and the Saxon struggled to stay in the saddle. He dragged the distressed beast backwards, and two more of his men kicked their mounts forward. Hildr shot one of those men in the stomach, and as his only protection was a leather breastplate, the shaft pierced him, and he fell screaming from his horse. Hrist shot the other horse dead in the eye, and it dropped in a twitching mass of horseflesh. The Valkyrie had struck without hesitation, and the day had turned to carnage. Hundr felt the hollow pang of fear deep in his belly, and he let it rise. He allowed it to creep up into his chest, and his heart beat faster. He would use that fear and twist it into rage. He set his face against the Saxons, mumbling a prayer to Odin and Thor, asking them to watch and see what he could do to honour them and earn a place in their Halls of the Dead.

The Saxons were in a panic. One man was

coughing blood and dying, and two horses were down with one braying and screaming. The man in scale armour had dismounted his injured horse and ordered his men to do the same. A few had shields, but they left them on the ground. Hurriedly they spoke between themselves as the two Valkyries had their next shots ready.

The Saxons had already made their first mistake. They should have charged their mounts across the bridge and ridden the Vikings down. Their leader had dismounted, and the rest had followed, so Hundr assumed they would now charge the bridge on foot. He had to goad them into a fight on that narrow bridge where their numbers did not matter. If they understood they should just push him back with their shields, it would be over, but they seemed indecisive, and that gave him a chance. Hundr took his axe from its loop and strode to the centre of the bridge. He shouted his challenge and beckoned the men to fight; he shouted curses he knew they would not understand and spat at them. They watched him, and he could see the snarls on their lips. One man, short but broad-shouldered, drew a sword and a seax in his other hand and marched towards the bridge. The Saxons cheered and chanted.

"Cwichlem, Cwichelm."

Cwichelm raised his blade in salute to his comrades, and reaching the edge of the bridge, he clambered over and around the fallen horses. He looked Hundr up and down and grinned at him. He saw a boy not yet twenty, who was tall but not yet filled out. Hundr held his shield low and off-balance and shifted his feet as though he was afraid. He crouched behind the shield as though petrified. *The trick had worked before, so why not try it again?* The Saxon laughed, and so did the others.

Cwichelm took a step forward and aimed a wild slashing cut at Hundr's shield. Hundr stepped backwards, and the Saxon blade clattered on the wood of the bridge path. The man looked up at Hundr in horror as he stepped in, slamming his axe straight and hard into his eye. He gave a jerk and fell dead. Hundr rolled him over with his foot and yanked his weapon free, spraying blood onto the old wood of the bridge. He had created a barrier that the Saxons would have to cross to get to him once they had climbed over their dead horses. The Saxons were silent and open-mouthed, struggling to understand how their man had died. Hundr grinned and stretched his axe and shield, arms wide in challenge, and he beckoned the fools on. They would have to come one at a time now, and any who tried to cross the river to get around him would be shot to ribbons by the Valkyrie. The Saxons had hesitated, and now they would die.

Hundr wanted to goad them on. This was his time now. He had trained his entire life to fight, he was better than these men, and he gloried in it. The battle fury was upon him. He kicked Cwichelm's body and curse and spat at it to provoke them, and the Saxons became enraged. Two of them surged forward and became crowded together by the narrow span of the bridge, they reach the corpse, and the first man jumped to clear it. Hundr banged him with his shield braced against his shoulder, and the man toppled backwards, tripping the Saxon behind him, who cried out as he used his sword arm to balance himself on the corpse. Hundr smashed the rim of his shield onto the back of that man's head. The warrior who had jumped tried to rise, and Hundr and drove his axe into his mouth, smashing teeth and lips.

Hundr was shouting to Odin and Thor now, screaming at them in his battle fury to watch his deeds, hoping he would catch their eye and they would bring him luck. Three more Saxons approached, with three more warriors close-packed behind them. Other men peeled off to cross the river. The Valkyries waited until the Saxons slid down the bank and then poured arrows into them, forcing them back in a welter of screaming and scrambling.

The six Saxons were ready to charge, but Hildr and Hrist shot arrows into those on the edges, and they bustled together to avoid their lethal missiles. Two men fell whilst one had an arrow stuck in his upper arm. They reached their fallen comrades on the bridge and thrust their blades at Hundr. He kept them at bay whilst arrows smacked into them, and the Saxons fell back, running in panic at the blood and death before them. They had been so confident of an easy victory, and all they had found was blood and death.

The Valkyries cheered, and Hundr was bellowing his defiance at the Saxons. The Saxon in the scale armour was gesticulating and shouting at his men. After some discussion, four men mounted their horses and rode off hard to the

East. The remaining Saxons settled in out of bowshot and sat and rested. Hundr stayed where he was but sat on the edge of the bridge to rest and catch his breath, watching as thick blood dripped from his axe into the river water. Ragnhild and Sten approached him wide-eyed and thrilled.

"You've some skill, lad," said Sten, slapping him on the shoulder, "that was a stand worthy of a song or two."

The old man was beaming and full of excitement. Hundr flashed a ghoulish grin, face splashed with blood, and as his heart rate settled, he slumped a little and rested his hands on his knees.

"What now?" he said.

"They have either gone to fetch more men, or more likely they will ride for the ford and attack us from behind," said Ragnhild, her one eye blazing.

"Bastards will try to trap us," said Sten, scratching his beard. "We must try to last 'till nightfall, then we can slip away in the dark."

"That depends on how far away the ford is, and if they realise they should just all-out charge us. Hopefully, they're as stupid as they look," she said.

Hundr rose from his crouch now that he had his breath back, and he loosened his arms again. He looked at the bodies in front of him, and he felt no pity or remorse. As a child, he'd been taught the difference between right and wrong. It was wrong to steal, wrong to curse the Gods. It was not wrong to kill in battle; a warrior should be able to defend himself. He looked at their weapons and mail, and there didn't seem to be anything worth taking, but one of the swords looked good and well made, so he stripped the belt and fleece-lined scabbard from its dead owner and strapped it to his waist. Armed with a sword, axe, and shield and protected by his hard leather breastplate, he looked like a warrior.

The sun had made a quarter rise across the sky before the riders returned. Each of the four had a man sat behind him, and each of those men had a bow. Ragnhild spotted them first, and she leapt to her feet.

"Archers. Only four, though, prepare yourselves."

Hildr and Hrist made themselves ready and had their arrows at easy reach. They had spent maybe a third of their arrows in the previous fight but had plenty left between the three quivers. The four Saxon bowmen looked like churls, their cloth was poor, and they were skinny and hunched. They were likely gamekeepers or hunters and carried the long yew bow that the Saxons favoured, powerful and able to shoot over a great distance. It took strength to draw such a bow, but the eastern recurved bows were also strong, and the Valkyrie were fast.

"They are going to drive you away from the bridge," Ragnhild said to Hundr.

He made himself ready with his shield and crouched behind the fallen warriors, using them as a grim and bloody barrier.

"You must hold, we will keep their archers at bay," said Ragnhild, Hundr was weary, and his arms were burning, but she was right; he had to hold. He glanced back at Saoirse. She was safe with Sten, but Hundr knew that she would be at their mercy if the Saxons made it across the bridge. The thoughts of what they would do to her washed the fatigue from his arms, and he set himself again. He would hold or die.

Four Saxon bowmen drew their bows. Before they could shoot, the Valkyries let loose, and a Saxon fell screaming with a shaft through his thigh. The other three Saxon bowmen got their shots away. One shaft thumped into Hundr's shield with a force he was not expecting. The point went straight through and stopped only a fraction from his face making him jerk back with surprise at the steel tip only inches from his eye. The other two shafts landed amongst the Valkyrie, but they were unharmed. For fifty heartbeats, arrows flew back and forth. Soon Hundr's shield became peppered with shafts. He couldn't stay where he was with the force of the arrows smashing into his shield and the timber of the surrounding bridge. So he edged backwards under the pressure, out of breath and wincing at each arrow strike.

The Valkyrie and the Saxon bowmen had backed away from each other to test the yardage on their respective bows' reach to see if there was any advantage. In doing so, they trapped Hundr in the middle of their exchange. A Saxon bowman was sinking shaft after shaft into either Hundr's shield or slapping into the corpses strewn on the bridge from the earlier fighting.

His shield was now heavy with arrows, so he balanced it on the nearest body to bear some of the weight. That Saxon had voided his bowels on death, which left Hundr breathing in the foul stench of blood and shit as he crouched for his life behind his only protection. Another arrow slammed into his shield, and a board broke loose with a loud snap, leaving a gap for the archer to aim at. *Bastards.*

Hundr couldn't hold the bridge. There was no way he could survive the longbow barrage, and he shuffled backwards again in a crouch, keeping his shield towards the enemy. The Saxon warriors gave a cheer at his withdrawal. Now all three archers focused their missiles upon him whilst Saxon warriors protected them from the Valkyrie shafts with their shields. As he slid backwards, an arrow made it through the broken board. It sank deep into the flesh of his thigh, knocking him over onto his back, scrambling, and another shaft punched through the shield and on through his left forearm.

The pain was hot and deep, but he did not cry out. That was not the way of the drengr. Instead, Hundr clenched his teeth and tried to open his eyes which were clamped shut. The pain was almost too much to bear as it pulsed upwardly from his leg and burned like fire in his arm. Hundr tried to rise, but his injured leg gave way as arrows skittered on the wood of the surrounding bridge. *I am done, Odin, please take me to Valhalla*, was all he could think, and he clutched hard at the sword in his free hand. Hundr felt powerful arms pulling him back by the shoulder and looked to see Sten bellowing and dragging

163

him across the bridge and then onto the grass beyond. They crashed to the ground, backs against the bridge posts where the arrows could not reach them.

"Can you walk, lad?"

"I don't think so, my leg's not broke, but I need to get the arrow out," Hundr cursed as he tried to move the shield pinned to his arm by the arrow, the weight of it straining through the bones in his arm. The Valkyries tried to provide cover, but they were running low on arrows, so the Saxons drove them back. Pain screamed from his leg and arm in pulsing throbs, and his breathing had turned shallow, so Hundr closed his eyes and tried to calm himself. A loud cheer followed a roar thundered out as the Saxon warriors made ready to charge the bridge and avenge their losses.

"You must run, take Saoirse and go. I'll hold them for a few minutes," said Hundr.

"Don't talk rubbish. I'll stay with you, boy." Sten stood and drew his axe from its belt loop.

Sten looked changed. He stood with axe drawn and face set against the enemy, looking for the first time like a Viking warrior ready to fight. Ragnhild was cursing like the roughest sailor as she rode her horse back and forth behind Hrist and Hildr, fearless of the missiles fizzing around her. She leapt from the saddle and drew forth her axe with her good arm. She marched over to Sten to stand with him. The pain in her shoulder seemed to melt away and became replaced with battle fury. She still had one good arm, and she was ready to fight. She said a prayer to Odin and turned to Sten.

"Are you going to use that now, old man?" She nodded at his axe, looking taken aback by the look in his eyes—the cold hard look of a pitiless warrior.

"I'm ready," Sten said, and he was.

Ragnhild grinned, and the two warriors stood shoulder to shoulder, ready to take the charge they could not possibly hold back. At that moment, a glint of light from the edge of the hill behind the Saxons caught Hundr's eye. Horsemen came into view, milling around for a few heartbeats at the peak of that hill, then formed a wedge and raced down the slope. The noise of their hooves pounded on the turf and thundered like the battle roar of Thor.

"Vikings, Vikings," called Ragnhild, a smile almost splitting her scarred face.

Hundr could not believe his eyes. A long score of mounted Viking warriors was charging the Saxon line like a flock of birds gliding down the hillside. Hundr laughed; he had thought he would die for sure as the powerful Saxon arrows had thudded into his limbs. Now, the sheer elation of surviving mixed with the battle joy still in his veins was a heady combination, and his head swam. The Saxon warriors turned, looked to their leader and then panicked. The scale-armoured leader tried to get his men to form a shield wall, but they were frightened beyond reason. The warriors ran but didn't know in which direction to turn. Hurriedly, their leader rallied a handful of them to brace themselves behind their spears while the rest of the Saxon force ran in a blind panic, either towards their horses or the river bank. Hildr ran forward, and with a curse, she loosed an arrow. It shot across the bridge at a low trajectory and thumped into the back of one of the Saxon archers as he looked at the oncoming charge, knocking him from his feet. She nocked one more and let fly, and seconds later, that shaft sprouted from the eye of another of the Saxon bowmen. Hrist followed her lead and began shooting her remaining arrows at the Saxon melee.

Hundr watched as Saoirse crumpled to her knees, sobbing. She looked at him as she wept, and he hoped it was because she had feared for his life, and he had survived. His heart lifted to see her safe and unharmed, but his joy soon turned to darkness. They had been rescued by Vikings, which meant they must return Saoirse to her husband. That thought made his head sag, and the pain from his wounds flooded his senses. Finally, he felt himself blacking out, yet he fought against the desire to close his eyes and sleep, and he forced his eyes open. This might be the last time he saw her, and he wanted the moment to last forever.

"It's Lord bloody Einar," said Sten beside him, and Hundr twisted around. Sure enough, it was Einar and the Seaworm crew milling around on the far bank, cutting down Saxons as they rode.

Hundr watched as Einar cut a man down with his spear and then turned his mount and called to the Saxon leader who had managed to unhorse a Seaworm man and was stabbing him with his sword and shouting. Hundr shifted his position to get a better view as Einar leapt from his horse and tossed his spear to the ground. He drew his axe and shook it, challenging the Saxon leader. The Saxon stood in his blood-soaked scale armour and went to meet Einar.

The slaughter had been quick, and Hundr couldn't see many Saxons left standing. Einar's men saw the confrontation of war leaders about to take place, and all stopped to watch the men, making way to create a space for the fight. The Saxon was brave, and he shouted his defiance, charging at Einar and rained down a series of wild blows. Einar struggled against the man's raw power, and each parry forced him a step back, but he got wide of the man's guard and cut his bicep open with his knife.

"Gut the bastard Einar," Hundr heard Halvdan shout.

The Saxon backed off then, and he and Einar circled each other. Einar didn't pause, though, and they traded blows for a few moments. The Saxon tried to cut Einar's throat with a broad sweep, but it left his belly open. Einar thrust with his knife, punching through the scale plates, and as the man doubled over, Einar drove his axe into the leader's neck. Finally, he raised his blood-soaked axe, and the crew cheered their Lord.

"Good fight that," said Sten, and so it was.

Einar barked orders which Halvdan echoed but with twice the ferocity. The men became busy searching the dead for anything of value and rounding up the Saxon horses. Hundr swallowed hard as pain pulsed through his body again, and he watched Einar stride across the carnage strewn bridge.

"Thor's balls, is that Hakon's wife?" Halvdan said from behind Einar.

"It is, old friend, and two Seaworm men to boot," Einar said, gesturing to Hundr and Sten. Halvdan took a few steps forward and shook his head.

"I don't believe my bloody eyes."

Ragnhild walked towards Einar and ruffled Hundr's hair on the way past.

"Odin has brought us luck today. You came just in time; how did you find us?"

"Their horses left a trail of shit," said Einar, "Did you make this stand?" He gestured at the fallen Saxons on the Bridge.

"No, I could not fight." Ragnhild nodded to her injured shoulder.

"The old man, then?"

"No, the boy there. He has great skill. They could not get close to him. Archers done for him in the end."

"Will he die?" Einar said, peering at Hundr, who realised that he must have made a grim sight indeed, sprawled on the grass covered in blood, only half of it his own, shield pinned to his arm by an arrow, and another skewering his leg.

"No, he'll recover," Ragnhild said, and Hundr snorted at her flippancy as he grimaced again at the pain.

"Let's put the little bastard out of his misery," growled Halvdan and took a step towards Hundr, but Ragnhild put herself between the bull-necked shipmaster and Hundr.

"He saved my life *and* our lives. I won't let you kill him."

"Very well," Einar said, beckoning Saoirse to follow him, "there are horses for you all. We will ride hard for East Anglia. Hakon misses his wife."

Saoirse glided past Hundr and picked her way around the blood and death on the bridge, where Einar took her arm and led her towards the rest of the crew. She did not even glance at Hundr as she passed him, and he rolled onto his back, allowing himself a groan. He feared he would never see her again. She would ride with Einar now and soon be back with Lord Hakon, and that hurt him far more than any pains from his wounds.

ELEVEN

The three Ragnarsson brothers, Ivar, Ubba, Sigurd, and Kjartan Wolfthinker, plus a handful of their retainers, stood in a yard behind the main hall of their East Anglian base. A greened and rotting fence enclosed the yard, and a twisted tree under assault from dark, sprawling ivy shaded it in one corner. Einar watched Kjartan. The wizened old seer always made him nervous. Kjartan had sailed and fought alongside Ragnar Lothbrok and now imparted wisdom to his sons. Einar wasn't sure of Wolfthinker's standing in the world, but he knew he was Sigurd's pet and was both clever and dangerous.

A burly Dane, one of Ubba's men, Einar thought, carried an armful of weapons over to a sturdy timber table set up before the brothers. The Dane couldn't see over the top of the clutch of iron in his hands and so let them go when he thought he was over the table, causing them to clatter and clang as they thudded onto the tabletop. The man had brought two swords, a sax and two axes. He now laid them out with elaborate care, his face turning increasingly crimson under the baleful glare of the Lothbroksson brothers. Once he had finished his arrangement, the Dane backed away to show no disrespect but then tripped and fell on his arse. Ubba grumbled something into his beard as the man turned and almost ran from the yard, and Ivar laughed, allowing a wide smile to break out across his handsome face.

Ubba picked up a sword from the table and swung it in two sweeping arcs. It was a fine blade with a ball of amber below the grip.

"Saxon weapons," he growled at no one in particular.

Einar watched him as he made the standard practice cuts, lunge, parry, thrust. Ubba was a broad, stocky man. With his mail and thick trews, he almost looked like a box, appearing to be as wide as he was tall. Ubba wore his moustaches long and had intricate plaits in his brown hair. Among drengr, it was a matter of honour to present oneself well, to project wealth and wellbeing. A polished and groomed warrior signalled he was successful and carried a reputation. Einar had never seen Ubba fight but knew he was notorious for relishing single combat like Ivar.

The brothers had summoned Einar not long after his return to the army. He hadn't noticed him at first, but Hakon was there skulking, leaning against the fencing, with the shadow of the ivied tree hiding his face. Next to Hakon stood the hulking captain of his men, Magnus No-Ear. With his bear-like black beard growing almost up to his eyes, he looked like a clothed and armoured bear glaring through matted black fur. Einar raised his eyebrows to Magnus in recognition and tried to ignore Hakon. Still, he could feel him staring, wanting to give Einar one of his knowing grins.

"The blades are good," said Ubba, turning to his brothers examining the length of the blade. Ivar picked up another sword and weighed the weapon in his hand. Then, he took two quick steps forward and lunged at his brother, who parried two cuts and then made an attempt of his own, which Ivar avoided. The two brothers laughed and examined the blades again.

"Good swords. Not as good as my Hugin and Munin, mind," said Ivar. Sigurd lifted a spear and examined the iron head.

"Better than steel from the North, but maybe not as good as Frankish blades," he said.

Sigurd was not a large man, nor did he have a great reputation for being a lover of battle, but he was clever. Eye-wateringly clever. He had a narrow face and quick eyes with the dark snake stain in his left eye that he had been born with. Men said it had the shape of a snake, hence his name: Sigurd Snake in the Eye. Einar hadn't looked at it close enough to tell, but if Sigurd said it was a snake, then so be it. Einar saw Ivar was grinning at him.

"Ah, here you are, Einar Rosti, I hear tales of Princesses rescued, and Saxons killed, and you in the front fighting as always." Ivar hefted the sword making cuts and slashes and grinning. Einar nodded his head in thanks. He looked at Hakon, who was whispering to Magnus and the big man made a guttural noise, and his shoulders shook as he chuckled.

"My son tells me you played no small part in the rescue of his wife," said Ivar. Einar clenched his teeth, the muscles on either side of his face working. Thor only knows what tale Hakon has spouted to his father of the rescue. Einar had not even known Hakon had returned to the army. The last he had seen of him was at the East Anglian town. Einar had avoided bringing the Princess to Hakon, wanting to deliver her to Ivar himself. Why shouldn't he reap the glory when he had done all the hard work? Any more time spent with the turd Hakon would have been un-bearable, anyway.

Ivar took off one of his arm rings and tossed it to Einar. It was a beautiful thing of silver with dragon carvings chasing around its edges. Einar slipped it over his hand where it joined his others, and he stood straighter and pushed his shoulders back. Always nice to get a reward. Arm rings were the mark of a good Lord, a good ring giver who rewarded his warriors with rings and wealth. They were also the mark of a warrior, and a good drengr had rings on each arm; they were signs of battles won and reputation built.

"Thank you, Lord Ivar," Einar said. *Best to not get into a conversation here. Odin only knows what tale Hakon has spun to his father. I don't want to give a different story.* Ivar nodded at him.

"How do they fight, these Saxon warriors?" said Ivar, placing the sword back on the table.

Einar shrugged.

"They have men who can fight, but their warriors are afraid. Not proper warriors. Back home, they would be farmers or traders." That was true. The man in the scale armour who fought at the bridge had been skilled and well-armed, as were a handful of the other Saxons. However, the rest of their soldiers were not skilled and had fled when faced with the charging Northmen. They were most likely local men forced to fight by their Lord when needed, but not full-time warriors.

"I look forward to meeting them in battle. What say you, brother?" Ivar said to Ubba, who puffed out his cheeks and rammed the point of the sword he was holding into the ground.

"We need a fight; the men need it. I need it," Ubba said in a guttural growl. Sigurd grinned, and Ivar nodded approval at Ubba.

"Ubba is eager to test his mettle against Saxon steel," said Ivar, "we will make a move into Northumbria in the next few days."

"Yes Lord, I'll...." started Einar, but Ivar raised a hand to stop him.

"I hear there was a boy who fought well, my son did not mention him, but a little bird tells me this boy stood alone against many and made slaughter among the Saxons."

Einar did not reply. He looked to Hakon to intervene, not wanting to contradict any tale Hakon had already told his father, but he was paring his nails with a short knife as though disinterested. The pause became too long, and Ivar's strange eyes were burning into Einar.

"Yes Lord, the boy held a bridge against many warriors and saved the life of Princess Saoirse."

"Saved her life, you say. I will have to meet this lad and hear the tale," said Ivar, "I also hear he has joined your crew?"

"Yes, Lord, we always welcome fighters, as you know."

"Where did he come from, this unknown warrior?"

"I took him on up North, on the way back from Vankjir. He was with the column ambushed in Mercia, Lord."

"I doubt my son has rewarded this young hero for saving the life of his precious wife, whom he saw fit to bring to war. So, give him this from me." Ivar slipped another ring from his arm and tossed it to Einar.

"You are most generous today, Father. You will soon run out of rings," said Hakon and laughed to himself. He was the only one who laughed. Before Hakon realised what was happening, Ivar was chest to chest with him, eyes boring into his skull. Hakon backed away and banged against the fence. Ivar shook his head, not bothering to conceal his disappointment, and turned back to Einar.

"Odin only knows where you were when men were fighting for your wife," hissed Ivar, and then he turned back to Einar, "I also hear that Sten Sleggya was there."

Shit.

"What?" said Sigurd. Ivar turned to him,

"You heard right, brother; he is alive. Einar bumped into him at a Christ Priest's hall somewhere, and now he is here with the army, is he not Einar?" said Ivar.

The old and thin Wolfthinker darted towards Einar, his rheumy eyes quivering under furrowed brows.

"Where is he?" said Wolfthinker, so close to Einar that he could see his stumpy brown teeth beneath his black and white streaked beard.

"Yes Lord, he is with my men," said Einar, looking at both Ivar and Wolfthinker as he spoke. Sigurd came close and edged past Wolfthinker, and Einar could not help but stare at the black dragon shape in his eye. Unfortunately, Einar was a head taller than Sigurd, which made it awkward as it forced him to look down to meet his gaze.

"You know who he is?" asked Sigurd.

"Yes Lord, he sailed with your father,"

"Rather more than that. He was everywhere with Ragnar, Paris, Frankia, everywhere. Ragnar's Champion. He was everywhere except at the end," said Sigurd.

"He is a coward and a nithing and refused to come and avenge the death of his greatest friend. That turd must pay," spat Wolfthinker. He twisted, holding his staff high, and it shook as he waved it in Ivar and Sigurd's direction, "I want him, I want that turd. I went to him when Ragnar died, I went to Sleggya, and he refused to leave his whore wife. He cast me out! I want that turd, Ivar. I cursed him and his whore," Wolfthinker was shaking, hopping from one foot to the other and spittle flecked his beard such was his fury. Einar took a step back from the wrinkled old terror. Anything to do with curses and Gods always spooked him.

Ivar came forward and put a hand on Wolfthinker's shoulder, trying to calm him.

"Sleggya was with us when we were boys, Einar," said Ivar, "he helped teach us to fight, taught me the tricks of the shield wall,"

"He left my father to die in the snake pit," said Sigurd, raising a finger to Ivar.

Einar and all Vikings knew the story. Passing between the sea off the Frankish coast, Ragnar had become caught in a foul storm and separated from his fleet. King Aelle captured him following a shipwreck on the Northumbrian shore. Aelle hated Vikings, and in revenge for the years of raiding and fear, he had prepared a pit of snakes and threw Ragnar into it, with no blade to hold as he died. As the snake's fangs sunk into his flesh and Ragnar swelled with the poison, he had roared;

"How the little pigs will grunt when they hear how the old boar died," those words had winged their way North, and now and here were Ragnar's little pigs with their Great Army.

"Yes, Lord," said Einar, not knowing what else to say.

Wolfthinker had spittle on his mouth and in his beard, and his eyes flicked from Einar to the brothers and back again. Sigurd had pursed his lips and crossed his arms, and the air seemed to have become heavy. Ivar balanced the sword across his hand as though solely focused on that and without a hint of anger. But that could change in a heartbeat.

"I want to see him, Einar, if it is indeed Sten," said Sigurd.

"I want his turd head on a spike," Wolfthinker said, his eyes almost jumping out of his head, bone trinkets jangling in his hair and beard, "I will use his skull for drinking ale. I will piss on his bones."

"Yes, Lord," repeated Einar, rearing his head back to avoid flecks of Wolfthinker's spit.

"So, bring him here, Einar," said Ivar, "we will move into Northumbria in the next few days, take your men and range ahead of the army. I want them provoked, do it as we did in Frankia. Take any towns and villages you can and report back if you find a city. There should be a city, Yovr, Yok, Yorvik or some such name two or three day's ride north. If you meet a large Saxon force, drop back to us and report. And Einar, deliver the Princess to my son."

Einar knew what they required of him; he had done it many times. Burn and pillage, try to get the Northumbrian King to come out and fight to meet them in the open. But first, bring Sleggya here, to this hornet's nest.

"Yes, Lord," he said.

"My son will range ahead before you. Leave as soon as you can,"

Hakon and Magnus exchanged looks that look made Einar shudder. *The Gods help the people of Northumbria.* Ivar wanted the king drawn out. He wanted bands of twenty or thirty men on horseback moving fast across the countryside, looting churches, killing men, burning towns and farms and leaving spoiling crops while also leaving food stores secure for the following army. He was cutting a swathe across the country. Hakon saw an opportunity for slaughter and rape, to indulge his terrible lust for pain and suffering. Einar was not soft, he knew the face of war and what that meant for the ordinary people, for women and children, and he knew Ivar would be indifferent to that suffering.

Einar would do the work of a drengr. He would ride hard and cut a swathe of fire and death across the Northumbrian countryside in a campaign to draw the army out into a pitched battle, but he would not kill women and children. That was not the way to build or keep a reputation. The Great Army was in a foreign land now. They had no supply lines and so would have to forage as they went, meaning Einar would secure livestock and food for the army to pick up on the march. The army had fixed numbers, and there were no reinforcements, so they could not afford lengthy sieges or battles they could not win. If Northumbria became allied with Mercia or East Anglia, then the Great Army would become outnumbered. If the odds were not favourable, then they would have to withdraw.

But before all that, he had to bring the old man to Ivar and Wolfthinker, and the thoughts of delivering Sten to this hornet's nest and Wolfthinker's fury made him shudder.

TWELVE

It was midsummer, and the Northumbrian countryside bulged with healthy golden crops, the dales bulging with yellows and greens. Hundr rode with the crew on a fine white dappled mare he'd captured from a Saxon warrior who had trained the beast for battle. She did not fear noise or the smell of blood and would fetch a good price if he wished to sell her. That Saxon had been wealthy enough to keep ten retainers, and they had fought well to protect their lands. Einar's men had raided three such places and a small town since leaving the army. Hundr had been determined to keep pace with the crew despite his injuries. Sten helped keep the dressings fresh and clean, and though he had a slight limp, he was well able to ride and fight. The crew rode laden down with spoils, laughter and joking rippling up and down the line. They had only lost one man and picked up no more than a handful of minor injuries. Although he thought of Saoirse constantly, it was good to be with the men on a campaign.

Einar had done as Ivar had asked and had cut deep into Northumbria. He had driven far North and three days ago had looped back Eastwards looking for more prime pickings. The crew had burned villages and killed men wherever they found them and had done all they could to spread terror across King Aelle's country. The Northumbrian Lord's would have raised the alarm by now and would have issued the command for their armies to assemble. Hakon and the other crews would do the same work, and Northumbria would be in a panic. They had not yet sighted the City of Eoforwich, Aelle's great Northumbrian City, where the King kept his court. Hundr and the crew couldn't twist their Norse tongues around the Saxon word for that place, so it became Yovrvik.

Einar had discovered the city's rough location from a captured Saxon. Still, the crew wanted to make themselves a little richer before joining up with the Great Army again, who were likely marching to Yovrvik. So they rode now half a day south from their Eastward path looking for one more plump spot to raid, then they would look to join up with the army again.

The column rode in good order, all mounted and laden with captured silver and iron. Hundr rode alongside Einar, who he thought had taken a bit of a shine to him since the fight at the bridge. He found the usually distant and grim Jarl talking to him increasingly as the days went by. Einar would offer advice on raiding and riding, and Hundr would listen, soaking up the information. He enjoyed being with Einar; it gave him some prestige amongst the crew and curtailed their cursing and foul looks.

Hundr looked at his new arm ring. He adored the thing, and he polished it whenever he had the chance. The ring made him wealthy, it was more than most Carl's of the army owned, and he could chop it into hack silver if he needed money. Moreover, the arm ring was a signal of prowess and a Lord's favour; only valued warriors possessed such jewellery. Along with the sword captured at the bridge and his axe and breastplate, Hundr reckoned himself to have risen fast. He was at least halfway up the pecking order in the Seaworm crew. Above Kraki Horse Face, at least. As he rode along, Hundr remembered how he had felt on that Roman hilltop on the Mersey in his poor travel-stained clothes and thought that he now looked like any other warrior of the army. He had left his home in the East to chase his dream of becoming a warrior, and indeed now he could say he had achieved that dream. The ring and the sword had not, however, helped with his popularity amongst the crew. If anything, his success had pushed the men further away. Only the stalwarts Bush, Blink, Brownlegs and the others were friendly toward him.

"Halvdan should be back before mid-day," Einar said, scanning the surrounding hills. Einar had sent the shipmaster and three other men off at daybreak to scout ahead for any farmsteads or villages with instructions to pick up the column when the sun was at its peak.

"Will we fight today?" said Hundr.

"If they have found a place, yes, we will. Then tomorrow, we will find the army."

"You hear that, Sten? One last chance to fight today before we go back to the army," Hundr said, leaning over his saddle to Sten, who rode behind him. Einar smiled at the joke. Sten just grumbled into his beard and mumbled.

"Fresh from his mother's tit and bastard thinks he knows it all." The surrounding men laughed, as did Hundr. The crew liked Sten; even though he was surly and talked little, he knew how to handle the men. Although he was a Christian and was ever fondling the cross pendant at his neck, it didn't seem to bother the men because the old-timer talked little of it.

At the previous night's camp, Hundr had spoken to Einar about Sten and his life. They accepted he was indeed Sten Sleggya but was not that man anymore. He did as he was told, would stand in

185

the shield wall but would not strike a blow. Einar didn't care about that. Few men were lovers of battle. Most men claimed to be and would draw their weapons and wave them around, but they would cower behind their shields, shitting themselves when it came down to it. Most men would only use their blades on a weaker foe or a foe in retreat. So, the old man did as good a job as most of the other crewmen and would hold the line in the shield wall, which was good enough for Einar.

Hundr had asked Einar how the Princess had been when he returned her to Hakon, but Einar would not talk of it—saying only that she went and that Hakon was as happy as a pig in shit to have her back. The thought of them together made Hundr itch all over. He knew Saoirse was unhappy, but there seemed little he could do about it. Einar said that Ivar and Sigurd knew Sten was in the Seaworm crew and that Kjartan wanted Sten and wanted him badly. Luckily, the crew had ridden out before they had summoned Sten or forced Einar to deliver him up. Hundr wasn't sure which it was, and he hadn't spoken to Sten of it.

"You should make more of an effort with the men, get them to accept you. One day you will need their shields to protect you in battle," said Einar as the column meandered down into a rock pitted valley. Hundr's brow furrowed.

"Why do I need them? Do I not fight better than any of them?"

"You do. But you can't fight alone. You need the others to fight with you, to watch your back and protect you. If you are ever going to lead men, you need to learn how to make them want to fight for you. You want to be a known man, to have a reputation. Others will despise you for that. In our world, that means death. You think only of battle and duels. But it's the knife in the dark that will get you unless others are watching your back. Also, if you don't get the crew to accept you, they will probably kill you." Einar flashed him a rare grin. Hundr looked at him and grimaced.

As they rode down and around the twisting coils of a wide river, a column of smoke appeared to the East, and Einar drove the column towards it. They pushed into a trot, and Hundr kept pace with Einar.

"Do you think it's the army?"

"No," said Einar, "a raided town or village. Bastards have beaten us to it."

"Yovrvik?"

"Doubt it. There would have been a siege or a battle. They would have sent for us. Halvdan's not returned, and they should have seen the smoke before us."

"Do you think something has happened?"

"Let's find out." Einar kicked his horse into a gallop, and his men followed him. The warriors thundered towards the pillars of smoke.

They did not have to ride for long before cresting a hedged rise where they could see down into another shallow valley. It sloped down to a thin brook, and on the slope was a huddle of thatched huts and livestock pens. As Hundr passed over the crest of the hill, he reined his mount in and came to a dead stop. The valley was chaos. The hills echoed with screaming, and warriors swirled around the buildings, running and shouting. Two of those buildings were alight, and the smoke drifted on the wind. At the edge of the settlement, in a muddy pigpen, huddled a group of captives, ringed by armed men. Hundr could make out the enormous baleful figure of Hakon's man, Magnus No-Ear. Some of the crew whooped and rode on past him.

"Hold," Einar shouted, and they followed his orders and formed a line on the hillcrest. "Hundr, Sten, Blink, and Bush, come with me." So they moved off, and the horses picked their way down the hillside towards the chaos below.

"Stay behind me; we won't stay long," was all Einar said as they approached. There was no glory in this kind of warfare. It did not make one a drengr to kill hungry farmers defending their children and women with pitchforks. When Einar raided, he did not think twice about killing the menfolk. He had told Hundr that it was their Lord's weakness for not protecting them, but he would not kill the women and children. It was beneath him as a warrior of reputation. Hundr had learned that lesson, the eagle and the mouse, from his weapons master back home, yet he had dismissed it as bluster. Now, much of what the old codger had taught him was resonating—the way of the drengr, how to care for weapons, etc. Most important of all, it had been his father's veteran warrior, turned into a weapons master, who had taught Hundr how to fight.

Magnus No-Ear made a pretence of not noticing the riders as they came close. He was laughing a guttural, cavernous laugh as his men prodded and poked at the prisoners with their spears and axes. Magnus was head and shoulders taller than any of his men and carried a huge double-bladed, long hafted war axe that he now had slung across his back. Hundr had heard that Magnus called that axe Warbringer. He boasted that on the day of Ragnarök, he would use it to kill Fenris Wolf, the gigantic wolf who guarded the underworld. Hundr watched as Magnus reached out with a giant hand and grabbed the hair of a young woman huddled in the pen's corner, and pulled her savagely towards him. Then with the blade tip of Warbringer, he ripped off her dress in one savage movement. She screamed and tried to cover herself as Magnus' men laughed and cheered. The Seaworm men came to a stop ten paces from Magnus. Einar spat on the ground as he leaned forward on the pommel of his saddle. Magnus glanced up at him, and his laughter subsided, a sour look spreading across his broad face.

"Einar Rosti, welcome to the feast," Magnus said. He had not let go of the girl's hair, and she just hung there quivering, trying to cover her nakedness. Einar matched Magnus' stare.

"Is Hakon here?" he said.

Magnus and his men sniggered like small boys as they exchanged glances.

"Back there doing Ivar's work," said Magnus, nodding towards the thatched buildings but without taking his eyes off Einar. Magnus grabbed the girl by the throat now and hauled her out of the pen with one hand. She screamed in terror as he forced her down to his knee. She continued in vain to cover her nakedness with her hands as she shook with silent sobs.

Screaming came from the buildings, and a woman darted from a doorway. She was trying to run but could not quite get her legs moving and fell to the ground. The woman picked herself up and clutched at a bloody stain on her clothing between her legs. She hobbled towards the pen, unsure of where to go. Hakon then emerged from the doorway, pausing and raising his arms as though in triumph, and his men raised their weapons and cheered. He gave a mock bow and began walking towards them, tying up his leather leggings as he walked.

"Ah," he called as he saw Einar, "Einar, my old friend, the war is in full flow, is it not?"
He carried his belt over one shoulder and stopped as he fumbled to draw his axe from its belt loop. The woman stumbled as she looked behind, and her whimpering turned into panicked cries as she tried to quicken her pace.

"So, it is Hakon, and you are a great warrior and no mistake," said Einar.

Hakon bowed again, and as he arose, he took three quick strides forwards and struck the woman across the back of the head with his axe. As she fell to her knees, he kicked and then bludgeoned her with the axe. He hit her repeatedly, the axe head ripping up chunks of flesh and spraying blood all over him. Hundr flinched at the attack, looking at the ground in front of him rather than witness the horror of Hakon's attack. Finally, after what seemed like an age, Hakon became tired of the slaughter, putting his hands on his knees, and gave an exalted shout. He then secured his belt around his waist and put the axe back in his loop.

"You look miserable Einar, have you had no fun making yourself rich these past weeks?" he asked, putting a hand back on one knee, trying to catch his breath.

"My men have taken much silver, Lord," said Einar.

"Have you roused the Northumbrians?" Hakon reached the edge of the pen. The prisoners shrank back and huddled in the far corner. The captive men tried to shield the women by making a half-hearted human wall in front of them.

"We have burned three villages and one church," said Einar. Hakon nodded in appreciation.

"You must be rich then if you burnt out those Christ weasels. We also found a church. They will not soon forget our passing," Hakon said, exchanging glances with Magnus, and the men around the pen laughed.

"We go to join the army Lord, we will meet you on the road to Yovrvik," Einar said, pulling his reins and clicking his tongue as he went to leave.

"You there," Hakon said.

Heat flooded into Hundr's cheeks; Hakon was pointing at him.

"I am told that you spent time with my wife, boy."

A silence fell over the gathered men—*Thor's*

balls. But the aloof, smarmy look on Hakon's face was too much to bear. Hundr's stomach lurched as he saw a vision of the potential repercussions he would face if this turned into a fight. Hundr said nothing but held Hakon's stare.

"I asked you a question boy, have you been talking to my wife?"

"Yes, Lord. We travelled together after the ambush in the West," said Hundr.

"You sound like a Rus," Hakon said and spat. "What did you talk about?"

"The weather, Lord," said Hundr, and some of Hakon's men sniggered, which made Hakon's face flush scarlet. Hakon reached for his axe and took a step forward, and Hundr grabbed the hilt of his sword.

"Enough," shouted Einar as he kicked his horse between the two men.

"He touched his weapon to me," Hakon was screeching, stepping back from Einar's warhorse as it pounded the ground with its forelegs.

"Hundr, get back to the others. Now," Einar said, stroking the beast's neck, calming it. Hakon had his axe drawn but was making no forward movements. Hundr wheeled his horse, with Sten following, and rode back up the hill away from the danger. He glanced back and saw Einar ride around in a quick circle so that he faced Hakon again.

"He touched his blade Einar," said Hakon, brandishing his axe, "I should kill him for insult, the impudent bastard."

"I apologise on his behalf, Lord", said Einar nodding his head in deference. It was no loss to his reputation to defer to the son of Ivar the Boneless for something so petty.

"Very well, Einar."

Hundr watched from the hilltop as Hakon put his axe back in its belt loop and turned to his men.

"What do you think Magnus, should I seek satisfaction from the whelp?" Magnus laughed in his low rumble and hefted his axe in two hands, pushing the girl away from him with his knee.

"Let's cut his balls off," the big man shouted, and the other men cheered. Einar yanked his mare's reins to twist her head around.

"If either of you shiteaters wants to fight, I'll fight you. It will be different to killing women and children, though. We can do it now. We can lay out the square."

Einar bared his teeth and was shouting. Hundr wasn't sure if he should ride down to support his Jarl. He held himself back, however. To ride down that hillside now would mean there must be a fight. The confrontation was a mistake; surely

Hakon would be Einar's enemy now. Hundr had touched his blade to Hakon, the son of the Champion of the North and the thought of making such powerful enemies sent a shiver down Hundr's spine.

Magnus took a step forward, but Hakon spoke first.

"No need to lose your temper Einar, if I had known the boy was so precious to you, I wouldn't have made the joke. We are only having fun with you. Go, ride back to the army and let them know we will follow today."

Einar spat towards Magnus and backed his horse away.

"Now Magnus, let's show my good friend Einar how we make war the Ragnarsson way," said Hakon as he strode towards his men. Magnus placed one hand on a top plank of the pen and vaulted inside. As he landed, he gave a shout and lay about him with his Warbringer. The prisoners screamed in terror as the blood flew, and some tried to clamber out to escape. Hakon broke into a run to head them off, and his men whooped for joy as they chased the helpless men and women down.

Einar rode up the slope with the sounds of the slaughter undulating behind him. He reached his men and kept on riding, his face grim and jaw clenched. Hundr caught up with him,

"What happened?" he said.

"I challenged Hakon Ivarsson and Magnus No-Ear to fight."

"I saw. Why?"

"It didn't come to that, thanks to Odin," Einar said, "you touched your sword to Hakon lad. He won't forget that."

"I don't care, he…"

"Don't be a fool. Hakon will kill you. This is not a game, and it is not some boy's dream of glory and heroes. This is actual life. Hakon is the son of Ivar the Boneless, who is my Lord. Hakon can kill you, and no one would stop him or punish him. You make enemies wherever you go Hundr, you need to make some friends, or you will find yourself dead in a ditch. So whatever that shit is about Hakon's wife, keep away from it, or you will get us all killed."

"But…"

"But nothing. Get back with the rest of the men, go."

Hundr saw Sten shooting him a disappointed look, like a father cross with his bed-wetting son. A pox on Sten's disappointment. It was enough that he was now the enemy of Hakon Ivarsson, who also was the husband of the woman currently occupying Hundr's head. On the one hand, Hundr was driving towards his dreams of reputation and success, and on the other, he had found love. But everything to do with that love seemed impossible and drenched in trouble. Hundr nudged his horse on. There was much to think about and much danger to navigate.

THIRTEEN

The army reached Yovrvik two days later. By the time the Seaworm crew arrived, the camp was already under construction. A ditch and a timber palisade were being erected, and long orderly lines of sailcloth tents had been thrown up. The smell of fresh-cut logs sweetened the air, and those logs stood in piles, gold and bright as warriors hacked at the ends to make sharp points. The large city lay at the coming together of two wide rivers, the Ouse and Foss. It was an old city built by the Romans, and the high walls were made of magnificently dressed Roman stone.

The camp's position allowed the Vikings an unobstructed view of the city's great Christ Minster, with its peaks rising far above the ancient stone walls. The Ragnarrsons had sent ships patrolling the west coast of East Anglia and Northumbria, and they now secured four ships on a makeshift dock to the South West of the city. Hundr's breath had caught in his chest to see that the Sea-worm was there, having been sailed around the southern Saxon coast by Ivar's men and on to Northumbria. The ships were the Vikings greatest asset, so having the sleek war vessels with the army allowed them to seal off access to the city by river and sea, as well as by land. Einar had been like a child running to the river when he caught sight of her. The two rivers ran through the city itself, and the old walls had gates on three sides, one facing to the south of the Ouse, one to the South East between the Ouse and the Foss, and then one to the North West. The Ragnarssons camped the army to the South of the city, ranging westwards to the edges of the Ouse. Their ships blockaded the river to supplies and support for the city, meaning that supplies and any reinforcements could only come from the North.

Hundr wandered along the riverside, taking care not to get too close to its marshy banks, which sloped down into the fast-flowing river. He had spotted Sten stood there alone, watching the river and gazing up at the vast Roman stone walls of the city. The river flowed swiftly by, and flies buzzed across its sleek surface, the long grass of its banks dragged along by the current. Hundr watched the reeds and grasses bend to the will of the water and stood next to the old warrior who had become his friend.

"What's on your mind?" he asked. Sten fingered at the wooden cross at his neck.

"Seen a few assaults on castles like this, more than most I'd wager. Never thought I'd see one again,"

"Do you feel much like your old self?"

Sten chuckled.

"No, lad. That part of me died long ago; I'm not that man anymore. Too long living in peace, too soft now for the bloody ruthlessness needed to live this life."

Hundr didn't think he sounded too convinced about that.

"You two vagabonds look weary," came a woman's voice behind him, "perhaps you need an afternoon nap near the fire, grandfather." Hundr turned and saw Ragnhild stood before him, smiling her gap-toothed smile. Her arm was out of its sling, and she looked well.

"I could use a nap. You got a warm cloak?" Sten said, and they laughed. Ragnhild came and stood beside Sten, the top of her head not even reaching his shoulder.

"How is the slayer of Saxons? I hear Ivar gave you a ring?" she said to Hundr. He grinned and held it up for her to see.

"I am well, Ragnhild. You look as fearsome as always."

"It looks formidable, does it not?" she said, nodding towards the city. Sten shrugged.

"When the Rome folk were here, it wouldn't have been easy to take this place. The stone is old now; depends on how well the Saxons have maintained it."

She nodded, "True enough. Have you seen a city of Rome before?"

"Seen a few bigger than this. Don't know if they've enough men to protect the walls all the way around. How's the shoulder?"

She rotated it around, "Getting better, should be good as new in a few days. That was some fight at the bridge, was it not?" she said to Hundr.

"It was," he said, flexing his own arm and feeling the soreness still there where the shield had been pinned to his arm in the fight.

"We would be dead if it wasn't for you," she said as they continued to stare at the city. Which was true, he supposed.

"How are Hildr and Hrist?" Hundr asked.

"Good, we rode many miles these last few weeks scouting miles around. Our entire company is together now, and our High Priest Vatnarr is here. We are ready to fight," she said, pushing her shoulders back and standing straighter.

"I don't doubt it," said Hundr. "Will we attack?"

To attack a well-fortified city like Yovrvik would mean many men would die. They would need to either storm the walls or smash down a gate and then fight within the city, guaranteeing chaos and slaughter.

"Yes, we will attack in two days maybe," said Ragnhild, "men are making ladders and rams at the moment; look," she pointed downstream. Hundr could see logs pulled along behind the ships there and the foremost being hauled ashore to be fashioned into siege engines.

"Will the Northumbrian King come?" he asked.

"His country is in ashes, and he skulks behind walls somewhere in the North. He does not protect his people. He is not a good King," she said and spat into the river.

"Lot of silver behind those walls," said Sten.

"And much glory to be had on the walls. Odin will watch us, Hundr," Ragnhild replied with a grin. She touched the spear amulet she wore at her neck.

"Where are you camped?" Sten asked.

"Close to the centre, over by the Ragnarsson's tents. We have to stay close if we want to be first over the wall. You should both come to our camp this evening. We will have meat and good ale."

"In that case, how could we refuse?"

Einar gave Hundr and Sten permission to travel into the Valkyrie encampment, and they left in the late afternoon as the day became cooler. They made their way from their own section of the camp and through the many crews who made up the Great Army. The majority of the men were Danes, but there were also Swedes, Norse, and men from Ivar's crews in Ireland and the lands of the Scots. They passed men playing knucklebones for hack silver; they passed men at makeshift smithies having fresh edges put on their weapons. There were laneways marked out between crews in what was an organised camp. Ragnarsson men had come to each crew and explained where they could go to shit and piss and not to do it close to the camp or in the river. The troops had been told to forage for their food but that ale would be provided. Two Irish warriors with their long plaid cloaks came towards Hundr and Sten, walking two abreast and taking up the whole laneway. Sten had to move the side into the mud to avoid bumping into them. Hundr tutted and shook his head.

"Why did you do that?"

"You rather I started a bloody fight?" said Sten.

"No, but at least stand your ground, Sten, don't be such a...."

"Such a what?"

"Never mind," said Hundr, "Let's keep going; it can't be far away now."

Hundr didn't want to upset his friend, but it had not gone unnoticed that Sten had not struck a blow in anger since they had both joined the Seaworm crew. He had stood in the shield wall and had not shied away from the fighting. Still, he had not so much as drawn his weapon, as far as Hundr had seen at least. Of course, there were others who didn't push to the front to strike at the enemy, so Sten got away with it, but Hundr had noticed. *How could Sten have been such a famous warrior if he was afraid to fight?*

"Why didn't you stand your ground back there?" he asked. Hundr just couldn't understand how a man could not take more pride in himself. Sten just shrugged and grunted, which was infuriating. Hundr stopped walking,

"Talk to me, Sten. Would Sten Sleggya move aside for two warriors and stand in the mud?"

Sten looked at Hundr and shook his head.

"In the old days, laddie, them two would have moved for me. But I ain't what I was, and don't look like it neither. Fact is, I don't mind stepping aside."

"But.." Hundr began, but Sten just held up a hand to quieten him.

"I know. A drengr moves aside for no man unless he fears him. You're young, and you haven't learned yet. To you, it's all about pride and fighting and glory. When you get old like me, lad, you realise that's all piss. Pride softens when you've seen so much death, so much loss."

They carried on in silence, and the camp sprawled before them, cooking fires lit up the early evening. Smells of pork and lamb roasting made Hundr's stomach twist with hunger.

"I hope Ragnhild has good meat for us. My belly thinks my throat's been cut," Sten said, trying to lighten the mood. Hundr laughed.

"Me too, I don't think my belly can take much more of Blink's cooking," Blink was still the self-appointed cook for the Seaworm crew, and his fare remained less than appetising.

"That looks like their enclosure up ahead," said Sten, pointing at a grouping of tents ringed around by a thick rope barrier tied to spears driven into the ground at twenty pace intervals. Two Valkyrie warriors stood watch at a break in the rope fence. They were both armed with spears which they lowered as Sten and Hundr approached.

"We're here at the invitation of Ragnhild," Sten said. The warrior to the left looked him up and down and then did the same to Hundr.

"The old man and the boy with the dog's name," she said, "Ragnhild is expecting you. Follow me," she said and led them into the Valkyrie camp. Mostly, it was the same as the rest of the Viking encampment, a collection of tents separated by marked laneways, but at the centre of the Valkyrie tents was a cleared square where a fire blazed and crackled, spitting golden embers into the darkening night. The Valkyrie warriors all sat around the edges of the square in small groups, talking and laughing, drinking and eating. The smells of roasted meats and wood ablaze washed over Hundr like a wave, and he breathed them in.

"Looks like we've come to the right place, lad," Sten said, slapping Hundr on the shoulder. Hundr grinned and rubbed his hands together. Shouts came from across the square, and three Valkyrie warriors approached around the fire. It was Ragnhild, Hildr, and Hrist.

"Welcome," said Ragnhild, spreading her arms wide and smiling. Hildr came and greeted Sten, and Hrist lifted Hundr's arm to check his wounds,

"It doesn't look too bad," she said.

"Must have been the way you looked after it, Hrist, thank you. The leg is also healing well; it's much better," Hundr said.

"Come, let's eat," said Ragnhild and led them over to where they could sit. Hundr sat, and she handed him a wooden plate of roasted pork, a juicy chicken leg and a pot of ale, which was like a gift from the gods, and he bit off a chunk of steaming chicken, grinning as the juices flowed down his chin.

"So," said Ragnhild, sitting cross-legged in front of them, "what have you two been up to since we last saw you?" Sten also had not waited, and he'd stuffed some of the pork into his mouth. The juices were running into his beard, so he held up a finger to excuse his inability to answer. Hrist laughed and raised her ale pot to him.

"We went out ranging and scouting with Jarl Einar, the Jarl of the crew who killed the Saxons at the bridge," said Hundr. "I heard you had been scouting far ahead of the army."

"We did," said Ragnhild, "we rode North past Yovrvik and round to the West looking for Saxons on the march."

"Northumbria is fine land, rich," said Hildr.

"Did you see any Saxon warriors?" said Hundr.

"No," said Ragnhild, "King Aelle is hiding in a fortress further North. He lets his people die, and his country burn."

"How did that man catch Ragnar Lothbrok?" said Hrist, and each of the Valkyrie shook their heads.

"Now," said Sten, having swallowed his food, and they all laughed. "Ragnhild and the lad here are both healing well, so here's to being safe with a full belly," and they all toasted to that.

"Praise to Odin that we survived at the bridge," said Ragnhild, "and you saved my life. I won't forget that," she placed her hand on Hundr's shoulder. The Valkyrie all touched their silver spear pendants and raised their eyes in thanks to Odin. Sten reached for his own pendant and looked down at the fire across from them, going into a daze.

"You will have some fine scars now," said Hrist to Hundr, "scars are good. They remind us of our deeds and give us stories to tell."

Hundr rubbed at his thigh.

"Ragnhild, tell us the story of how you lost your eye," Hundr said. She stared at him for a few moments with her one good eye but then smiled and took a drink of her ale.

"I will tell you," Ragnhild said, "but then Greybeard here must tell us a tale of his adventures with Ragnar."

"You have many scars, Sten," said Hildr, "tell us their tales."

Sten took a long pull at his ale, "We'll see. You first Ragnhild."

"I had been a Valkyrie warrior already for five years, " Ragnhild said, leaning forward, her good eye catching the firelight. "My father had brought me to the Order when I was a girl, he had too many daughters, and so I was given as a sacrifice to Odin. I was trained and had fought many times before my eye was taken.'

'Have you seen them since?' asked Hundr.

'Seen who?' said Ragnhild.

'Your father, your family?' said Hundr,

"This is my family," Ragnhild said, sweeping her arm around the campfire, 'Odin is my father. So, we were fighting in the South of the country of the Danes, there were Christians there spreading their poison to good people, and they sent us to expel them. There were many warriors with their black Christ Priests, warriors wielding good Frankish steel and skilled fighters. I was fighting one such warrior, and I misjudged his reach, his sword point flicked up, and I felt the sharp bang of it opening my face up and my eye was gone." She lifted her eye patch to show the long straight scar that went from her top lip through the empty, withered red eye socket and on through her eyebrow. She took a drink of her ale, putting her patch back in place.

"What then?" asked Hundr.

"Then I sent him to the afterlife," Ragnhild said. "Now I have one eye like Odin All-father, but alas, I did not get the power to see into the future," she said, and Hilda and Hrist laughed.

"Your turn, Sten," said Hrist.

Hundr watched his friend take another pull at his ale, which the Valkyrie had refilled twice already. Sten sighed and belched, looking around at them all from under his frown and creased brows.

"Bloody Hel," said Sten, as he adjusted his seating position for more comfort. It was surprising how relaxed Sten looked. Whenever there were questions about his old life, Sten would usually close up like a sea chest.

"There're many tales I could tell, for I have sailed far and wide. I've been South to where the sun burns men's skins black and West to the misty edge of the world."

"I like this story already," said Hrist.

"I'll tell you the tale of how I killed Ketil the Black. Of course, you young pups won't remember old Ketil, but he was a famous warrior once upon a time," said Sten.

"Here, Sten, fill your cup whilst you talk," said Ragnhild as she poured him some ale. Ragnhild was clever; the ale had loosened Sten's tongue. Hundr hadn't heard the old dog talk so much in all the time they had known one another.

"So, Ragnar and me had sailed deep into Frankia. We were young then and just taken a huge haul of silver from a Frankish King, who

Ragnar had persuaded to pay us to not attack his city. Wolfthinker, the sly bastard, had come up with that plan, and it had worked." Sten wagged a finger at the Valkyrie, "we never had enough men see, always Ragnar worried we would lose too many men in fights and have to sail home. Wolfthinker would always have a plan, some bloody scheme to avoid fighting unless he were sure we would win."

"This is the Wolfthinker who advises Sigurd and Ivar?" asked Hrist.

"Aye, that's him, little bastard with bones and trinkets in hair and beard," said Sten. "Anyways, we were all rich with silver and set to sail home, but one of the Norse Jarls sworn to Ragnar was a bastard spawn of Loki named Ketil the Black. Ketil was the Lord of a few shit islands in the far North and had three ships under his command, had a reputation for brutality did Ketil and his crews were fierce fighters. Anyway, we had made peace with the Frankish King and were ready to sail away, but Ketil got it into his head that he would make a better leader than Ragnar, and so he challenged Ragnar's leadership as Lord of the North."

"I haven't heard this tale before," said Ragnhild, "you tell it well, here take some more ale."

Sten drank again and wiped the ale froth on the back of his sleeve. He was enjoying himself now, leaning forward and gesturing with his hands as he spoke.

"So bloody Ragnar was away sealing the peace with the Franks, so Wolfthinker met with Ketil and agreed that there would be a fight to determine who was leader, and it was left to me to fight him in Ragnar's stead." Sten leant closer to the group, "At the time I half thought Wolfthinker, the rat, had planned it that way; Ragnar gone, black bloody mad-as-a-bull Ketil and only me to fight him."

"Was Ketil a skilled fighter?" asked Hundr.

"He was bloody mad, lad, and fought with that reckless madness. Not much blade skill, but plenty of bloody madness," Sten grinned, "the entire army gathered to watch Ketil and me fight, the square was made and off we went. No surprise, Ketil fought like he was possessed by Loki, and his axe broke more than one of my shield boards, but I had the better of the bastard, and he was bleeding from his shoulder and his leg. I closed in to finish him, but Ketil was a sneaky bastard. He barged me back to the edge of the square with his shield, where one of his black-hearted crew stabbed me twice in the back above the rim of my brynjar. You can see the two scars here, look,' said Sten, and he showed them the thick scar tissue there.

Hundr looked at the sheer size of Sten. He

hadn't met a man as tall and broad, and he had hands like shovels. He had still not seen Sten raise a weapon in anger, but should he decide to take up his old fighting ways again, there couldn't be many who could match him.

"Sly bastards," said Ragnhild.

Sten nodded and licked his lips.

'So, they hurt me bad, and Ketil pressed me more with his axe, knowing I was losing blood and my strength was flooding out of me. I knew it too, and so I had to end the fight quick. I couldn't get past his shield with my axe, and so I let him hit me with his axe, and it bit deep into my shoulder. Like getting bit by a bloody dog, it was. I dropped my axe and grabbed his head, and got both my hands around his jaw," Sten shot his huge hands out and clasped them together, "I can still hear Ketil's screams now as I crushed his bloody skull. The bastard died badly. So that's how I got some of my scars, and the story of how I killed Ketil the Black,' said Sten.

The Valkyrie and Hundr gave a cheer and raised their cups in a salute to Sten's story.

"What happened then?" asked Hundr; the story couldn't just end there.

"What do you mean," said Sten and drained his cup, which Ragnhild refilled.

"What did Ketil's men do?"

"Turned out Wolfthinker had planned it all. He had put the seed of challenge in old Ketil's head. But I killed Ketil, and his men swore an oath to Ragnar, which gave him more crews and lands in the North surrounding one of his rivals back there. Can't even remember the bugger's name now." Sten said, scratching his beard.

Hundr watched Sten, old and hulking, as he flexed his hands, feeling at the missing finger, then rolling his shoulders and grimacing at the stiffness there. It had been an incredible story for a night such as this, but it had been a cruel plan Wolfthinker had cooked up. Ragnar away, Sten left to fight. If Sten had lost, then Ketil would still not have defeated Ragnar, but if Sten won, then the challenge went away, and Ragnar had the lands and warriors he needed. Maybe Sten had seen that at the time and didn't care, or maybe not. Either way, it was hard for Hundr to see his friend as a great Champion; he just seemed too gentle.

"That was a great tale Sten, although it's hard to imagine the Sten we know today in such a famous Holmgang," said Ragnhild, laughing, echoing Hundr's thoughts.

"Tell us, Sten, how did you leave Ragnar's service?" asked Hrist, smiling.

An air of awkwardness descended on the group as Sten sat back and slumped, staring into his ale. In all the time Hundr had known Sten, he hadn't been able to get him to open up and talk, but it seemed this night the ale had loosened his tongue, so Hundr just stared at this friend, hoping he would share another story, the story Hundr was itching to learn; how Sten had gone from a famous warrior with wealth and power, to scratching around in the soil with Christ Priests in Northumbria. Sten sighed, his broad shoulders rising and falling into a deeper slump. He looked up towards the fire, and Hundr thought he saw the firelight glistening against wet eyes in the old man's face.

"I met her," Sten said. The group leaned in to hear him, "My Ralla. I met her, and everything changed." It seemed he would say no more, but then he sniffed and cleared his throat, fingering at his wooden cross pendant.

"I was like you all," he said, sweeping his arm towards Hundr and the Valkyrie, "all I had ever known was Odin, battle, glory, reputation. I had grown tired, bloody Wolfthinker growing more powerful. My life was less of the simple things I loved, sailing, fighting and the like. Too much bloody skulduggery, deep thinking and planning. Ragnar were all caught up in it, wanted to be a King," Sten trailed off and looked into his empty ale pot.

"I've drunk too much, said too much," he said and rubbed his eyes, "Well, one day I met my

Ralla, and it all changed. She brought me peace, and I didn't want to fight anymore. So I just left. I stayed in the Saxon lands with her, and we lived a quiet life. I left my men, and they sailed back to Ragnar. She was like a bright star in a world of darkness and slaughter."

"She was a Saxon?" Hundr asked. He had so many questions but didn't want to stop Sten from talking,

"Aye, she was. A Christian, showed me the way to God. I swore to her I wouldn't kill again, and I haven't. We were happy." Sten shook his head, his lips folding in against his teeth.

"Few years back, she died. Sickness took her. Took her little body a whole Winter to die."

"Sten, I am sorry," said Hildr and went to him and put her arms around him.

"It's alright, don't worry," he said. He put his pot on the ground and tried to rise but fell and had to steady himself with an arm on Hildr's shoulder, "too much bloody ale. So, she died, I buried her and went down the hills to help the brothers. I stayed there for a while, and then you lot came and bloody killed the lot of them, and now here I am. Come on, lad, let's get going," he said, nodding to Hundr. They said their thanks to the Valkyrie for the fine feast and began the journey back to the crew. Sten was unsteady on his feet and put an arm around Hundr's shoulders.

"How did you learn about Ragnar's death?" Hundr asked him as they walked. Sten grunted and belched,

"He came to see me, came to my home and told me. Asked me to go back and fight."

"Who came?"

"Wolfthinker."

"Did you go?"

"No, I stayed. He cursed to all Valhalla, cursed my Ralla, said he would beg Loki to put worms in her belly. He always hated me Wolfthinker did."

"Does he have power from the Gods?"

"Maybe, he always reckoned he did the slimy little bastard. Enough talk now, lad, just get me to where I can sleep," Sten said. He would say no more.

Hundr walked with the old man, helping to keep him upright. So Sten had given up his oath to Ragnar and become a Christian, all to be with the woman he loved, but who had then been cursed by Wolfthinker. *How had Sten not wanted revenge for that curse?*

As he went to sleep that night, Hundr closed his eyes and imagined the Sten of old, armed and dressed for battle. He wished for a second he had known that man but then checked himself. The Sten he knew was a good man; truth be told, he was more of a father to Hundr than any other

217

man in his life. Sten looked after him. He made sure there was food, made the fire every night, and more than once, it had been Sten's shield protecting Hundr from enemy blades. As sleep pulled him deeper, he almost envied Sten's quiet life with his Ralla on a Northumbrian hillside. *Could there be such a life with Saoirse?*

Hundr fell into a deep comfortable sleep, ale and a full belly, helping the hard ground feel like a soft, warm bed. They woke him early the next morning because that day, they would assault the walls of Yovrvik.

FOURTEEN

Hundr woke with a thick head from the ale supped with the Valkyrie; he groaned and rolled over in his bed. It was a day for sleeping and nursing his head. He curled up and closed his eyes again, but Halvdan woke him fully with a kick up the arse and a growl.

"Get up, you lazy bastards, we attack the city today," he said and moved on to the next man.

Hundr opened one groggy eye and watched Halvdan leave. *Miserable bastard*. Sten coughed and groaned, searching around their quarters for some ale to break his fast. Hundr stretched.

"Today is the day," he said through a yawn.

Sten was moving blankets and lifting belts.

"Any bread left?"

"Who needs bread? Today we can fill our bellies with glory," said Hundr, rising onto his elbows.

Sten looked at him and shook his head.

"Daft bugger. Fill our bellies with arrows and blood more like," Sten continued his search for bread, "bloody fool boy." Soon enough, thoughts of the day ahead cleared Hundr's fuzzy, hungover mind. The prospect of impending death, or horrific pain and injury, would do that to a man. But today, he would see the entire army mobilise and attack Yovrvik, which meant an opportunity for Hundr to make a name for himself in the onslaught, and also be part of an actual battle. He had been in skirmishes and fought well already, but a battle was something completely different.

"It was a good night last night," he said.

"Too much bloody ale, talking bloody shite," Sten grumbled and coughed.

"Always so grumpy, old man. Don't get killed today."

"I'll do my best, don't get me killed is all I ask. Do nothing stupid."

They gathered together their clothes and weapons. Bush and Hrafn were nearby, also readying themselves. Bush was spitting on and polishing his helmet with his elbow. The helmet was his finest possession; it was a magnificent piece, well-crafted and ringed with runic inscriptions. The camp was like a kicked beehive; men were marching and jogging across the muddy laneways, and captains on horseback shouted instructions.

"Get into your crews and move towards the river. Hold on to your weapons today, lads!"

Hold tight, thought Hundr as a reflex. *Hold tight to your weapon or lose your place in Valhalla.* The crowd buzzed around them, some men excited, but more were ashen-faced and lost in wide-eyed dazes. Only a few would relish the climb up the ladders. Fear and a spear point in the arse from their captains would drive more up there, but both would die just as easily.

"I think I see some more of our lads over there by the smithy," said Sten, pointing.

They crossed the laneway between tents and joined up with the Seaworm crew. Two of them were getting fresh edges put onto their blades. The others were checking straps on shields and drinking ale. Blink was serving up some slop from a cooking pot, fussing around the crew with his bow legs shuffling and long open face smiling.

"Here, there's some left boys," Blink called over.

"Maybe we should throw this shit at the Saxons," said Brownlegs, and then men laughed.

"Give it back then if you don't like it. Ingrate," said Blink.

"Get it into you lads, settle your stomachs," said

Bush, now wearing his fine helmet polished to a gleam, standing a little straighter. In truth, it looked a bit out of place against his old leather breastplate and faded trews. Horse Face was there also, helping Ulfketil with a shield strap.

The crew set off towards the river, looking for the right place to stand. They moved in and out of groups of Danes, Svears and Norsemen. Hundr could feel the twin senses of excitement and fear amongst the men they passed. Some were laughing and joking; others were worrying at straps and blades. Sten, being as big as he was, could see over most men, and he spied Einar twenty paces away. Einar, also being tall, was visible among the throng of soldiers. The Seaworm crew all shuffled together and made a space for themselves with Einar and Halvdan at their centre. The field stank already of sweat and piss; men would piss where they stood rather than sloping off to find a secluded spot and risk not finding their shipmates again.

"We are so far back," said Hundr, standing on his tiptoes.

"That's good," replied Sten "first ones up will die in droves."

"Halvdan," called Bush, " there's rumour of a prize for first to scale the wall."

Halvdan turned his thick neck and nodded, "Aye, a silver arm ring from each of the Ragnarssons for whoever gets up first."

"Three arm rings," said Hundr to Sten, "that would make a man rich."

"Do nothing, stupid lads," said Einar over the din of shields banging together and spear shafts clattering above their heads as men tried to keep the forest of spear points steady. "Calm down, and we wait our turn. We go up with Ivar, not before."

"The first up will be the allies of the brothers, expendable crews who got to prove their worth. Irish and Scots," said Sten. "They'll earn their silver today. Wolfthinker will have them up there faster than a beggar on a hot chicken leg."

The sun continued its journey across the morning sky, and no news came from the Ragnarssons. As time wore on, men grew more febrile as fear and anticipation gnawed at their bellies; some men crouched, and some sat. Games of knucklebones broke out, as did songs and riddles among groups.

"When will we cross the river and attack?" said Hundr for the tenth time that morning, convincing himself that the hollow feeling in his belly was hunger and not fear.

"When the Lords tell us to. Must be waiting for a sign. Maybe Sigurd's waiting for his Odin priests to tell him the omens are right," said Bush, his helmet under his arm now as he scratched at his bald head beneath the old helmet liner.

"Omens, what a load of shite, boys," said Blink "just attack and be done with it," he blinked even faster than usual, looking around at the others.

"Lots at stake here lads, thousands of lives, if we lost more than a few long hundreds, war could be over. Time's got to be right to attack. The little pigs will have learned from the old boar; they'll know when," said Sten.

"How would Ragnar have done it?" asked Hundr. Sten thought for a minute.

"We stormed a few castles like this in Frankia, old Roman forts fallen to disrepair. We would have scouted the walls and looked for weaknesses, maybe a few probing attacks to check the defences. Then attack. A few fake attacks to force the enemy to spread their defenders thinly across the walls. Whatever way you do it, climbing them ladders is grim, bloody work. Luck's what's needed today, lad."

Hundr was about to reply when a messenger rode down the line shouting, and Einar raised his axe.

"Now boys, across we go. Stay together and regroup on the far bank. Wait there for my signal."

The crews roared and leapt to their feet. Hundr picked up his shield from where it rested on the grass and slung it on his back. He lurched forward at a slow jog, keeping pace with the crew. They walked and jogged a few feet, but then the line stopped as men clattered into each other's backs as they paused in the front lines to wade into the river. Finally, when Hundr's turn came, he stepped in, and the water came up to his waist. The icy chill of it took his breath away.

"Odin's balls it's freezing," said the man next to him, making little jumps through the water as if to reduce its coldness.

Hundr looked at Sten, and he was silent, focused on the steps in front of him, eyes fixed on the walls ahead. They scrambled up the far bank, churned to a muddy slop by the men in front, and Hundr slipped four times before a man behind grabbed his foot and helped push him up over the mud-splattered bank. Hundr grabbed some weeds and hauled himself up. They trudged forward again and then halted. They could hear the roar from the city now; the attack had begun. Hundr felt his stomach churning again, and he needed to piss.

"Can you hear that," he asked, "what's happening?"

"Attack's begun, our turn soon," said Sten, short of breath from the climb up the riverbank.

The old warrior unslung his shield and strapped it onto his arm. They could see arrows and rocks pouring down from the towering city wall facing them as three ladders rose in long arcs against it. Those ladders wavered and then made it to the wall's face. The defenders pushed one away, only for it to be replaced by another. Men around them cheered and brandished weapons. Hundr had his sword drawn and was waving it around his head, shouting, not realising he had even drawn it, lost in the attack's adrenaline. He heard Einar shouting above the din.

"Now boys, follow me; we attack to the right. Look to Odin now. Let's win some glory," he bellowed. A great roar went up from the crew as they followed their captain sprinting to his right.

They ran towards the North-Eastern corner of the fortress, right into the recess where two walls met. Hundr saw a score of ladders go up, and as quick as rats up a mooring rope, men streamed up them. The defenders had been massing on the front gate, and they now rushed back across the battlements to meet the fresh attack. Men fell from ladders, and arrows whipped overhead, thudding into shields, they were in range now, and an arrow clanked off a helm close by. The man next to Hundr fell to his knees cursing with an arrow in his shoulder.

"Heads down, lads," Sten shouted. Hundr grabbed his arm.

"Look, the Boneless."

They could see Ivar's green cloak whipping in

the wind as he scaled a ladder.

"Now, now, now!" roared Einar "to Ivar."

The men surged forward, and Hundr felt the power in them. He felt, too, the thrill of battle rising from his belly, the excitement of seeing their Lords attacking the Saxon fortress. There was pushing, and fiery breath on his neck as the weight of the army drove him towards the ladders. The press was so tight that his shield locked to his side, trapped there between the surrounding men. Hundr looked around for Sten but could not see him. He set his jaw and let go of the shield. He didn't need it. Hundr closed his eyes and whispered a prayer to Odin. *Watch me now, watch me, Odin and bring me luck.*

Hundr's eyes burst open, and he surged forward, shouldering past the warriors in front. They didn't resist. Most didn't want to climb up the timber ladders with arrows and rocks pelting down; most stood back, hoping others would make the climb. He shouldered past another man and tripped as his foot caught on a dead body stuck with arrows. Keeping his balance, Hundr took a few more paces forward, ignoring the scream of pain as a Viking tumbled from the wall above him. Another step and his hand was on a ladder, its rung slick with blood.

Men were screaming on the surrounding ground with terrible injuries; heads split open and crushed limbs. Shipmates tried to pull them back from the carnage as brave men tried to succeed where the injured ones had failed. Hundr was breathing hard now, heat surged in his chest, and his heart was pounding. He stuffed his sword into the back of his belt in case he needed to draw it whilst on the ladder. He puffed out his cheeks and launched himself up the rungs as quickly as he could. After two rungs, the man above him fell and came within a whisker of dragging him off, but Hundr held on with grim determination.

Hundr climbed five more rungs with his head pressed tight and low and felt he was close to the top when a spear blade flashed in front of his face. He swung, darting to the side, clinging to the ladder with one leg and one arm. He shot out his right arm and grabbed the shaft of that spear, and yanked it from its owner above him. Reversing it, he jabbed it upwards and felt it jam on flesh and bone. Resistance gave way, and he launched the spear over the battlements. He took the next rungs two at a time and then sprung over the lip of the battlement, bellowing and cursing. *Not first up, but up and alive.*

Before he could get a chance to look around him, a man with foul ale breath barged him and shouted, spittle flying into his face. Hundr headbutted him twice, whipped out his knife, and shoved the blade into the man's soft belly. He clung to the man and pivoted in a circle, using the dying Saxon as a shield and feeling his hot blood wash over his knife and hand. Hundr spun to see what was happening around him, whipping his sword free of the belt as he did so.

Other Northmen had also made the climb and were driving the Saxons back from the ladders. Hundr seemed to be the last Northman at his end of the wall, and so he swung his attacker back towards his enemies, still using his body as a shield. The man tried to pull himself off the knife, groaning, but Hundr twisted it, making the Saxon yelp and jerk sideways. He launched a savage kick to force the man away from him and attacked the charging Saxons with wild fury. His fierceness held them back and gave enough time for two more Vikings to scale the battlements and join the fight. Hundr stepped back and looked for the Ragnarssons. He could not see any that stood on his side of the wall, but he spotted the green cloak of Ivar swirling at the front of the attack close to the corner wall turret. Ivar shouted a challenge and leapt from the blood-slicked wooden fighting platform to the dusty ground inside the fortress. He rolled to cushion the fall and rose to brandish his famous swords out at either side of him. The sheer daring of it took Hundr's breath away.

There was a knot of twenty Saxons facing Ivar in the ground space between the fortress walls and the nearest houses of the city. The Saxons crouched into fighting stances and braced themselves.

"Who wants to fight with Ivar," the Boneless shouted at them "where is your champion?"

"Mad bastard," said Hundr under his breath. No one had leapt to join Ivar. The Vikings were so hard-pressed on the wall that they had not yet noticed that Ivar's battle fury had led him into the fortress itself.

Hundr watched as two Saxons charged forward with spears levelled, and Ivar danced between them with his swords whirling. He let one man past him and cut the other down. *The Boneless, now I see how he earned that name.* Then turning on the first man, he made quick work of that foe as well. Finally, Ivar turned back to face the remaining force.

"Who is next? Where is your champion? Come and fight with Ivar," he challenged.

Time stopped for a moment; battle cries and clanging of weapons went quiet. *There is an opportunity here, an opportunity for reputation.* Without another thought, Hundr jumped from the battlement and landed with a roll, coming up brandishing his weapons just as Ivar had. He ran forward as six men converged on Ivar, and Hundr attacked the flank of that group, cutting and slashing with his sword and knife. *They are all so slow, and I am moving so fast.* Blood pounded in his ears as he cut down two Saxons, and the group backed away. Ivar had attacked three others, and the Saxons were wary now of the danger of the two Vikings who had leapt into their city. One Saxon had dropped a sword, and Hundr sheathed his knife and picked it up, it wasn't a great sword, but it still felt good to feel the familiar heft of the long blade in his hand. He had two swords now, just like Ivar, and the Boneless turned to him, grinning.

"Come, boy, Odin is watching. Let him see what we can do," and the two men advanced on the Saxons together. Hundr ran ahead, slashing at them. More Saxons had joined the group which Hundr attacked. Big men barged their way to the front, and those men locked shields and presented a solid front. *Here are the proper warriors.* Hundr bent low and slashed at their shins, and as their shields lowered, he cut at faces and necks, and the Saxons shuffled backwards from his fury. Ivar was at his shoulder now, and the two backed away, grinning and raising their blood-drenched weapons. He felt men surge past him, and Northmen closed in around him and Ivar, making a shield wall.

"Well done, boy," growled a big man in front of him, gripping his shoulder. Hundr looked up to see Einar beaming at him with a blood splashed face, "Kill the bastards," Einar shouted, and the shield wall surged forwards.

Hundr gasped for breath, and his arms ached from wielding his weapons. He'd fought back to back with Ivar and had jumped into the fortress following the Champion of the North. Hundr smiled; *this was what I was born to do.* He gripped his two swords and took deep breaths, the iron smell of blood flooding his senses. For as long as he could remember, Hundr had wanted to be a warrior, to be a man with a reputation, and this day must have brought him both. He charged ahead, following Einar, into the Saxon capital of Northumbria, now lost to the forces of the vengeful sons of Ragnar.

FIFTEEN

Hundr drank deeply. The Saxon ale was sweet and smooth, and he gulped it down, slaking his thirst and washing the dust from his throat. Once the fighting had stopped, the looting and rapine had begun in earnest, and hungry Northmen flooded the city of Yovrvik. Hundr, Sten and a few other members of the Seaworm crew had found a deserted Saxon tavern in the city and an empty table within. Other crews had also discovered the tavern, and drinking and singing songs of victory had started. Hundr was sitting with Sten, Thorvald, Brownlegs, Blink, and Bush.

"Thor's balls, Hundr, you fought like a berserker today," said Thorvald.

Hundr looked up from his mug of ale and nodded at his shipmate, uncertain that he had fought like a mushroom-drunk wild man but happy that he had fought well. He had blood crusted on his face and hands, making his skin feel stiff. Since the fighting had stopped, he had felt shaky and tired. But, of course, the assault hadn't lasted long in real terms. Yet if time had slowed and allowed Hundr to see every moment replaying before his eyes, he'd see how he could have died a dozen times that day, how blades and missiles missed him by a hair's breadth on the ladder, on the wall, and inside the fortress. He gulped down more ale and tucked his hands under the table, so the others couldn't see them shake.

"Lucky to be alive, you daft bugger," Sten said, wiping froth from his moustache.

"The whole army's talking about you, aren't they boys?" said Blink, leaning towards Hundr and blinking even more rapidly than usual.

He had met with the Seaworm lads once Einar had charged past him inside the fort. Most of the crew had survived the attack. The major casualties had come in the first assaults, and the Ragnarsson allies had carried them out, not the sworn Viking crews.

"Where did you learn to fight like that?" asked Thorvald.

Hundr shrugged. "In the East, where I was raised,"

"I've fought in the East, never saw a man fight on the same level as Ivar the Boneless, but you did today," said Thorvald.

"Maybe he was breastfed until he had his first shave, and it made him stronger," said Brownlegs, and they laughed.

Bush leaned over and messed up Hundr's hair. It felt good to be with these men. They were his friends, and their recognition made him feel like one of them, like he was part of something. He thought back to his childhood and how he had longed for that feeling of acceptance.

The door to the tavern burst open and slammed back on its hinges. A group of Norsemen fell in, shouting and singing and dragging four captured Saxon women with them. Those women were shaking and weeping, stripped to the waist and beaten bloody. The Norsemen moved to the nearest table and kicked and shouted at the men occupying it to move. They did so with no argument.

"Those lads gave up their table a bit too easily," said Bush, leaning back with one hand on his paunch.

"Those are Guthrum's men. Better to do what they say," said Brownlegs.

"Guthrum's not a son of Ragnar," said Sten.

"No, but he is the pet of Hakon Ivarsson," said Brownlegs.

"Hakon and Guthrum. Didn't see much of them on the walls," said Thorvald, spitting into the floor rushes. Bush nodded.

"Cross them two, and it's more likely we'd find you in the river with your throat cut than face a man to settle an argument."

One of Guthrum's men spoke broken Saxon and was shouting at the women and pointing to some nearby ale barrels. The women were sobbing and crying but ran to their task and returned with mugs of ale. The Norsemen grabbed the women and molested them as they drank.

"Share the wenches around, lads," said a warrior from a table nearby.

"Get your own women," came the curt reply.

"Come on, lads, let's toast the victory," said the warrior again.

"Bloody seal shagging Norsemen," said one of his mates.

One of Guthrum's men rose from his seat and threw his tankard at the man. The thrower was a short, wiry man with a bald head and a wispy beard.

"Get your own women, I said, nithing," he shouted in challenge.

"Brave when you know you won't be challenged back," said Thorvald in a whisper. The bald man strode over to the man who had shouted and slapped him hard across the face.

"Lost your tongue now, haven't you, turd?" the bald man said. The slapped warrior was about to rise, but his mates held him down.

Hundr kept his head down and looked into his ale. There had been enough fighting today; anyone who wanted to show their prowess should have done it already in the battle.

The door of the tavern was still open where Guthrum's men had kicked it in. Then, through the open door came a big man, blocking the light for a second, making it hard for Hundr to see who it was. The big man had to duck under the door frame to get in. Another man followed behind him, and they paused to survey the room. As they moved into the gloom of the tavern, Hundr could see it was Einar and Halvdan. Einar saw Sten and the others and walked over to them. Guthrum's bald wiry man blocked his path and pushed a finger into Einar's chest.

"Before you get any ideas, you can get your own..." but before he could finish his sentence, Einar grabbed him by his leather breastplate, lifted him off the ground and delivered a savage head-butt. Einar grunted and tossed the man aside like an old rag.

"Stop me whilst I'm walking again, and I'll cut your bastard balls off," Einar growled and kept walking.

Guthrum's men rose from their table, bellowing

in indignation and charging towards Einar. He and Halvdan turned on them without hesitation, and there was some pushing and shouting. Their man's face was destroyed as Einar was still wearing his helmet from battle, and the rim had done terrible damage. Hundr and the others had also jumped up to help their Lord, but by the time Hundr had got across the table, the confrontation was already over. Halvdan was brandishing his axe and kicking men out of the door. Two Norsemen were clutching bloody wounds as they charged into the street.

"Norse bastards," muttered Halvdan.

"Who is their Lord?" asked Einar to no one in particular.

"They are Jarl Guthrum's men, Lord," said Thorvald.

"Bastards," said Einar, moving to close the door. "Show's over, lads, back to your ale." He clasped Halvdan and Thorvald on the shoulder and led them back to the table. They set more ale upon the table, and the men sat down. Hundr watched as Einar drank deep. Their Jarl pulled at his beard and removed his helm. His head was still sweat-soaked from the battle, and he ran his fingers through his wet hair. Halvdan also watched his Lord.

"Those seal shaggers will be straight off to Guthrum to tell their own tale of what happened here," he said.

"Aye, well, can't help that now," said Einar, still deep in thought.

"What is happening in the town?" asked Sten. Einar took a long pull from his ale.

"The brothers are holed up in the central keep now talking about what to do next. A few more days to get the city in order, scouting around and about, and then the army might meet," Einar said, drawing his axe and knife so he could be more comfortable and laying them on the table, still crusted with blood from the battle.

"So, what of the King of Yovrvik?" asked Bush. Halvdan shrugged.

"Bastard wasn't here, but don't worry, lads, there are a few other Saxon Lords here for the brothers to have fun with." Halvdan grinned, which twisted his scarred face, being such an unusual expression for him.

"Did we lose many men?" asked Bush, touching at the hammer amulet at his neck, warding off the bad luck of the dead.

"Not too many; the walls weren't heavily defended," said Einar, "looks like most of the best Saxon warriors had already left. Bastards must be gathering an army somewhere."

"What about the booty Lord? Did we take much?" asked Thorvald, and for the first time,

Einar himself grinned.

"There are churches here, Thorvald, and fat Christ Priests. Lots of big houses and gold and silver."

"We will be rich lads," said Halvdan, raising his cup and splashing ale over the table. The men gave a cheer and clashed their cups together. As the men laughed and drank, Hundr noticed Einar was staring at him under his heavy brow, that flat hard face making him uncomfortable.

'Ivar asks for you, boy,' Einar said across the table. Hundr said nothing. He was too weary to contemplate an audience with the Boneless. He just stared at Einar.

"There will be a feast tonight in the Great Hall, and Ivar asked for you," Einar said.

"He asked for me?" asked Hundr.

"Not by name, boy, he asked for the drengr who fought beside him like a hero from Odin's top table."

"Odin's top table," said Thorvald "fine praise indeed, lad."

"Drengr my arse," growled Halvdan, turning away in disgust. Hundr ignored him.

"You fought well, boy," said Einar, "a match for Ivar himself." At that comment, the men all looked at Einar and were silent.

"It's about time we gave you a decent name, lad," said Brownlegs "can't have you going around with this kind of reputation, being a Seaworm man, and having a name like Dog. Bad for the crew." The other men nodded.

"What about Ballbag," said Thorvald to much amusement.

"Or Tiny Cock," said Brownlegs, and then men laughed and banged their mugs on the table.

Einar did not laugh, he continued to stare at Hundr, and Hundr pretended not to notice and went along with the joke. He also pretended not to notice the baleful glare Halvdan was aiming in his direction. Hundr wasn't sure why the shipmaster was angry with him, but Hundr's limbs were aching, and his eyes stung. He had fought hard that day, and so he continued to ignore the stares and drank his ale. Hundr had other thoughts to occupy him, and as the ale flowed and his mind fogged, it dawned on him that he would actually meet with Ivar the Boneless. It turns out he hadn't needed Sten to get him an audience; he had made that happen on his own with skill and bravery. Hundr thought back to his old friends, his old masters, what he would give for them to see him now. The laughter of the crew swirled around his mind, and he remembered himself as he was when he ran away from home; ambitious, alone, angry and disregarded. He thought of going back there, back East to show them, to show them he now had a reputation of his own.

The next day, a gentle kick in the ribs awoke Hundr.

"Come on, up. Time to meet the Boneless." It was Einar towering over him.

Hundr had slept most of the day, his stomach sour and his head pounding from too much ale the night before. He got up and made himself somewhat presentable, and along with Einar, they made their way through the streets of Yovrvik. The city was quiet now after the savagery of the battle yesterday. Crews had found quarters in abandoned houses and were sleeping off the celebrations of the night before. There were still bodies littering the streets and the city stank of blood and death. If Einar was feeling the same effects from the ale, then he didn't show it. He walked straight-backed and had cleaned his brynjar until it shone. They trudged along in silence, past a group of warriors asleep in the open streets. They stepped over discarded clothes and other belongings strewn across the city during the looting. Hundr hadn't noticed amongst the thrill and danger of the assault, but during the battle, he'd picked up some deep cuts on his forearms and one on his calf. Blink had cleaned and wrapped them for him the night before, and those wounds ached now as he walked.

The grey walls of Yovrvik's Great Hall loomed into view, standing out in contrast with the yellows and browns of the thatched rooftops of houses and merchants buildings. They trudged along until Einar broke the silence.

"Ivar will want to talk to you," he said, "might reward you for yesterday."

"What shall I say?" Hundr asked, his heart lifted at the prospect. Ivar was perhaps the most famous Viking warrior of the day, and there was a chance Ivar would show favour to him. Hundr's mind tumbled over the potential routes the meeting could take. Should he keep his mouth shut and smile happily, should he ask Ivar outright for a higher place in the army, should he push his luck and ask for command?

"You thank him and say it was an honour to fight beside him," said Einar.

"Should I ask him for anything?" Hundr asked. Einar stopped and frowned at him.

"Like what?"

Einar was looking at him with a raised eyebrow. Hundr swallowed hard; he didn't want to antagonise Einar. On reflection, asking Ivar for something wasn't a good idea; but would there ever be a better time to ask for a command or a place on Ivar's own crew?

"Nothing, I'm just not sure what to say, that's

all."

"Just say thank you, Lord. Then get out of there. Ivar is unpredictable, and you are young and don't yet know the ways of dealing with him. Think of him as a dragon; if you stand in front of him, you might get burned, so don't eyeball him, and don't stay in front of him too long."

"So I'll just say thank you." *Asking for a command, what am I thinking?*

"That's right," Einar said and put a hand on Hundr's shoulder. Hundr almost flinched at that touch which came unexpectedly. "You have come far since we met on that dock up North. When I saw you there, something told me there was something different about you, and I'm still not sure what. Already you're a known man in the army, after what you did at the bridge, and now yesterday. Your reputation will soon go beyond even my own." Einar paused and scratched at his beard as though looking for the right words.

"Thank you, Lord," said Hundr to break the awkward silence.

"I tell you this not to blow smoke up your arse, but because whilst some of the lads are fond of you, most of them are not."

"Halvdan?"

"It doesn't matter who. I'm telling you this so that you watch your back. With reputation and wealth also comes jealousy. Men will kill you if they hate you, Hundr. I told you once before you need to get the crew to respect you, they don't have to like you, but you need them to not hate you. You are young, and you think only of glory and reputation, but you have to understand how men think. This life isn't just about songs told by poets at the fireside; it's also about knives in the back, men thrown overboard, and throats cut for a few pieces of hack silver."

Einar became stone-faced again, and it seemed he would say no more. His words had come as a surprise. Hundr knew that Kraki, Toki, Halvdan and some of the others didn't like him; they hadn't made a secret of that. But he didn't think they would kill him, though. Hundr decided he would listen to what Einar had said. Maybe he was still wet behind the ears, and maybe he was letting recent events get the better of him. He felt his cheeks reddening. Only a moment ago, he had considered asking Ivar for a command, which was foolish.

They walked up a piss stinking lane between lanes of houses, with groups of Vikings passing on either side. Some were drunk and shambling along, while others were armed and heading out on patrol. Some nodded in recognition at Einar, and some at Hundr too, much to his de-light. *They are acknowledging me; they know who I am.* He pushed his shoulders back and tried to walk straighter despite his ale-induced thundering head and watery stomach. Warriors he didn't know had recognised him. This was what it meant to be a known man. Hundr nodded to himself. *Men know who I am, and I have earned their respect.*

They approached the Yovrvik's central keep, which was now the feasting hall for all the leaders of the Great Army, and as expected, two of Ivar's warriors guarded the place. Einar gave over his axe and knife to the men. Hundr took a step back, not wanting to hand over his hard-earned sword and axe.

"They won't keep them, lad; you can have them back on the way out. No weapons in the feasting hall. A drunken man with a sword at his hip is not a good combination," said Einar. Hundr gave his weapons over, and Einar chuckled, "Cheer up, you are about to eat with the greatest lords and warriors of the North," he said, striding forward.

They stepped into a narrow entry corridor, and Einar wiped his muddy boots on a length of wood fixed to the floor for that purpose, so Hundr did the same. Einar did not have his helmet but checked his braids and smoothed his beard.

"Got to look the part lad when among the great and the good," Einar said and flashed a grin at Hundr as he pushed open two wide doors. A blast of heat hit Hundr as he followed him in; the noise of men laughing and shouting filled the room. The cavernous space towered above him with a smoke-blackened roof, and its smoke hole funnelled an ashen plume flecked with embers into the sky. There were many tables in the hall, each piled with bread, meats of different sorts and horns and cups of ale. Saxon women scurried from table to table, pouring more ale and trying to avoid the grasping hands of hungry Northmen. Einar stopped and surveyed the room, scratching his chin.

"Need to find the right place to sit, sit too close and piss off men who rank higher than me, sit too far away, and bastards get ideas." Einar continued to look around, pulling at his beard when a roar went up from the other end of the hall.

'Einar, Einar Rosti,' boomed the voice. Einar bowed his head, and the hall went silent.

"Lord Ivar," he said. Hundr could feel a hundred pairs of eyes on him. He scanned the room and saw grim warriors with grizzled beards and great Lords dripping in gold and silver. He forced himself to stand straight, despite his gut twisting with nerves and his mind telling him to turn and run out of the door and away from the fierce focus of these men. Every man in the hall was a killer, Lords who paid men to join their ships, braving the dangers of the Whale Road to carry their blades in search of silver and reputation.

"Don't skulk at the back there; come here. Ah, the sword warrior has also come," Ivar called, slapping the table with his hand. As they moved forward, Hundr could see Ivar seated at a raised table facing out towards the rest of the hall. There were six other men sat at the top table. He did not recognise any of them except Ivar the Boneless and Hakon Ivarsson, who sat further to the left. They approached the table, moving through the crowd, and Hundr noticed some men raise their horns to him as he passed. They stopped, and a few of the men at the top table nodded at Einar.

"Welcome, Einar. What is your name, lad?" asked Ivar. His cheeks were flushed scarlet, and the table before them crammed with roasted meats and pots of ale brimming with froth.

"Hundr, Lord," he said and cleared his throat, cursing to himself. He had croaked the reply when he should have spoken clearly for all to hear.

"Hundr, you have a dog's name? Where are you from, Hundr?"

"Yes Lord, I am from Jomsburg in the East," Hundr said, swallowing hard and feeling sweat forming on his brow.

"Jomsburg! Sounds like some shithole in the back arse of nowhere. Hundr, the dog of back arse," shouted a voice from the end of the high table. Hundr turned to see it was Hakon Ivarsson. A few men laughed; a big man with a black beard tied with rings a few tables back roared with laughter until Ivar stood and frowned at his son.

"Wherever it is, Hundr of Jomsburg fights like one of the Einherjer and jumps alone into a fortress full of Saxons. Where were you, my gentle son, when men fought at the front to take this city?" said Ivar.

The laughter stopped, and Hakon's face went puce. He took a sip from his ale with a shaky hand and fixed Einar and Hundr with a baleful stare. Ivar took two arm rings from his left arm and tossed them to Hundr. Surprised, he caught one well enough, but he fumbled and almost dropped the second one. Ivar spread his arms wide.

"Let it be known that this man has sword skill and bravery. Therefore, Hundr of Jomsburg, find a seat here with the Drengr of the Great Army." The Champion of the North raised his horn and drank deeply until the ale poured down his chin and soaked his beard. All men in the room stood and cheered, all except Hakon Ivarsson.

"Lucky bastard, two arm rings from Ivar the Boneless. Three you have from him now. Men would kill for such an honour," said Einar as they made their way over to the warriors' tables. The rings were as beautiful as the one Ivar had given to him before, fine silverwork with runes and beasts. *I have more arm rings now than most men in the army. I have made it; I am a warrior.* An enormous man wearing the plaid of Ivar's Irish warriors, with white hair and thick white eyebrows, was beckoning to them.

"Sit with us boys, make room, you bastards," he bellowed in his lilting accent, and his men shuffled along the benches to make room. The big man grasped Einar by the forearm and then did the same to Hundr;

"I saw you on the walls and inside the walls, Hundr of Jomsburg. I was up there fighting at the front, and I saw your deeds. Let's drink and be friends. Cormac is my name."

Hundr sat and drank from a horn, the big man pressed into his hand. He had always dreamed of being accepted by warriors, as a warrior, and here he was. He wiped the sweat from his brow and gulped down a mouthful of ale. The table brimmed with pork and beef and fresh fish from the river, and Hundr ate his fill and mopped up the grease with freshly baked loaves. He had never eaten so well. The surrounding men were fearsome, and the talk was all about fighting and who had done what great deeds and what deeds they would do in the campaign ahead. Cormac and his men were Ivar's fearsome Irish warriors from the lands he had conquered there. They'd been the first over the walls of Yovrvik and took most of the casualties and most of the glory. The Irish warriors were friendly and full of cheer, and Hundr talked through his meal with Cormac, who was their leader.

"Do you know Princess Saoirse's father?" Hundr asked.

"Aye, he is my Lord and my kin. You rescued her, or so the tale goes?" replied Cormac.

"I did, she told me of her home and of Hakon."

Cormac frowned and nodded.

"That one is no match for our fair Princess," Cormac said and tore into a mouthful of beef from his plate.

"Did the marriage end the war with Ivar?"

"Aye, it did. We are allies now, and we are here fighting to seal the alliance and keep the peace. She shouldn't be here."

"Why wasn't she left in Ireland?" Hundr asked. It was difficult to understand the reasoning behind Hakon bringing her here into the middle of a war when she could be safe at home.

Cormac shook his head.

"Your man is careful with his prize," he jerked a bone in Hakon's direction, "best not to talk of it. Let me see those rings," Hundr passed them to him and looked up at the top table; Einar saw his head turn.

"There you have all the power in the North-lands, Scots lands, Ireland and now Saxon lands," said Einar, "this army is the first time the Great Lords of the North have come together to fight as one. Normally they are at each other's throats, fighting and killing each other for land and silver."

"Who is the leader?" asked Hundr, fascinated. All these men were dangerous. Hundr knew it must take a man of dominant power to have brought them together and keep them together.

"Good question. Ivar is the King of Ireland and some of Scotland and is the greatest warrior, the Champion of the North. Kjartan Wolfthinker and the Snake Eye are the closest and deci-sion-makers, they are not Kings of anywhere, but they are the smartest. They have the power and wealth, but not the responsibility. Ubba just loves being a Viking, fighting, raiding, drinking. The other Lords at the table are not on a level with the Ragnarssons or Wolfthinker but are still powerful," said Einar.

"What about Hakon?"

Einar grimaced.

"He is the son of Ivar and works to make his own reputation. Ivar has another son, Ivar Ivarsson, who is younger and left in Ireland to rule whilst Ivar is on the campaign."

Hundr knew he was asking too many questions about Hakon, but the bastard was husband to Saoirse. It was a strange thing that Hundr had gained everything he had wanted; he was sitting here with the greatest warriors in all the North, accepted as one of them and lauded by their champion. Yet, his mind was consumed with how lucky Hakon was to have Saoirse. It nagged at him and made him uneasy. Hundr was wealthier than most men in the army, holding three arm rings and a fine sword. He had hoped he would feel content and happy with these achievements, but he did not. Instead, his thoughts turned to Saoirse. They had only had a short time together, but he couldn't get her out of his head. Every moment he wondered what she was doing, where she was. He watched Hakon at the high table eating and drinking; he had done nothing to earn Saoirse's hand. They gave Hakon Saoirse and his place at the top table only because he was the son of Ivar.

"He doesn't like you. Hakon, I mean," said Hundr, picking at his food.

"No, he doesn't," said Einar, "he likes me even less now after Ivar just slapped him down."

Einar took a swig of ale and grabbed a leg of lamb from the table.

"Mind Hakon, boy, he is driven to madness over his wife, and he will be suspicious that you and she travelled together. It will turn over in his mind, eating away at him. He also won't have forgotten that you touched your sword hilt to him. He won't fight you, but he can kill you. Be careful."

Hundr's thoughts drifted back to those days with Hakon's wife on the run; they had been good days. She had understood him, and he, her. He had never had affection like that from a woman before. Hundr wanted to see her again; he thought about Saoirse all the time, yet the risk of being caught was too high. *But I have to see her again.*

Cormac handed Hundr back his rings and nodded in approval.

"Fine reward, Hundr," he said and raised his cup. Hundr nodded thanks.

"Do you and your men only fight for Ivar because Hakon married your Lord's Princess?"

"Their son will be our King," Cormac shrugged, "My Lord has no sons, only Princess Saoirse. So we fight for Ivar and our future King."

"Do you love Ivar?"

"He is a great warrior and a good Lord. The Danes came to our land in the time of Ragnar, and since then, we have not known peace. This marriage gives our people that peace and unites the Danes and our people. So we sail and fight with Ivar. Enough questions, now let's drink!" Cormac shouted, and his men cheered and all drained their ale.

Hundr continued with the feast, trying to suppress his melancholy and enjoy the celebration. They brought more platters of meats and loaves of bread to the tables along with an endless supply of ale. They mostly ate in silence, surrounded by Irish warriors who became more raucous as the evening drew on. They were not out of place, though, as most of the hall was falling into a heaving mass of laughter, singing, and the occasional brawl. The Irishmen talked and laughed in their own language, and Hundr noticed Cormac was always at the centre of the jokes and singing. His men appeared to like and respect him. Hundr saw that and knew Einar was right; he had to get the men to respect him if he wanted to be a leader.

"Food is good," Hundr said to Einar to break the silence, and Einar grunted and raised a half-eaten leg of lamb to acknowledge the point.

"Have you always served Ivar?" Hundr asked, keen to understand what path Einar had taken to get command of the Seaworm.

"Man and boy," Einar said.

"How did you become a Sea Jarl," Hundr asked, and Einar snorted a laugh.

"I fought hard, always at the front where I could

be seen. Then, one day, one of Ragnar's old Sea Jarl's died, and I took his place."

So it was as simple as that. Einar belched.

"Don't worry, lad, keep doing what you're doing. You're doing alright."

Cormac shouted over to challenge Einar to an arm wrestle, to which Einar agreed. As he moved out of the way of the two Jarls, he cast another glance at Hakon and felt a pang in his belly and throat once more. That bastard would stumble back to his quarters soon, and Saoirse would be waiting there for him. Hundr closed his eyes and could see her back on the Northumbrian hills, laughing and smiling, and the thought of their time together warmed him. That time with her had completely changed the way Hundr saw his future. Until recently, all he had ever wanted was to be a known and respected warrior, but now all he wanted was to be with her.

He supposed Saoirse was right; she had a duty to her people, but Hundr wanted to be with her. He could think of little else. For that to happen, though she would need to forsake her people, Ivar would lose his Irish warriors, and war would rain down in Ireland. Hundr would need to run away again, as he once fled his home to chase his dreams of reputation and glory. He would need to run away from Sten, Einar, and Ivar and the world of the Northmen. Hundr pictured himself with Saoirse, living out their years on a hill-top farm, just like Sten had built with his wife. That thought made him smile. They would live out their years in peace together, just the two of them, away from armies and Lords. It was a dream beyond his reach, but so had been his dream of becoming a warrior, and look at him now. Perhaps it was possible if he could just reach out and grasp it.

SIXTEEN

The Great Army settled in and wintered in Yovrvik. The Northmen still couldn't pronounce the Saxon word for the place, Eoforwich, so it had become Yovrvik first, and then just Yorvik. The army was content with most men richer than they had been in the Spring. Campaigning would stop now for the Winter, and men would stay warm and safe through the cold months and prepare for the feast at Yule as the new year dawned, and then make ready for the next season of campaigning in the Spring. There was still no sign of King Aelle. The rumour was that he was skulking in the West, and some men told stories of a vast Saxon army waiting to pounce and throw the Vikings back into the Sea.

Hundr and Sten spent their time trying to keep warm, gambling at knucklebones with their shipmates, and taking their turns on patrol or in forage parties. There were a few skirmishes with the Saxons, but nothing on a large scale. Hundr had asked Einar to let him work with the crew, to show them some fighting techniques from East. Einar had allowed it, and Hundr enjoyed working with those who wanted to join in, usually Bush, Blink, Thorvald, Brownlegs, and those who were friendly to him. But Kraki, Toki, and the others scoffed at their efforts and did not take part at all. Hundr showed them how to form a skirmish, how to wrestle, and methods of fighting with different weapons. Of course, they already possessed these skills, but Hundr tried to teach them as he had been taught. The techniques were different, and the men enjoyed the training. Hundr enjoyed setting the training drills and sparring sessions, and he believed they helped bring him closer to the Seaworm crew. His three arm rings, breastplate and sword, marked Hundr out as one of the Seaworm crew's main fighters after Einar and Halvdan. There was great fun to be had in wrestling practice, where even the biggest of the men fell to his holds and twisting grips.

Once Winter set in, Hundr had taken to looking for the women's quarters to catch glimpses of Saoirse. His longing for her had not abated as the seasons changed. Hundr wanted desperately to see her again and share the closeness he'd felt with her during the march following the ambush. He had seen her once walking with her maids close to the Ragnarsson enclosure within the walls of Yorvik. The sight of her, though she was beyond his reach, set Hundr's heart racing just as fast as it had when scaling the ladders in the assault on the city. He had watched again over the next week and had noticed that a pattern had emerged. The same day each week, Ivar's Irish warriors escorted the women for a walk outside the city and down close to the river for exercise. During the third week of watching, Hundr had concealed his appearance in a long cloak borrowed from Blink and a broad-brimmed shepherd's straw hat bought in Yorvik's market. He had waited for the procession to pass and then stumbled his way into the line of women pretending to be drunk. He had taken a few kicks from the Irishmen, but as he passed, he caught Saoirse's arm and lifted the brim of his hat and tipped his face in her direction.

"It's me, put two candles in your window this evening, and I will come to you," he whispered.

He didn't give her time to respond and shambled away as the Irish warriors cursed him and punched him clear. Hundr knew it was a considerable risk; the warriors would have killed him on the spot if they suspected he was trying to talk to the women. Even so, the desire to see and talk with Saoirse burned like a fire inside him, and to Hundr, it was a risk worth taking.

That night he waited until the streets of Yorvik

became quiet, and he made his way to the Ragnarsson quarters at the centre of the city, passing houses glowing inside with firelight. There was a sliver of a moon that night, and the sky was thick with clouds. Hundr could not see any stars, which he thought was a gift from the Gods because other than street corners lit by torchlight, the city was dark, and he could conceal himself in the shadows. Hundr moved from one shadow to the next, and more than once, his senses tingled, warning that he was being followed, but when he waited behind a corner or turned to catch who was there, he could see no one. He was on edge, more than aware of the risks of being caught trying to talk to Saoirse. Capture meant death for him and for Saoirse. Not only that, but Hakon and Ivar would see a betrayal, and her father's peace treaty would be in tatters, plunging her people back into war with the Vikings. It was that fear and knowledge that made him feel watched; he was sure of it.

Hundr knew the risks, but he didn't care. He had taken such a risk when he had left home to pursue his dreams, and the Gods had rewarded him. He hoped they would reward his daring again. The Ragnarssons and their men had taken quarters around the central keep of the city. The Warriors were in lesser houses, and the brothers and their Jarls were in the bigger buildings that had belonged to Saxon nobles, wealthy merchants, and important men of Northumbria until the capture of the city. The Aesir Priests of Uppsala had taken the vast church across the square from the keep, and the Christ Priests were either dead or had fled the city. Hundr hid in a dark alcove behind the keep's hall, the same hall where Ivar had feasted and rewarded him following the assault on the city. Hundr looked at all the buildings, and it was impossible to tell which one would house Saoirse and the other women. He said a prayer to Thor that she had heard his message and would light a candle for him.

He kept to the darkest places, being careful, and did a complete circuit of the buildings he thought were occupied by the sons of Ragnar. Finally, Hundr came upon one building with fine carved wooden doors and built of the neat dressed Roman stone. That building's perimeter was guarded by the Irish warriors, distinctive with their plaid cloaks. This place, he decided, was his best bet to find Saoirse. The building was broad but not too deep and had one guard who patrolled the front and the rear and then one on each side. There were braziers lit at each corner, which meant that on this frosty night, the guards spent more time at the brazier warming their hands than they did patrolling up and down the front of the building. Hundr assumed they believed no one would be foolish enough to attack this place, knowing that inside was

Ivar the Boneless or one of his other fearsome brothers and a hive of grim and skilled warriors waiting to welcome any trespassers.

The building had two stories, and Hundr could see the warm glow of fires seeping through the wooden shutters of the bottom floor to illuminate patches of the gloom on the surrounding terrace. Most of the windows were dark on the top floor, but some had the dim glow of a fire or candle within their walls. Hundr focused on these. If she could, he hoped Saoirse would give him the signal of two candles in the window. He waited, drawing his cloak around him; it was a worn woollen thing taken from the Saxon house the crew slept in.

The cloak was musty, but it was thick and warm and helped keep the frost from his bones. Hundr had left his breastplate and weapons at the house, not wanting to arouse suspicion as he wandered the streets of Yorvik at night. As he crouched in the shadows, he felt vulnerable without the heavy leather armour and his sword. Still, what he lost in feeling unprotected, he gained in speed and lightness on his feet, and this night he must be silent. The clanking and chinking of iron and heavy sword belts might give him away, and that would mean death. It would mean death because that night, he planned to sneak into the quarters of Hakon Ivarsson to talk to his wife. *I must be mad.* But he had to do it, he had to speak to her and see if she felt the same as he, and if he could think of a way to make it possible, would she run away with him and build that life, the dream that occupied Hundr's mind night and day? Would she escape with him and build a simple life together on a hillside somewhere? Hundr had to ask her. He had to see if she would risk all and run away with him and make a life together, a quiet life away from her husband and her unhappiness. They could be happy together; he was sure of it.

As he watched the house, a pair of shutters in the North-East corner of the second floor opened halfway, and he saw the flickering light of a candle ebbing with the breeze. Hundr raced across the wall, keeping tight to it and in the shadows. His breath caught in his throat. Two candles were there clear in the open window, fluttering in the light wind but shielded by the open shutters. Two flames, dancing and in danger of blowing out. *She wants to see me; she feels the same as I do. Shit, how do I get up there?* His heart thumped, and he swallowed hard, trying to suppress the knot of fear in his belly.

The guard was at the opposite corner of the building, warming his hands talking to the guard of the adjacent wall. Plumes of steam lifted from their mouths in the frosty night as they breathed and talked, huddled around a couple of flaming logs in the iron brazier. Hundr sprinted and made it across the terrace in a few long strides. He knelt with his back to the cold stone of the Ragnarsson building, holding his breath for ten heartbeats. Nothing, no voices raised in alarm, no charging Irish guards with weapons drawn. He took a deep breath and started the climb. The Roman stone was so well dressed that there were few finger holds, but he braced his foot against a window ledge and reached up, searching for a gap to get his fingers into. Finally, after much effort, he found a hold and thanked Odin and Thor. His fingers burned, holding his weight as he dragged his right foot up to the top of the window shutter. Extending then to his full height, he could get both hands on a branch of ivy as thick as his wrist. He tested its strength and then pushed off with his foot. The branch took his weight, and he leapt up, and with his right hand, he grabbed at what had to be Saoirse's window ledge.

The ledge protruded from the wall allowing Hundr to get a solid grip. He clung to it with his fingertips, cold biting into his skin, and for a split second, he thought he must fall when a pale hand snaked out and grabbed his wrist. His stomach sank, thinking it might be a guard, but then Saoirse's face popped out the window, eyes and mouth wide with alarm.

"Pull yourself up," she whispered, her voice clipped with urgency. Hundr moved his other hand up to the ledge and pulled his body square with the window; he managed to swing one leg up and onto the ledge. One more push, and he was over and in. He rolled over the ledge and landed on a wooden floor. Hundr sat with his back against the stone wall panting for breath, and she sat with him. Her face was white, and her eyes as wide as full moons. She swallowed and bit at her bottom lip.

"Thank you," he said.

"Be quiet," she whispered, "thank you for what?"

"For seeing me, for grabbing my hand, for..."

"You shouldn't have come. It's too dangerous," she said. Her eyes were still large and fearful as she glanced at the door to the room. It was a large room with a four-post bed and a dark timber table and chair in one corner. There was a fireplace opposite the bed with three logs aflame, making the room pleasant and warm.

"I had to see you again," Hundr said.

"Why?"

"I haven't been able to stop thinking about you. Since we've been apart, all I have wanted is to talk to you again," he said. Her hand was resting on the warm oak floorboards, and he put his hand on top of hers, but Saoirse whipped it away.

"I am married, Hundr. My husband is here. If

we're caught talking like this here in my room, they will kill us," she said.

"Then why did you put the candles in the window?" he said, and her face reddened, and she turned away.

"I don't know. When I saw you today, and you asked me to do it, I promised myself that I wouldn't. Then night came, and I was alone, so I just did. I have a husband, Hundr, and I have a duty," she said.

"A duty? Saoirse, listen..."

"Yes, a duty," she said, cutting him off, "It's not a game, my father married me to Lord Hakon to make peace between our peoples, and I must be a good wife. But this is not what a good wife does."

"But you don't love him; I know you don't," he said, moving towards her. She raised a finger to stop him.

"Love has nothing to do with it. Love is a foolish thing for children and young girls. This is the real world, Hundr. I was raised for this life, and this is my lot. I must be a good wife to Hakon, have his children, and peace will reign in Ireland."

"What about what you want?" Hundr said, and Saoirse shook her head.

"Are you that naïve, Hundr?" she said, "how do you know what I want? What I want doesn't come into it, this is my life, and I must do what is necessary."

"I'll go then. I am sorry I bothered you," Hundr said and made for the window.

"Wait," she said, lunging to stop him. He turned to her. She had tears running down her face. But, she wiped them away, "don't go, not yet."

So he stayed, and they talked in soft whispers. Saoirse was sure that Hakon would not come to her room that night; he rarely did. There were whores and Saxon prisoners who amused Hakon and his men. He often spent his nights with Jarl Guthrum, Magnus, or his men drinking and whoring, which was not unusual for the Lords of the army. Saoirse was the only Viking wife here, so her lot was to sit in her room with her maids and take her weekly walk around the city. They talked long about her life now, her life in Ireland, his life and their dreams. He asked her to come with him, to run away and make a life somewhere, but it was impossible, and she would not go. Hundr's heart plummeted, but he knew she was right. It was just a dream, a foolish dream that could never be.

They talked so long that they feared the sun would rise, so Hundr watched and waited to make sure the guards were still not diligently patrolling and slipped out of the window. Before he made the climb, they looked at each other one more time. She was beautiful, but it could not be. As Hundr ran through the streets of Yorvik towards his quarters, he tried hard to ignore the wrench in his heart, but the cold wind drew tears from his eyes as he ran. It was just the cold, he told himself and ran harder.

SEVENTEEN

Einar was at weapons practice when the summons came. He had practiced with his weapons every day since he was a boy, as did all Northmen who sailed the Whale Road and wanted to stay alive. With his crew, Einar practised manoeuvres and single combat. They practised shield wall formations, spear and axe skills and holding a shield high and wide to build strength. Einar had joined in with and enjoyed the practice drills Hundr had been showing to the men. The lads who had trained with Hundr had become more organised as a unit and better able to switch between different fighting formations—practising daily ensured that when weapons clashed for real, that fighting came as second nature. Hundr had brought in new drills for the men, and most had taken to it with delight, especially after the battle for Yorvik. Many of the men had a new respect for the boy now, and he had become friends with some of the more popular members of the crew, such as Thorvald, Blink and Bush. It seemed to Einar that Hundr had taken his advice, and through his training, the men looked on him as one of them. However, there was still a small group who practised away from Hundr's drills; they were Kraki Horse Face, Toki, Hrafn and a few of their mates. Halvdan did not join in either, but he had always practised alone and would only spar with Einar.

Einar had finished practice for the day and was sharing an ale skin with Bush, who had just finished polishing his fine helmet, and was tracing the runes around its rim as he drank. He saw Bush nodding back over his shoulder. Einar turned around and saw two warriors approaching armed and wearing mail. Blink came and stood next to him, still holding his practice axe.

"That one is Ivar's pet," he said, nodding at the man on the right.

"An Irishman," said Einar.

"Aye, they look serious, Lord," said Bush, which was true. Einar watched their frowns as they made a beeline in his direction.

"Einar Rosti?" asked the Irishman with that strange lilt to his accent which all the Irish followers of Ivar possessed.

"Yes," replied Einar.

"Lord Ivar would like to see you."

"I'll be there soon. I'll just...."

"Lord Ivar wants to see you now," said the Irishman. He fixed Einar with a flat stare, challenging and belligerent. Einar said nothing, but he stared back at the Irishman. There was an uncomfortable pause, and the second of Ivar's warriors glanced at his comrade and then back at Einar.

"Let's go," said the Irishman. Blink twitched his practice axe and edged forward, his bow legs shuffling. The Irishman dropped his hand to the hilt of his sword. Einar put a hand on Blink to reassure him and walked forwards between the two Irishmen.

"Come on then, wouldn't want to keep Lord Ivar waiting," Einar called to his men over his shoulder. Einar tied his hair back and winked at Bush. Out of the corner of his eye, Einar saw Halvdan talking with Kraki and Toki. Einar thought it strange that his shipmaster had not leapt to his side at the approach of the Irish warriors, but he shrugged it off as nothing and followed Ivar's men.

Einar's mind turned over as he marched along with the Irishmen. They made their way, twisting and turning through Yorvik's lanes and alleys. This was urgent. Any other time he would have assumed that Ivar was sending him out on some sort of mission, but the demeanour of the two warriors had unsettled him. They had not greeted him with the respect he was due, and there was no small talk as they walked. He was a Jarl, and they were just Carls of the army, and it was not for him to make conversation with them, so they continued on in silence.

Since Winter had come to Northumbria, Einar had taken on his crew's share of foraging and patrols, but in truth, he was bored, and he hoped that despite the attitude of these two Irishmen, Ivar had a job for him to do. He had only seen Ivar a handful of times since the fall of the city. Maybe there were new orders. Still, it was normal to be bored in Winter, and he expected little to happen now until the Spring came and the war would start again. They turned a bend coming from a narrow street of thin grey stone-built houses into the great open square, and on the opposite side was the Great Church of Yorvik, and next to it, the Roman stone keep where the Ragnarssons held court. The three walked across that square, which on two days in every five was a bustling market square. It had been a market day yesterday, and so Einar stepped over rotten cabbages and piles of animal shit as they make their way to the keep. It had surprised Einar how quickly life had returned to normal for the Saxons and how they had mingled with their new Viking rulers. Markets had traded again; men had returned and reclaimed houses for their families. It had been a peaceful transition, the peace in no small way aided by a vast occupying army of Vikings.

They reached the keep, and Einar's two escorts grunted at their Irish compatriot door guards as they went in through the old weathered timber doors. The nail reinforced boots of the two warriors clicked with heavy steps on the stone floor of the hallway, and they emerged into the wide reception hall with its hearth ablaze in the centre. The Irishmen stopped walking and allowed Einar to pass between them. The lead man who confronted Einar earlier turned and smirked at him. *Not a good sign.*

Einar scanned the room and saw Ivar sprawled on a bench with one of his swords laying flat across his chest. Four of Ivar's warriors sat drinking ale at a neighbouring bench, and next to them was Hakon Ivarsson, along with Magnus No-Ear and Jarl Guthrum. At the seating opposite Ivar was the wizened and baleful figure of Kjartan Wolfthinker. The hairs on Einar's neck stood up, and he shifted his feet. *This is a strange gang to greet me.*

Hakon saw him first and sprang to his feet.

"Einar, lovely of you to join us," he said, turning his gaze to his father. Ivar rose with the cat-like litheness from which he had earned his name. He stood and rested his blade on his shoulder.

"Einar," Ivar said, his handsome face grim and serious. Wolfthinker grunted as he slid himself from his bench and shuffled around to stand next to Ivar, the bones in his hair and beard clanking together as he moved.

"Lord," replied Einar, not hiding the suspicion in his voice. "You asked to see me, Lord," he said, straightening himself and pushing his shoulders back.

"A Lord of East Anglia came to see me this morning, Einar," said Ivar, "he wanted to know why I had not kept my part of the bargain we had made with his King."

The bulk of the Great Army had landed in East Anglia, and its King had struck a bargain with the Ragnarssons to buy them off with horses and chests of silver. In return, the brothers had sworn an oath not to attack East Anglian lands. This was an excellent arrangement for East Anglia, but not for the rest of the Saxon kingdoms. Einar and his men had ridden those horses in their campaign North towards Yorvik. Because of that peace, the Vikings had become mounted and could strike deeper into Northumbrian lands, softening them up for the major attack. Einar looked at Hakon and Guthrum, and he saw Guthrum glance sideways at Wolfthinker. *Something is wrong here.*

"What do you know of that, Einar?" said Ivar.

"I know of no raids in East Anglia, Lord. You had given your oath to King Edmund." *I am in danger here; I can feel it.*

Ivar took two steps forward and pointed his sword at Einar.

"I know men raided in East Anglia, and I know it was you, Einar. You would make an oath breaker of Ivar Ragnarsson?" The sound of Ivar's shouting echoed around the hall. Einar felt panic rising inside him and raised his hands, palms facing out.

"Lord, I had nothing to do with this. I give you my oath on it."

Einar forced himself not to step backwards in front of Ivar's fury. He saw Hakon rise. *That sneaky bastard is behind this. I know it.*

"Liar, I told you he would say that, Father," said Hakon. The four warriors rose from their benches and grabbed for axe and spear. Wolfthinker beckoned them on to stand with Ivar.

"No man calls me a liar and lives," said Einar, fighting to keep his voice level and calm. Then, he pointed at Hakon and Guthrum, "You two cravens know the truth here, and I won't be called a liar, even by the son of Ivar."

"Guthrum and my son swear it was you, Einar, and they can call on other men of reputation to swear it," said Ivar, looking at Hakon and then back to Einar.

"I'm sure they do, Lord. My men will also swear to the truth of the matter."

"Come in here, don't skulk at the back there," said Hakon. He waved to the rear of the hall. Einar saw three men emerge from a gloomy doorway, men he recognised. Halvdan, Kraki and Toki walked to stand with Hakon. Halvdan had his eyes fixed on the floor, but Kraki was smirking. Einar set his jaw. *How could Halvdan have gone over to Hakon after all their years together?*

"Well, speak. Halvdan, are you not Einar's shipmaster?" said Hakon. He had one hand on his hip, chin jutted and pointing at Einar. Halvdan nodded.

"Speak up!" shouted Hakon, his voice becoming shrill.

"Yes, Lord," said Halvdan and raised his eyes to meet Einar's.

"Did you raid an East Anglian town?"

"Yes, Lord," said Halvdan.

"Who ordered that raid?" asked Hakon.

"Einar did, Lord. He led us there," Halvdan said. He met Einars gaze but could not hold it.

Einar just stared. His own men were betraying him. He felt anger overtaking him and clenched his teeth together, keeping eye contact with Halvdan, who looked belligerent now.

"Your men confess it, Einar. How can..." Ivar said, and Wolfthinker began waving his staff in Einar's direction, shaking with fury, interrupting Ivar mid-sentence.

"Your crew are outcasts and oath breakers. I know you, Einar Rosti; you have always been a rotten apple in the barrel. You have welcomed other rotten apples into your crew, and you have broken the word of Ivar. Do you think you are above the word of your Lord, whom you are sworn to obey?"

Einar looked around the room.

"What is happening here?" he said, "Halvdan, my old friend, Toki and Kraki. Many times we have fought together. Have you sold me to these creatures? Odin sees all, and he will repay you," Einar said, fighting to remain calm. *They have set me up, and all are aligned against me.*

Einar turned away from Ivar and took a few slow steps towards Hakon and Guthrum. Hakon took a step back and looked to the warriors on his right, then Magnus moved his enormous bulk in front of Hakon. The other four warriors lowered their spears and proceeded to get between Einar and Ivar's son.

"Be careful, Einar," said Ivar.

"He called me a liar. You know the truth of this in your gut, Lord. Lord Kjartan here has sided with Hakon and Guthrum, and they are coming against me with lies. They have turned my own men against me. Either way, I won't have this from your son or any man, we will make the square, and Odin will show you the truth of it. I'll fight you, Hakon, you coward, and you Guthrum, you fat bastard. The victor will be the truth sayer."

He had insulted them in front of Ivar; they had to fight now. Ivar growled and shouted curses at the rafters.

"Einar; Hakon and Guthrum have sworn to me, and they have witnesses from your own crew. Of course, you can produce your own witnesses. Still, I can't go against my son, Einar. You have served me well, and we have won many victories together, but now you must find another Lord, Einar. You cannot serve me anymore."

Hakon grinned at Einar. He had won, and Einar was laid low. Cast out by his Lord and a masterless man. That left him outside of the law and with no Lord to provide him with silver or protection. *What about my men, what about the Seaworm, what will we do for the Winter?* Ivar had not finished.

"I can't let you fight my son."

"It is my right, the right of any man under the eyes of Odin." Einar had a sick feeling as he felt at the empty belt loop where his axe should be; he had come to the meeting unarmed. He closed his eyes and cursed his foolishness.

"I know that, Einar, but I can't let you fight him," said Ivar.

"Any man can challenge to fight where there is a dispute."

"I know, Einar, but there won't be a fight," Ivar looked at the four warriors, and they spread out and took steps towards Einar with spears lowered. Einar saw Hakon smiling from behind Magnus, and it was too much to bear. *If I am going, I go like a drengr.* Einar darted forwards, and in two long quick steps, he grabbed a spear shaft and yanked its holder towards him. As the man tipped off balance, Einar rolled his shoulder around that warrior and sprang away, spear in hand. There was shouting now, and Einar was through the spearmen. Magnus went for his double-bladed axe at his belt, but he was slow, and Einar was fast. Einar raised the spear and slammed the shaft into Magnus' nose, and the big man reeled away, blood spurting from his face. Einar opened up his body and launched the spear across the hall, and it flew wide of Halvdan and thumped into Toki's chest. Toki fell to his knees, gasping, and blood poured from his mouth in a bubbling dark red flow down into his beard.

The hall echoed with shouting and movement. Einar was all savagery and fury now. They had betrayed him, but he wouldn't die easily. Einar watched Hakon's eyes widen with terror, and in another step, Einar was within reach. He reached out, and Hakon closed his eyes and lifted his hands to protect his face, but Einar grabbed his tunic and thundered into him with his head, fists and elbows raining short but hard blows down all over Hakon's body. Hakon whimpered and cried out for help. Einar heard steps behind him and ducked to avoid a spear thrust. He let Hakon go and swerved away from a scything axe blade as it thudded into a bench next to him. A sharp thud exploded across the back of his head, and Einar staggered with a bright white light, blinding him. He felt himself being thrown across a hip, and he crashed into the floor, head spinning from the blow. His vision cleared, and Ivar knelt on his chest. Of course, it was Ivar who had brought him down.

"I can't let you fight my gentle son," Ivar said into his ear, "but I won't let them kill you. You have been a fine warrior for me. Find a new Lord, Einar, find a new Lord and live. Forget about all this; let it go." Ivar stood, and he stalked between the spearmen and disappeared into the gloomy rear of the hall. Einar rolled to his side, but kicks and spear staves rained down on him. He saw Halvdan reverse his axe and smash the haft into his ribs, and pain flashed there as though a horse had kicked him. Einar curled up to protect his head, and he heard Hakon shouting,

"He is mine, mine! Look at the fierce warrior now, Einar the Brawler, lying on the floor broken and alone. I am Hakon Ivarsson and no man crosses me. I am Hakon Ivarsson." Hakon was triumphant as the blows came hard and sharp. They dragged Einar to his feet, but he couldn't straighten as pain lanced his ribs. A hand grabbed his beard and yanked his head up.

"Look at me, bastard," Hakon said, spittle flecking Einar's face, "Look at me. I will let these men take your brynjar, your helmet, your belt and your boots. Your weapons are mine, and so is your silver. I can't kill you here; my father forbids it. But when you are grubbing for food scraps behind whore houses and shivering in the cold, remember who laid you low." Hakon stepped away, and an axe haft cracked across Einar's forehead, and he slumped to the floor as his legs collapsed and fell out from under him. Einar reached again for his missing axe at his belt and then felt for the handle of his eating knife. If he was dying, he had to hold a blade, any blade. A boot crashed into his jaw, and his head pounded off the hard stone floor. He clutched at the small knife handle as he fell and held it tight. All went dark. *Please, Odin, let an eating knife be enough. I am holding the knife. Let me into Valhalla.*

Einar woke to the gentle sound of running water. He could hear birds chirruping and the distant sound of people talking and bustling about their business. The smell of piss was overwhelming. His left eye was closed shut, but he could open his right eye into a small slit, and even that sliver of light made his head explode. Einar lay crumpled with his face pressed to the cold, hard ground. He put his hand down to help roll himself over, and stabbing pain shuddered across his rib cage as his hand pushed deep into sludge and slime. He rolled over, and through the slit of his eye, he saw he was lying in the middle of the laneway in a pool of piss, and Odin only knew what else. Einar coughed, and again his rib cage flashed with pain. Einar moved his fingers, and none seemed broken. He could move his arms, and his legs felt badly bruised but not broken. Einar knew he had broken ribs from the pain there, and his head was beaten up and swollen to what felt like twice its normal size. He did not think they had stabbed him, but something inside him was broken, and he could feel it screaming from within. His breathing was shallow, rattling in his chest. Einar used his legs to push himself back through the sludge against a barrel. Even that effort left him panting, so he allowed himself to sit there until he got his breath back and rose to his feet. He could not stand up straight but could rest his elbow on the top of the barrel and take the pressure of his ribs. He grunted and clenched his teeth; *I am still alive.*

They had taken everything. Einar had no boots on, no belt, no mail coat, nothing. He was barefoot and left with only his trews and an undershirt stained with sweat and whatever mess he had been lying unconscious in. Einar was in danger. Although Ivar had forbidden his death, he was a masterless man now. That meant he was nothing, outside of the law, and any man could kill him or make him a slave without fear of repercussions. *Let them try. I am not an easy man to kill; men have tried before.*

He took brief steps, gasping with each shuffle, to find something to help him recognise where he was and how to get back to his men. His feet sank into the mud, and he could feel the soft thickness squelch between his toes. Einar almost toppled over as the pain in his head lanced behind his eyes, and his body screamed at him to curl up into a ball. Instead, he took more steps, stopped again, and took some more. Men moved away from him as he sidled along, and he tried to straighten his back. He had his left arm tucked in to support his screaming ribs, and he knew his face was a mess. He had been a man of reputation, a head taller than most men and well known among Northmen as a fighter and a man of Ivar the Boneless. But now that bastard Hakon had reduced him to a piss-soaked beggar stumbling around a conquered city.

"I have to get to my men. I have to warn

them," he said under his breath over and over as he edged forwards. Einar worried for his crew; he knew Hakon would come for them. Halvdan had gone over to Hakon, and he would want to take over the Seaworm. Without question, they would likely kill any that resisted. Three men walked past him.

"Out of the way, scum," one said, and they laughed. Einar ignored them and pushed ahead.

"Did you smell him? He'd pissed himself," he heard another say as they walked away. He looked up to find his bearings again, and through the slit of his left eye, he saw the familiar rising battlements of the South Gate. *Still alive, and things are getting better.*

"Head west, and I'm safe," he whispered, and so he continued.

EIGHTEEN

Hundr watched as Sten used a soaked cloth to dab away the crusted blood from Einar's face.

"You did well to make it here," Sten said as he tried to remove thick clots from Einar's forehead. Einar had stumbled into their quarters half-dead and covered in dark black blood like something from a nightmare. Hundr and Sten carried him into a room and cleared the men out so they could check his injuries and try to patch him up.

"Is my eye bad?" asked Einar. He spoke in a muffled voice due to the swelling around his mouth.

"It's alright, you will see again tomorrow. I need to sew up your head and your cheek here," Sten said.

"Do it. We can't stay here for long. Bastards will come for us," Einar said with difficulty.

Sten reached down to the table and took a bone

needle, which he had threaded with a bowstring.

"Hundr, hold the skin together here," he said. Hundr did so with a grimace.

"Frigg's tits," he hissed as warm blood sheeted across his hands. Hundr had never seen a wound bleed as freely. The blood gushed and poured in a torrent of deep crimson. Einar was hurt bad, and it was a wonder he had made it back to their quarters at all, having lost so much blood.

Sten passed the needle through the flaps of skin and brought the wound together. He then did the same with the cut that ran from under Einar's eye across to his ear. Once they had Einar sewn back together, Hundr gave him some boots and a clean shirt and trews.

"They took my brynjar," Einar said, fumbling the sounds out through the painful swelling around his face. Hundr knelt and pushed on the new boots, and Einar grunted and clutched at the pain in his ribs. He put a hand on Hundr's shoulder to brace against the pain.

"They took everything from you, Lord. Hakon, Guthrum, Wolfthinker, and Magnus, treacherous bastards," Hundr said through gritted teeth.

"Except your life," said Sten, washing his hands in a bowl of water which was now more filled with blood than with water. Einar laughed, his breath rattling and catching in his chest.

"Took that brynjar from a warlord in Sjaelland. I fought him on a sandbank; he was as tall as me and strong as a bull. I killed him in the shallows and took his mail coat, his axe and his silver," he said, wheezing through his nose.

"You will win another," said Hundr, "You must tell us what happened, Lord."

Einar seemed to wake from a dream, and his head jerked up, flitting between Sten and Hundr.

"We have to get the lads away from here," said Einar, "it was Halvdan and the others. They'll come today with Hakon," he tried to get up but crumpled from the pain.

"Stinks of that bastard Wolfthinker this does," said Sten.

"He was there, with Hakon, Jarl Guthrum, No-Ear, and our lads," Einar said, casting his gaze to the floor.

"What lads?"

"Kraki, Toki."

"I'll warn the lads outside," Hundr said, "Sten get him up and moving." He dashed to the door and burst out into the cold winter daylight. The Seaworm crew gathered there. Blink and Bush came to meet him.

"What's happened?" said Blink, a panicked look on his face.

"Halvdan, Toki, and Kraki betrayed Einar. They are with Hakon now. We have to leave this place and move somewhere safe," said Hundr.

"But, how did.." Bush said, taking off his helmet liner and scratching at his bald head, worry etched on his face.

"No time for this. We have to move now!" Hundr said, and the crew rushed around, grabbing weapons and belongings. Sten emerged from the doorway, supporting Einar as he limped. The crew rallied around their Lord.

"Someone's going to pay for this," Brownlegs said, but before anyone could say any more, a shout came up from the entrance to the small square of their quarters.

"Right then, shitworms," came the shout. Hundr spun to see Halvdan leading a large band of Hakon's warriors. Kraki was there, leering over Halvdan's shoulder.

"In case you haven't heard yet, I'm the captain of the Seaworm now," Halvdan growled. "Any of you turds is welcome to stay on; any who don't want to can go now."

The crew looked at one another in disbelief.

"You're a traitor Halvdan, I won't follow you," shouted Bush, and Halvdan grinned.

"You were always too far up Einar's arse, Bush. You can go. Go on, piss off."

"Can we go freely?" asked Blink.

"You can, for now. Lord Ivar has given Einar his life. Any of you scum can go too."

Kraki Horse Face took a step forward and pointed his spear at Hundr.

"Not him. I want that little shit, and his bloody arm rings," Kraki leered.

Hundr stepped forward.

"Come and take them, you Horse Faced coward," he said, and men on both sides shouted and jostle, hurling insults.

"Stop!" Einar bellowed in his strange, muffled voice, "We go now. Anyone who wants to stay with Halvdan is not my enemy. Make your choice." Then he and Sten shuffled towards Halvdan, and the bullnecked warrior had his men move to the side.

Hundr followed, as did Bush, Blink, Brownlegs, Thorvald and the Kveldsson brothers. The rest stayed.

"Sorry," said Bjarni Lackbeard, "A man must have a Lord." Then, as they passed Halvdan, Kraki spat at Einar, and the thick glob of it stuck in Einar's blood crusted hair, and Kraki laughed.

"Not so high and mighty now are you, Einar the Brawler," he said, elongating the final two words.

Einar didn't stop or react to the insult, which

made Hundr's heart sink even further. He hadn't ever known a prouder drengr than Einar. The Jarl would fight any man who challenged his reputation, yet his beating and humiliation had reduced him to this. Hundr paused and stared at Kraki.

"You will die for that," he said.

Kraki just laughed again, and the procession continued out into the city. More than half of the Seaworm crew had stayed with Halvdan and Kraki. That must have pained Einar more than his humiliation at the hands of Ivar and Halvdan.

"I think I know a place we can go," said Brownlegs, so they followed him. They wound their way in silence through the streets of Yorvik until they reached a half-derelict Roman stone building on the East side of the city where a section of the wall had crumbled. The Saxons had tried to repair it with timber beams and thatch, but the thing was full of holes and drafts.

"Sorry it isn't anywhere better, lads," said Brownlegs.

"It will do, for now. Let's get Einar settled," Hundr said.

The remaining crew made themselves busy trying to make the place more comfortable. They cleared a space for straw pallet beds and tried to scavenge what they could from nearby crews to make the place liveable. Finally, as the day drew on unto evening, Hundr walked outside and leaned against the front of their new quarters where the other men had already gathered.

"How is he?" asked Thorvald.

"They hurt him bad, but he'll live," said Sten. The men all nodded.

"It's not right what they done, Einar's done nothing to cross Ivar," said Bush.

"Bastards turncloaks," said Kari, spitting across the street.

"And us now left in the shit with no Lord and no master," said Rollo Kveldsson and was rewarded by pushes and shouting from his shipmates.

"We swore to Einar, and we stay with him," growled Thorvald. Sten moved away from the group and sat on an old milking stool. Hundr followed.

"They take his mail and weapons?" asked Hundr. Sten nodded,

"That and more lad. Taken away his reputation, which were all he had,"

"Why did they do it?"

Sten shrugged, "Accused him of a raid of some sort."

"I would not have thought a drengr and Lord like Ivar would beat one of his Jarls and leave him humiliated like that."

Sten snorted and stood, "What d'you know of it, boy?"

Hundr clenched his teeth.

"I'm not a boy. I've three arm rings and..."

Sten laughed and stood, towering over Hundr.

"Boy, I've killed many men. Killed women, too. Killed men with axes, swords, spears, these bare hands, killed a man with a filthy rock once," he said, holding up shovel hands. "Killed men in war, when I was drunk, in the dark, and when they were crying. Burned people in their homes. All kinds of shit, terrible things and men thought me a drengr. Piss on that." Sten spat and stalked off.

Hundr watched Sten's back as he left. He wasn't sure where that outburst had come from. Likely Sten was getting used to being around men of war again after living so long away from the life of a Viking warrior. Hundr was still getting to grips with it himself. In his dreams, he had imagined the world of a warrior to be all about honour and glory, but the more he was around these men, he could see it wasn't that simple. Nothing was as simple as he had imagined or hoped it would be. Strangely, he had come to admire the old man. He had given up the life of a wealthy and renowned warrior to be with his love. Maybe Sten felt pity for Einar, just as Hundr did. The Jarl had lost everything he had worked his whole life for, but what struck Hundr the most was that outside of that life, Einar had nothing. He had no wife, no children, no home outside of that which Ivar provided. It was a precarious existence to live at the whim of a Lord, especially one as unpredictable as Ivar.

Hundr was about to check on Einar when a horn blared from the Western rampart, a long deep sound, followed quickly by another horn blast. Men stopped what they were doing. It sounded like an alarm or a call to arms. Warriors ran past Hundr across the laneway, going to rejoin their crews and arm themselves for whatever threat had come to Yorvik. Sten came lumbering down the street with his enormous shoulders rolling as he ran.

"Bloody Saxons," Sten said.

"What?"

"Scouts say a bloody Saxon army is here, now," said Sten.

NINETEEN

King Aelle had brought his Saxon army to attack Yorvik and get his city back, which surprised the Vikings because it was nigh on impossible to mobilise and feed an army in the cold winter months. The Vikings themselves were settled in at Yorvik for the Winter, with no thoughts of fresh campaigning until the Spring. The Saxon army had formed up across the South river the same way the Northmen had only three months earlier. King Aelle himself was there, sitting short and plump on a fine horse, he who had thrown Ragnar Lothbrok into the snake pit and earned the wrath of Ragnar's sons.

The Saxons were at their captured city, ready to take it back from the invaders, steam rising from the horde of men and horses. Pennants and battle standards were hanging lank on that still, frosty day. The Vikings had formed up on Yorvik's walls and inside the city, in the open spaces between the walls and town proper, spaces meant for fighting and killing attackers who scaled the ancient walls. Viking scouts who had spotted the advancing Saxons had given the Ragnarssons enough time to form up their army and make ready for the assault.

Hundr stood on the wall, his teeth chattering and steam blowing from his nose. He had wrapped his hands in scraps of cloth to keep warm, and every so often, he loosened his sword in its fleece-lined scabbard, worried that it might stick in the frost.

Despite Ivar casting Einar aside, the remnants of the Seaworm crew still loyal to Einar formed up at a gap on the rampart between a band of young Norsemen and a crew of Sigurd's Svear allies. Hundr and the others hadn't known what to do as the army formed up. Ivar did not hunt them, or they would already be dead. No orders came, so they just headed to the walls and found a spot to defend. Hundr stood on the wall next to Bush and Sten, the big Dane armed only with his shield as always. Bush had his shining helmet tight on his round head and every so often would finger the runes at its edges for luck, whispering prayers to Odin and Thor with his hammer pendant in his other hand.

Bush and Sten flanked Einar so that the Jarl could lean on Sten, and because Bush demanded to stay with his Lord. Einar had insisted on coming to the battle despite his injuries, and none of the crew wanted to deny him the fight. Hundr looked again at the massed Saxon ranks.

"Looks like they want to fight."

"They ain't come here for nothing," said Sten.

"These walls won't serve us any better than they served the Saxons," said Einar, still slurring his words because of the swelling in his face. He pushed some loose masonry over the top of the rampart with his foot.

"Why didn't we repair the walls, or at least strengthen them?" asked Hundr. All they had taught him as a boy told him they should have strengthened the defences to make their base secure.

"Maybe the little pigs learned something from the old boar," said Sten.

"What's that supposed to mean?" asked Hundr.

Sten sniffed and stiffened.

"Well, in the old days, we'd take a city like this but never wanted to hold it, didn't have enough men most times. Ragnar knew the bastards would want their city back, so we would trick the attackers and let them think they had beat us on the walls and lure them into the city. Fighting in the streets is murderous work; numbers don't matter."

'If we can beat 'em, why not just do it on the

walls?" asked Bush.

"Their army looks big, but they are farmers called up to fight by their Lords," said Einar, "their proper warriors are the Lords' household troops, but more are farmers. We here behind these walls are all warriors, fierce men trained to fight with swords and axes. If we can get the farmers into the city, we will slaughter them once and for all, hand to hand in the streets. Defeat them on the walls, and they retreat to fight again another day."

Gates further along the wall creaked open, and Hundr leaned over the rampart and watched as warriors streamed out and formed into lines.

"Let's see if you're right, old man. Them's the Snake Eye's and Ubba's lads down there," said Bush.

A rider halted his mount behind them in the castle's inner perimeter and shouted up at the massed warriors.

"When our boys come back through the gate, everyone is to retreat, fall back to the city. Fight them in the streets, lads, slaughter the bastards." Then, with his message delivered, the warrior rode on twenty paces to deliver the message again. Hundr looked up at Sten. The old man shrugged, winked, and looked ahead.

"As I said, the little pigs learned from the old boar."

"Hey Einar," Thorvald called out from down the line, "we should just show the Saxon's your face and scare the bastards away," the men laughed, and so did Einar.

Hundr looked across at Einar, and indeed he was a mess. His face was swollen and bruised, and Sten's stitching made him look like one of the Loki brood from a fireside story. Stripped of his brynjar and belt, he looked like any other Carl of the army now. The crew had offered Einar some spare kit and weapons, but he had refused and armed himself with a simple spear in one hand and used his other hand to cradle his broken ribs. Looking at Einar felt to Hundr as though he was looking at himself through Odin's one eye, which could see into the future. *Was the destiny of the Warrior not taken for Valhalla, to be cast aside like an old rag, alone and with no home or security for the future?* Einar had given his whole life to Ivar, serving him, chasing his dream of becoming a landed Jarl. Einar's beating and humiliation also carried over onto the men who not stayed with Halvdan, which for Hundr meant he was sworn to a Lord without a ship and with only a handful of men to command. Nevertheless, he still had the reputation he had earned, or at least he hoped he did.

Hundr watched the warriors marching out of the gate in well-dressed ranks, and his mind turned to Saoirse again. He knew he had to try once more, to try harder to convince her of the life they could have together. *Maybe I am a fool, and she would never leave with me. Maybe I should have never left home. What now of my reputation and standing with the army?*

As he stood on the battlements and breathed in the chill of the air, he steeled himself to that thought; it was just a boy's dream of love which was not destined to be. As foolish as his dreams of a warrior's honour and glory. Saoirse had been very clear that she was where she wanted to be, her duty to her people was everything to her, and he must accept that. *But what better way to take my mind off her than killing a few Saxons.* He clutched the hilt of his sword for comfort.

The warriors who had marched out of the city formed into four ranks headed by Ubba and Sigurd. Last of all came Ivar the Boneless riding through the gates on a fine white stallion with his green cape billowing behind him and clear for all to see. The warriors on the walls cheered and clashed weapons in salute as Ivar rode past, showing his horsemanship by controlling the beast with his knees and waving his swords Hugin and Munin overhead. Horns sounded from the Saxon lines, and they advanced down the same bank the Northmen had crossed in the summer. The Saxons came on splashing through the river, and Hundr did not envy them the cold bite of the water and slippery climb up its bank.

"Why don't we attack them as they come out of the river?" Hundr asked no one in particular.
Blink leant forward from further down the line, a smile splitting his long face.

"Don't worry, young savage. You'll get your chance soon enough." The men laughed.

Hundr needed to piss, and the day was wearing on as they stood and watched from Yorvik's walls. The Viking lines did not move, and the Saxons reformed into their own organised lines on the city side of the river. Riders rode up and down those lines calling out to the Saxon warriors, trying to give them hope for the assault to come, and then they charged.

The Saxons roared as they charged, and the sound of so many men raging for blood made the hairs stand up on the back of Hundr's neck. If the Saxons won today, there would be no quarter shown to the Viking invaders, and they would be butchered or sold into slavery. The thought made Hundr swallow hard, and his stomach churned. He looked around him, and all the men on the walls seemed calm, as though certain that they would not die that day. He tried to use that confidence around him to quash his fears of how the day would end.

The Saxons charged, and their lines smashed into the Ragnarsson shield wall in a thunderous clash of timber, shield on shield. Straight away, the howls of pain and injury melded with the shouts of challenge and defiance. The Viking shield wall held, and Hundr watched as Ivar dismounted and pushed his way through to the front ranks. Warriors on the ramparts cheered, but not Einar's men. Hundr heard the Snake Eye bark an order, and the Ragnarsson lines gave a mighty short, clipped shout and shifted two paces back. They braced themselves again, and the shields clashed as the Saxons surged forward into the space made by the backward steps. Sigurd roared the same order, and again the line shifted back two paces. Then the Vikings suddenly ran, pouring back through the main gate.

"Frigg's tits, they will be murdered as they retreat," said Hundr, gripping the stone rampart and peering over the edge.

"Come on, lads, back into the streets," said Einar.

Hundr turned and watched as men along the wall lowered ropes and ladders from where they had rested unnoticed against it. The Vikings retreated through the enormous gate, and the warriors atop the walls descended on the ropes and ladders to avoid a clamour at the gate's mouth where it and the wall's stone stairways converged. If there was chaos there, it would allow the Saxons to slaughter the retreating Vikings as they became jammed in the gateway. The Saxons were already cheering their victory and piling across the river to join the rout. Hundr followed the Seaworm crew down the ladders from the ramparts and across the open ground into the streets of Yorvik. There was an air of controlled panic amongst the men. It was evident that this was the plan to draw the Saxons into the streets, but to see thousands of enraged Saxons charging at the city was enough to make any man panic, and Hundr resisted the urge to just sprint away from the attack as fast as he could.

Einar could barely walk and was being helped by Sten. Hundr rushed over and ducked his head under Einar's other arm to help him move along. The Jarl grunted at the pain in his ribs.

"Sorry Lord, let me help you," Hundr said, and Sten grunted.

Warriors rushed past them, and the Seaworm crew went deep down an off-shoot street from the main road into the centre of Yorvik.

"Here, stop here," Einar said as they reached the middle of that street.

"Here," Hundr shouted, and the crew turned to him.

"We make our stand here," he said. The men who had stayed loyal to Einar were the group Hundr had been training over the last few weeks. They knew the drills now as well as he did, and he hoped they would obey his commands. Hundr could hear the roar of the Saxons as they raced through the gates, and that sound was drawing closer as though borne on the wind.

"They're only farmers and shit shovelers, boys," shouted Sten, "not killers like you lot."

"Let's kill the bastards here and have done with it," said Bush. The men drew weapons and made themselves ready.

"Tight shield wall like we practised," said Hundr, "keep it tight, and they can't get through. Wait for my orders, and we'll butcher the bastards," said Hundr with a confidence he didn't feel. There was a pause, and for a moment, he thought they would ignore his orders, but then they formed up with Hundr stood in the front row alongside Bush and Blink. Their three shields interlocked to cover the street's width, and Sten was behind Hundr with his shield in another row of three. Einar was pushing his way through the men, and he shoved Hundr aside to take his place next to Bush.

"You are in no state to fight, Lord; please stay at the back," said Hundr.

"I fight at the front, boy," Einar growled, "always I have fought at the front. Better to die today and go to Valhalla than skulk around the back like a nithing."

Hundr was about to reply when the first of the Saxons came hurtling around the corner. They came in a roaring, furious surge, teeth bared and eyes wild. Hundr could not tell how many there were.

"Keep it tight. They can't get through us," Hundr shouted and braced himself.

The Saxons charged, and some fell over each other in the eagerness for Viking blood. They were uncoordinated, which caused them to bash shields and weapons together, unable to raise them as they became funnelled into the narrow gap between houses on either side of the small street. Hundr could see the wild ferocity of those men bent on slaughter as they smashed into the small shield wall. The Seaworm crew formed ranks and took the force of the attack.

"Hold," shouted Hundr, "Hold," and they held them.

Hundr crouched behind his shield as he felt blades crashing into it and bodies trying to shove him backwards. He could smell stinking sweat and foul breath and hear the grunts of the Saxons as they pushed at the Viking shield wall. He also felt Sten's shield lying on the top of his shield and saw that Sten was also covering Einar's head to protect from blows coming over the top.

"Now," Hundr called, and the Seaworm men took one big step back in unison just as they had practised, and the Saxons who pressed against their shields stumbled forward.

"Push," Hundr ordered, and they slammed their

shields into the off-balance Saxons and then pulled back again.

"Open," he said and felt Einar and Bush's shield give way either side of him.

Hundr surged forward from behind his shield, cutting and stabbing with his sword. Saxons screamed, moving away from his vicious blade, and he pushed into the gap laying about him as he went. He took a big step forward and found that he was through them; the Saxons were now trapped between him and the crew. Hundr saw the panicked look on their faces. They were not warriors by trade these men, and they thought to kill some retreating and panicked Vikings but found themselves faced by trained killers in the narrow Yorvik street.

"Kill them, Kill them all!" he shouted.

Hundr threw down his shield and drew both of his swords, the second inferior sword he had taken in the battle for Yorvik he had strapped to his back. The rearmost Saxons turned to face him, and he slashed savage cuts at their eyes and faces. He gloried in his speed and skill. They would have seen a young warrior with rings and reputation carrying two swords and wearing a breastplate which only the most successful of warriors could own, and of the ten Saxons they were fighting, only one had armour. They would have seen a Viking warrior in all his glory, and so Hundr laughed. He slashed his blades and laughed with battle joy.

In a few quick minutes, it was over. The Saxons were dead or dying. Einar had bloodied his spear but was now leaning against a wall clutching his ribs, panting. Blink looked to have taken a cut to his thigh, and Brownlegs was nursing a bloody nose, but that was all the damage they had taken.

The fighting continued this way for most of the day. The Saxons had been reckless, charging into the city smelling Viking defeat and slaughter, and it was as Sten said it would be, farmers against warriors. Hundr had only seen a handful of actual Saxon armoured and equipped warriors amongst the rest. That day had seen great slaughter, and Vikings were now chasing Saxons through the bloody streets of Yorvik as their broken army tried to retreat out of the gates and across the river. The Seaworm crew loyal to Einar kept together and held their street. It had been simple butcher work of keeping the shield wall solid and then breaking out to attack any Saxons who attacked them. They had lost no crew members, and there was plenty of Saxon dead to plunder for coins and weapons of value. Hundr sat against a wall with Sten.

"So he made it through today," said Sten, nodding at Einar, who sat against the opposite wall with Bush.

"There is that," said Hundr, "but what next?"

Sten shrugged.

"You should wash the blood off you, you look like a bloody Loki Demon."

Hundr wiped his face with his hand and sighed.

"I meant what next for Einar, for the crew and us?"

Sten scratched at his beard.

"Odin only knows laddie. I bloody don't."

Three young Danes walked up their street from the gate side entrance. They were carrying a looted mail coat and had an armful of weapons taken from the Saxons.

"We routed the Saxons," said a tall slim youth, "we have their King, the Northumbrian King who put Ragnar in the pit," he raised an axe and gave a shout, and they went on their way.

"Did King Aelle really put Ragnar in a pit of snakes?" asked Hundr.

"He did, or so Wolfthinker tells it anyway."

"What will they do with him?"

"The King?" said Sten, "Ivar will have something planned."

Hundr watched the young Danes reach the end of the laneway and disappear to the right. Then, from the left side, came another band of warriors turning and walking towards Hundr and the rest. These warriors were well-armed, and some had good mail and swords. More appeared from around the corner, and Hundr could make out around a score of them. The foremost of the men drew their blades, and Hundr stood as he recognised the bullnecked warrior at the front of the group. That man shouted a challenge as he chopped his axe down into one crewman who sat resting at that end of the street. It was Halvdan, and he had just killed Bjarni Lackbeard. Blood now flowed into Bjarni's long blonde plait. Hundr scrambled to his feet.

"It's Halvdan, the bastard," he said, and as he lifted his shield, he thought he saw Hakon Ivarsson in the middle of the attacking group.

"Ambush, ambush, shield wall, shield wall," Hundr shouted.

Men shouted, and panic ensued as they readied their weapons. Sten surged to his feet and charged forward with his shield. Hakon's warriors were attacking in force now, hacking with swords and axes at men who were exhausted from a day's fighting. Blood splashed red onto the wall of a house as Magnus No-Ear sunk his enormous double-bladed axe into Asbjorn Lucky Feet; Hundr banged his shield next to Sten's.

"Shield wall now," Sten was bellowing.

Another shield joined to theirs, and their wall

now stretched across the street. They walked forward, and Seaworm men scrambled to get behind them. Hundr looked over his shield to see that Bush and Styrr were hard-pressed by warriors as they tried to move Einar back towards the shield wall. Einar was almost unconscious from the day's exertion. Magnus slashed his axe down across Styrr's shoulder, and Hakon whooped with delight as he thrust his sword through Styrr's belly. Bush roared and pushed Einar back towards the Seaworm shield wall. He swung his axe at Magnus and missed but followed it up with a savage kick which drove Magnus back into his own men. Halvdan cut down a man to his left and slashed his axe backhand across Hundr's shield, and the force of it pushed the iron rim into Hundr's face. *We are dying here. If we don't do something quickly, we are all dead men.*

Einar tripped and fell between the two shield walls, and Hundr looked up in desperation as Halvdan leapt forward, but Hundr didn't see it in time to stop him from reaching the fallen Jarl. Halvdan, however, did not strike at Einar. Instead, he spun and held his shield over his old Lord and Jarl, defending him from Hakon's men.

"What are you doing, traitor?" came a shrill cry from Hakon.

Halvdan turned to look over his shoulder, and pain was written across his grim face. He looked down at Einar.

"I am sorry, Lord, forgive me," he said to Einar and then growled back at Hundr.

"Get Einar out of here. Go now," Halvdan said.

Sten broke ranks, forcing himself out of the shield wall. He grabbed Einar by the collar and yanked him back behind the safety of Hundr and Bush's shields. Once he was through, Hundr and Bush made the wall solid again, Bush blinking against the sweat pouring from beneath his helmet.

"Fall back on my order," Hundr shouted.

He glanced back and saw that Sten had lifted Einar over his shoulder and was carrying him back to the other end of the street.

"Step," Hundr shouted, and the men grunted and took one step back together. "Step," he yelled again, and they moved again.

Ahead, Hakon's men were hacking into the remaining members of Einar's crew who had not made it behind the shield wall. Halvdan was backing up, so he stood between Hundr's shield wall and Hakon's men and stooped to pick up a fallen axe from the ground. He raised his two axes at Hakon's men and roared his challenge.

"My name is Halvdan Hreidersson. I have sailed South to where the sun burns like a furnace and North to where the sun does not set. For twenty years, I have fought with axe and spear. I betrayed my Lord, but I must right that wrong. I am ready for Odin's judgement and for Valhalla, come and die bastards," and he banged his axes together, snarling at Hakon's men.

Hundr kept the men moving back. Halvdan had betrayed Einar to Hakon on the promise of the Seaworm and promotion. Hundr could only imagine that Halvdan could not live with his decision and now saw a chance to make things right before the Gods. Hundr had despised Halvdan for his betrayal, but looking at him now, outnumbered and welcoming a warrior's death, he thought he had never seen such bravery.

"Kill him quick. I want Einar dead; kill them all," Hakon shouted.

Two of Hakon's men charged at Halvdan, who parried their blows and darted inside them, chopping his axe into one attacker's face. The other attacker lunged with a spear, and Halvdan cried out as it pierced his side, but he spun and slammed his axe hard into that spearman's chest.

The Seaworm crew were now at the end of the street where it opened onto a wider thoroughfare, and there were other Vikings around to witness the attack. Hundr turned back to see Halvdan fall with a spear through his neck, and Magnus No-Ear had his huge long-handled war axe buried in Halvdan's shoulder, and as he fell, his attackers swarmed him, stabbing and chopping. Hakon's cronies charged towards the Seaworm men, but when they reached the end of the street and spilt into the thoroughfare, they halted. The space was too open, and there were too many witnesses. By attacking Einar, Hakon had broken his father's order. His hope must have been that the attack would be passed off as casualties of the battle, but now out in the open, Hakon would not risk his father's wrath. Hakon strode ahead of his men, laughing.

"We got a few of you this time; we'll finish you soon," he said, walking with a swagger. "Einar, I know you are there somewhere. If you are not dead yet, there is still time for you to run. Maybe the Christ Nuns will take you in, and you can be their arse wiper," said Hakon, and his men laughed.

Hakon waited a moment for a reaction, but there was none, and so he gave a mock bow and led his men away. Hundr looked at the remnants of the Seaworm crew around him. They were a ragged bunch now, and certainly not enough of them left to crew a ship even if they wanted to sail away. Good men had fallen that day, and not to Saxon blades. Once again, that dream of a warrior's honour was tarnished and trampled.

The crew kept close together and made their way back to their quarters. They walked in silence, supporting the injured as they went. Sten carried Einar across his shoulder. Hundr knew his friend was strong, but Einar was a big man himself, and Sten carried him like a bag of grain. All seemed lost as they trudged back to the ramshackle house which was now their quarters. They moved through the celebrating army like defeated men. Reaching the place, the Seaworm men slumped on the benches and pallets inside, and Einar lay unconscious on a straw bed. Sten waved Hundr outside, and they went to sit with Bush, Blink and Thorvald.

"We can't stay here. Hakon will come for us again," said Bush, wiping blood from his face and hair with a rag and squeezing the sweat from his helmet liner before putting it back on to cover his baldness.

"Where do we go? Einar can't even bloody walk," Thorvald said.

"Seaworm's here, we can take her," said Bush, but Thorvald shook his head.

"Even if by some gift of the Gods we could get her and sail her with the lads we've got left, we'd never make the coast. There will be roving bands of Saxon warriors everywhere on the river after today."

"Ship or no, we have to get out of this shithole, or we're dead men, boys," said Blink rubbing his eyes, blinking at an even faster rate than usual and shaking his head.

There was not much they could do, and Hundr knew it. Blink was right that they should leave Yorvik if they wanted to survive, and Thorvald was right that they would never make it to the ship, never mind back to the sea. They could try to find a new Lord, but who would take them on with Hakon Ivarsson set against them or risk the displeasure of Ivar? Hundr stood.

"Let's try to get this lot ready to move. Let them rest for now and get some food into them. Hakon won't come for us today. They have the Northumbrian King Aelle, so there will be a feast tonight, which will keep him busy. Tomorrow we decide what to do," he said.

"Can't believe Halvdan's gone," said Thorvald.

"Bastard traitor," said Blink, and he spat for good measure.

"Come good in the end, though," said Bush.

"Lackbeard gone too," said Bush.

Thorvald stood and slammed his knife into the side of the old timber frame house.

"Bloody Hakon and that no-eared bastard Magnus. Can't let them get away with this," he said, shaking with fury.

"That bastard Horse face was there, skulking at the back, I saw him," said Bush.

Hundr stood; he had to get some air, to think. Sten went after him.

"Where you going lad, it's not safe out there," he said.

"It's not safe here either," said Hundr.

"We need to stay together to have any chance of getting out of this alive."

"I have to see someone first, in case we leave," Hundr said. Although their situation was desperate, he knew he had to try Saoirse one more time. He hoped she had changed her mind with time to think, he had to see if she would leave with him or he would never see her again. Without question, Hakon would hunt them again, and he would want Einar dead, and Hundr too, for good measure, no doubt. To stay was to die, but to leave meant a return to ignominy, and he could only contemplate that if she was at his side. Sten put a hand on his shoulder to stop him.

"Hang on a second. I know what that bloody means. I've seen you sneaking out to spy on the womenfolk. The other lads know it too. I also know that you're a headstrong, stubborn bastard."

"Just leave it alone."

Hundr shook off Sten's hand. "Einar's finished now, and Halvdan is dead. Hakon's out to get us all, likely Ivar too. We have to leave this place quick if we want to live. I need to do this one thing. I need to see her one more time, Sten." He looked the old warrior in the eyes. Sten dropped his head and sighed.

"At least be careful, lad," he said.

"I will," said Hundr, and he turned and strode away.

TWENTY

Hundr lay flat on the thatched roof of a stable, the tight-packed straw was rank with damp, but he ignored the smell and kept his eye on the building ahead of him. It had not been hard to make his way here. There was still daylight, and in the evening, he saw the city packed with warriors celebrating the victory of the Saxons and the capture of King Aelle of Northumbria.

The last time he had made that journey, it had been at night, full of fear of capture, and he had approached the buildings where the Ragnarssons housed their followers and their women. This time though, he had walked through the busy streets weaving among the different crews as they drank ale and sang songs of victory. The time for fear was over. He had to make his dream a reality.

As he made the journey, Hundr's head swam

with the profound changes in his fortunes. In a matter of months, he had gone from being all but a beggar to a Carl on the Seaworm, then to recognition from the Champion of North, and now to an uncertain future. He belonged to Einar's crew, but Ivar had cast Einar out and beyond the protection of the laws of the Northmen. More than that, he had left home with an unshakeable longing to prove himself and become a renowned warrior with a reputation, but that dream had shattered the day he had met Saoirse. Since then, she was all he wanted. So there he lay, watching.

From his vantage point, Hundr could see the outbuildings and all comings and goings from the large stone house to the towering Roman wall which butted onto the river. However, he chose not to watch the side facing the great square and where he had made the perilous climb to Saoirse before. Now it was light, and that way would be wide open to all the people in the square. So he focused on this more secluded area, hoping to find a way in.

For what felt like hours, he had watched the guards as they came and went serving women, going back and forth for water and bringing out food scraps. There had to be a way in; it was high risk, but he had to see her once more. Everything now was high risk. Death from Hakon or Ivar could come at any turn, so what more danger could he be in even if they caught him? Still, as he lay there, Hundr knew this might be his last chance to persuade her to steal away with him, to make that life they had spoken of and he had dreamed of, the life Sten had lived with his wife. If she refused to come, he would leave with Sten, Einar and the others and find their fortune somewhere else. Hundr only knew one thing for certain; he would not die in this place or at the hand of Hakon.

He waited until sunset, and the shadows grew long. Hundr had watched most of the evening and could not see any way into the building without being seen. In the end, he resolved to take the risk. He had taken risks before, and they had always paid off. *Maybe Odin likes risk-takers and rewards them with luck* he through to himself as he slid from his hiding place.

There was no other way in that Hundr could see, so he had to take a desperate chance again. He was waiting until the guards were lighting their braziers at the building corners and re-solved to do it the way he had done last time. He searched for the same finger holds and hauled himself up the wall. The thick ivy vines that sprawled across the stone held his weight, and he inched his way across to Saoirse's window. He managed to pull himself onto the stone ledge, and crouching into its corner, he opened the painted shutter just a sliver. Through the thin crack he had opened, he could see the back of a woman facing towards a fire in the grate. He opened the shutter wider and jumped through, landing with a thud on the floorboards. The woman spun, and a look of horror twisted her face. *Shit, it's not her.*

Hundr leapt forward and grabbed the girl, putting his hand over her mouth to stifle any scream.

"Be quiet," he hissed, "Saoirse," he said as loudly as he could allow himself. She came from her antechamber startled.

"Hundr is that you… what are you doing here…? It's too dangerous. Guards will come for me soon."

He reached out for her hand and cradled it whilst not letting go of his grip on the handmaid. Saoirse recoiled, and he realised he had not washed since the battle. His hands caked in dried blood and gore, and he knew his armour, face, and hair were also filthy. He felt ashamed to come to her like this. She was pale and sweet-smelling and beautiful, and he, a filth covered warrior reeking of desperation.

"I'm sorry, I had to come. Hakon attacked us during the battle. He will come again. I know what you said before, but.."

"Hundr.." She tried to stop him, but he just had to get the words out.

"I love you, Saoirse, and if we ever want to be together, if we want to leave together, it must be now."

Saoirse looked at her handmaid, who was still in Hundr's grasp, and the Princess' eyes grew wide with fright. It had dawned on Saoirse that the maid knew Hundr had been in her room, and she would talk.

"It doesn't matter now if she knows or not. I have to leave this place today. Will you come?" he said.

Saoirse took a few steps back and sat on a wooden stool with her hand over her mouth. He went to follow her, and the handmaid twisted out of his grasp and made for the door. He let her go and kneeled before Saoirse, reaching for her hand.

"It's too late, Saoirse. We must go now."

"Where would we go? How would we live?" She was sobbing and rocking on the stool.

As he looked into her eyes, he could see that he could not change her mind. Again, he had built a future and a life in his dreams, but it was just that, a dream. She could not leave her life and her duty to her people; she could not leave Hakon. This was the life her birth dictated, the daughter of a Clan Chief wedded to a great Viking Lord. Not to be left for a childish fool with nothing to give but his love.

"Come with me, please. I can't leave you," Hundr breathed.

"He will kill us both; he and Ivar will hunt us down. I think I love you too. You have filled my thoughts since you saved my life. But love does not matter in this world. It just cannot be. We could never make it Hundr." She put her hand on his cheek; it was soft and warm. He took her hand in his and kissed it.

"We can go to my home, my father he would…."

Before he could say another word, the door burst open, and two guards burst in wearing the plaid of Ivar's Irishmen. They were both armed with spears and lowered them at Hundr.

"Get away from the Princess, turd," said one in his guttural, accented Norse.

Hundr rose and moved away from Saoirse. She was sobbing still. The guards took a step towards him, and he darted forwards, grabbing a spear and twisting around to elbow the guard in the face. He continued the twist into a full circle, drawing that man's knife from his belt and buried it into the back of the second guard. Then, without stopping, Hundr drew his own knife and smacked the first guard across the head. Both guards were writhing on the floor, groaning and trying to rise as Hundr dashed to her.

"We don't have time; come now, Saoirse, please-." They could hear heavy boots thundering down the hall towards them. She stood and pulled him close.

"We can't Hundr, you must go. Go and live," she said, her face wet with tears and eyes wide in despair. Hundr pulled away.

"If you change your mind, I will wait in the small shepherd's house closest to the river gate. It's got black rotten thatch for a roof, it's full of holes, and it's painted faded yellow. I will wait until first light. You can't live your life like this. Come with me." Hundr took one more long look at her, trying to drink in her beauty, and then ran for the door.

He jumped over the fallen guards and only just made it before more guards skidded around a corner of the hallway and shouted the alarm. He sprinted back into Saoirse's room and turned to drop feet first out of the window when he caught sight of Magnus No-Ear in the hall bursting into Saoirse's room. The huge Dane pointed at him and bellowed in red-faced incoherent fury. Hundr dropped backwards and grasped for an ivy vine. He found one and swung down, smashing into the wall with his knees; he dropped to the floor and ran for his life.

As his steps pounded through the streets of Yorvik, tears streamed down his face, tears of regret, embarrassment and despair. What had he done to Saoirse? What would Hakon do to her now? A man in her bedchamber, and Magnus recognised him. Hundr ran into the night knowing they would come for him, knowing his reckless actions had only added to his plight and that of the crew.

Hundr raced back to the Seaworm's quarters. His heart pounded, and his mind flitted from one terrible outcome to another. Magnus had seen him, and Hakon would come filled with rage. It also doomed Saoirse to the severest of punishments unless she could convince Hakon that Hundr had entered her window unlooked-for to attack her. He met Sten outside the Seaworm crew's house. Some of the men were heading to the fields outside the city. Tonight the sons of Ragnar would exact their revenge on King Aelle. Hundr thought that the gathering would buy him some time as Hakon would need to be present at the big event. Perhaps that was what Saoirse had meant when she had said guards would come for her soon. He just needed time to think.

Einar stayed at the house with Blink and Thorvald. He was conscious but not able to rise, and they would guard his life. The rest of the surviving crew, including Hundr and Sten, had donned hooded cloaks and went to the gathering. Ivar had called the army to assemble. It was time for the sons of Ragnar to fulfil their oaths of vengeance. They had captured King Aelle of Northumbria, who had thrown their father in the snake pit, and they had laid waste to his kingdom, exacting fierce revenge on their father's killer.

Sten and Hundr stood by a birch tree and kept their hoods up, watching as Ivar whipped the crowd into a frenzy. They had built a platform from fresh-cut wood. It stood twice the height of a man so all could see what took place. Sigurd rose to the platform first, exclaiming his gratitude to the Jarls and Lords of the army and listing the conquests of the sons of Ragnar. Then some wealthy-looking Saxon prisoners shambled onto the platform to be executed in short order. Men carried up treasure which was shown to the gathered army, and they gave awards of honour and bravery to heroes and Jarls who had taken part in the forming of the Great Army and the victory over Northumbria. The Ragnarrsons were now the rulers of that kingdom, and it was theirs to do with as they would. Wolfthinker came onto the platform, hunched and scratching at himself, trailed by his huddle of witches. Sigurd had been granted lands to the west of Yorvik, and the old man and his Volva's grinned and cackled. Other Jarls that Hundr recognised came forward to be rewarded with lands and wealth in the conquered Viking kingdom.

It was only recently that he had been so honoured and celebrated by Ivar. Hundr felt the arm rings under his cloak, cold to the touch. Somehow now, they did not make him as proud as they had. He had got all he had ever dreamed of, and now he had thrown it away. Without a doubt, after being spotted in Saoirse's room, his time with the army and the sons of Ragnar had to be over. No reputation, no crew, no Lord. He had also lost Saoirse. Hundr had been so sure she would just leave and run with him to the life he had planned in his dreams, but she would honour her duty. Life was not as simple as he had imagined.

Ivar the Boneless strode back onto the platform as the army roared with approval. He beckoned to the wings, and Hakon mounted the steps and waved at the gathered army. Ivar clapped his son on the shoulder and presented him with a fine bright sword.

"This is Soulstealer," Ivar called. "It is not a looted sword; I had it made in Frankia for my son. Frankish smiths crafted it from the finest steel, and it will be a sword of kings," he held it aloft, and the crowd cheered their approval. "I give this weapon to my son, Hakon. I also grant my son rich fertile lands in Northumbria to rule as Jarl and, and he will be as a King here among the Saxons."

Ivar handed the blade to Hakon and raised his arm. Hakon was beaming from ear to ear, and he held the mighty sword aloft like a conquering hero. *I hate you, Hakon Ivarsson; one day, I will watch you die. I swear it here; I swear before the Gods. You have everything, and I nothing. I will take your life from you and send you to Niflheim.* Hundr made that oath and closed his eyes tight. Watching Hakon made his guts wrench. Hakon had everything Hundr had ever wanted and had ever dreamed of. It had not been too long ago that it would have been more likely to be he or Einar up on that platform being made wealthy and respected.

"Bastard's rich now," grumbled Sten, "rich and untouchable."

Then King Aelle was dragged out. Ivar made a great show of stripping the fat Saxon King naked and parading his feeble white body around the platform. He showed the King his torture tools as his Irishmen laid Aelle out face down on a table. Next, Ivar took his axe and chisel and did his grizzly work, cutting and chopping at the man's back, blood flowing freely across the platform's fresh wood. King Aelle screamed and wept; the cutting lasted a fearfully long time, and the King was still alive when they strung him up. When Ivar had finished, they raised the King up by ropes tied to his hands, and Hundr saw the famous Blood Eagle of Ivar the Boneless. Ivar had cut the King's ribs away and opened out his back with the skin, and ribs spread wild like grisly eagle's wings. The crowd was hushed.

"Never seen the like before. A King killed like that. Maybe it's a sign," said Sten. Hundr looked at the grim, bloody spectacle again as various High Priests of Odin, Thor, Njorth and the other Gods pranced on the platform, shaking sticks and skulls and praying to the Gods of the Aesir.

"What sign?" he said,

"A sign from Odin, that we are a great people, we are conquering kingdoms and sending the souls of Kings to the Gods." His eyes were bulging and his mouth agape.

"What happened to the Christ God and your oath to your wife?"

Sten just stared at the Blood Eagled King. Hundr had given Saoirse one last chance to be with him, one last chance to make the dream come true. He had to see if she would take it.

The hut had been uninhabited for some time; it was a piss stinking rat hole, and various animals enjoyed its dark and secluded protection from the elements. Hundr sat crouched against the back wall of the hovel and watched as a gigantic rat scurried across the opposite wall. It was fat and fast, and it ran for its life from the man crouched in its home. It was dark and raining outside. Drips of water fell from the patchwork rotten thatch roof at various points and pooling on the packed earth floor. He had found a dry spot and waited. He had promised himself that he would wait until dawn to see if Saoirse would come and then go back to Sten and the others, and they would run for their lives. Most likely, she either did not want to leave Hakon and would stick to her duty, or she wanted to leave but couldn't and was under heavy guard. Either way, Hundr would leave Yorvik. His time with the sons of Ragnar was over, and with it, his ambitions of reputation and glory. Hakon being made a landed Jarl made him more powerful and therefore more dangerous. And with Einar outside of the law and open to attack by anyone in the army without fear of repercussions, it made Hundr's and the Seaworm crew's position in Yorvik impossible.

Hundr looked out at the stark wet night, his thoughts twisting and turning around the various scenarios of what might have become of Saoirse after he fled her room. She could be dead already, slain by her husband for suspected infidelity, she could be a prisoner, or she could turn the corner any moment running to him and to their dream life together. Magnus had recognised him, so Hakon would know by now, and no man would suffer another man being in his wife's bedchamber. Hundr's only hope was that she had found some way to escape from Hakon and make her way here. Then they would slip out of the river gate and away to a future together.

However much he tried to envisage a positive outcome, and however much he stared at the corner up ahead, wanting her to appear there, he always came back to his worst fear. If she was dead, it would be his fault. He had sneaked into her room, and her death, the death of the woman he loved, would be on his conscience. Muffled voices outside roused him from his thoughts, so he scrambled to his feet and ducked out under the doorframe of the hovel. As his head came up, and before he could see in front of him, someone kicked him savagely in the ribs, sending him sprawling in the mud. Hundr scrambled to find his feet coughing and gasping for breath, but the heavy haft of an axe clattered him around the head, and he fell to the ground again, splashing and flailing in the mud. He heard a scream and looked up, gasping and shuddering as a nightmare came to life before his eyes.

Saoirse was there. On her knees in the pouring rain, with her hair gripped in the fist of Magnus No-Ear, who towered over her, huge and terrible. Hakon Ivarsson was also there, shouting and flailing his arms, accompanied by at least ten armed warriors. They pulled Hundr to his feet and dragged him through the mud towards Saoirse. He looked up and saw the twisted hatred on Hakon's face, and there leering next to him was Kraki Horse Face.

Hakon stepped forward and slapped Hundr

hard across the face, and kicked him in the stomach. Hundr doubled over, but a powerful hand grasped his hair and dragged him back up.

"I knew you had been rutting with my whore wife," Hakon shouted in his face, "all this time you have been sneaking into my house and having your way with her. Rutting like pigs and laughing at me," spittle flew from his mouth, and his eyes grew wild with fury as rain cascaded down his face.

"Do him now, kill the runt," Kraki said, almost jumping with joy at Hundr's capture.

A warrior cut Hundr's breastplate away and took his weapons. Hundr was hollow, the rain washing all hope from him and draining away his dreams of happiness in the maelstrom of Hakon's spite and hate.

"Well, now you are mine, now you will both know what it means to betray Hakon Ivarsson," Hakon said and drew his knife. He cut Hundr deep across the chest and shoulder in one long slice, shouting as the blade tore through Hundr's skin. Hundr didn't cry out, but he gritted his teeth against the burning fire of the wound and looked into Saoirse's sad-eyed face.

Hakon turned and half slipped in the mud. He took two long steps and punched Saoirse in the belly, and kicked her as she fell. Hundr called out to her, but they met his cry with a crunching blow behind his ear, and all went dark. As he drifted into that bleak darkness, he knew his world had ended.

TWENTY ONE

Einar woke groggily in his bed of straw. He had slept well, and in the fog of half-sleep, he almost forgot that the bastards had beaten him close to death. The sharp, crunching pain in his ribs served as a brutal reminder of that fact as he tried to sit up, as did the throbbing vomit-inducing pain in his face and skull. Finally, he got to his feet, but that effort felt like fighting a battle, covering his face and body in a sheen of sweat. Einar braced himself against a rickety stained table and cursed Hakon, Ivar, Guthrum, Kraki, Odin, and anyone else he could think of worth cursing. Those bastards had laid him low, an entire life of service gone to shit. He remembered Halvdan above him, protecting him in the battle for Yorvik's streets. At least he had remembered his honour as a drengr at the end, but Einar wasn't sure Halvdan's sacrifice was worth it.

It felt strange that Halvdan was dead. The taciturn, fierce warrior had served Einar well for longer than he could remember, and Einar had never suspected Halvdan would betray him. It must have been the promise of the Seaworm or a sparkling future taking Einar's place as a Sea Jarl. It didn't really matter now, Einar supposed. Poor bastard is a corpse. Likely in a pit outside the city walls with the rest of the battle's carrion. Despite his betrayal, Einar hoped Halvdan had made it to Odin's hall in Valhalla or Thor's hall in Thruth-vangar. He had always fought well and had died with a blade in his hand. *Save a place for me, brother.*

Einar looked around the room inside the ram-shackle hovel, which now served as their quarters, the quarters of masterless men. Blink, Bush, and the others were asleep, dotted around the hard-packed earth floor. Brownlegs was happily snoring like a boar in one corner. Sten ducked his monstrous frame in through the front door and slumped at the table next to Einar. The old man looked even more morose than usual, he had a frown with more furrows than a tilled field, and he fingered at the wooden cross around his neck.

"Any ale in that?" Einar said, pointing at a pitcher next to Sten's right hand.

Sten grumbled and pushed the pitcher towards Einar. He lifted it, and there was liquid in it. Einar sniffed it, and it smelled like shitty ale, but he drank it anyway, hoping it would help dull the throbbing aches swamping his senses.

"Any sign of him?" Einar asked. Sten shook his head and clenched his fist.

The crew had not seen Hundr since the army had gathered to watch Ivar cut the grizzly Blood Eagle on King Aelle the night before. Einar had missed it, having only returned to consciousness when most of the men had already left. He was glad he hadn't seen it; it would be hard now to look upon Ivar. The men had told Einar that Hakon was now a landed Jarl with a fortress and vast lands in Northumbria, which made him feel worse than any of his physical wounds. *That should have been my bloody fortress, my vast bloody lands.* Hakon had taken everything from Einar with his lies. He clenched his teeth, but that made his face ache, so Einar tried to banish any thoughts of Hakon. Hate burned inside him like the white-hot belly of a forge, but he needed a clear head to think about that properly and decide what, if anything, could be done about it.

The rest of the Seaworm crew had agreed that today would be the day they left Yorvik. To stay meant death. The attack from Hakon after the battle was an unmistakable message that they were to be hunted, so it was a simple choice of run or die. They had not yet discussed where they would go, with no ship and in a hostile foreign land.

"We have to leave soon," Einar said, "soon as we get the lads together." Hakon the turd could find them at any moment.

"I know," said Sten in a low growl. Sten looked up at Einar, and there was sadness in his eyes, and his lined face looked strained with worry. "I'll have to find him first, can't go without him," Sten said.

"These lazy bastards won't wake for ages, I'll come with you," Einar replied. He couldn't let Sten go out into the city alone. If any of Hakon's men found him, he would be a dead man. All were familiar now with the story of Sten leaving Ragnar Lothbrok's service to be with his Saxon woman, and the oath he had given to her not to fight and instead take up the ways of the Christian God. Sten had told the tale to Hundr, and then he had told Bush, and then, of course, the entire crew had heard the story. An old warrior who wouldn't fight wouldn't last long in a city full of Viking warriors flushed still from the thrill of yesterday's battle. Although in the state he was in, there wasn't much Einar could do if they did run into trouble. Still, he borrowed an axe from one of the sleeping men and tucked it in his belt, and the two set out into the city.

Einar and Sten trudged through the streets of Yorvik, picking their way between Saxon corpses and sleeping drunken Vikings. The place was eerily quiet, and Einar could hear pigs grunting and chickens clucking somewhere close, and on the breeze was the iron tang of blood as a reminder of the previous day's slaughter.

Sten was never one for engaging in conversation, but Einar was sure that wandering around was both pointless and a good way to get them both killed.

"Any ideas where he could be?" he asked.

"He got it into his head to talk to her again," said Sten.

"Talk to who?"

"Bloody Princess."

"Hakon's bloody Princess?"

Sten just frowned again,

"So we head up that way," Sten said, nodding towards the spire of the church as the centre of Yorvik, which was also where the sons of Ragnar quartered. Einar stopped walking and sighed.

"Hang on. You want us to walk right up to where Hakon and his men are?"

"Come, or don't," replied Sten with a shrug and pressed on.

It was one thing to look for Hundr, Einar was fond of the lad, and he had proved himself a fearsome fighter, but it was another to march right into the Hakon's jaws. He couldn't let the big lump go alone, so he grimaced again against the pain in his ribs and caught up to Sten. Walking made him feel better. It lessened the stiffness in his limbs, so he was glad to keep going, even into the maw of their enemies.

They continued in silence. Einar watched Sten and wondered where he would be at that age. Until a few days ago, he had been sure that he would earn his goal of a proper Jarldom and be able to settle down and find a wife, maybe have a few children to pass his wealth on to. That had always been Einar's future, earn lands of his own, or earn a place in Valhalla. Now he had nothing, no ship, no Lord, no future. He supposed it had been much the same for Sten, serving Ragnar and then settling down with his woman.

"Do you miss her?" Einar said and then regretted it as Sten shot him a murderous look.

"All day, every day," Sten replied to Einar's surprise.

"She must have been a great woman."

"What do you mean?"

"Well, for you to leave Ragnar, she must have been worth it."

They turned a corner into a wide laneway which must have seen heavy fighting the previous day. Einar had to sidestep to dodge a puddle of dark blood, and there were three corpses slumped against a wall.

"Leave what... this?" Sten said, nodding towards the corpses. "This is the life we choose when we take to the seas. We all know it. If you don't like it, stay on the bloody farm. We kill and steal, betray and burn, go to another place, and do it again. Jarls fighting each other, fighting foreigners, making alliances and breaking them. She showed me another way. A better life."

"Was it better?"

"You don't know no different, Einar. Like me back then, with Ragnar. But there is another life, simple work, love, a hand to reach out on a cold night."

It stunned Einar what the old warrior was saying. What was love to a drengr? A warrior could take a woman whenever he chose. Then again, maybe Sten was right; he just didn't know any different.

"You are fond of the boy," Einar said to break the awkwardness of Sten's words.

"Aye, I am."

Sten stopped and turned to Einar, his face flushed crimson, "I never had a son. We tried, her and me, but God never gave us that blessing. Hundr's a good lad, brave and honest. If anything's happened to him...." Sten's eyes blazed, and he fingered at his wooden cross pendant.

Einar knew little about the Christ God. It made

no sense to him, a man on a cross, a ghost and a woman. He knew that look in Sten's eyes, though, the look of a killer. *Takes one to know one.*

They came within sight of the keep and the great church but were reluctant to get too close for fear of being recognised. Sten asked a few people who passed by if they had seen a young warrior alone, but none had seen him, and most did not know who he was when Sten described him. Einar saw smoke swirling from a low, dark, thatched building across the square which looked like a smithy, and he nudged Sten towards it. They ducked under a low lintel and into a blacksmith's yard, which backed onto the rear riverside of the city. The smith was at his bellows, getting his furnace hot and so not yet working with hammer and tongs, which meant that Einar could hear the river swirling beyond Yorvik's great stone walls. Einar greeted the smith, and he was a Dane, who must have taken over the forge from its Saxon owner.

"Just firing up, won't be hot for a while, mates. What do you need?" the smith asked as he went again at his bellows.

"Don't need smith work," said Sten. "We're looking for a friend, a young warrior, has three arm rings and wears two swords."

The smith stopped at his bellow and scratched his chin.

"There was a lad taken last night. I thought it was him that fought back to back with Ivar when we took this place," said the smith.

"Taken how?" asked Sten, bunching his fists.

"Taken by Hakon Ivarsson, there, by that hovel over yonder," said the smith, "Gods only know what he was doing in there."

Einar looked at the yellowed, crumbling building by the back city gate visible through a wide entranceway at the rear of the smithy.

"There was a half a crew. They gave the lad a hiding and dragged him off. There was a girl as well; she got a kicking too," said the blacksmith.

Einar looked at Sten, who just stood still and shaking.

"You think it's him?" Einar asked, but Sten ducked back under the entrance and stalked away. Einar thanked the smith and followed. The lad in the smith's story was Hundr; Einar could feel it. Hakon, the bastard, had taken Hundr to the Gods only knew where, and to do the Gods only knew what. The turd was a landed Jarl now with his own land and crews, and there was something beyond madness between Hundr and Hakon's Irish Princess. Einar caught up to Sten, who was heading back across the square.

Einar's head was spinning at the thought of Hundr's capture. Was he in the Ragnarsson quarters here, only a stone's throw from where they now walked? They headed down a merchant's street with awnings stretching across the cobbles. Two men came around a corner and headed towards Einar and Sten. They were two of Ivar's Irish warriors, big men, and one barged into Sten as he passed. Sten slipped on the cobbles and rose, steadying himself. The Irishmen who had barged Sten stopped to adjust his plaid cloak where it had come loose from the collision.

"What are you looking at, you old bastard?" said the Irishman.

Einar looked at Sten and saw the corners of his mouth turn down and his shoulders stiffen. His brow furrowed, and his jaw jutted. Sten closed his eyes, and then a thin-lipped smile crept across his face, as though a welcoming cloak was warming him after a night out in the cold.

Sten lunged forward faster than Einar thought possible for a man of his size and punched the big Irishman in the stomach, hitting so hard it lifted the man off his feet. Einar heard air whoosh from the man's lungs. Sten continued moving forward to headbutt the other Irishman brutally full in the face, and Einar heard the crack of bone as the man grunted out of consciousness. Sten had put all the strength of his neck and shoulders into that blow, muscles built over a lifetime of pulling oars and hefting weapons. That Irishman crumpled to the dirt, his face mangled and smashed.

Then, as the first Irishman doubled over clutching his stomach, Sten grabbed his head and savagely twisted it, breaking his neck with a sickening click. The head-butted man was lying still on the cobbles, and Sten knelt and pulled a knife from the man's belt and stabbed him four times in the chest and neck, short, brutal thrusts. Sten kept the knife, took the belt, and took an axe from the first man, slotting it into the loop of his new belt. Sten stood and grimaced slightly as he stretched his back like an old man rising from sitting at the fire too long.

Einar, rooted to the spot, realised his mouth was hanging wide open, stunned at Sten's ferocity. Sten looked up towards the sky and closed his eyes. He tore the cross from his neck and threw it in the pool of blood that had formed around the stabbed Irishman.

"I'm sorry, my love," he whispered, "for I must be who I was again."

"Sten... what are you...." Einar said, but Sten looked at him. In that look was pure fury. Einar could almost feel the violence pulsing from the big man.

"Time for peace and God is over. We need the others," Sten said, and stepping over the two corpses he had just made, he strode up the street.

Einar followed, and for the first time since his betrayal, he felt alive. Sten had killed with ruthless efficiency, and the warriors he had taken down were no mewling peasants either. If the boy was alive, they would get him back, and if the boy was dead... well, then they would kill them all.

Einar and Sten reached the new sorry-looking Seaworm quarters as the sun was rising to mid-morning, and the crew gathered outside, packed and ready to leave. Bush was securing his pack with rope and looked up at the sound of their approach.

"No sign of him then?" he asked.

"Hundr's been taken, him and his Princess," said Einar.

The crew gathered around at that news.

"Taken him... who?" asked Brownlegs.

"Hakon," said Einar, and he could see their faces change from resigned men about to flee from danger to a group of angered warriors.

"Bastard. Taken him where?" asked Bush.

"We don't know yet," said Einar.

"I see you have taken up arms, my friend," said Bush, pointing at the axe and knife at Sten's belt.

Sten ignored him and ducked into the house. He emerged again with a whetstone and sharpened his new knife.

"What do you plan to do with that?" asked Bush.

"Sten has taken up arms again," said Einar and waved the men to silence whilst Sten focused on his knife. He could see them passing puzzled glances between each other.

"If he took him, the lad's alive. He would have killed him on the spot otherwise," said Sten.

"Maybe, but what can we do about it?" said Blink, "we've got to get out of here before we're dead men, boys."

Sten stood up to his full height, towering over the others and raised his axe, passing across the group,

"We get him, like he would do for any of us."

"We're already outlawed," said Thorvald with a snort, "half of us are dead, and the rest are all banged up. So what can we do... do you even know where he is?"

Sten tested the edge of the knife with his thumb, cut his long hair in hanks, and then shaved his grey hair close to his scalp around his ears. Einar and the rest of the crew just watched Sten, bemused that he had chosen this time to cut his hair.

"Is now the right time for that?' asked Thorvald.

Sten paused and snarled at him.

"Since you lot came and killed my friends the brothers, I've taken your shit and let you treat me disrespectfully...."

Thorvald interrupted him, "hang on a second..."

"Never interrupt me," Sten bellowed, "from now on, when I talk, nobody else does."

Sten stared down each of them, including Einar. Einar raised his hands to calm the situation. Sten resumed scraping at his head with the knife until the shaved skin around his ears and at the base of his skull revealed tattooed dragons and axes, whirling dark blue against his white skull. Sten stood and dipped his head in a barrel filled with rainwater. Einar nodded and moved to clap his friend on the back.

"Looks like the Sten Sleggya of legend is back. Let me help you with that," he said.

Sten sat and allowed Einar to take the knife and shave his head where he had missed patches. He shaved the sides and left the top part long. Einar handed the knife back to Sten and then tied the remaining hair in a long braid. He did this in silence whilst the crew continued to look on speechless; they had made ready to leave Yorvik but now waited for a command from Einar, yet he waited. Finishing Sten's hair had been soothing, a transition from an old world to a new one. Ivar and Hakon had stripped everything from Einar, and now they had taken Hundr, whom Sten loved like a son. Einar felt purpose flow through him, he had become lost in the pain and melancholy of his humiliation, but as he plaited

Sten's long hair from the remaining patch at the top of his skull, he felt purpose. Get the boy back and kill Hakon. He and the crew had nothing else to lose; they had no Lord and no protection from Hakon or any other bloodthirsty crews. They had no ship in which to leave the lands of the Saxons. If they fled Yorvik, they would be prey to vengeful Saxon warriors and had nowhere to go. Einar would not run. A drengr did not run.

Sten stood and went back into the house and came out with a mail coat that belonged to Rollo, who had looted it from a dead Saxon the day before. Sten took off his old jerkin, cut the sleeves from it, put the jerkin back on, and pulled on the mail coat. His muscled arms were now bare, revealing the old and faded dark blue tattoos writhing up his arms and onto his cleanly shaven head. Rollo didn't object to losing his coat of mail.

"Let's go visit Jarl Guthrum," said Sten.

TWENTY TWO

Hundr couldn't open his eyes, yet he could feel the surrounding darkness, oppressive and close. *Am I dead? Is this the Skuld world of the nithings*? He rubbed at his eyes and tried to control his breathing, which had become fast and shallow in fear of the darkness. His breathing slowed as his encrusted eyes opened, and then a sharp, hot pain shot through his head from the wound on his scalp. The blow from the axe haft on the back of his head had split his skull, and blood had soaked his hair and face in a thick crusty mess.

Hundr retched with the pain and would have vomited had there been any food in his belly. As it was, he just heaved, and a thin line of spittle dripped from his mouth, and the pain of retching made him want to vomit even more. The clotted blood on his face came away in little flakes as he continued to rub at his eyes with his knuckles. He needed to see where he was and get his bearings, but as he tried to sit up, the pain in his ribs made him gasp and curl up into a ball, retching again.

He could feel gentle, rhythmic swaying beneath him, and the surface he lay on was smooth planking, which stank of old vegetables. *I am in a cart of some sort. Where are they taking me?* Damp straw covered the surrounding planking, and it tangled in his hair and stuck to the crusted blood on his face. He pulled what he could free and crawled over to look through slits in the dark side panels of the cart. Mounted warriors surrounded the cart, and they seemed to be travelling through open fields. The brightness of the sun made him wince, and he could see the different shades of greenery on the bushes and trees around the horsemen.

He sat back against the panels and closed his eyes. The images of when they had taken him and the horror of seeing Saoirse punched and dragged away had become etched into the forefront of his mind and replayed repeatedly. Every time he blinked, he saw that picture of Saoirse punched by Hakon. Hundr swallowed the dryness from his mouth, and as he thought of her pain, he could have wept. He had to get to her, if she was still alive. Hundr was unsure why he was even alive; he had been certain that Hakon would kill him in Yorvik. What reason could there be for Hakon to have spared him? He hoped that whatever reason it was, it had also spared Saoirse. His head slumped into his hands, and again he forced back the desire to weep at his fate. How far he had fallen, feted by the Boneless and so sure of his future, to this.

He had to get free and get to her, get her out of this mess. Hundr crawled to the rear of the cart, ignoring the pain from his wounds. He rested with his back against the cart, feeling its swaying motion. Closing his eyes, he could hear the warriors talking outside, but he couldn't make out their muffled words. He thought about chancing a look over the back of the cart but decided against it.

He must make a run for it. If he was free, then he had a better chance of finding Saoirse. Without hesitation, he put a hand on the rear of the cart and vaulted over the back, landing and rolling on hard-packed grass. He heard horses snort and the scrape of weapons drawn. Hundr came to his feet and looked around in desperation for a route in which to dash. Surrounded by horses and with no clear path of escape, fear flooded his mind. He raced to his left but bounced off a horse's flank and felt a boot kick in his back, he scrambled in the opposite direction to get free of the riders, but a hand grabbed the back of his hair and lifted him off the ground tossing him to the turf. He rolled again, and holding his ribs, he rose gasping for air and wild-eyed, but two warriors grabbed his arms, and another punched him in his injured ribs, and Hundr cried out at the pain. The warriors laughed. He could hear Hakon Ivarsson shouting and laughing.

"He looks hot, relieve him of his jerkin and tie him to your horse. He can run the rest of the way."

The warriors pulled Hundr's jerkin from him and tied his wrists with a rough hemp rope. They lashed the other end to a saddle pommel, and he felt the huge tug as the horse started forwards. He kept his eyes on the dirt track, shame stopping him from facing his captors. His heart sank even lower at the sounds of their laughter.

The power of the horse jerked him forward, and the rope burned and pulled at his wrists. Hundr tried to keep up, jogging and walking, but too often, he fell, and the weight of the horse dragged him along, his chest and back scratching and cutting on the stones and undergrowth of the track and fields. The warriors laughed again and mocked his nakedness. Spear shafts clattered across his shoulders, but he had to keep going for Saoirse. He fought to keep up, running and being dragged along, until he could no longer. He was being dragged along, humiliated, his arms and shoulders on fire, and he allowed the warm embrace of darkness to envelop him.

Hundr awoke in a familiar place, a place from long

ago. He was floating or flying like a bird looking down on the scene below him. In an expansive room of carved pillars and soft woven rugs, a woman sat playing with a small child. They were playing with carved animal toys, and the woman belly-laughed at the child's impressions of sheep and cows. The sound of her laughter made Hundr smile. The room was familiar; he knew this place. Hundr drifted around the scene so he could see her face, and yes, it was his mother. Her hair auburn and shining, face open and kind. The child was him, Hundr, before he had a dog's name, when he had another name. He remembered playing with his mother like this; it felt like happiness and warmth and safety. He wanted to float down and stroke her hair, to hug her and feel that comfort, but he could not. Whatever force had brought him here held him fast where he was. Finally, the doors to the room opened, and a man entered, and with him came a strained look on his mother's face. She sat straighter; her smile evaporated as she fussed at her hair and put a protective arm around the child. The man was broad-shouldered and black-bearded; he wore a colourful embroidered tunic above bright trews and fine calf-skin boots.

"You are too gentle with the child, he won't grow strong," said the man in a deep voice. Hundr knew that man and that voice.

"He will grow strong, like his father," he heard his mother say.

"You must come to me tonight, after the feast," the man said.

"What about our son?" she asked.

"Your son," the man corrected her, "What of him?"

"I know I can never be a wife to you, my Lord, but he is your son. You must recognise him, allow him a place with your other sons," she said.

"The son of a concubine is not a son. How many times must we have this tiresome discussion." the man said. His tone became angry, pointing at her in warning, "you will come to me tonight." He left the room, leaving them alone again.

Hundr looked at himself, the small Hundr before he was Hundr. He felt the child's sadness, the hollow feeling of rejection. He knew how that would grow and change into a desire to impress, to prove his worth.

"Do not worry, little one, you will be a great man one day like your father," his mother said and gave the child a kiss.

Hundr reached out a hand to the mother and child. He wanted to touch her, to smell her. He had lost her long ago, taken from him and gone forever. But, as he reached out, Hundr felt himself being pulled away from the room towards the sky. I have failed; I have become a failure. He tried to recall his mother's face, but it faded, and all that remained was the perfumed smell of her hair, her kindness, and his *pain.*

Hundr woke again, lying in thick, stinking mud and still stripped to the waist. A shiver racked his body, and he closed his eyes to force away the pain from his head wound. He curled up for a moment, hugging himself tight and shaking with his mother burned into his mind. It was just a dream, and he was still alive, for now at least. Hundr pushed all thoughts of her and of home to the recesses of his mind where they had rested for so long.

Hundr tried to kneel up, slipping in the mud but rising to his knees, he looked around and saw that he was in a square mud-soaked courtyard surrounded by timber buildings made from dark wood, stained even darker by the recent rainfall. Hundr tried to raise his hands to feel his head wound, but they had tied him to a post fixed deep into the earth. Looking around again, he saw armed warriors and men were busy at their work, crisscrossing the open space with buckets and arms of firewood. Men noticed he was awake, and some laughed, pointing at him, enjoying his plight.

Hundr sank back down again and tried to flex his hands and fingers. The rope had tightened after being wet, and his hands were stiff and blue. He heard footsteps squelching in the mud and looked up to see Hakon approaching with

Magnus No-Ear and three of his men. Hakon was smirking, his eyes glinting with joy and his stride cocksure and confident.

"Welcome to my estates, dog," said Hakon smiling, "I hope you are enjoying our hospitality."

Hundr grunted and sat back against the post. *Why doesn't the gloating pig just finish me and have done with it?*

"You are wondering why I haven't killed you yet," said Hakon. Hundr just looked at him and spat mud out of his mouth. *Obviously, you turd.*

"When a new Jarl comes into his lands, we must sacrifice to please the Gods. We want the harvest to be good, and so Freja and Frigg and the rest must be honoured." Hundr just stared. He wanted the arrogant fool to take a few more steps forward, just a few more steps, and he could get reach him. He could die happy if he could take Hakon with him screaming into the afterlife.

"And what better way to make the Gods happy than the sacrifice of a young and healthy fool and his whore Princess," Hakon continued. "A Princess sacrificed in my honour will surely please the Gods, even if she is a filthy whore who has rutted with half of the army. I have brought along one of Wolfthinkers witches, a Volva to do the thing right, for luck."

Hakon made a slight turn to grin at Magnus, and Hundr leapt forward using his legs to launch himself as fast as possible, Hakon leapt backwards, gasping, but the rope went taut and snapped Hundr backwards.

He shouted in impotent rage and kicked mud at Hakon and yanked at the post.

Let me free, give just a moment with him before I die.

One of Hakon's men was scowling and watching his Lord flinch as the mud spattered his fine cloak. Hundr shot out in his direction and kicked out at that man's legs and caught him, the man toppled back, and Hundr was on him like a feral animal. He elbowed the fallen man in the face and began head-butting him, feeling his nose crunching under his forehead, but then Magnus kicked Hundr in the head, and two more warriors grabbed him and pulled him back. They kicked him, their heels and feet pounding his head and face. As the light dimmed behind his eyes, Hundr could taste the bitter iron blood in his mouth; the smell of leather and the sweat of his attackers swarmed his senses.

Don't let me die now without a weapon, not now. Grant me revenge Odin, help me. Please....

When Hundr next woke, it was because he was being slapped across the face. He blinked and shook his head. Pain racked his entire body and his tongue stuck to the roof of his mouth. He tried to swallow, and the dryness of his throat cracked like parched leather.

Still alive.

A rough gloved hand slapped him, and he jerked to twist away from the blow, but they had him tied fast in a standing position. He couldn't move his hands and feet, and as he became more lucid, he felt the hemp rope biting again at his wrists and ankles. They had lashed Hundr to a stout post in the middle of the fortress courtyard. Facing him was Hakon, this time with Jarl Guthrum glowering and scratching at his vast belly. To their right was Magnus No-Ear, who was holding Saoirse.

What have I done? How could I have brought her to this end?

She was in a plain brown rough spun dress; her face bruised, and she was shaking. Hundr twisted and pulled, but his bonds were secure.

"See before you the animal you chose over me, whore," Hakon said to Saoirse. "You must pay the price for your choices. What was it, I wonder, that made you betray me? Was it his noble birth? No, he's low born and more than likely a bastard. Was it his wealth? No, he has no lands, no ships, no warriors to call upon. It must then be his soft face and handsome eyes, is it not?" he said. "Well, we can remedy that."

Hakon strode over to a brazier where a thin-faced warrior stoked a bright fire. The warrior handed Hakon a rag wrapped around the hilt of a long knife that rested in the flame. Hakon drew the blade and held it up for Hundr and Saoirse to see. Its tip glowed an angry orange-red which stood out against the drab browns and greys of the fortress. Hakon walked towards Hundr but first turned to Saoirse.

"Behold your handsome Prince," he said.

Hakon grabbed Hundr by the hair and pinned his head back against the post.

"Cuckold me, would you, dog?" Hakon spat.

Hakon held the knife up to Hundr's face, and the heat from the blade was overwhelming. Hundr couldn't move his head, and Hakon held the knife close to his skin. Sweat beaded on Hundr's face, and it was all he could do to not cry out. Finally, Hakon touched the knife's blade to Hundr's forehead and dragged it down his face to his chin. The blade seared through Hundr's left eye, sizzling as it tore away the eyeball. Hundr screamed and wept as the white-hot pain exploded inside his skull. Hakon's eyes blazed with delight as he turned, held the knife in the air. Cheers erupted from the watching warriors around the fortress. Hundr's chin sagged to his chest, and he shuddered as the tears from his right eye dripped down his cheek.

Hakon turned back to Hundr and lowered the blade again,

"I am Hakon Ivarsson, I have a reputation, and I will be respected," Hakon whispered those words to Hundr through clenched teeth. Then he pushed the knife blade against Hundr's chest and dragged it across to his shoulder, directly above the cut he had made in Yorvik. Hundr sucked in a deep breath and smelt the burnt hair from his chest and the sickly smell of his own burning flesh. He screamed again, and he wept for himself, and he wept for Saoirse. As he gave himself over the sobs of despair, he heard Hakon and the others laughing, laughing at him and his suffering. Once more, darkness overcame him, and the laughing and pain drifted away with the light.

What a fool I have been, a childish, selfish fool. Look at what I have done to us both. Dreams of love and a life together....the world is no place for such foolish dreams. Those dreams must die. I must replace them with hate and fury and death.

TWENTY THREE

Einar was walking more freely, but his ribs still jabbed like knives whenever he twisted or stretched too far. He could see a little more through the slit of his damaged eye, and he found that opening his mouth as wide as possible felt satisfying even though it pulled at the swelling around his face. It did not take long for the crew to reach Guthrum's quarters. Guthrum had six crews and lodged in a row of houses, the largest of which was at the end of a street and had fine stone walls and a broad courtyard where warriors sat in front of a fire drinking ale. Einar paused at the opposite end of the street and halted the crew.

"What now?" asked Blink.

"We need to figure how to get past that lot and into the hall," Einar said, feeling at his swollen face and opening his mouth wide again to stretch out the pain.

Sten did not break stride and walked past Einar towards the big house.

"What are you doing?"

Sten wasn't even pretending to show any guile. He was just marching up to Guthrum's men, straight and bold.

"Shit," said Einar, "Come on lads, we can't let the old fool die alone," and he strode after Sten.

"Gonna talk to Guthrum," said Sten over his shoulder.

"I can bloody see that," Einar replied, "but...."

Sten seemed even less in the mood for talk than usual. He marched towards the courtyard fire, and two of Guthrum's warriors with their backs to the street rose as they saw their shipmates staring. One sniggered.

"Look, it's the big man who won't fight, had a haircut...."

Before he could finish his insult, Sten had punched him square in the throat, and the man fell choking. The other warrior was still twisting around as Sten hit him with a savage kick knocking him over the bench.

Einar supposed this was as good a way to get Guthrum's attention, and he smiled to himself, enjoying Sten's ferocity. It wasn't so long ago that it would have been Einar launching into the fray without thought. Maybe the beating had taken that out of him, taken the brawler out of him. He hoped not. Guthrum's men shouted and rose from their seats. Sten smacked a mug of ale from one man's hand, and as he reached the fire, Sten kicked at the burning logs spraying the fire at the men to his left. They yelped and jumped back as a man's greasy beard caught fire, and he screamed in panic.

A warrior drew an axe, but Sten grabbed his hand before he could raise it. Sten head-butted that man and snatched his axe in one fluid motion, back cutting it across the face of the warrior whose ale he had spilt. This all happened in the blink of an eye. The Seaworm crew were running now to catch up to Sten. Einar found it hard to believe this was the Sten he had been commanding for the last few months; this was a different man. This was the Sten Sleggya of legend. *I like this Sten much more.* Guthrum's warriors backed away.

"Is Guthrum the fat in there," Sten said, pointing his bloody axe at the hall.

Guthrum's men just stared; some of them tried to help their shipmate put out his flaming beard. That man was making a strange mewing sound, and the other men Sten had felled were groaning and writhing on the ground. The Seaworm crew flanked Sten, and Einar couldn't help grinning, even though it hurt his injured face. His humiliation at the hands of Hakon, Guthrum, and

Magnus had laid him low, but he was Einar the Brawler, and he felt his pride returning watching Sten at work.

One of Guthrum's men pointed a shaking finger at the hall.

"I like the new Sten," said Einar as he warned the enemy back with his axe, "what now?"

Sten was already making for the hall, and he pushed open the big double doors and stepped forward into its gloomy entrance.

"Blink and Thorvald, watch these bastards. Rest of you follow me," Einar said, and followed Sten into a narrow dark entrance hall without a torch to light it. There was light up ahead, but Sten's vast frame blocked most of it.

"Guthrum," Sten shouted, and the noise echoed around the hall. Einar could hear men scrambling and benches scraping on the stone floor at the other end of the gloom. Sten strode into the vast expanse of the hall and approached a small fire at its centre. The crew followed him in, and Einar stood next to him, axe in hand. There were warriors dotted about the hall's benches but no sign of Guthrum. Einar felt power pulsing up his arms from the feel of the axe, the familiar weight of its haft and blade rejuvenating him and washing away the pain of his wounds.

"I've left men outside to watch the door, so Guthrum's other crews don't follow us in. If they do, we'll end up trapped in here with them," said Einar, "let's be quick."

Sten was searching the room with the axe he had taken hanging loosely at his side, dripping blood onto the floor rushes.

"No, these Norse sheep shaggers will end up trapped in here with us," Sten said, and bellowed for Guthrum again.

Five men approached from the back of the hall; four of them were warriors armed with swords or axes, and in the middle of them was Guthrum, red-faced and sweating.

"Who do you think you are coming into my hall like this? I'll have you whipped like dogs," Guthrum said, his jowls trembling as he spoke.

"What did Hakon Ivarsson do with Hundr?" said Sten. A smile crept across Guthrum's face.

"Hopefully, he cut his throat and threw him into a dung pile." Guthrum looked at Einar and gave a low laugh. "How is your face Einar, it looks sore? I see you have new boots. I think I gave your old pair to the Saxon who empties my shit pail."

"Where's the boy?" said Einar.

He fingered the axe in his hand. How easy it would be to kill Guthrum right there, how simple to whip the life from his chest. Einar thought of his humiliation again, waking lying in piss with no boots on, stripped of all his wealth. He hefted his axe, but then a wizened, thin figure leapt between the warriors and began gesticulating at Sten.

"I see you, Sten Sleggya, I see you turd of Loki. You wouldn't help your Lord, your oldest friend Ragnar, but here you are begging for your boy lover's life," it was Kjartan Wolfthinker, and he was raving mad.

"Wolfthinker, stay out of this, you weasel shit bastard, piss off back to the shadows. This is warrior work," Sten said.

"Warrior work," sneered Wolfthinker and spat to the side, "says the man who lives in the mountains with his whore, hiding from the fighting behind her skirts. You have forgotten the old days, the days of legend and glory," Wolfthinker said, and Sten laughed.

"Glory days. I remember the old days well enough, Kjartan. It was murder and theft. I remember attacking and killing them who couldn't protect themselves, and I remember Ragnar and me with blood on our faces and silver beyond compare. I remember you don't like to fight Kjartan, but you can fight me now if you wish. Otherwise, shut up and piss off."

Wolfthinker spluttered and wrung his hands.

"Why are you here in Guthrum's hall, Wolfthinker?" asked Einar.

Of course, he was here. Of course, the old snake had been part of Hakon and Guthrum's plan of setting Einar up for the raid in East Anglia. A raid he knew nothing of. It was surely beyond Hakon to come up with such a plan, but it was bread and butter for Kjartan Wolfthinker. These two insects reeked of it; they reeked of stealing Einar's reputation and his promise of landed Jarldom; they reeked of his humiliation and of Hakon's sly rise to power.

"Why shouldn't I be here with a fellow Lord? You, Einar, are a masterless man, an outcast. Your ship is taken, your Seaworm. Hakon's men sail it North to his lands as we speak. You have nothing except this ragged band of crusty Nithings and an old coward for company."

My ship, Hakon, has taken my beautiful ship.

Einar's heart beat faster. He loved the Seaworm, her curves and her power, her beast head and his steerboard platform and the feel of the sea beneath his feet. He couldn't bear the thought of Hakon the turd having the joy of the Seaworm. Einar could not allow that, would not allow that.

"Where is the boy?" Einar said again, but with menace this time.

"How should I know where the little shit is," said Guthrum, "get out of my hall before I turn my men loose on you. You are masterless men, we can kill you all right here, and no one will care."

The two warriors flanking Guthrum stepped forward and raised their weapons, but Sten did not hesitate. In a blur, he exchanged blows with the first warrior in a clang of iron on iron and shouldered the second attacker away. Einar took a quick step forward and smacked the blade of his axe into the throat of the second warrior and saw that Sten's foe had wheeled away wounded. Einar smiled a grim smile, feeling strong again, feeling himself.

The room erupted into a melee of shouting and pushing around him.

Einar took three steps between the crowd and reached forward to grab Guthrum by the throat. His guards were not close enough to intervene, and before they could react, Einar had him in close. Guthrum was flapping and clucking, so Einar hit him with the haft of his axe whilst Sten bullied back the rest of Guthrum's men.

"Tell me where Hakon Ivarsson has gone with the boy, and you can live," Einar said. Guthrum's men stopped fighting, and so did the Seaworm crew.

"Tell them to back off, or 'I'll open your pig throat," said Einar.

"Back off, back off," choked Guthrum, waving his arms at his men.

"Move to the back of the hall," Sten ordered them.

"Do it, do it," said Guthrum, becoming panicked. Guthrum's warriors shuffled backwards, and Wolfthinker went with them. Einar walked backwards towards the door.

'Now, where is he?' said Sten to Guthrum, now that there was a safe space between them and Guthrum's warriors in the hall.

"He... he went...." Guthrum gasped, licking his lips, eyes wide, "he went to his new lands. He left this morning with his men and three of my crews; one crew sailed your Seaworm up the coast."

"Was the boy with him?"

"Yes....yes, he was. Him and the whore princess."

"Where are his lands?" said Einar.

"North, close to Grimsby, a place called Fareton."

"Wait here," said Sten and turned back into the hall. "Wolfthinker!"

The old man skulked back into the light of the fire.

"What do you want, coward?" the old man said through gritted teeth. Sten tossed his axe towards him, and it clattered on the stone floor, echoing around the silent hall.

"Pick it up," he said. Wolfthinker stared at the axe and crossed his arms, jutting his chin out.

"Pick it up," Sten said again.

"Come on, Sten, we have to go," said Einar. Any minute now, Guthrum's crew would come swarming into the hall and butcher them, so if they wanted to get Hundr back, they had to leave immediately.

Sten stepped towards Wolfthinker, and Wolfthinker bent down and grasped the axe. Wolfthinker stood and held it before him, the weapon shaking in his bony arms.

"You've always wanted to kill me, Kjartan, so do it now. You have always cursed and boasted and stood behind the warriors with your witches and your Gods. You cursed my Ralla. Kill me now, you piece of shit," Sten said and started towards Wolfthinker. The little man raised the axe and let out a howl as he charged at Sten. Wolfthinker swung a blow at Sten's head, but Sten just caught the axe. He caught it and ripped it from Wolfthinker's grip, and grabbed him by the throat. Sten's meaty fist clenched hard, and his knuckles went white. The wiry little man croaked and shook in his grasp.

Sten pulled Wolfthinker backwards towards the Seaworm crew, then lifted him from his feet, slammed his head once into the cold stone wall, and dragged his limp body out of the hall. Einar released Guthrum and turned to walk out of the door. Guthrum backed away wide-eyed.

"Guthrum," said Einar, and as the Jarl turned towards him, Einar punched him on the nose, and as he fell, Einar grabbed a fistful of Guthrum's hair and hacked it off with his knife. Guthrum screamed as Einar sawed the blade back and to. Once the hank of hair came away, Guthrum crumpled to the floor, and Einar kicked him in the belly and spat on him. He could feel himself shouting and cursing incoherently, afire with rage. He kneed and punched Guthrum until the Jarl was whimpering like a child. Einar tore the Jarl's brynjar over his head, pulling and yanking until it came free. He clutched the brynjar and kicked the Jarl again. The Seaworm crew backed away from the hall and went back the way they had come.

"Why'd you do that to his hair?" asked Thorvald.

"I don't know," shrugged Einar. It had been pure uncontrollable hate and rage, and it had worked, and indeed, it had felt bloody good. He felt like a warrior again as he held Guthrum's brynjar close to his chest, the cold iron rings feeling like a fortune in his hands, like reclaiming his reputation. Thorvald nodded and shrugged his shoulders.

"Fair enough,' said Thorvald, "but what now,

Lord? We can't go back to the house. It will be like a nest of wasps before we can say Thor's balls."

The crew emerged into the open where the men Sten had assaulted earlier stood with weapons drawn.

"Your Lord needs you inside," said Einar, and the warriors dashed through the entrance, giving Sten a wide berth. Sten stood, chest heaving, with Wolfthinker still hanging limp in his grasp like a rabbit caught for the pot.

"We go get the Valkyrie. We need Ragnhild and her warriors," said Sten, "I'll meet you outside their quarters," and he stalked away, dragging Wolfthinker along with him.

"Where in Odin's name are you going now?" Einar asked.

Sten called over his shoulder,

"To see Ivar and Sigurd. I'll meet you there."

Einar stood and stared. What was the old fool thinking walking into the hornet's nest like that with Wolfthinker? Einar thought of going after Sten and then thought better of it.

"Where the bloody hel's he going now?" asked Blink, his head darting from side to side like a chicken and his eyes blinking at a furious pace.

"You don't want to know... come on, let's go," Einar replied.

"Go where? We've got to get out of here, Lord....Guthrum will send his men after us. We are dead men," said Thorvald, throwing his hands in the air.

"Let's go to Ragnhild and her Valkyrie. Come on," Einar said, and so they set off. Einar could hear the crew whispering behind him about Sten and how he had suddenly changed into a different person. He had indeed changed, and all for the better as far as Einar was concerned. He pulled the heavy brynjar over his head. It was too broad, likely forged for Guthrum's considerable girth. Still, he tied his belt around it and welcomed the familiar weight of the armour and the status it gave. Einar already felt the pain of his wounds lessen, and his back grew straighter. Bush scurried up beside him and grinned.

"Feels good, eh...?" he asked, nodding at the brynjar.

"It does," Einar replied.

"Some show back there, Sten was like an animal."

"Easier to see the legend in the man now and no mistake."

Bush nodded and glanced back towards Guthrum's hall.

"Hakon's gone now, right?"

"Yes, North."

"So, we got rid of one enemy, and we've just made another?"

"Guthrum was our enemy already; it was him and Hakon who set me up and lied to Ivar."

"Well, yes... but Lord... but, well, maybe now's the time to slip away..all quiet like?"

Einar frowned down at Bush. He was getting old like Einar. He had silver streaks in his beard and a face lined and creased like worn leather. Bush had sailed with Einar for many years, and he had tied his fate to Einar's. No family, no wife, living life on the sea following Ivar's orders. Einar supposed the men had the same worries he did about the future, where they had dreamed of settling down with Einar in his landed Jarldom and living out their years there. Yet here they were, they had nothing and no prospects. Still, there could be no running now. There was nowhere to run to. No, they would help Sten get Hundr back. There might be a good death in that, and a place in Valhalla, or maybe another opportunity would present itself, such as the chance to kill Hakon. That thought made him smile.

"No running Bush, we help Sten get the boy back. We're going to get Hundr and kill Hakon. We're going to kill that miserable turd of Loki and take his silver and his ship. So tell the lads, because this is how we'll get out of this mess, by doing all we know how to do... killing and taking what we can."

They did not meet any resistance as they passed through the streets of Yorvik. The Seaworm crew made their way through the west gate to the Valkyrie encampment. They had formed up as Hundr had taught them, with archers at the front and rear protecting the main body of warriors, small enough though their number had become. Finally, they came to the looming crumbling west gate of the city, outside of which was the Valkyrie Camp. Einar waited on this side of the gate for Sten.

Einar's face was still sore, and he touched it, flinching at the sensitivity. He opened his mouth wide to stretch it, which still gave him a perverse relief even though it hurt like Hel.

"How is it, Lord?" asked Thorvald, who leaned against the wall next to him.

"Better. Not sure there aren't bones broken in there somewhere, though."

"A few lumps and bumps will give you more character, Lord, make you look more fearsome," said Thorvald, grinning.

"A kick up the arse might give you more character." Einar winced again at the pain in his face as he smiled.

"Why aren't they following us?" asked Bush from further down the line, and Einar shrugged.

"Don't know. Guthrum has either gone to Ivar and found Sten there, or he has panicked that Wolfthinker might spill the truth of the lies about the raid in East Anglia and has left to join Hakon. Hard to say."

"He'll want to kill you, Lord, after you took his brynjar and did that thing to his hair. Hurt a man's pride that would," said Thorvald, laughing.

"He wanted to kill me anyway, and they would have killed me if Ivar had not forbidden it." Which was true. Only but for Ivar preventing it, Einar would still be in that piss-soaked ditch but with his throat cut.

They waited in silence. Much had happened that day, but it was not yet noon. The city was quiet, the Saxon inhabitants still lying low after the battle and the celebrations afterwards. Although it was almost Winter, it wasn't too cold, and Einar enjoyed the feel of the sun on his face whenever it broke through the clouds. It felt good to have a purpose again. He might be a masterless man, but at least he had a plan. Kill Hakon, take his silver, get the boy back. Then there was the Seaworm. The thought of Hakon at his steerboard, stood on his deck, enjoying the power and speed of that beautiful ship, was almost too much to bear. She would be there, at Hakon's new fortress, moored at a dock or in a bay somewhere. If he had the Seaworm, then anything was possible. Einar could sail and raid or pledge his loyalty to a Lord in need some- where, some embattled Jarl, knee-deep in a war and in need of men and ships. There were al- ways wars, and Einar was a man to fight them. All he had to do was get out of Yorvik alive, at- tack Hakon's new Saxon fortress and kill him, kill Hakon's men even though he knew not their number, steal back his ship and sail away. Either that or die trying. He looked down the line at his men resting against the wall. There were only six of them left now, but excellent fighters and killers all. Einar owed them for sticking with him when Halvdan and Kraki and the rest had be- trayed him; these men had stayed loyal. He owed them at least their ship back, or if not, then a good death.

Sten came from a shadowed lane and awoke Einar from his thoughts. He seemed to have mis- placed Wolfthinker on his travels but seemed none the worse for having gone to see Ivar and Sigurd.

"Well?" Einar said.

Sten leant against the wall.

"Any ale or water?" Sten said.

They passed a skin of ale up the line, and Sten took a draught. Einar waited until he had fin- ished, yet the delay in hearing what had taken place with Ivar, the consequences of which would impact their chances of living or dying, becoming excruciating. Sten finished and wiped his mouth with the back of his hand,

"Right then, let's go see Ragnhild," he said,

"Hold on... what happened with Ivar and the Snake Eye?" said Einar.

"Ivar knew his son had left, but not that he had beaten his Irish Princess and carried her off in chains."

"She's his wife; he can do what he wants with her."

"Not when her father's warriors have four crews with Ivar, he can't. Fierce Irish warriors to a man, who won't like that their Princess is all beat up and in irons."

"And?"

"Ivar loses four crews, war's over," said Sten.

Einar caught on at last. If Ivar's Irishmen knew how Hakon had treated their Princess, he would have a mutiny on his hands here in Northumbria and a war at his back in Ireland.

"So... what will he do?"

"I don't know," said Sten with a frown, as though the question was absurd.

"Well, what happened with Wolfthinker? What will Ivar do about Hakon?"

"I left Kjartan there. Who knows what Ivar will

do. He won't kill us, though. He owes me that much."

"What does he owe you?"

"A lifetime of fighting for his father."

Which Einar supposed was true.

They went through the open gate and out into the fields enveloping Yorvik, nestled against the two wide rivers which surrounded the city walls. The Valkyrie camp was to the West of the city but inside the wide turn of the river. It had been untouched by the Saxon attack because it was not visible from the Northern side from which the Saxon's had made their assault. And also, because the Saxons had been so focused on the massed Danes outside the city walls, they had paid its wings no attention. Just as when Sten and Hundr had visited for the feast before the assault on Yorvik, two Valkyrie warriors guarded the camp entrance.

"Will they help us, Lord?" asked Thorvald.

"Hundr saved Ragnhild's life twice, so she owes him." Einar shrugged.

"Do you think the lad is even still alive, Lord?"

"I don't know, seems strange to take the boy if you were going to kill him. Maybe he wants him alive? I don't know. If Hakon was going to kill him, he could have just done it when he caught him. Why wait?"

"Knowing Hakon, the little turd, whatever his reasons are, they won't be good ones," said Thorvald.

Sten approached the guards, who nodded at him and admitted the crew to the camp. Whether the Valkyrie agreed to help them rescue Hundr or not, Einar would go anyway. He would take back what was his or die in the attempt.

Sten and Einar sat on stools in the Valkyrie training ground, which was a long strip of open grass with targets for archery practice, and stacks of blunt spears and other weapons for combat training. The Valkyrie had brought food and ale, which the crew devoured, and afterwards engaged in archery and axe throwing practice with the Valkyrie warriors.

The Valkyrie camp contained tents used for sleeping quarters, the practice grounds, and then another space for sacrifices and prayers to the Gods. Northmen did not have the religious zeal that the Saxons and the Franks possessed for their Christ God. The Gods of the Northmen were all around them in their daily lives and squabbled and fought just like ordinary people. The Holy Men of the Svear at Uppsala, however, were different. They were devoted to Odin and the rest of the Aesir. They generated wealth and power from the Jarls and Kings who paid homage to the Gods at their great temple looking for favour in war, marriage, or crops. Einar had little time for worship and prayer, but he honoured Odin and Thor, and all sailors honoured Njorth from fear of drowning.

He sat on a stool and watched Sten pacing back and forth in front of him, fists clenched and jaw set. They were waiting for Odin's High Priest Vattnar, and Sten wasn't able to contain his impatience. Einar left the huge warrior alone; he was a man of few words anyway and didn't appear in the mood to talk. Meanwhile, the rest of the crew seemed happy to be distracted from the turmoil of the last few days as they spent time throwing spears and shooting bows, albeit to varying degrees of success. At least, it lifted the pressure and fear of Hakon and Guthrum hunting them. For now, they were within the security of the Valkyrie camp, and for that, Einar was grateful. His men had been through a lot, Hakon had brought him low with lies and deceit, and he had not seen it coming. Over half of his crew gone now, Einar knew he should have thought faster and fought better to protect them.

Einar used the time to sharpen his axe and knife, and he found a handful of rough gravel nearby to give his new brynjar a polish. After a while, Vattnar approached, flanked by Ragnhild. The High Priest was a tall man, though not as tall as Sten or Einar. Still, he was taller than most men and as thin as an oar. His head was bald, but what white hair remained around the edges grew long, and he had it tied back in a shimmering ponytail. He had a long white beard, tied here and there with charms and trinkets. Vattnar wore clean bleached white robes and carried the heavy ceremonial Gungnir spear of Odin. Sten nodded to Ragnhild, who nodded back in greeting. She looked as fierce as ever, her one eye glowering in her scarred face.

"High Priest Vattnar," said Sten and bowed his head. The rest of the crew stopped what they were doing, as did the Valkyrie warriors, and all bowed to Vattnar. Then, he motioned for them to return to what they were doing with a graceful wave of his hand.

"What news, Sten?" he asked, "you are more like Sten Sleggya today than yesterday, I think."

"Hakon Ivarsson has taken Hundr to his new Jarldom. They took him with violence," said Sten, getting straight to the point.

He looked at Ragnhild to see her reaction, and she shifted her stance, resting her hand on the top of the axe looped at her belt. Her face, however, did not change and gave nothing away.

"Is this Hundr, the man with a dog's name who fought back to back with Ivar the Boneless?" asked Vattnar.

"The same, High Priest," said Einar, "the same man who fought alongside your Valkyrie and caught the eye of Odin fighting many Saxons."

Vattnar turned to Ragnhild and raised a pointed eyebrow, but she kept her gaze fixed on Sten and Einar.

"I hear that you, Einar Rosti, are cast out by Ivar Ragnarsson and are now a masterless man," said the High Priest.

It flattered Einar that Vattnar even knew who he was, but then he supposed his fall and humiliation went hand in glove with Hakon's rise to Jarldom, and so it was the talk of the army.

"That is true, High Priest," said Einar, bowing his head.

"So, you and your men," Vattnar said, glancing at the Seaworm crew and drawing out the last word as he looked them up and down, "are outside of the law of our people, so Hakon Ivarsson can do what he wants with this Hundr? You know our laws as well as I, Sten Sleggya."

"He can," said Sten frowning, "I know the law. But I owe Hundr my life, such as it is, and I'll fight Hakon Ivarsson to get him back, if he still lives."

Einar watched Ragnhild, who also owed Hundr her life, but she remained still, and her gaze remained steady.

"So, you are not a thing of the Christ God any longer, Sten?" asked Vattnar.

"Meaning?" said Sten, in a low voice.

"You were seen wearing a cross at your neck,

not a hammer or a spear, but a cross,"

"No longer. I serve Odin as I did before," said Sten and his face became flushed, "You know me as Sten Sleggya, and so you know I sailed and fought with Ragnar Lothbrok, beloved of Odin. We went where Northmen had never been before. Always I fought at the front, always I struck first. I daresay I have earned my place in Valhalla, and I daresay I have my place among the Einherjer or in Thruthvangar, the hall of Thor. I daresay I have filled more than a few benches in Valhalla. Hakon Ivarsson does not strike with the blade; he works in the shadows and is a slaughterer of women and children. He is no drengr.' Sten looked to Ragnhild for support, but still, she remained quiet.

Einar did not recall Sten stringing so many words together before, but if he wanted Ragnhild and her warriors, then he needed Vattnar's say so, and he wouldn't get that by antagonising the indifferent Priest of Odin.

"What say you, Ragnhild of the Valkyrie, would it not catch the eye of the Gods if we were to take back Hundr who fights with the favour of the Gods? Is a life debt not owed?" Einar said. *No point beating around the bush.*

"Hundr is a warrior with Odin's favour, and if it were not for him, many of us here would be dead," said Ragnhild, deigning to speak, "Hakon

Ivarsson is not beloved of Odin."

Vattnar shot her a sharp look.

"Is that true?" he said, but she didn't reply.

"Look," said Sten, raising a thick finger and pointing at Vattnar, "are you going to bloody help us get the lad back or not?"

Vattnar peered at the finger and then tutted at Sten. For a moment, Einar thought Sten would attack the High Priest because he leaned forward, but sense prevailed, and Sten mastered himself.

"So, what do you want of the warriors of Odin?" asked Vatnarr.

Einar looked at Sten and saw the muscles in the jaw working as he clenched his teeth. *I'd better speak quickly before Sten makes us even more enemies.*

"We would have the warriors of Odin ride out with us to rescue Hundr. Let us do this bold thing and catch the eye of the Gods in Valhalla. The Great Army might fight no more now that King Aelle is Blood Eagled. The sons of Ragnar are kings here now, and there will be tributes of silver paid by the Saxons to keep the army at bay. The Ragnarrsons will keep this land, and it must therefore be settled. So that means waiting for ships in the Spring with families from Norway and Denmark, but no more souls for the Einherjer," said Einar.

"Tell me then," said Vattnar, "how would fighting Hakon Ivarsson further the cause of our Gods in their fight against the plague of the Christ God? How would it serve Odin All-father for his warriors to earn the enmity of Ivar Ragnarsson the Champion of the North by attacking his son?"

"Sometimes, you have to catch the Gods' attention. You who are the Priest of Odin are here in Northumbria to honour him by sending the souls of warriors to his hall," said Einar. He saw Vattnar's eyes narrow. *I'm on to something here.*

"What other reason are we here than to be the playthings of Odin and the other Aesir? If all we do is follow Ivar and camp here for Winter, settle farms and distribute land, does that amuse Odin? Does it cause Thor to give pause and look at what we are doing? You know more than most that as we speak, the great serpent gnaws at Yggdrasil in the depths of the Earth and Ragnarök will come upon us one day. So then who does Odin want in Valhalla or Thor in Thruthvangar? Does he want fat, rich farmer Danes? Or does he want warriors who sail into the unknown, warriors who fight when they are the few against the many, warriors who will stand in the front line when Loki and the frost giants fall upon the world of men? What great deeds are there left in this war, Vattnar? What tales of heroes and champions will you have to take back to Upp-sala?"

Now give me warriors and horses so I can drench myself in Hakon's blood and piss on his bones.

Vattnar nodded at him and stroked his beard.

"The All-father does indeed want the greatest of warriors for his host. You argue well, Einar Rosti. I will consider your request. Meet me here this evening." The High Priest turned to walk away. Ragnhild watched him go and turned to Sten and Einar.

"You have lots of enemies," she said.

"It has always been so," Sten shrugged.

"They will try to kill you before long."

"Many have tried, fiercer and worse bastards than these whelps."

Ragnhild smiled and clapped Sten on the shoulder.

"I like the new Sten, you are like a drengr now, old one. I will help you if I can, but we must wait for Vattnar."

As they waited for Vattnar's decision, the crew continued to practice with the Valkyrie, who supplied them with a steady stream of meat and ale, which all ate. Sten remained silent and grumbled in his direction when Einar laughed as he watched Thorkild lose at throwing axes again to Hrist.

"Thor's balls, these women are good," he said. Sten nodded.

'They are. That's why we bloody need them. Old bastard better come back soon.." said Sten.

"If he says yes, then we'll leave straight away. They have horses enough here. If he says no, then what?" said Einar. He looked across at the Northumbrian hills in the distance to the North. They rose in browns and greys towards a clear sky, where the sun sat low and warmed them despite them being well into Winter.

"If yes, then we go now as you say, we can follow the tracks Guthrum left as he rides to meet Hakon. But, if Vattnar says no, we go anyway," said Sten.

Einar looked at him and sighed. He stood and stretched, still sore from the beating he had taken, but he was feeling strong again now. He could raise his arms without his ribs burning with pain. He picked up a practice spear and hefted it above his head, and stretched with both arms, trying to loosen the soreness in his torso.

"Assuming Ivar has granted his worthless shit of a son a fortress or at worst a hill fort somewhere, then how should the six of us attack it?" said Einar. Sten stood and also picked up a training spear. He, too, stretched a little and then beckoned Einar to practice. They went through a drill with the spears of lunge and parry, high and low strikes. The shafts clicking and clacking as they struck, blunted blades flashing in the sunlight.

"You can break into a place without going through the front door," said Sten, panting and with beads of sweat springing out on his brow.

"Meaning?"

"We want the boy back, that's all; you're thinking we need to kill Hakon and all his men."

Einar stopped the drill and placed his spear butt on the ground.

"I want that bastard dead," he said with more venom than he had intended and lunged again. Sten parried and swung around the butt of his spear as though to crack Einar's skull, but he ducked to avoid the blow but was now off-balance, and Sten had a heel behind his foot, and he fell on his arse.

"If Vattnar doesn't help us, then we slip into the fort, take Hundr, and slip out. Catch Hakon off guard. If we get a chance to kill the bastard, then we take it," said Sten, reaching down to help Einar up.

Einar dusted himself down and nodded over Sten's shoulder; Vattnar and Ragnhild were approaching. As the High Priest drew closer, Einar could see dark blood splashed on his fine white robes, blood from the sacrifice, no doubt. Einar had never believed that these Priests could see the future in the entrails and organs of birds and squirrels. Vattnar was wiping the remains of whatever animal he had opened up from his hands with a cloth as he walked.

"Well, what does Odin say?" Sten asked.

"Thank you for waiting," said Vattnar. Einar thought the haughty bastard would talk down his nose if he didn't have to look up to speak to him and Sten. "You should know that Ivar Ragnarsson sent a man to me today asking why we are harbouring criminals. He wants me to turn you all over to him, and he will kill you for assaulting Jarl Guthrum and Kjartan Wolfthinker."

"But he also wants no trouble with the Gods. Otherwise, Ivar would have marched in here and taken us," said Einar.

"Likely so, Ivar does not command here."

"So, you talked with Odin?" asked Sten, gesturing at the bloodstains.

"One does not talk to Odin All-father. I made the sacrifice and hoped the Gods would hear me."

"Did they?" asked Einar.

"It seems you have caught their attention; the omens for your task bode well. Unfortunately, however, I cannot allow the Valkyrie to ride with you against Hakon Ivarsson."

"You mean you're afraid of bloody Ivar and do his bidding?" snapped Sten.

Vattnar frowned.

"I wish you luck in your quest, Sten Sleggya." The High Priest turned and strode away, leaving Einar staring at his back.

"That's it then," Einar said.

"Do not give up, Einar Rosti,' said Ragnhild, "Vattnar cannot support you, but he cannot stop me from riding out with you. Nine of my warriors and I will go North,"

Einar could have hugged her if he didn't firmly believe that she would cut his throat if he tried.

"You'd disobey the High Priest of Odin?" said Sten.

"I would repay a debt of honour to Hundr, and my warriors will help. Vattnar stays here with the rest to support the sons of Ragnar."

"So Ivar cannot blame Vattnar, and he can claim you have gone against his wishes," said Einar.

"Just so," said Ragnhild, "we ride to battle."

TWENTY FOUR

The afternoon was cold but bright as Einar and Sten rode North with the remaining Seaworm crew and ten Valkyrie warriors. It was a good war band; they had Blink, Bush, Thorkild, Thorvald, and the Kveldsson brothers. In addition, Ragnhild had brought on Hildr and Hrist and seven fearsome-looking warriors.

It had been a simple thing to pick up the horse tracks of Jarl Guthrum and his men. They had ridden out from Yorvik soon after Sten's attack. The large numbers in Guthrum's force had churned the roads to mud and horse shit led the way. It was cloudy but warm, with a breeze shaking the green treetops as Einar rode. The pace was easy; they did not want to catch Guthrum on the road but follow him to Hakon's new stronghold. Einar did not enjoy riding. He was a sailor, not a horseman. His arse was sore, and the insides of his legs ached already. They rode two abreast along the muddy roadway; Sten and Ragnhild led the column with Hrist out in front, picking up the tracks. Einar rode alongside Thorkild. He looked across at his shipmate and thought that he looked old. His grizzled golden hair had receded almost entirely from the top of his head. Einar could not recall how many summers they had sailed together. Their villages were close to each other in the south of Norway, where fjords rose from the cold seas and men either took to the sea to fish or to go Viking.

"What are you looking at?" asked Thorkild as he rode. He adjusted the bow slung across his back. Einar grinned.

"I was just thinking how young you look," he said, and Thorkild laughed.

"About as young as you, Lord, your face has more wrinkles than my grandmother's arse," he said. Einar smiled.

"So, we ride to certain death, old friend," said Einar. He had no right to be cheerful, given that he had lost everything and was likely riding to have his head caved in by some stinking Norseman. But Einar felt good; his troubles were behind him in Yorvik, and in front was revenge.

"Not for the first time, Lord. This time seems worse, though, I'll grant you."

"It does. Many of the lads gone, brave men. Halvdan." said Einar.

"Men we have sailed the world with, Lord. Shame how Halvdan turned out, the arsehole. He was always a miserable so and so. It was not your doing, though, that Hakon is a spawn of Loki shit and no mistake."

"We are not dead yet, Thorkild. They tried to take everything from me, from us. We'll kill that turd Hakon, might even get the old Seaworm back."

"Is that why we ride, Lord, to kill Hakon? Thought we were rescuing Hundr."

"We will help Sten rescue the boy, but if we get close to Hakon or Guthrum, then they die, I swear it by our dead brothers."

"We're with you, Lord. Remember, no man would like to have you as an enemy. You think you have lost your reputation, but you've not. I have seen you fight many times, in the shield wall, in ship fights, in the square. There aren't many who could stand against you. Apart from me." said Thorkild, and Einar smiled at his friend's jest. Thorkild was a great storyteller but no lover of the Holmgang square.

"I daresay we have earned our place in Valhalla, Thorkild. We are old now for warriors of the Whale Road. But, if it comes to it, then what better for us than to die with our axes in our hands and take our places in Valhalla with our ship-mates," said Einar.

"We're not dead yet, Lord. Let's get this done and see where the next ship takes us. Does anybody know where Hakon is and what we'll be facing?"

Einar had thought about that. Ivar would have granted his son a fine swathe of Northumbria, the fortress that commanded it would need to be high and stout.

"Ivar would not send his son to a shithole; it will be a fortress. He has his own crews plus those of Guthrum, so maybe six or seven long scores."

Thorkild blew out his cheeks.

"Good job there are six of us then, and ten of these blood-mad women,"

"They might be mad, but they fight well. We won't be fighting Hakon in a shield wall, and we don't need to kill two hundred of them. We just need to get in, kill Hakon and Guthrum and get out," said Einar.

"And rescue Hundr."

"Yes, and that."

"If we can get the lad free, it's like having another five men, Lord, you know that."

"Yes, you might be right, but he must be alive for us to rescue him."

"He's alive. No way Hakon took him North to kill him straight away; he has plans for the boy. What will we do, Lord, when this is over?"

Einar patted his horses' powerful neck.

"I had always thought Ivar would make me a landed Jarl, that we would stay on that land and settle down. Wives and children, all of us."

"Ivar wants to kill us now, Lord, so that's not happening."

"So now we get this done, we get our ship back, and we make our own destiny. We have always fought and raided and coughed up the majority to Ivar. Now we take some for ourselves."

I need one chance, just one chance, to get close to Hakon. Then, should I get a sight of him, no man could stop me from killing him. If I live, then I take my ship back. If I die, then I take Hakon and as many of his men as I can to Valhalla with me.

****

Hundr slumped against the pole, his bonds keeping him upright as he slipped in and out of consciousness. Some moments he was lucid and could see men milling around him at their daily tasks; other times, he drifted into the dream world. He watched as men worked to erect a fresh, bright yellow timber platform at one end of the open square inside the fortress. He coughed, and his ribs ached. As he raised his head again, the pain from the wound on his face made him retch again. Hundr heard movement to his left and turned to look. He had to crane his neck right around to see with his remaining eye. Hundr saw a short, squat man shambling over to him, carrying a bucket of water sloshing with the man's rolling gait. He also had a bowl of food, Hundr could smell the meat, and his belly gurgled at the prospect.

"Got to feed you up," the man said through blackened broken teeth, "Keep your strength up for the big show," he said and cackled. The man lifted a ladle of water to Hundr's lips, and he drank.

"More," he croaked, and the man laughed again and gave him more. Finally, after five more ladle fulls, Hundr could feel the sweet coolness of the water flowing down his neck and revitalising his body. The man then spooned the bowl of stew into Hundr's mouth.

"What's the show?" Hundr asked between spoonfuls.

"The Jarl must bless his new land. There must be an offering to Freja and Odin," he said.

"What offering?"

"A blood offering to please the Gods, a man and woman together for a good harvest."

A man and woman. Hundr knew what that meant; Hakon planned to sacrifice him and Saoirse. Hakon would make a big show to keep his men happy and to copy his father's famed Blood Eagle. Hundr had to get free. He pulled and twisted at his bonds, and the man laughed.

"No way out of those sailor's knots, boy, them ropes won't break. Made for long voyages, they are. Too strong for a cut-up whelp like you," he said and cackled again as he shuffled off.

Hundr coughed. Too much food and drink too fast. He thought he would vomit, but his head fell to his chest, the darkness of the dream world overtaking him again.

Hundr found himself again tied by hand and foot, but this time, however, it was not a post. Instead, it was an enormous tree. The tree was monstrous, and as he looked downwards, he could see a dark and shrouded plane below him to a distant horizon. As he looked up, he could see an airy plane stretching out parallel to the shrouded lands below. This was Yggdrasil, the tree of life, the tree that bound the worlds together. He heard a crow caw and felt hard talons gripping his skin and realised that he had a raven on each shoulder. He was Odin, pinned to Yggdrasil with Hugin, and Munin sat on either side of his thought and memory. Odin had sacrificed an eye for a drink of the pool of knowledge. Hundr could sense his Odin mind sprawling across what was and what would come to be. He tried to force Odin to look into his own future, but the God just laughed, a booming and terrible sound. Hundr felt himself expelled from the mind of the God. He fell, tumbling past Yggdrasil's huge branches, past the screaming terror of the Hel world, and he glimpsed the hulking form of Fenris Wolf, chained and snarling. Hundr looked down and saw the coils of the great serpent Nithhog gnawing at the tree, and its cold eyes turned to him, and he could not bear its gaze. He screamed and fell into blackness.

TWENTY FIVE

A slanting shower of fine rain spat across the hills and dales turning the road and tracks into a muddy mess, making it more difficult to follow Guthrum's tracks. They passed some small farmsteads and asked the owners if they had seen the horsemen; the farmers shaking and wide-eyed just pointed to the North East. The Vikings had not yet raided that part of Northumbria; otherwise, the farmers would have fled for safety along with their valuables and livestock upon hearing the hoofbeats of Guthrum's force. They travelled all day, and as evening drew in, Ragnhild ordered a halt, and so they dismounted and made a makeshift camp in the shadow of a great hill covered in tall grasses and topped with pale rocks. The grassy hill made for excellent fodder for the horses, and the band could use bunches of the long grass stalks to rub their horses down and made small fires to dry their boots and clothing, which were soaked through.

Sten had fidgeted and grumbled all day. Einar knew Sten just wanted to get to wherever Hakon had Hundr, he needed to know the boy was alive, and every minute meant another minute during which his friend could face torture or death. After some debate, they had persuaded Sten to accept the need to camp for the night. It was treacherous to ride at night, and they would risk injury to the horses. Ragnhild had sent Hildr and Hrist on ahead to scout for sight of Hakon's new Jarldom. Those two were excellent scouts and would travel fast and unseen by Guthrum's men. Ragnhild was sure that they would be back early the next day with news on Guthrum's progress, and Einar hoped they would have the location of Hakon's fortress.

Einar warmed his hands at a small fire. The damp bark was giving off more smoke than he would have liked, but on a wet evening like this, he would rather be warm and dry and fight a horde of Saxons than be cold and wet waiting for news of their enemies. Sten had finished rubbing his horse down and came to sit.

"Seems as good as place as any to camp," he said, groaning as he sat.

"Hildr and Hrist should be back early tomorrow," said Einar, adding another damp branch to the fire.

"It'll be good to know what we're up against."

Sten delved deep into his pack and pulled out a fist-sized crust of bread, which he tore in two and handed half to Einar. Einar nodded his thanks.

"It will be some sort of walled fortress. If Hakon is to rule this part of Northumbria, then his fortress will be formidable. It has to be to keep the Saxons at bay once the war is over. We won't be able to attack it with this force."

Ragnhild joined them and sat cross-legged. She shivered and held her hands out, enjoying the warmth.

"We were talking about Hakon's fortress; we won't be able to assault it," said Einar.

"Hildr and Hrist will tell us more tomorrow if they have been able to find it," Ragnhild said.

"It surprised me, Vattnar allowing you to ride with us," said Sten. He passed a horn flask of ale to Ragnhild, and she took a draught.

"He didn't openly allow it, remember. Our duty is to serve Odin," she shrugged, "so we go where the fighting is."

"If we kill Hakon, Ivar will know the Valkyrie were here; he will want vengeance against you," said Einar. The fire crackled, and its quivering glow passed shadows across Ragnhild's scarred face.

"If we kill Hakon, then yes, Ivar will want blood. However, he won't come against the temple at Uppsala because Vattnar will condemn my riding with you. Also, I don't think Ivar would want to risk the wrath of Odin. He won't simply refrain from doing something, though. If you both live, then the Boneless will hunt you to the ends of Miklagard for killing his son," she said, grinning.

"Ivar has other sons," said Einar, "his eldest son Ivar Ivarsson is in Ireland minding Ivar's lands there. He has another son then fostered with a Sea King Jarl in Jutland. Hakon is a shit weasel; he is better off dead."

"Ivar will still want something, though," said Sten.

"He will," said Einar.

"So, tomorrow when Hildr and Hrist return, hopefully, they have seen the fortress, and we can make a plan to get into it somehow. We are here to get Hundr out, not to kill Hakon and Guthrum," Ragnhild said, fixing Einar with her one fierce eye.

"You and Sten can rescue the boy. I must kill Hakon and Guthrum for what they did to me."

"Maybe we can get in and out without killing either of them, then there is no feud with Ivar," said Ragnhild.

Einar finished his bread and washed it down with a swig of Sten's ale. He stared into the flames as they danced and flickered, and a light breeze blew across the camp.

"All my life, I have tried to live as a drengr, to follow the warrior's code," said Einar, "I daresay I had a reputation as a fighter and a man of honour. I have served Ivar well, and I was his loyal hound. Ivar would send me to do his dirty work, to punish people, to make sure Ivar was respected, and those sworn to him kept their oaths. He gave his Seaworm to me, a beautiful ship cut from the finest forests in Norway with curves and lines fine and true as though carved by the Gods. He made me a Sea Jarl, a position of honour and respect. That bastard Hakon was always jealous. He longed for Ivar's approval, but his father despised him for his weakness. So Hakon conspired with Guthrum and likely with Wolfthinker. Hakon wants to build his reputation, so he raided East Anglia and blamed it on me. They took me by surprise and beat me, took my weapons and my brynjar and humiliated me. They would have killed me, but Ivar would not allow it. So now I have no Lord, no ship, just this handful of warriors to show for a life of fighting. For that, Hakon and Guthrum must die, you can rescue the boy, but they will die for what they did to me."

"Very well, I won't stop you, Einar. What say you?" Ragnhild asked Sten.

"Don't care. I've got to get the boy out. If we have

to kill them all to do it, then so be it."

"He means a lot to you," said Ragnhild.

Einar watched the old man's lips curl inwards together against his teeth, and Sten dipped his head.

"I never had children. We tried, Ralla and me, but it never happened. She always wanted a child. I know the lad can sometimes be a pain in the arse, but he saved my life and yours too. He's the closest thing I'll ever have to a son. I won't let him die in some Saxon shithole so that Hakon bastard Ivarsson can emulate his father's bloody torture spectacles to build his reputation."

Einar and Ragnhild nodded and watched the flames dance. They had eight members of the Seaworm crew left and ten Valkyrie warriors. Einar knew it wasn't enough, but maybe they couldn't get into the fortress and do what needed to be done. This was all he had left, so he would help Sten get the boy Hundr out, and once in the fortress, he would kill Hakon even if it meant he would go to his death doing it.

"If we get this done, and we get out alive, what will you do then, where will you go?" asked Ragnhild. Einar smiled.

"I haven't thought that far ahead," he said, "my ship might be there or somewhere close. If my Seaworm is there, and if I can, I will take her and sail her away."

"Where, though, do you have a wife or children?" she asked.

"I had a wife once, when as young as Hundr. She lived with the other women in Ivar's lands back in the North, but she died of the pox. Had no children. I was never in any place long enough to settle down. What about you?" As shameful as it was, Einar thought little of that woman. It had not seemed important back then, not as important as being with the crew and doing the work of a drengr.

"What about me?" said Ragnhild frowning.

"Didn't you ever want a husband or children?"

Ragnhild laughed, throwing her head back.

"I am devoted to Odin and to battle. Valkyrie do not think of such things."

"Well, if you ever change your mind..." said Einar, grinning, and Ragnhild laughed again and kicked out at Einar. She was as heavily scarred and as tough as any warrior Einar had ever known. Thor help any man who asked to settle down with Ragnhild.

"Sten, what will you do if we live?" Ragnhild said.

"I've lived both lives, the life of the warrior and the life of peace with my Ralla. I'm here now, returned to the warrior's life. I'll free the boy, then who knows. Maybe Einar needs an old man to help pull an oar. I broke my oath to her and to the Christian God. So I'm stuck in this world now, no chance of getting to heaven."

"You would be more than welcome aboard. We can always use a living legend to help with the rowing."

They sat for a while longer, comforted by the fire. Einar thought about the fight to come and about his life. He hoped the Gods were pleased with the fate the Norn's had woven for him. Maybe they were. It had all come down to this. Whatever awaited them, however formidable the fortress, they would win, or they would die. *Maybe we will catch Odin's attention. Odin, let me have my revenge.*

Sten, Einar and Ragnhild sat astride their horses at the edge of a bracken covered wood filled with tall spindly trees. That wood stretched across a hill throughout the valley from the larger rise where Hakon's fortress perched. It was a log palisaded fort built atop an earthen mound surrounded by a ditch. Einar thought it well placed overlooking the land around and out across the river to enable an early view of attacks from the sea. The wide river Humber wound lazily around the contours of the hills at the valley bottom and meandered away to the East.

"It's a stout-looking place," said Einar, "they can

see anyone approaching for miles around."

"So they can. We just need to figure out how to get in," said Sten. The three looked in silence. Hildr and Hrist had found the fortress and reported that Guthrum and his men had entered the day before. The Seaworm sat in the river, moored at a planked jetty below the fortress with its beast head snarling towards the fort. Einar looked out over the valley spreading below them. There were some wooded areas dotting the valley defile and thick hedging separating small farmsteads. Then up the gentle slope of the hill was clutches of thatched wattle and daub buildings.

"We can make our way through the valley and remain hidden," Sten said as he nudged his horse up a slippy bank.

"We are eighteen warriors; they will see us," said Ragnhild.

"The villagers will notify the fort as soon as they spy us," said Einar.

"We could travel through the valley at night and get over the walls as the sun comes up," said Sten, but Einar knew he was right, and they could not do it that way. Sten must have known it too. He stroked his beard with his free hand and frowned.

"We are only thinking of going at it straight on. The way into this place isn't with a heavy hammer. It is with a bit of cunning," Sten said.

"This is no time for riddles. What do you mean?"

"We should head downriver, find a boat to carry us as though merchants or fishermen heading for the sea. We go as night is falling and then jump ashore in the dark. Then we can get to the walls before the sun comes up. Bastards won't see us. They won't even be looking," said Sten.

Einar laughed and clapped him on the shoulder.

"Seems like a good plan to me, you wily old fox."

"How do we catch a ship?" asked Ragnhild.

"Same way you catch anything, with a trap. But more likely with silver," said Sten with a shrug.

They travelled back through the eerie quiet of the skinny trees and skirted in a wide loop around the valley, and headed back towards the river, being careful to stay undercover as much as possible. Ragnhild had Hildr and Hrist ride ahead, looking for any danger and dropping back at intervals to ensure the group went by the safe and unseen paths. Riding in the open would allow any local Saxon spying warriors on the loose to notify the fort, and the game would be up.

"We are Danes, people are afraid of us. We look the same as the men in the fort," Einar had said, and so it had proved to be.

Anybody they had seen had fled or hid behind their doors. Once they had reached the river-bank, they followed it until they reached a tiny fishing village. It comprised of five hovels with woven netting spread wide to dry between posts sunk into the earth. The village sloped onto a shale beach with one small coracle for river fishing, but it also had one larger vessel for sea fishing. They anchored it just beyond the shale, and she had a short mast and four oars. Men from the village greeted them cautiously, their eyes standing bright against their deep brown wind burned faces. Those men came stinking of fish and scratching at the lice in their matted hair and beards. Sten and Einar had tried to converse with the fishermen as best as possible. The men spoke the Saxon tongue but could pick out a few of their Norse words. They offered the men all of their horses and whatever silver they could put together between them, which was a few pouches of hack silver. That offer would make the fishermen the richest men in their valley. Einar wanted to just take the ship by force, but Sten said that the fishermen or their families would scamper away upriver to the fort, and he was probably right. The fishermen were dumbfounded at their new wealth and were initially reluctant to part with the larger ship, but once Einar began shouting and waving his axe, the negotiation became simpler. Sten and Einar waded out to look over the vessel with Blink and

Thorkild.

"She is no beauty boys," said Blink, picking at black slimy mould on the hull.

"More like an old scrubber," said Thorvald as he felt the lines of her caulking.

"She's caulked, and the ropes look alright," Einar said, which was true. These men make their living catching and selling fish, so they looked after their ships. "She will do to get us upriver."

"Thank Njorth we don't have to take to the Whale Road in her boys," said Blink.

"She is not the Seaworm," Einar said, running his hand along the bow.

"I miss the Worm," Thorkild said, shaking his head.

"We all do. She was a beautiful ship."

Einar thought of the glorious lines of the Seaworm again as he held the tiller of their new wide bellied fishing boat. They sailed up the Humber, allowing the slow summer current to pull them along. How he loved his old ship. She was close. All they had to do was sneak into a hilltop fortress to kill Odin only knew how many men, get out alive and recapture her. Simple.

"Let her out a bit, Bush," Einar called, and Bush let the heavy wool sail out so that it bulged in the light wind just enough to carry them waddling upriver. They had all stowed their mail coats and weapons in the bilge, wrapped in an old half-rotten sailcloth to protect them from the foul water which sloshed around the ballast stones. Ragnhild turned to him.

"Will it be dark before we pass the fort?" she asked.

"Almost, we will pass it just as the sun is setting," he said, "they won't be able to make us out. We will just look like another dark outline of a fishing boat heading out to deep water. Make sure you all cover your hair," he called to the Valkyrie.

They had huddled as low as possible, but their fair hair would be a sure giveaway, and so they would throw another old sailcloth over the warriors as they passed the fort. Ragnhild called over Hrist and Hildr to come and sit with Einar and Sten.

"Tell us what you saw," she asked the scouts.

"We got close enough to the walls," said Hrist. "It was easy, no one saw us."

"It is a ditch and earth bank topped by a palisade with a fighting platform where the guards stand. There is a gate facing to the south and a smaller one to the north with a path leading down to the river where it rounds around the valley," said Hildr.

"They must use it for collecting water," said

Einar.

"We could wait for them to open it and force our way in," said Ragnhild.

"They will have guards there. So it will be too easy for them to raise the alarm," said Sten.

"We could not see how many were in the fort, but it is large," said Hildr, "maybe four crews in there, a long five score. They don't have anyone patrolling the walls."

"They must feel safe," said Einar.

"There is a wharf on the Eastside, but only one ship," said Hrist.

"The Seaworm, my ship," said Einar. Even the thought of other men sailing her around the Saxon coast to Yorvik had troubled him, but that Ivar had given to her to Hakon was unbearable.

"They are confident in their numbers and feel safe. So what we will do is this..." Sten said, and they listened to his plan.

"You have done this before," said Einar.

"Many times, my friend, many times," said Sten, "they are confident and arrogant, so don't have guards, so they won't see us, and we can be in and out before they even know it. We might not even have to kill anyone."

"That would be a shame," said Ragnhild, and they laughed. *We will have to kill many*. Once they were inside, Einar would find Hakon Ivarsson and kill him, and if possible, Jarl Guthrum would also die. That would bring the warriors out in force. Einar ardently hoped it would be a sword and spear day, a blood day.

"If they see us, and there is a fight…" said Hildr.

"Then we make the shield wall," said Ragnhild, "and we make a song for Odin's hall."

"Once we have Hundr, we make for the North gate, then down the hill," said Sten.

"If the boy lives," said Einar. No doubt if Hakon had brought the boy all this way, then he had some sort of Ragnarsson torture in mind, and it could already be too late.

"What if he's already dead?" said Ragnhild. Sten looked at each of them carefully.

"Then we slaughter as many of the bastards as we can," he said, "we take their silver, and their weapons, we take their arm rings and their brynjar, and we put them in the ground."

"I like this plan better," said Ragnhild. Einar did not want to see the boy dead, but he would kill his enemies either way, no matter what they agreed here. So, the Valkyries would get their wish, and there would be a slaughter.

As the sun went down, the fishing boat continued its ponderous journey along the wide river. Earlier in the late afternoon, Einar had dropped the stone anchor to make sure they did not approach the fortress whilst there was still pleasant light. Once the day waned, they hauled the stone aboard again and carried on their way. The Valkyrie warriors crouched in the bows, keeping their fair hair and weapons out of sight. The sun was setting behind the fortress on its hill, and it cast a red glow over the valley. Its burnished orange reflection shimmered beautifully on the river. They had rounded a bend in the water and were in sight now if Hakon had posted any sentries. Einar stared at the fort, its grey silhouette stark against the orange band the sun cast across the lower horizon and the dull iron of the sky above. He could see heat glowing within the place; fires had been lit to keep the warriors warm. More than likely, they were drinking and feasting to celebrate Hakon's new Jarldom. *Drink you bastards, drink yourselves stupid.* The Valkyrie had made a black paste from riverbank mud and Thor knew what, and they spread it now over their faces and hair and wherever they showed bare skin. Einar and his men also applied it. The paste stank of mud, soot, and shit, but it was a good idea to make themselves as dark as possible and blend in with the night.

"We will be like the Huldufolk, the hidden people of the deep forests and mountains back home," said Thorkild as he smeared his face. Einar watched Sten apply the stuff on his bare arms, his muscles writhing as he worked.

"We are going around the fort now; seems like we have escaped their interest," said Einar.

"I think so. I don't think they saw us," said Sten. "Let's double back now, to that rocky outcrop we saw at the bank back there."

As they had entered the fort's valley and the river bent northwards, they had noted a useful mound of rocks which tapered into the river and where they could leave the boat and wade ashore. A low hillock covered in hedge and gorse would keep the boat out of sight from the top of the hill. Einar gave the order, and they came about in the river.

"Cover your weapons. Cut up the old sailcloth there. Wrap the steel, any glints of moonlight might give us away," Sten said. The Valkyrie warriors moved like cats, keeping low below the sheer strake. They cut the old cloth and wrapped their weapons and those of the Seaworm crew.

"You know all the tricks, grandfather," said Bush.

"Experience, that's all," Sten said, "a sentry will spot the moon glinting off an axe or spear blade."

"When we go, we stay together. Do not break off into groups," said Ragnhild. She had applied the dark paste to her face, and it made her one eye shine bright against the darkness. "Hildr and

Hrist will go over the wall first and open the small gate. Then, once we are inside, we should wait in the shadow of the walls whilst they scout the inside of the fort," she said. Sten nodded.

"A good plan. We don't know what awaits us inside those walls," he said.

"Once we have found Hundr, we can free him and get out of there," said Ragnhild.

"What about Hakon?" said Einar.

"What about him?"

"You all know I want to kill the bastard, I won't be leaving this place whilst he lives."

There was a silence.

"First, we get the boy, then we see," said Sten.

Bush and one of the Kveldsson brothers rowed the boat in close to the rocky outcrop, and they dropped the anchor. Bush hefted the thing, which was just a big rock tied around with rope, and got it as close to the river surface before dropping it in to avoid a splash. The crew then slipped over the side into the knee-deep water and waded to the shore, and began the wet footed trudge up the hillside towards the fort. Traversing the hill was difficult in the darkness, and more than once, someone slipped and cursed, only to be hushed by another. Finally, once they got within sight of the glow of the fires inside the fort, they huddled together, lying low.

"Let's go now," said Einar. He could feel the anger welling up in his belly already. He was ready to fight; his enemies and his ship were all within touching distance and there for the taking.

"No, we stick to the plan and go as the sun comes up," said Sten.

"Do it now. Bastards will be drunk, and we can get in and do them whilst they snore," Einar insisted.

"Stick to the plan," Ragnhild hissed, "we wait for the sun to come up. Night fighting is bad, bad for us and bad for them."

Einar shook his head. He could taste his revenge, and the sweetness of it made him impatient.

"Let's wait there," said Ragnhild, then pointed over to a straight row of hedging which separated two fields and which would keep them hidden until the sun rose. So they kept low and moved over to the hedge where some sheep huddled there. They drove them out of the way and used the warm, dry ground the sheep had left to curl up under their cloaks and try to sleep.

Sleep did not come for most of them, but some were lucky and could get a few hours of rest. Brownlegs had gone out like a flame, and it had forced Einar to kick him awake more than once when the rumbling rhythm of his snoring grew too loud. Einar watched the horizon as birds became visible, flitting above the tree line on the opposite bank. Eventually, the sun seeped a wan slither of red light above the horizon and pushed back the night.

"Red sky in the morning, shepherd's warning," he muttered, pulling his cloak around him. It always seemed colder after a night without sleep. "Looks like rain, lads. Time to go."

They readied themselves and began the climb up the hillside towards the fort. Hildr and Hrist had been right, there were no sentries on the walls, so they reached the ditch without a problem. The war band scuttled up the ditch's bank, keeping low, and hauled themselves over its ridge. Einar thought the place was old and not in good repair, its timbers looked rotten in places, and the road leading to the gate was overgrown with weeds. They dashed across the hilltop, hoping that the waning darkness and the favour of the Gods would keep them hidden. Einar ran in a low crouch and sat panting with his back against the knotty staves of the palisade.

"All sounds quiet inside," said Einar.

"Sleeping off the ale," said Sten.

"Hildr, Hrist over the wall and let us in," said Ragnhild, and the two Valkyries checked their weapons and readied themselves. They had bow strings tucked behind their belts to keep them dry, and bending their curved bows behind their legs, they hooked the strings over the horn tips of their recurved bows. Hildr and Hrist slung those bows across their backs and tucked axes in their belts, ready to grab when needed. Sten and Einar were the tallest, so they stood with their backs against the palisade and made cups with their hands. The two women placed their feet in the cups, and on a count of three, the men launched them upwards. Hildr and Hrist vaulted themselves at the same time and grasped the top of the wall. They scrambled upwards and disappeared over the top.

"So, it begins," said Ragnhild, flashing a grim smile beneath her mud smeared face.

TWENTY SIX

They huddled together and listened, but no sound came. It felt to Einar like they had waited half the night for a sound that Hildr and Hrist were working their way through the fortress. But he supposed no sound meant they were doing their work successfully, and he tried to be patient. Einar and the others shuffled around to the point of the wall where the small North gate stood and waited. Sure enough, after the sun rose on its journey across the sky, they heard a wooden catch lift, scraping against its latch, and the door opened.

Einar went in first. He looked left to see Hildr with her hand over a warrior's mouth as he bled out from a cut throat; the dark blood sheeted from the terrible wound and poured down his light brown leather breastplate. The rest of the band filtered in, and before they closed the gate, Sten dragged the dead warrior outside and left him beside the ditch.

"We will wait behind that building," said Ragnhild, pointing her spear at an extensive structure backing onto the rear wall.

The two scouts nodded and headed off, running low to the ground. They had their bows in hand with an arrow each nocked and ready to shoot. The group waited, leaning against the building. Although there was still no noise and no alarm, they heard some coughing coming from the west, and a dog barked somewhere to the North, but the barking stopped with a squeal.

"Nothing surer than an arrow in the throat to shut up a noisy dog, boys," said Blink, and there was a low chuckle across the line. The sun had crept up beyond the walls now, and the early red light had settled into a dreary overcast morning. Einar saw the first of a few raindrops landing on his boots. Then, as the rain spots turned into a drizzle, Hildr and Hrist returned.

"They have Hundr tied to post in the central open square, fifty paces from here. No guards, everyone is sleeping," said Hildr with a grin.

"Right, let's go. We will guard the square, and you free him, meet back here when it's done," said Ragnhild. They nodded, and Hrist led the way. The Valkyrie jogged towards the square and Ragnhild whispered orders, sending her warriors around the perimeter. Einar took the coverings from his weapons as he marched and watched the vast back of Sten moving before him as he also took the coverings from his axe blade. They walked between dripping buildings and emerged then onto the square. It was wide and open, and the ground was turning to mud in the rain. At one end was a platform of which its golden fresh wood gave away its newness, and in the centre of the square was a post to which the pitiful shape of a man was tied and slumped.

"Hundr," said Sten and surged forward. The Valkyrie were in position now, and the Seaworm crew followed. As they reached Hundr, Sten knelt to lift Hundr's face by the chin, and they all gasped.

"What have they done to you," growled Sten.

Einar thought he heard the big man's voice catch in his throat, and he looked with horror at the ravaged mess that was Hundr's face. Bruising had swollen the left side of his face to twice its normal size with a blood-red, blistered cut running from his forehead to his chin and where his eye had once been, there was an empty, angry puckered socket.

Sten drew his knife and cut the boys bonds; as he started cutting, a shout went up from somewhere in the surrounding buildings. The outcry was cut short by a sharp thrum from a Valkyrie bow. Einar turned to that sound and saw a warrior fallen to the ground and another enemy warrior feathered with three arrows. The Valkyrie closed in on the centre of the square. As they moved, they stayed in a crouch with the bows strung, all the time facing outwards with their arrows threatening any enemies who showed themselves.

"That's it now, lads, ready yourselves because the bastards will be on us soon," said Einar drawing his axe and knife. Sten lay Hundr in the mud and stood with axe and knife drawn. In haste, Hakon's men poured to the square now that the first shout of alarm had peeled out.

"Kill them all," growled Sten as he lay Hundr in mud and strode forward. The black paste streaked across his face by the rain, twisting his features into a demonic snarl. Three men were stumbling from a building befuddled from last night's ale; one of them fell with an arrow in his chest, one ducked and scrambled back into the building, and the third shouted, holding up his hands. Sten ran towards that warrior, two arrows flew by him, and one hit the man in the shoulder, and he spun around. Sten leapt up a step to the building and backhanded his axe into the falling man's face, and did not break stride as he charged into the building.

"What now, Lord?" asked Rollo Kveldsson, panic in his voice.

"Stay, lads, hold fast. Our best hope is to form a shield wall here," said Einar.

"We didn't bring any shields, Lord," said Bush.

"We can make the wall behind your belly then," said Blink, and the warriors laughed. It was always this way with warriors. At the moment of most peril, they would still find a joke. The Valkyrie were close around the Seaworm crew and were firing at any enemy who showed themselves. Shouting and screaming came from the building into which Sten had charged, and then all went quiet as Sten came back through the door. He flung a shield towards the crew and then threw three more, each skidding on its side in the mud. Sten stalked back across the square, his axe dripping blood and his face set against the chaos of enemies swirling around the edges where they shouted threats. Yet they hung back, waiting for the brave amongst them to attack the invaders.

"Odin preserve us," said Thorkild, watching Sten.

The old warrior had blood covering his forearms and splashed across his brynjar, and his face was still a fearsome mask of black mud but now streaked with blood. Brave enemy warriors gathered at the North end of the square, calling for their comrades to stand with them. Those warriors advanced with spears levelled, and shields overlapped to make the shield wall. There were five of them, and they came on, peppered with Valkyrie arrows as a reward for their bravery. The Valkyrie took up the shields Sten has thrown and made a small wall in front of the archers facing to the North. Shouting reverberated around the fort, and a metallic bell was clanking. Soon Hakon and Guthrum themselves appeared and stood open-mouthed, gaping at their attackers. Magnus No-Ear shouldered past the Jarls bellowing and waving his giant double-bladed war axe.

"Well, well, look who joins the festivities," shouted Hakon, "Einar the masterless and a ragged band of whores and outcasts."

Magnus strode forward, roaring to his men.

"Shield wall on me. Listen to me bastards, fall in on me." He twirled his axe around as though it were as light as a wand, and warriors gathered around him, locking their shields together.

"I am Magnus, and this is Warbringer," he shouted, pointing his axe at the invaders.

"We need more shields," said Einar. Ragnhild ignored him.

"Form line on me, you four form up to our rear so we don't get outflanked. Then, you four form a line behind and pour arrows into them," she said.

The Valkyries formed up without hesitation.

Sten knelt with Hundr again, cradling his head and trying to catch rainwater in his hand and pour it into his friend's mouth. Einar felt his blood rush; his enemies were all here. His stomach tightened, and his knuckles whitened on his axe handle.

"This is it, boys. I want those bastards dead, but to do it, we need to get through that wall," Einar called to his men. He walked forward and joined Ragnhild's line behind the four shields. Magnus came on. He had formed a shield wall ten men across, with more now joining them in the rear. Magus was shouting and clashing his axe on the shields around him

"Brace yourselves," shouted Einar.

"For Odin and Valhalla," screamed Ragnhild, and the Valkyries let out a blood-curdling scream. "Loose," she shouted, and the archers let loose at the advancing men. They closed to ten paces, and Einar set himself for the clash, but Sten knocked him aside, roaring as he went.

"Come and fight, come and fight with me, come and die," he shouted and elbowed past the line and broke into a run.

"Mad bastard," said Bush.

"Don't break the line," Ragnhild shouted after Sten.

A spear flew from behind the advancing enemy

line, but it sailed over Sten's shoulder and thudded into a Valkyrie shield. Sten smashed into the enemy shields shoulder first and drove them back, weapons struck at him, but his bulk drove him through, sending Magnus spinning and then he was among them slashing with his axe and shouting. Einar bared his teeth and surged forward.

"They are in the open kill them, kill kill kill," he shouted and ran to cut at an enemy's face with his axe, blood splashing into the rain-soaked mud.

The others heard him and charged forward. If the shield wall breaks, pour into it and get amongst the warriors. The panic will drive them to flee and slaughter whoever breaks first. That was shield wall warfare. *I am drengr, and this is where I belong.* He slashed at another man and then ducked as Magnus No-Ear's axe whipped over his head; Einar kicked the big man towards the Valkyrie and charged forward again. He cut and slashed at the attackers and could see Sten circled by warriors afraid to close on him. Sten was begging them to come and die, and bodies lay dead or dying on the surrounding ground.

Magnus No-Ear was laying about him with Warbringer. The enormous axe arced low and sliced through Rollo Kveldsson's belly and chopped deep into the shoulder of Jari Kveldsson. Einar cried out as his men fell, brothers gone forever.

Two more Seaworm men were dead. There was a pause as warriors stepped back from a flurry of blows exchanged and the clang of steel on steel. Einar turned to see Ragnhild fighting Magnus No-Ear. Magnus stood head and shoulders taller than Ragnhild, but what she lost in size, she made up for in skill. Blades whirled and clashed, and Magnus was bullying her backwards, yet Ragnhild parried or swerved away from his blows. Finally, she got inside the reach of his axe and cut across his belly with her knife, but he dropped the axe and lifted her by the throat, head-butting her twice. Einar thought she must die, but then someone attacked Magnus with fist and feet and screaming. Magnus dropped Ragnhild, and she rolled away, rising again without hesitation to swing her axe in a wide circle, slicing at the warriors around Magnus. Einar wiped the rain from his eyes. It was the boy Hundr who had attacked Magnus.

Hundr had awoken to the sound of weapons clashing and the noise of battle. Forcing his remaining eye open, he saw fighting in the fortress square. It took a few moments for his mind to understand what he was seeing, but as the haze cleared from his eye, he saw Ragnhild and Einar Rosti fighting against Hakon's warriors, and then he saw Sten swinging an axe with his eyes wide and bright with battle fury. *How can this be, Odin?*

Have you answered my prayers? He was no longer tied to the post; he was free. Hundr staggered to his feet, his bare feet sliding in the mud. As he steadied himself, he saw that Magnus No-Ear had Ragnhild in his grip. *What was she doing here?* He closed his eye, and the vision of Magnus gripping and dragging Saoirse flashed before him. The blood fury welled up within him, coursing through his body with new power and strength, the strength of vengeance. Hundr howled to the heavens and threw himself, charging at the giant Magnus. Hundr could feel himself screaming, but he couldn't control it.

There were warriors around him, yet none attacked. He slammed his elbow into Magnus' kidney, and No-Ear dropped Ragnhild and swung a ponderous arm around. But he was all size and power, not speed. Hundr felt the strength flow through his body like molten steel. *He is slow, and I have the speed of the Gods.* As the arm went past him, Hundr smashed the heel of his hand into Magnus' throat, and he choked and clutched at his neck, then Hundr aimed a savage kick into his groin and shouted into Magnus' face as he dropped to his knees. He jumped at Magnus and plunged a thumb into each eye, gouging and tearing, gripping his gigantic head and forcing the thumbs deep until the jelly gave way. No-Ear screamed like a wounded pig and fell, writhing on the floor with blood pouring down his face.

He looked up from the bloody mess of Magnus' face and watched as Ragnhild disembowelled one enemy and twisted past another's spear, slicing her axe down hard on that man's arm.

A warrior screamed a challenge and rushed from Hakon's side into the fray. He was running hard towards Hundr; that warrior was Kraki Horse Face, the Seaworm traitor. In his fury to reach Hundr, he had not considered how close he had gotten to Ragnhild. She tripped Kraki Horse Face, and as he landed, arms splayed in the filthy mud, she buried her axe in the back of his skull.

"Sten, Sten Sleggya," Hundr shouted, and his friend turned to him, and amongst the welter of battle, Sten smiled. Hundr stooped to pick up Magnus' double-bladed axe and threw it towards Sten, who found himself surrounded by enemies. Warbringer landed on its side and skidded, splashing through the square's churned mud. Sten charged an enemy out of the way and dropped his own weapon to take Warbringer from the ground, and he swung it around, forcing his enemies backwards. Sten grinned and beckoned them onto his new axe. Hundr himself knelt and scrabbled in the mud to pick up two axes from the ground nearby, dropped by a Valkyrie warrior who had fallen to Magnus' attack. Hundr beat the two axes on the earth and then stood with the weapons held wide in challenge. At last, there were enemies to kill, and the torture was over, so he ran forward to embrace killing, to make them pay for all that he had endured, all that Saoirse had endured.

Hundr moved among the enemy warriors who had sprung to life now after the shock of seeing Magnus fall. He slashed and cut, ducked and weaved. He cut the legs from a man and picked up his fallen sword, dropping an axe. As he closed his grasp on the sword grip, he wept from his remaining eye, the salt tears mixing with the rain as it coursed down his ruined face. The grip was twisted around with leather, and the feel of the sword in his hand was overwhelming. The joy of battle washed over Hundr, and he had a chance now to achieve that which had been impossible. *Where is Saoirse? Is she alive?*

Hundr could hear Hakon shouting shrill orders over the din of the battle, and his men moved back and organised into a new shield wall. Sten edged backwards towards Hundr, and once he was clear of the fighting, he grabbed Hundr in a tight embrace, his enormous arms feeling like home and warmth. Hundr allowed himself to press his face into his friend's chest. *Thank you, old man, I have been a fool, and you have come for me.*

"What have they done to you, my boy," Sten said.

"You came for me."

"I couldn't leave you here with these whoresons, could I?" said Sten. Hundr saw Einar and Ragnhild marshalling their remaining force into a circular shield wall as enemy warriors surrounded them. There were only ten of them left now, of the Valkyrie and the Seaworm crew. Many had fallen in the battle, but more of the enemy lay bleeding in the rain and blood churned mud.

"Shields, archers there," said Ragnhild, pointing to the top of a stable where two enemy archers knelt and began shooting, but the Valkyrie raised shields just a moment too late. A Valkyrie warrior fell with a shaft in her throat, and Thorkild cried out as an arrow slapped into his thigh.

"Bastards have us now," said Einar.

"Stop," came a shout from behind the enemy shield wall. Hundr peered over the Valkyrie shields, and to his horror, he saw Guthrum had Saoirse by the hair. She was in a soiled and soaked brown dress, and her face looked swollen and bruised.

"Throw down your weapons, or she dies," shouted Jarl Guthrum. Ragnhild looked at Hundr snarling, but he shook his head.

"We won't be throwing down our weapons," he said.

"We have done well; we are only outnumbered three to one now," said Einar, grinning. He was right. They had killed so many of Guthrum's and

Hakon's men that the odds had shifted.

"That's still terrible odds," said Thorkild through gritted teeth as he cut the shaft from the arrow in his leg.

"If we can kill Hakon or Guthrum, the rest will fold," said Sten.

"Drop your weapons," shouted Guthrum again. Hakon shouted and berated his men to move closer to the Valkyrie shield wall. "This is your last chance, drop them now, or the Princess dies, and we will butcher all of you," called Guthrum, "surrender now, and we will let you live."

"Why don't you come and fight, fat man, show your men how much courage you have," shouted Einar.

"Hakon Ivarsson, how much courage do you have? I will fight you now, man to man. Show your men what kind of Lord has their oath," called Hundr.

"I'm going to gut you, worm," said Hakon as he drew his sword Soulstealer, the gift from his father. Her blade shimmered blue as he held her aloft and joined his men in the shield wall, which edged towards the Valkyrie wall.

"They are only ten paces away now," said Einar, "a little closer, and we can charge them."

Hundr watched Guthrum. He was sweating and looking around him, calling to his men waving and wheezing.

"He's panicking. He is going to kill Saoirse," said Hundr.

"Let them get closer, and we will charge," said Ragnhild.

But he could not wait. Hundr took two steps and launched himself over the Valkyrie shield wall and ran towards Saoirse; he ran along the face of Hakon's shield wall and then skidded in the mud once he reached its end.

There were enemy warriors who stood with weapons drawn around the square, but Hundr believed these men were not fighters. They were afraid and would wait until the real fighting was over and then might join in to hack at their enemies. So as he reached the end of the shield wall, he ignored those men.

An arrow whipped past his face, and he moved into a running crouch. He then heard the thrum of Valkyrie bows behind him firing at the enemies on the rooftops. He took a few more steps forward and saw Guthrum's eyes widening as he watched Hundr get closer. Saoirse cried out and twisted in Guthrum's grip, she wriggled free, but Guthrum caught her hair and dragged her back. Guthrum stabbed with the knife, slashing down her forearm, but she pulled free again and fell to the ground.

Hundr dropped his sword and passed his axe

to his right hand, which he threw overhand, with all his strength and pain channelled into the throw. The axe spun through the raindrops and sunk into the broad chest of the Jarl. Guthrum staggered backwards and slumped to the ground, pawing and gasping at the weapon. Hundr ran again towards Saoirse. A warrior had stepped in front of her and swung an axe, but Hundr rolled underneath it and reached her. He turned and grabbed the axeman's arm on the backswing and hip threw him into the mud. He followed the man's fall, kneeling on his chest and clawing for the knife in that warriors' belt. The man scraped at Hundr's face, but he got the knife free and stabbed it in short bursts into his guts and through the leather breastplate. The warrior's arms gave way, and Hundr rolled free to grab Saoirse. She clung to him, cradling her wounded arm. There was not an enemy close to him now, and he was behind Hakon's shield wall.

He saw that Sten and Einar had charged Hakon and were hacking at his shields. Ragnhild followed up with the remaining Valkyrie, and there was a savage fight there in the rain-soaked square. He held Saoirse tight, and she put a hand to his ravaged face, her warm, gentle touch felt like a salve, but it was not over yet.

Einar charged shield first and smashed into the enemy shield wall with all his weight and strength, but they held. So he used his axe to hook down the shield of the warrior in front of him. It came down a fraction, enough to see a red-bearded grunting enemy behind it, and Ragnhild's axe tore across that man's face. She screamed in defiance as she reached over Einar's shoulder to land the blow. The fighting here was fiercest where he and Sten held the middle of the line, and they were hard-pressed. Einar heard a scream to his left and saw that another crewman had fallen to a spear thrust. More enemies joined Hakon's shield wall as he shouted orders at the timid men who had stood back on the edges of the fight.

"Time to get out of here, the boy is free," shouted Ragnhild over the din.

"No, no retreat. Hakon must die," said Einar, hacking at the shield wall again. Each time his axe thudded into the enemy's stout wooden boards, it sent a judder up his arm.

Ragnhild ignored him and gave the order. The Valkyrie made backward steps. Then, as the shield walls disengaged, neither side pressed the other. Einar edged back but couldn't let his revenge slip away now.

"No, Hakon must die. I want that bastard dead," He couldn't leave whilst that worm lived. Guthrum was dead, Magnus was dead, but Hakon yet lived. Einar's men and the Valkyrie edged back along the path they had used to enter the square and were almost at the small gate now. *Odin, bring me battle luck, grant me vengeance, and I will give you my axe this day for your Einherjer.*

Einar glared over the iron rim of his battered shield and watched as Hildr and Hrist darted around the enemy shield wall and reached Hundr and Saoirse. They sped back across the square's western edge and formed a rearguard behind the Valkyrie and Seaworm shield wall, and they moved back towards the small gate which led to the river. They moved between the stables and followed the route they had taken into the fortress. Hakon and his men followed and threatened but did not attack. Einar had no choice but to follow Ragnhild's orders and moved back in quick steps in time with Bush and Blink, who flanked him. Sten had been there, but he had dropped to the rear with Blink taking his place, bracing himself on his bow legs. Two enemy warriors tried to block the gateway behind them, but Sten was there laying about him with his blood-drenched axe to clear the way.

Hildr opened the gate as Hakon shouted for his men to attack and kill them all. The space between the stables was too narrow for a shield wall, and so the enemy warriors came on in pairs of two. The gate was open, and the Valkyrie and remaining Seaworm crew poured out into the open. Sten and Ragnhild were fighting the attackers in their pairs but were being pressed backwards.

"Go, Ragnhild, get everyone away. I will hold them here," said Einar, wiping sweat from his brow between attacks.

"We go together or not at all," she said.

"Go," bellowed Einar. A warrior lunged a spear, and Einar turned it aside and smashed his axe down through the man's parry and into his shoulder. He kicked the falling warrior into the path of the attackers and created an obstacle for them to get over before they could attack. Ragnhild ran out of the gate, and they were all clear except for him. He couldn't go until Hakon was dead, even if he had to kill a hundred warriors to make that so.

"Where is Einar?" asked Thorkild. There were only eight of them left, including Saoirse. Hundr couldn't answer; he had Saoirse and had to get away from the welter of death inside the fortress.

"He holds the gate," said Ragnhild.

"Did he fall?" asked Thorkild, but the group all shrugged. Thorkild limped back towards the gate, but Ragnhild grabbed his shoulder.

"He won't be coming out of there if he isn't with us now," she said, "we need to go while he blocks the gate. They can still charge out of the south gate."

Hundr had a tight hold of Saoirse and was moving down the hillside led by Hildr and Hrist.

"What now?" asked Saoirse, eyes wide with terror. She was limping and cradling her wounded arm. Hundr was supporting her, but he could barely support himself. They were heading downhill towards the long jetty and a ship. But not just any ship. They were headed towards the Seaworm.

Einar held the gate, and Hakon's men shrank back from his fury. It was too small a space for them to rush him, and to do it, they would have to clamber over the bodies of the fallen and knew that Einar's axe would be there waiting to take them to the afterlife. He could see Hakon behind the first line of his men, shouting and screeching and pointing but not fighting.

"Hakon, you stinking coward, come and fight, come and die!" he challenged, but Hakon did not come forward. Einar took the risk of a glance over his shoulder and saw Ragnhild, Sten and the others racing down the hill towards the Seaworm. He felt a pang of regret that he might never get to take her to the open sea again, to enjoy the power of her speeding through the wind and spray, for to kill Hakon, he must die here in this gateway.

"Archers, archers, someone get a bow and kill this bastard," he heard Hakon calling, "Get up on the walls, surround him."

Einar saw a stocky man in a bucket helmet forcing his way through the crowd of warriors, clutching a bow. This was different. They could pick him off where he stood with a bow, and he would never get to Hakon. Warriors were also clambering up the walls, from where they could lunge spears at him or simply drop over the other side and surround him. Einar knew it was over; he would not get to kill Hakon that day. He would be dead in moments.

"Bastards!" Einar bellowed, and snatched up a fallen shield and slung it across his back, turned and ran down the hill towards his beloved ship. He might not get to kill Hakon, the filthy turd, but he would get to sail in his boat again. He heard the enemy clamouring and shouting behind him. An arrow shaft whipped past his head, and Einar instantly tucked his head into his shoulders and quickened his pace. Another shaft thudded into the shield on his back and knocked him over, but he leapt back to his feet and pushed ahead.

Einar was puffing as he ran, his teeth bared and heart pumping. He was almost at the crew and could see Blink waving him on. Then, a long low sound rang across the Saxon hillside. It rose in pitch, paused and then sounded again—a horn. A horn to sound a ship's arrival. Einar tore his eyes from the Seaworm and looked to the river beyond. Sure enough, there were two Longships rowing across the still glassy surface. One of those ships was enormous; he only knew of one such ship that size. He looked and saw a raven banner fluttering from her mast.

Ivar had come.

Hundr saw the ships approaching. He was in touching distance of the Seaworm, heartbeats away from escaping. He gripped Saoirse's hand tight; she looked at him and then back at the on-coming warships.

"Odin's balls, it's Ivar," said Bush.

They were on the jetty, and the Seaworm was right there. But to board her now meant they had to slip past Ivar's ships which would be im-possible without Ivar being able to board and at-tack them. Hundr's head dropped. The Gods were cruel to play this last trick when he was so close to freedom.

"What now?" Saoirse asked again.

"The ship, untie her, let's go!" shouted Einar as he drew closer, panting from his dash down the hillside. Bush went to untie the mooring ropes, but Sten stepped across him.

"Leave the ropes," Sten said and twitched War-bringer, blood dripping from her twin blades.

Bush looked back to the others and then back to Sten.

"What are you doing? We must go now!" he said, his face drawn long with panic.

"We stay," Sten said, his face implacable.

There was no time to argue the toss now, for Einar had reached them gasping for air, and Hakon's men had poured out of of the fortress and formed up at the end of the jetty. Hakon walked ahead of his men, grinning, his annoying smug grin, the same grin he had on his face when he took Hundr's eye. It was too much to bear.

Hundr took his arm from Saoirse and stepped away; she looked at him puzzled, but he couldn't explain. He had a chance now to be avenged on Hakon, to bully the coward. A chance to fight now that there was no way out for Hakon if challenged, not without carrying the shame of cowardice with him for the rest of his days. His men and his father would all see him refuse the challenge.

"Hakon, son of Ivar," Hundr called and walked towards his enemy.

"Throw down your weapons, whelp, we have you now," Hakon said, his eyes gleaming with triumph.

"I challenge you to fight Hakon. You and I here in front of your men and your father," Hundr shouted as loudly as possible, so all could hear the challenge.

Hakon laughed and shook his head.

"Why should I fight you? I have won; you are mine!"

"If you don't, then you are a coward and a nithing. Your men will know it, and your father has always known it." Hundr hoped that would push the bastard to fight, and sure enough, Hakon licked his lips and looked around him, but his men just watched him. There was no way out for Hakon now.

"Very well, turd..." he began but stopped and grinned as Hundr heard a thud behind him.

Ivar's ship had reached the jetty, and men had jumped ashore, Ivar foremost among them, his two famous swords drawn. Big Irishmen landed heavily on the timber jetty, clad in their long plaid cloaks and armed for battle.

"Sten Sleggya," Ivar said. Hundr saw Cormac, the white-haired leader of Ivar's Irish warriors, flanking him.

"Ivar," nodded Sten. Sten rested his axe haft down on the jetty and wiped the blood from his face with his hand. A tiny figure jostled and shoved its way through Ivar's men, and in a jangling of trinkets and talismans, Kjartan Wolfthinker came to stand next to his Lord.

"All the rats in a trap," Wolfthinker said, grinning beneath his long grey beard.

It seemed it was over. Hundr saw Einar look from Ivar to Hakon, and fearing Einar would attack Hakon and steal his revenge, Hundr spoke out.

"I made a challenge. You and I, Hakon Ivarsson. Will you shrink away from the fight because your daddy is here to protect you? You are a coward and child and are nothing without your father, you nithing."

"The challenge is made," Ivar said, shrugging his shoulders.

"Kill the worm," said Einar.

I intend to.

Hakon swallowed hard, he looked again to his men, but there was no help there, and so he stepped forward and raised his new sword to fight. Hundr smiled. He felt all of his pain and troubles lift and float away. This was what he knew, what he was born to do. If he was to die here on this Saxon shoreline, he would first send Hakon screaming from the world. So he stepped forward with his sword and axe raised, ready for vengeance.

Hakon looked like he might cry, his face drawn and his sword unsteady. He looked to his father again for one last chance to avoid the fight, but seeing no way out, Hakon charged, screaming at Hundr. It was a clumsy attack. Hundr parried the sword with one axe blade and tripped Hakon with his sword. Hakon sprawled on the jetty and cried out in panic. He flipped onto his back and was about to raise his sword, but Hundr slammed his axe into his thigh and stabbed the tip of his sword into Hakon's shoulder. Hundr tore the blades free, and Hakon screamed and sobbed, writhing in pain and holding a hand out towards Ivar. He turned and crawled towards his father, leaving a smear of blood slicked on the dark planks of the jetty.

"Father, please, help me. Father!" he begged.

Hakon had left his sword Soulbringer on the jetty, so Hundr dropped his weapons, blades thudding on the wooden planking, and picked up Hakon's sword. As Hakon crawled away from him, Hundr reversed the blade and stabbed Hakon through the back of the neck. He thrust the blade with so much force that the tip went straight through Hakon's neck and stuck into the wood below. As the blade passed through Hakon's body, Hundr let out a cry. He felt the raw animal sound leaving him, a release of fury and anger and hate. Hakon made a gurgling sound and died as he should have, without a blade in his hand and forbidden from Valhalla. Hundr looked across to Einar, who nodded.

"He killed your son," came a shrill shout, "let's kill these spawns of Loki where they stand and be done with it. Kill them, Lord, kill Sten!" it was Kjartan Wolfthinker who was hopping from one skinny leg to the other, shaking his staff at Sten and Hundr.

All eyes were on Ivar, but the Boneless displayed no emotion. Instead, he stood still, staring at his son's corpse. He put a hand on Wolfthinker's shoulder.

"Quiet Kjartan," he said, "it will be over soon. Now Sten, let's have this done with," Ivar beckoned to Sten, and the old warrior nodded.

Saoirse had stood with Sten whilst Hundr fought Hakon, and Sten whispered something to her which Hundr couldn't make out. She turned to Hundr and gave him a wan smile, and a tear rolled down her cheek. She left Sten's side and walked towards Ivar, and Ivar held out his hand, smiling.

"Saoirse!" Hundr said and took a few paces towards her, but Sten lifted Warbringer across his path.

"What... what are you doing? Where is she...?" Hundr said, but he could barely get the words out.

"Let her go. This was the price of your life, yours and Einar's men," Sten said.

Hundr looked at Sten, searching for a sign that this was surely not true, but all he saw there was a coldness in his friend's face.

"What are you talking about... Saoirse!" Hundr called after her, but she stood with Ivar now. Ivar kissed her forehead and turned to Cormac.

"See, it is as I said it would be. She will be my wife, and I restore the peace," Ivar said. Cormac nodded and pointed his spear at Hakon's lifeless body.

"He's paid the price for hurting our Princess, we agree, Lord, the peace is restored," said the Irishman.

Ivar gave Saoirse's hand to one of his men, who put a fur cloak around her shoulders and led her back towards Ivar's ship. Hundr started forward, but Sten stopped him.

"We arranged it, laddie, can't you see? For you, Einar and others to live, Ivar had to have his Princess. It had to be that way for Ivar to keep his Irish warriors. If he lost them, the war here was all but over, and there would be war back in Ireland. Hakon broke the peace when he beat her, and once the Irish knew he was going to kill her, Hakon had to die."

"You did this, Sten, when you went to Ivar," said

Einar.

"Why... we are friends?" said Hundr. He dropped to his knees. She had gone without a second look. Perhaps it was her duty to her people, or maybe she hadn't loved him after all. Hundr couldn't tell. Who could blame her after all the suffering he had brought upon them? But Sten, how could he have done this to him, and when did he make this bargain with Ivar?

"You saved my life, but I was happy before you and Einar came to my home. I've had to break my oath to my woman and my God. I won't see her in heaven now. What I've done here is give you your life, so learn from it. Life is hard, reputation isn't worth shit, and no one is your friend. So take what you can, when you can and trust no one," Sten said and turned to Ivar. "Let's finish this."

Ivar nodded and took a step back, and Sten hefted Warbringer. Then, without hesitation, he brought her around, turning in a circle and with a scything backswing, he took Kjartan Wolfthinker's head. The head toppled and bounced on the jetty, spurting blood into the water, and Sten kicked it into the river. Next, he spat on Wolfthinker's corpse and kicked that into the water as well.

Ivar nodded and sighed.

"So it's done. Sten, you will come with me as agreed. Einar, my old friend, the Seaworm is yours. Go where you will. If I see you or this pup again, I'll kill you both myself." Ivar smiled and turned on his heel, and stalked back to his ship. Sten followed, resting his enormous axe on his shoulder.

"No," said Hundr. It couldn't end like this, not with this betrayal.

Hundr stood and gripped Soulstealer. He pointed it at Ivar.

"I killed your son, and he died weeping like a child. He was a coward and a nithing," Hundr said.

"Leave it… we have our lives and the ship, let's go," said Einar, reaching out to put a hand on Hundr's arm to stay him.

Hundr shrugged it off, clenching his teeth.

"I challenge you, Ivar Ragnarsson, I killed your worthless and son, and I will kill you too,"

Ivar stopped and turned, his face no longer calm but twisted with anger, odd eyes burning under a furrowed brow.

"Very well, pup," he said and hefted his two blades.

"This was not…." said Sten, but Ivar waved him away.

"The challenge is made. Get back," Ivar said, and his men moved back towards his ship, and Sten shuffled backwards.

Hundr moved forward, but Einar put a powerful arm across his chest and thrust him backwards.

"Hold him," Einar said to Ragnhild, and she grabbed Hundr and held him tight.

"No!" Hundr called, twisting in Ragnhild's grip. She held him fast with arms as strong as iron. Einar turned and faced Ivar.

"I'll fight you, Ivar, for my humiliation and for a life's service cast into the midden pit. The boy is wounded and has suffered at the hands of your hel whelp, but I am healed."

Ivar grinned and beckoned him on.

"Come then, Einar Rosti," he said, and his blades flicked out like the tongue of a mighty serpent.

"This is my fight!" Hundr shouted, still wriggling in Ragnhild's grip, but she held him fast.

Einar edged forwards, leading with his shield and with his axe ready to strike.

"Gut the bastard," growled Bush.

Ivar lunged forward with eye-watering speed, and the tip of one of his blades rammed Einar's shield point, first thrusting it back into Einar's body, crowding him. Ivar's second blade then thudded down onto the rim of the shield, hammering it down. Einar dropped to one knee just in time to avoid Ivar's blade whipping a cut in the space where Einar's throat had been. Einar roared and charged at Ivar, trying to bang him with his shield, but Ivar sprang back as light as a feather, and Einar almost tripped. Ivar twirled his swords and raised to his men behind him, who cheered. Sten was one of those men now. Hundr could still not understand what had happened, how had his friend could have gone over to Ivar.

Einar came on again and attacked Ivar with a flurry of axe blows, but Ivar parried them. It looked as though Einar was getting the better of Ivar until Ivar slammed both swords on one side edge of Einar's shield, driving it wide, and then lunged with speed almost too fast to see. Before Einar could recover, Ivar's blade was in his belly.

Einar dropped his blade and sank to the jetty, hunched over the iron in his guts. Ivar looked at Hundr, smiled, and then pulled his sword free. Einar slumped to the side, his blood spilling across the narrow planks and on into the river.

"Lord, no!" shouted Bush and dashed forward to drag his Lord back from Ivar's reach.

Hundr shook off Ragnhild's grip. Faced with losing everything again, he stepped forward.

"No, Hundr, let it go now. There's been too much death today," she said, but he ignored her.

"Are we done here?" asked Ivar, waving his

sword across all gathered at the water's edge. On the landward side were Hakon and Guthrum's surviving warriors, and on the seaward side of the log jetty were Ivar's men. Most of those had stayed on their ships, but a few had jumped ashore with their Lord. Sten was there also, silent and baleful, watching as his plan unravelled before him.

"See now what your cunning had wrought," Hundr called to him.

"It had to be this way, for you to live," shrugged Sten.

"You are Ivar, son of Ragnar Lothbrok, and your son lies dead from my hand. You have taken my woman and turned my friend against me...." Hundr snarled at Ivar.

Ivar snorted a laugh,

"Your woman? She was never your woman, you fool. She is a Princess of Ireland and could never be with a worthless bastard like you. And your friend Sleggya here.... he came to me. It was Sten who told me where you were going and what I must do to save my war. So my son is dead, I have a new wife, and my Irish warriors stay here in Northumbria. Sten got to take Wolfthinker's life as revenge for the curse he put on his wife. The world is cruel, boy, and you must be as cruel as it is. Sten was right; this had to happen as it has this day."

"Maybe you are right, but you are wrong about one thing. I am not a worthless bastard. My father is a Prince of the Rus, my home in the East is the city of Novgorod the Great, my mother was the daughter of a great Viking Jarl. So I will kill you now, Ivar the Boneless, and go back to my people as the slayer of Ivar Ragnarsson."

Hundr raised Soulstealer; she was a beautiful blade forged by the greatest smiths in Frankia. She was perfectly balanced, and her blade gleamed almost blue as he held her before him. He had lost an eye, he had lost his woman and his friend, but he had a chance now to win the greatest reputation of all, to be known across the world as the slayer of Ivar the Boneless. He knew he must adjust for his lost eye, he would be vulnerable on that side, but the sword felt like power in his hand. A lifetime of training had brought him here. A lifetime of rejection by his father because his mother was a concubine and not a recognised wife.

Ivar came on, his blades whirling and lashing out with inhuman speed; Hundr swayed away from one strike and parried another. Then, rapidly, Ivar struck low, and Hundr lifted his leg, allowing the blade to hiss by. Then he attacked himself, all his pain and fury in those blows, pressing Ivar backwards. The self-satisfied grin had gone now, and Ivar's jaw set firm. Hundr even thought he saw sweat on the champion's brow.

"You have grown slow, Ivar, too slow to be the Champion of the North," Hundr said.

Ivar snarled and came on again, and the world seemed to slow. Everything, including Ivar, moved in slow motion. All was slow, but he was fast. Hundr dodged away from Ivar's attack, the blades fizzing around him. Even on his blind side, Ivar could not get close to him. Hundr stepped in and head-butted Ivar, and the Boneless reeled away. Hundr followed him and slammed Soulstealer hard close to the pommel of one of Ivar's blades, and it fell with a clatter onto the wooden jetty. Ivar was off-balance, so Hundr kicked him, and the Champion fell on his arse, skidding backwards.

Hundr knelt and picked up Ivar's fallen blade.

"Is this Hugin or Munin?" he said, "I hope it is thought and not memory. When I kill you now, I gain a reputation, and with your sword, I gain the cunning of Wolfthinker, Sleggya, or Ivar."

Ivar roared with rage and surged to his feet. He lunged at Hundr with all his might channelled into that one huge disembowelling blow, but Hundr parried it with Soulstealer and swung Munin at Ivar. The blade slashed across Ivar's chest, breaking the links in his brynjar and cutting the skin beneath in an angry red wound. Ivar fell back, and Sten leapt forward and grabbed Ivar, dragging him away.

"What are you doing? No!" Ivar bellowed.

"You must live, Lord," Sten said, and then looked across to Hundr, "and you must go, sail away with Einar and Ragnhild. You kill Ivar, and they'll hunt you forever."

Hundr leant his new blade against his leg and placed a hand over his good eye, so it seemed that he saw now through his dead blind eye.

"I see you all," he said, looking around at the gathered warriors, "Remember me. The dog who is a Prince of the Rus, the man who defeated the Champion of the North, the man who killed Hakon Ivarsson," he said. They all just gaped at him open-mouthed.

"I see you all with my Odin eye. I see your lives and your deaths. Any man who attacks us now dies. My blade will drink his soul and send him screaming to Niflheim."

Hundr let his hand fall and watched as Sten dragged Ivar backwards, the mighty son of Ragnar thrashing in his grip. Sten pulled Ivar towards his ship, where Saoirse awaited him.

Hundr watched the coast of Northumbria retreat into a haze beyond the glitter of wave peaks where the coastline met the horizon. The wind blew cold and stung at the lurid wound on his face, and his empty eye socket leaked fluid onto his ravaged cheek in long tears. The Seaworm's sail snapped taught as the ship tacked to cut North, away from the lands of the Saxons and away from Ivar's vengeful fury.

Einar and the remaining men of the Seaworm's old crew gathered at the steerboard, where Einar Rosti stood tall at the tiller, held up by Bush. His strong hand kept the long sleek power of the Drakkar warship on its course. Einar's face was strained and pale, his terrible wound bound tight by Hrist, he had insisted on steering ship away from Northumbria even if it killed him. Ragnhild sat next to Hundr. She had sung a loud and sonorous song to Odin as the crew and her surviving Valkyrie warriors rowed the Seaworm upriver and out onto the Whale Road. Oars were stowed and oar holes filled with their circular timber plugs. For now, they just headed North, with no decision on their destination other than that. North, back to their homelands.

"Was that true, what you said back there?" said Ragnhild.

Hundr looked across at her; she was cut and swollen from the battle. Blood had begun to crust on her hands and face, only some of it her own.

"Which part?" he said. He wasn't sure why he had looked at the enemy warriors through his dead eye. He hadn't planned or thought about doing that. It just happened.

"About Novgorod."

"Yes."

"So you are a Prince of the Rus?"

"My father is. I am his bastard."

"Will you go there now?"

He could go home, back to his father, but he knew in his heart that he had never been welcome there. Growing up as an unwanted bastard had been a solitary and hard way to spend a childhood. Hundr had no great longing to return to that place, all it held for him was sadness. His father had given Hundr only one thing, his skill with weapons.

"No," he said.

"Where then? Ivar might have agreed with Sten that you could kill his son to save his war, but he won't forget that you beat him. He will hunt you."

Hundr supposed that was true. He clenched his teeth and looked across the vast grey sea. When he had made the journey south, it had been as a boy, innocent of the world with thoughts only of glory and reputation. He had been forsaken by the woman he loved and his only friend, and together they had turned his heart into a stone. Hundr left Northumbria with two good swords, and he had defeated the Champion of the North in single combat. He had lost an eye and his heart, but he had gained a reputation. So he would sail with Einar, and they would do the only thing they knew how. They would fight.

BOOKS IN THIS SERIES

The Viking Blood and Blade Saga

The Wrath Of Ivar (Book 2 In The Viking Blood And Blade Saga)

If you like Bernard Cornwell, Giles Kristian, David Gemmell, and Griff Hosker you will love this epic Viking adventure, packed with battles, treachery, blood and gore.

866 AD. Saxon England burns under attack from the Great Heathen Army. Vicious Viking adventurers land on the coast of Frankia hungry for spoils, conquest and glory.

Hundr and the crew of the warship Seaworm are hunted by Ivar the Boneless, a pitiless warrior of incomparable fury and weapon skill.

Amidst the invasion of Brittany and war with the Franks, Hundr allies with the armies of Haesten and Bjorn Ironside, two of the greatest warriors of the Viking Age. Ivar the Boneless hunts Hundr, desperate to avenge the death of his son at Hundr's hand. To survive, Hundr must battle against fearsome Lords of Frankia, navigate treachery within the Viking Army itself, and become a warrior of reputation in his own right.

Hundr must navigate the war, survive Ivar's brutal attacks, and find his place in the vicious world of the Vikings in this unputdownable, fast paced adventure with memorable characters.

The Wrath of Ivar continues the unmissable Viking historical fiction saga series which began with Peter Gibbons' debut Viking Blood and Blade.

CHAPTER ONE OF THE WRATH OF IVAR, BOOK 2 IN THE VIKING BLOOD AND BLADE SAGA

866 AD.

Hundr stared down the long deck of the warship Seaworm and twenty pairs of hard killers' eyes stared back at him. He had brought these warriors to the mouth of a wide, silted river on the coast of Frankia to hunt and kill. Most were veterans of the war in Northumbria, where the sons of Ragnar Lothbrok fought to control Saxon England. Hundr's thoughts slipped to that Saxon land, a short voyage across the Frankish sea, but the memories were too painful, so he banished them from his mind to concentrate on the battle at hand.

Their minds must be keen, and their actions clear if they were to overcome their dangerous prey. The Seaworm lay in wait, sitting shallow in the river water, dragon-headed prow snarling out into the estuary. Hundr and the crew of the Seaworm waited, tucked away from sight of the river's bends, for fellow Viking raiders. Vicious and merciless warriors trained in warfare from the time they could stand. The Seaworm waited in a hidden inlet on a wide river to catch the Sea Wolves returning from their inland raids. Crews of hungry Vikings used rivers like Roman roads, sailing deep inland hunting for silver and slaves. Hundr and his crew of fighters planned to ambush and slaughter another crew of the most brutal fighters in the world, men just like them. Their prey would be fat with plunder and weighed down with silver. Hundr wanted to take it all from them. He wanted to strike with his sword and hear their screams; he wanted to feel the battle joy coursing through his veins. Most of all, however, he just wanted to hurt someone, for someone else to feel pain like he did, and distract his mind from its suffocating cloy of betrayal and suffering.

The Seaworm crew sat at their oars, gripping the smooth timber shafts with white knuckles. Each man had their eyes fixed upon Hundr, waiting for his order to row and launch into the attack. The crew licked their lips and shuffled, shifting their weight and unable to keep still as they waited for the order which must come soon. Hundr rubbed at the dark pit of his dead eye, which itched constantly. It had been a year since Hakon Ivarsson, son of Ivar the Boneless, had cut the eye from his skull with a red-hot knife. Hakon had died screaming when Hundr snatched his life away with Hakon's own sword. That blade sat belted at Hundr's hip. Soulstealer was its name, and he put his hand on her cool iron pommel for battle luck.

"Shouldn't be long now," said Einar Rosti, Einar the Brawler, leaning on the ship's dragon prow and peering downriver. The dragon gave the Sea-worm her name, the fire-breathing giant worm of nightmares. Einar had been Hundr's Jarl, his Lord, before they had fought Hakon. The Sea-worm belonged to Einar, and Einar had taken Hundr in when he had nothing. Hundr had begged him for a berth upon his warship at a dank and miserable port in the Jutland penin-sula. In those days, Einar was sworn to Ivar the Boneless and served him for many years as a Sea Jarl and war captain before Ivar and his son Hakon betrayed, humiliated, and dismissed him. They left Einar with nothing, no future, and nothing to show for his years of service but his life. The Seaworm belonged to Einar, but Hundr was the leader of the crew.

"I'm going over first," Hundr growled, and Einar nodded. Hundr craved battle. He hungered to lose himself in its mad fury, where he would either kill or be killed himself. Only in those moments, where blades flew and blood flowed, was his mind clear. No images of the war in Northumbria hurting his brain, no thoughts of her, his lost love. He wanted, and needed to go first so he could cut, slash and kill and dampen his own pain in the suffering of others.

"There," said Einar, pointing downriver and then wincing as he clutched at his stomach. It was only a year since Ivar the Boneless had plunged his blade deep inside Einar's guts, and Hundr knew it was a gift from Odin that Einar had survived that terrible wound.

Hundr followed Einar's finger, and sure enough, a long sleek Viking drakkar warship poked its beast-headed prow around a bend in the meandering river. Murmurs rolled down the Seaworms' deck, and Hundr heard the clicking and scraping of weapons loosened in scabbards, the clank of helmets on the hull where men lifted them, preparing for the fight to come.

"Wait," Hundr said, and the ship went quiet.

Einar grinned and drew his axe from the loop at

his belt. Hundr thought his friend looked gaunt; his face, which was usually an implacable slab of rock, looked hollow at the cheeks and his skin pale. The ravages of Ivar's wound still taking their toll.

"We fight for ourselves now. We serve no one. Anything we take is ours. A man must be the master of his own destiny if he is to be truly free," said Einar. It was the promise they had made to each other as they left England. They would make their own future and never again live at another's whim.

Since sailing away from Northumbria, they had become pirates. A lone ship preying on other Sea Wolves. They could do as they wished, and they had gathered much silver. The men were content, and Hundr supposed that was enough. For now.

The oars of the approaching longship dipped into the river's glassy surface, and Hundr heard the splash as the ship surged forward, slicing through the water like a knife.

"Now. Go," said Hundr.

Einar turned and repeated the order, and the Seaworm crew grunted. They dipped their oars and pulled. That first pull was the backbreaker, the huge heave to get the ship moving. Hundr felt the surge under his feet as the Seaworm lurched forward.

 "Faster, pull, pull," Hundr turned and saw gritted teeth and red faces as the men leant into the stroke. Then another stroke. Now the ship wasn't lurching; she was racing. Racing forwards to intercept her prey. Three more strokes, and they were in the river proper, heading into the path of the approaching longship. If they kept on this trajectory, they would smash into the hull of the approaching ship, but that collision would damage the Seaworm as much as it would the other. Hundr waited for a few more heartbeats, one more long stroke.

 "Now, bank now!" he shouted. Ragnhild, the Valkyrie warrior, nodded back from the steerboard at the rear of the Seaworm. She grinned across her scarred face and leant on the tiller.

 Hundr heard shouts of alarm erupting from the enemy ship. Those men pointed at the Seaworm and looked to their Lord for a command. But it was too late. The Seaworm's oars came up with a grunt at the effort. Ragnhild steered the ship into a sharp turn, and the Seaworm came about just as her bow reached within a stone's throw of the enemy vessel. Hundr saw the surprise on a bearded face across the water, mouth dropping open as he realised what was about to happen.

The Seaworm came around in a shallow arc until she was alongside the enemy ship. Hundr felt the jolt as the impact came, and he braced himself against the prow. Heat rose from his belly, and he allowed himself a smile as the Seaworm's curved prow crunched across the line of enemy oars. Hundr gripped the hilt of his sword and held it tight. He watched as the broken line of oars in the enemy ship snapped viciously. The force of the Seaworm racing across the oar blades in the water caused the handles of those oars to snap forwards into the oarsmen at their benches, Hundr winced at a high-pitched scream as one such oar handle crushed a man's ribcage like an overripe fruit.

"Kill them, kill them now. Take everything from them. Their lives and their silver are ours!" Hundr bellowed and launched himself across the gap between the ships. For a moment, his heart stopped as he thought he would fall short, but then relief came as his feet landed on the timber deck of the enemy ship. Bearded warriors all around him now, snarling and shouting. A boot connected with his back, and Hundr sighed as the cloak of battle calm descended. He whipped Soulstealer free from her scabbard and slashed it at a gap-toothed face. Blood splashed across the deck in thick gobbets like jewels, and Hundr barged a warrior out of the way and whipped a knife free from his belt to plunge its blade into the chest of the warrior who had kicked him. A blade came towards his chest, but Hundr batted it aside with Soulstealer's hilt and bellowed with joy as he head-butted a red-bearded warrior full in the face and dragged his dagger backhanded across that man's throat.

"Odin!" came a shout from behind.

Hundr turned and grinned as Ragnhild leapt onto the enemy ship and lay about her with her axe, shrieking like a demon. It was over then in a few heartbeats, the Seaworm crew swarmed the enemy, cutting and slashing at the Sea Wolves until they were dead or knelt in the bilge. A gap appeared at the stern of the ship where an enormous man stood with an axe in each hand, challenging his enemies to fight him one against one. Hundr stepped forward, wanting to fight the giant. The killing had stopped but hadn't yet sated his thirst for blood. He was too late. Ragnhild already accepted the single combat, and the Valkyrie warrior keened her high-pitched war cry and launched herself at the big man. The gigantic man was stripped to the waist, and his torso rippled with muscle, but Ragnhild moved with extraordinary speed and skill: she danced around the giant cutting at his arms and legs, whilst her enemy slashed wildly at spaces she had occupied a fraction earlier. In a blur of flashing axe blades, the big man dropped to his knees with Ragnhild's axe buried in his forehead. She looked to the heavens and sang a prayer to Odin, then, after wrenching her blade free, she dipped her hand in the blood of her fallen foe and wiped it across her face. Ragnhild cried out again to Odin and kicked the big man's corpse into the river.

The ship was theirs now, all resistance crushed in the time it would take a man to eat his breakfast. The Seaworm crew whooped for joy and searched the ship for treasure and plunder. Hundr sat back on a rowing bench and sighed. The fight had finished too quickly. The battle joy had been fleeting and had now subsided, leaving him with the familiar hollow cavern in his heart. He heard a squeal behind him and turned to see Guthmund, one of the newer Seaworm crew, pull a woman up by the hair from where she hid beneath a bench, caked in mud, and her blonde hair matted and filthy. They had bound her at wrist and ankle, and she sobbed wide-eyed in Guthmund's grip. Hundr closed his eyes tightly as a memory of his own time as a captive flashed before his eyes. He remembered himself dragged behind a horse for miles, falling in and out of consciousness, and then tied to a post where his tormentor cut at his chest with a blade, sheeting his torso in blood.

"Leave her," Hundr said, snapping his eyes open.

"What? Let's take the bitch, give her to the lads," said Guthmund, leering, showing brown teeth in his grizzled beard.

"I said leave her. Put her down." Hundr rose from the bench and fixed Guthmund with his one eye. The warrior let the prisoner go, and she scuttled back into her hiding place. "No one is to harm that woman. Drop their prisoners over the side. They can swim to shore."

Hundr picked his way down the ship, over bodies of fallen enemies and shards of broken oars. Three surviving warriors crouched beneath the ship's mast, where Einar spoke to them, brandishing his axe. Einar turned and nodded as he saw Hundr approach.

"A chest of silver and some slaves. Not bad," said Einar.

"I let the slaves go. Who were they?" asked Hundr, nodding to the cowering warriors.

"Raiders, Danes," Einar shrugged. "They say there is an army of Vikings upriver."

Hundr peered around Einar's shoulder at the three men. One wore a Brynjar mail coat, which meant he was a warrior of note. Like a sword, a coat of mail was rare and expensive, and only Lords or warriors with reputation could afford one and be able to stop others taking it from them.

"An army, you say?" Hundr said to the warrior in mail.

The warrior was middle-aged, and his hair was receding across his skull, making his forehead shine in the midday sun. He licked his lips and looked into Hundr's eye.

"There's an army, led by famous warriors. I'll tell you all about it if you cut me loose. Let me join your crew, Lord."

Hundr punched the warrior in the face and slammed his head back against the mast.

"Strip his mail, cut his throat and throw him in the river," said Hundr. Einar grabbed the man by his hair and dragged him away. The warrior whimpered and so Einar kicked him in the belly. Hundr turned to the two remaining survivors.

"Now. Tell me about this army."

The two survivors sang like birds, and they told a tale of Vikings fighting deep in Frankia alongside a Frankish Lord in his war against a rival. Hundr probed them, wanting to learn as much detail as possible.

Since leaving Northumbria on that rain-soaked day a year past, since the day he had fought and beaten Ivar the Boneless, Hundr and the crew had sailed aimlessly up and down the coasts of Saxon and Frankish Kingdoms. They had raided here and there but with no real purpose or plan. The Seaworm was short of crew upon leaving Northumbria, and so they had taken on new crewmen at a port in Northern Frankia. Guthmund and his men were a band of masterless men, a mixture of Danes and Norsemen, looking for a Lord to serve. Hundr and Einar had taken them on to bring the Seaworm up to her full strength and allow for faster sailing and more effective raiding. Having no purpose other than raiding here and there had allowed Hundr to wallow in his pain. He knew he had allowed the darkness of his betrayal by those he loved and the physical pain he had endured to overwhelm him.

The prospect of an army and a war to fight caught Hundr's attention. A war would allow him to immerse himself in that conflict. He would have a purpose again. When he was younger, all Hundr thought about was reputation, how he had to leave his home in the East and prove himself as a warrior. He had fled and joined Einar's crew and fought for the sons of Ragnar Lothbrok in the war against King Aelle of Northumbria. Hundr dared to say he had a reputation now. He had fought Ivar the Boneless, the Champion of the North. Hundr had taken one of Ivar's swords that day, along with Soulstealer. He had two fine swords to show for all that suffering. Another war meant battle and purpose, but the decision was not his alone to make.

Hundr leapt back aboard the Seaworm and called to Einar and Ragnhild to join him. The three stood close to the steerboard and watched as the crew loaded the ship with the fruits of their attack.

"Good haul this time," said Ragnhild. Their previous raid on a small fishing hamlet had yielded nothing but dried fish and stale bread.

"Aye. Still not enough silver though," said Einar.

Einar and what remained of his old crew had fixed on a plan to gather as much silver as possible. He had been serving Ivar the Boneless on a promise of becoming a landed Jarl in the newly conquered Northumbrian lands, but that promise had turned to ash on the fire of Hakon Ivarsson's treachery. Einar and his men were past middle age, and so they had looked forward to settling down and becoming farmers and starting families. A warrior cannot keep on fighting forever. He either finds his place in Valhalla, or he settles down. Hundr owed Einar his life. Einar and Ragnhild had stormed a hilltop fortress against impossible odds to rescue Hundr from Hakon, and Hundr would do anything he could to repay them for that. So, he had sworn to help Einar find enough silver to buy a swathe of land somewhere where he and his men could settle.

"At this rate, it will take many years to get enough silver," said Hundr.

"How much is enough?" said Ragnhild.

"Four times what we have now, maybe more," said Einar with a shrug.

"The prisoners say there is an army upriver, a Viking army," said Hundr. He glanced at Ragnhild and Einar. Ragnhild scratched her chin, but Einar frowned, creasing his hard slab face.

"And?"

"War means silver," said Hundr.

Einar shook his head.
"Surely you have not forgotten already what it means to serve another? We swore never to serve another Lord; we are the Lords now."

"I haven't forgotten," said Hundr, tapping his finger on his missing eye and ravaged face.

"Who leads this army?" said Ragnhild.

"A man called Haesten. A man with reputation, they say."

"I have heard of him," said Ragnhild. "He sailed far to the south, to the land of the Blamen whose skins are burned black by the sun."

"I have heard of him," said Einar. "He has a reputation alright, for trickery and battle luck."

"So, he sounds like an interesting man. We don't need to swear an oath to him, Einar."

"He sailed south with Bjorn Ironside. Son of Ragnar Lothbrok, and brother of Ivar the Boneless."

The sound of that name, Ivar the Boneless, spoken aloud made Hundr's guts twist. He spat over the side, watching the crew secure the chest of silver in the bilge.

"Take their weapons, everything of value," Hundr shouted to the men. Weapons could be sold and traded just like silver. There were two slaves, both women, and Hundr wasn't sorry he had let them swim away. It had cost him some grumbling and sideways glances from Guthmund and the newer crew, but he had been close to a slave himself and so wouldn't see those women continue to be ripped from their homes and families and forced into continued servitude upon his ship.

They poled away from the defeated ship and rowed back upriver towards the sea and away from Haesten's army. Hundr didn't know in which direction to sail. He wanted to sail upriver and join with Haesten. He wanted to fight and forget about Ivar and Northumbria. Hundr knew Ragnhild wanted that fight. She was born for battle and had trained her whole life for it. But he owed Einar his life and wouldn't go against his friend. So, they sailed again in search of silver for Einar's dream.

ABOUT THE AUTHOR

Peter Gibbons

About The Author Peter Gibbons Peter is an author originally from Warrington in the UK, and now based in Kildare, Ireland.

Peter is married with three children, and is an avid reader and writer of historical fiction, fantasy, and science fiction novels.

If you enjoyed this novel, please visit Peter's website at www.petermgibbons.com where you can subscribe to Peter's mailing list and keep up to date with latest releases and news.

35584530R00281